Dedicated to my loving parents

THE
GULCH
JUMPERS

Contents

PART ONE

"The Constitution protects the sanctity of the family precisely because the institution of the family is deeply rooted in this Nation's history and tradition. It is through the family that we inculcate and pass down many of our most cherished values, moral and cultural."

-Justice Powell, writing for the majority, Moore v. City of East Cleveland, Supreme Court of the United States, May 31, 1977

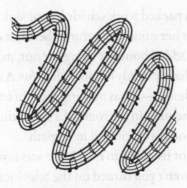

CHAPTER ONE

THE DAY OF THE BLIZZARD

Ellie Sanders stood in her flannel pajamas, phone to ear, and blinked sleep from her eyes. She took stock of the scene from her bedroom window. *Not good.*

"Just great. Traffic's going to be terrible—I have court this morning—and I'm already late." She ran her hand through her untamed chestnut hair as she spoke into her cell. "I should be okay with my four-wheel drive, right?"

"El, that's what I'm trying to tell you," Mike's voice came through the phone. "I'm watching the Cleveland weather here from New York. I know you don't want to hear this, but everything's closed: schools, government offices, *courts*. You're snowed in, my lovely little lawyer. You aren't going anywhere today."

"But I've got a trial today, I have to start getting ready." Heart pounding, Ellie felt anxiety rising like a sickening lump in her throat. *I cannot stay alone in this house today!* Her silent scream drowned Mike's next sentence into white noise.

So much willpower required to forge ahead, to simply put one foot in front of the other. Would it ever get easier? Ellie had carefully planned the few days Mike would be out of town so that she would be consumed with a packed work schedule, not sink into the dark place. Staying busy kept her mind from things best not dwelled upon. And work offered the added bonus of tiring her out, making sleep possible.

But her plans had certainly not included *this*. A day off, her husband away, this empty house—it was nothing short of terrifying. She peered out the window, helpless in the route of a springtime snowstorm, boorishly insistent upon disrupting all in its path.

"Ellie, you're not listening to me," Mike was saying. "No trial today. It's a *blizzard*. Haven't you turned on the television yet? They've even *named* the storm—they're calling it Jason."

"*Jason*? What kind of name is that? And I thought only hurricanes are given names."

She flipped on the morning news. The weather forecaster was dissecting the path of the storm, gushing with self-importance and issuing dire travel warnings: *If you don't have to go anywhere, don't.* He pointed to the map, explaining how lake effect snow is peculiar to only a handful of places in the world: the Baltic Sea, Japan, the Great Lakes. When cold Canadian air passes over the shallow, warm water of Lake Erie, everyone knows it's going to snow relentlessly.

"Oh, you should see this weather guy— they love this type of thing. I think they're all exaggerating." She started to pace. A list of school closings crawled along the bottom of the television screen, then came business closings, government offices. She saw that Mike was right, the courthouse was indeed closed.

"Ellie, just stop. You're the only person I know who isn't happy to have a day off. I know it's hard to slow down, but you're safer staying put today." His voice got softer, kinder: "I'll be home tomorrow. You'll be fine. Work from home or just take a break and relax."

Ellie froze, momentarily panicked and unable to find her voice to answer her husband. No, she was quite sure she would not be able to relax. No, she was quite sure she would not be fine. Too much unscheduled time on her hands was an emotional minefield. She plunked down quickly on the side of the bed and tried to breathe.

"You can always clean out your closet if you get really bored," Mike teased. He cleared his throat and went on. "And, sweetheart, if you start having a rough day... you can call me back..."

The weight of all that remained unspoken hovered between them. Mike was trying to offer an opening. Ellie loved him for that. But she wasn't ready. For a moment she considered asking him to come home, to cancel his meeting, but that wasn't fair, he'd worked so hard on this new account, and it was silly for a grown woman to freak out about spending a day in her own home. Of course, it was too dangerous for him to travel either, and probably impossible anyway today; all the flights would surely be canceled.

She pulled on yoga pants, pony tailed-up and grabbed her slippers, balancing the phone between her shoulder and ear. There would be no conversation about rough days. "Did you actually just suggest I clean out my closet?"

Mike laughed, relief in his voice. "That closet could be declared an environmental disaster zone. I bet you'll be amazed what a difference it would make if you gave away just five things. Five articles of clothing, five pairs of shoes..."

"Give away five pairs of shoes? What kind of husband are you?" She chuckled softly. "I'll call you back. Love ya."

Ellie pressed speed dial. Her paralegal Jessica lived in the apartment above Ellie's downtown law office and forwarded office calls to her own line after hours. She was on top of every case in the firm and often more than a few steps ahead of her boss.

"Don't even attempt it," said Jessica. "All appointments are cancelled—witnesses are called off, court is closed. Just stay home like everybody else. You have the Johnson discovery file to keep you busy if you really feel like work." Ellie could picture the worry line between Jessica's eyebrows. "And did you hear they named the blizzard Jason?" Jessica added. "Too funny."

"I know," said Ellie, resignation in her voice. "'Jason.' Sounds like the kid who bags my groceries, not a mass of freezing precipitation that's shut down the whole damn city."

After Ellie hung up the phone, she took a deep breath and straightened her shoulders. She just had to stay very, very busy. Mike was right: there were worse things in life than a quiet day marooned at home. The plow had not come down their street yet and, truth was, icy driving scared her. Put one foot in front of the other. She made coffee, then busied herself chopping carrots, garlic and onions to start a pot of white chicken chili.

With dinner simmering in the slow cooker, she considered her briefcase and the files she had brought home: interrogatories, deposition transcripts, bank statements, appraisals. Setting up at the kitchen table would probably be a better work space, but how lovely to curl up on the couch next to Gracie, her loyal shepherd-terrier.

"We'll keep each other company today," Ellie told her as she sat down on the couch. Ellie absent-mindedly ran her hands through the pup's soft fur as she reviewed the financial holdings of her client's soon-to-be-ex-husband. It was a dry and uninteresting case, but the rhythm and flow of the work steadied her.

Sometimes a mundane case was a relief. Ellie was a repository of sad stories. The domestic relations cases, distasteful at best, could be truly upsetting. People who once loved each other reduced to warring over the house, the kids. Was it better to be the subject of battling parents who both wanted you, or be simply forgotten and neglected, not fed or played with or even noticed? She focused on the clear-cut legal arguments and detached herself from any heartache that veered too close to her own sad story.

By early afternoon, she finished reviewing the paperwork and stood to stretch.

"Done with law for today, girl," she announced to Gracie. Now what?

Ellie meandered through the house, unsettled, footsteps echoing on the hardwood floors. The old house shuddered in the howling wind. She paused by the front window to fret over the accumulating snow, pretending for a moment that she didn't know full well where she was headed. Powerless to resist, she climbed the stairs and went directly to the second bedroom door, which normally remained closed.

Opening this bedroom door was always a mistake, she knew that. But the pull of heartache was too strong.

She pushed the door open a crack, then a bit further, and took a tentative step into the room. Her stomach tied into knots and her hands shook as she struggled against the familiar tidal wave of despair. Her finger absently ran along dust atop the dresser, creating a meandering line, and for a moment, she daydreamed how different things might have been. If only.

"I'm not going to do this today," she said, taking a deep breath. Once she allowed the downward spiral to start, it was so, so hard to climb back out. She forced herself to turn and walk toward the door, shutting it firmly behind her.

Mike was right—she needed a project.

Ellie continued down the hall to her own bedroom and the dreaded closet, every inch crammed with clothing, shoes, belts, purses, coats, scarves—much of it unused for years. Mike had given up long ago, moving his things to a closet in a spare bedroom.

She could bag some of the extra clutter for that homeless shelter near her office in the city. She couldn't remember the name of the place, even though she drove by it almost every day. It didn't matter. This was a good project.

"Let's see, Gracie, how about Earth, Wind and Fire?" It was unthinkable to do any kind of housework without music, and it had to be loud. Gracie cocked her head to the side, watching her master. Ellie gave her a pat on the head. "I'll take that for a yes."

Start small, Ellie told herself. She picked a corner and started pulling items off their hangers and sorting into three separate piles: keep, throw away, give away. She broke it down further, tossing jackets, suits and career clothes in one section, athletic and workout things in another. The music buoyed her mood and she quickly fell into the swing of tossing her garments into the growing piles on the floor.

Her eyes settled on the upper shelf. Ellie couldn't remember when she had last used anything stored up there: mostly out-of-season shoes, garment bags, and who knew what else. Probably best to sort out those items as well. She had to use a step stool to reach all the way to the back. Her fingers groped blindly along the shelf until, sure enough, they bumped against one last box, pushed all the way to the back of its perch. She stretched to reach and pulled down a battered-looking brown cardboard shoebox. There was no label, and the container was weathered and faded. The box was not from any brand of shoes Ellie could remember purchasing. In fact, she was sure she had never seen it before.

She carefully opened the lid.

Several varnished, old-fashioned pieces of costume jewelry nestled in the top tier of the box: cameo pin, glass bead necklace, and clip-on golden drop earrings. Ellie picked up each piece in turn, the light catching on the glass as she turned them over in her hand. *Interesting*. She didn't recognize any of it. She registered vague pangs of guilt for rifling through what was not hers, but quickly dismissed these thoughts, too intrigued to stop. After all, it was in her own closet, wasn't it? She rummaged below the divider that held the jewelry on the top tier, expecting to find more vintage treasures underneath.

"What in the world?"

Her hands ran over a thick stack of folded and yellowing papers. A few broken crayons lay beneath. Old letters, correspondence between past lovers, perhaps? A forgotten diary? A discarded school notebook?

Ellie unfolded page after page of handwritten lines and verses. She paused to sit on the floor and flip through the papers, reading snippets on each page. Poetry. All painstakingly set out in the same careful print. A little thrill shivered down her spine. She was holding something important, something significant and intensely personal, that someone, somewhere, had spent countless hours to create. She pried herself away long enough to pour another cup of coffee. This time it was easier to march down the hallway past the second door, head forward, resolutely carrying her coffee, eager to read more of the poetry. When she returned, steaming mug in hand, she nestled into bed, propping up pillows so she could read in comfort while the snow swirled outside the window.

Going back to the first page, Ellie started reading more carefully:

Come to town, oh sweet Doris Brown
   We'll ride to the moon, tumble softly on down
Our love is real
   No one gonna hold us down
Color blind, just follow the sound
   My heart is yours
Darling, don't let me down.

She flipped to another page, and read a different verse.

Song of the Hills
   You call my name, tender morning reverie
Echoing down the canyon, whispering through the coal fields
   Baby girl, singing so sweetly
   Country child of the hills.

The rhymes were simple and nostalgic, rich in sweet sincerity.

Losing herself in the melody of the words was somehow healing, comforting, and Ellie drew strength from allowing her mind to quiet. It was a relief to listen to someone else's story, even if she didn't know who the someone else was.

Shuffling further through the verses, Ellie found several drawings. A sketch of a guitar, then a banjo, with detailed shading around the strings and pegs. She turned a page and gasped at the next drawing: an exquisite pencil sketch of a young woman posing by a window in a cotton shift dress, hands folded in her lap, dark hair pulled back in a bun. The woman's level gaze was challenging, almost defiant, while her smile offered a hint of humor and kindness.

Ellie held the paper to the light by her window, admiring the beautiful face in the portrait while taking care to handle the fragile paper carefully, by its edges. Who was this woman? Was she the author of these verses—or the poet's muse?

More than an invasion of someone's privacy, this was an archeological dig into someone else's life.

She dialed Mike's cell, and he answered on the first ring.

"Ellie? Everything okay?"

"Mike, I found the strangest thing while I was cleaning: an old box in the back of our master closet—like a time capsule."

"A time capsule? In *our* closet? Well, what's in it? Instructions for building an ancient space craft? Any cash?"

"Vintage jewelry, drawings of musical instruments, and poetry—page after page of handwritten poetry. Sorry, no cash. No space ship blueprints. Seriously, Mike, it's extraordinary. Is it yours?"

"A box of poetry? Definitely not mine."

"There's also a sketch of a young woman."

"Someone you recognize?" Mike asked.

"No," Ellie said. "Not at all. I don't know if the artist and the poet are one in the same, but whoever created all this has an amazing talent. I'm going to call the realtor. All I can think is it must have been left behind by the prior owner."

The prior owner of the house did not leave a forwarding address and had only communicated through the realtor. There had been no face-to-face meeting, no walk-through with conversation about little nuances of the home. *This light switch turns on the outside porch as well as the hallway. Sometimes this floor creaks. I hope you'll be as happy here as we've been.* At the time, Ellie thought it unfriendly, but perhaps she had judged too quickly.

She retrieved the realtor's number from the list of contacts in her phone and dialed, but it just rang and eventually went to voice mail. Ellie hung up. The snow had shut down the realtor's office, just like everything else. She would try again tomorrow. For now, the box could go into the back of her SUV. If the roads were plowed and passable tomorrow, she would look over the poetry once more at her office and try that realtor again.

Ellie allowed herself a relieved moment of self-congratulation. She had filled the hours without veering over the cliff into the chasm of darkness, thanks to the distraction of the shoebox of treasures. She felt better. Control maintained, at least for one more day.

***

Following a pretrial hearing, Ellie was at the office the next morning by ten. "How was your snow day?" she greeted Jessica.

"Loved it," said Jessica. "Joe and I lounged around and watched movies all day. Old spaghetti westerns from the Duke to Clint to Sharon Stone. I didn't even get out of my PJ's. Can't beat it."

Ellie poured a fresh cup of coffee and sat down at her desk. The next two hours flew by as she returned phone calls, caught up on emails and reviewed incoming motions and court entries.

She was ready for a break by noon. "I'm heading out," she yelled to Jessica. "I've got a trunk full of bagged clothes to drop off at that shelter. You know the one, on the corner of East 30th. What's the name?"

"Mission of Hope!" Jessica called from her desk.

"Right, that's it. Mission of Hope. I'll be back in an hour."

Ellie picked up takeout for lunch and then proceeded to the Mission of Hope Homeless Shelter to deposit the donations from her closet. She slowed her car, eyeing groups of homeless men and women standing on the corner, shuffling about in the cold. Some of them furtively glanced her way, their breath visible in the cold air. She gave fleeting thought to locking her car doors to prevent a grab of her purse, but was determined to prove she was not a narrow-minded sheltered suburbanite who could only think about getting mugged. There was a drive-through where she pulled up her car to drop off the donations. She jumped out to open the trunk. A volunteer came out to help unload and provided a receipt to claim the tax deduction. "Thank you, and God bless," he told her.

"You're welcome," Ellie replied, and then glanced again toward the unfortunate souls milling about on the corner. Had she just imagined the face? Blue eyes, dirty blond hair, the contemptuously knowing "what kind of trouble can we get into today" smirk. No, it was impossible. No one Ellie knew would be loitering outside a homeless shelter. She must be seeing things.

Ellie hopped back in her car and drove off feeling good about herself, self-righteous even. She went into law to try to make a difference in the world rather than chase the dollar. She'd worked hard to build her firm, become a reasonably successful attorney, and here she was, donating some quite nice, just-slightly-worn articles of clothing to the less fortunate, doing the socially responsible thing.

As she pulled away, she popped on her satellite radio and cranked it up, enjoying the warmth of her heated leather seat, deciding to pick up a latte before returning to the office.

But when she returned home later that day, her mind returned to the little collection of old-fashioned rhymes, and she searched for her recently discovered treasure box. It wasn't in the car and couldn't be found in the house. How could she have lost track of it so carelessly?

She couldn't remember carrying it into her office, so she searched back through her day. The volunteer—the one at the shelter who had helped her unload her SUV—must have grabbed the shoebox along with the clothes.

The words from one of the poems turned over in her head as she set out leftovers for dinner:

Baby child, baby o' mine,
*   We rock softly under the elms, the wind keeping time.*
Come evening I'll strike out to earn me a dime,
*   Making music to bring home treats so fine.*
Catfish, cornbread, berries on the vine,
*   Common time with a walking beat, for sweet baby o' mine.*

She had really wanted to show the poetry to Mike, especially this one, which seemed to speak to her somehow. She quickly jotted down the verse while it was fresh in her mind. Damn. She would have to go back.

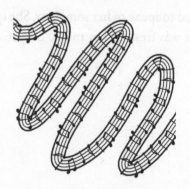

CHAPTER TWO

Homeless

Ray ate his oatmeal and toast by the window of the shelter dining hall, quietly sipping his tea. The morning sun was warm and forgiving as it fell upon his weathered face. He savored its warmth, the simple pleasure of late winter sun falling upon him like absolution. He ate slowly, watching a cardinal perch on a tree outside the window. The light played through branches that bowed under layers of snow. The hot oatmeal reminded him of eating grits in the South so long ago.

If you were lucky, you might be remembered for about a hundred years. That was assuming there were children, and then grandchildren after that. If you lived long enough to meet your grandchildren, you could tell them some stories. Perhaps sing them a bit of a song. A generation, maybe two at best. But who today could tell you anything real about a person who lived more than one or two generations ago? So many stories lost, never told and never remembered. Soon, Ray would be lost and never remembered. He was an old man living in a homeless shelter. He had no one to teach his songs to. No wife. No child. No grandchild. No overlap. Too many people lost even in this lifetime.

To get more than one hundred years, he figured, you had to be famous. Everyone knew the names of the great musicians. More importantly, everyone knew their music, their tunes. Ray admired those who immortalized their inner selves this way.

He could appreciate it, but he had none of it. His people were gone. The boys in the band were gone, their songs silenced like an old mine shaft filled with earth and forever entombed. Nobody remembered The Gulch Jumpers were ever around. These days Ray's music served simply to ease his pain. To ease the pain of the miserable men and women filling the tables around him. Not to be recorded or taught to another.

As he ate, he saw the junkie get up and sneak out the side door. He had noticed her earlier, arguing with the staff while waiting in line to check her plastic storage bin at the counter. "This is bullshit!" she had announced loudly, scanning the crowd for an audience to agree with her. Number 23, Ray had noted. Each bunk and bin was assigned a corresponding number. Residents made their beds before breakfast and then checked their belongings, wearing the keys on lanyards around their necks. "Come on Brandy, don't hold up the line," a counselor scolded the angry blonde. "You know if it doesn't fit in the bin, you can't store it here. You can play by the rules or you can be out in the cold."

The blonde noticed Ray watching. "Hey you—old man. Don't you think all these rules are BULLSHIT?"

Ray had averted his eyes. The shelter was crowded, tempers were short and fights quick to erupt. He didn't need any trouble. Still, he closed his eyes and wondered about Miss 23, so thin and wild-eyed. What was her story? What had she lost? She may even be about the same age as his Sally...

Every day he looked into the faces of people who came and went from the shelter. He searched the faces he passed on the street, hoping to see some flash of familiarity. Was she somewhere safe, warm? Did she have a family? Had she ever fallen in love? Was she happy?

Ray stood to clear his plate from the table and read the chore assignments posted on the wall. Today he would be working in the

donation and shelter shop. Unloading and sorting old clothes was
better than cleaning the bathrooms. Working for his keep kept him
honest, less ashamed about taking handouts.

He joined the group unloading bags from the drive-through load-
ing dock. Some of the donations were clean; some were stained and
musty. The workers used handheld laundry steamers on the clothes,
and then sorted into men's, women's and children's sections. They
discarded what was too worn or dirty to be given new life and worked
to arrange the rest on hangers, making the unwanted look presentable
and wanted again. The items were then set out in the shelter "shop"
and residents could earn shopping time to browse for personal items.
Warm clothes were especially desirable now, in the cold weather.

Unload, unfold, hang and steam. Three folks worked alongside him,
and one of the counselors walked through with "Good Mornings" to
all. It wasn't long before Ray's familiar, bass voice broke into song. He
started with hymns and then progressed into the old time music he
loved. His co-workers nodded and smiled.

"How about some Johnny Cash, my man?" called Pete.

But Ray had fallen silent. His mouth gaped open as he gazed into
the box he had just opened. The color drained from his face. He staggered and grabbed the side of a chair for support.

"You okay there, Ray?" asked Pete.

Ray stared dumbly into the open box he held in his hands.

"Yessir, I'm just fine," he mumbled weakly, struggling to recover.
"Just not much up for singing anymore today."

Pete nodded and turned away, and Ray quickly glanced around to
find his co-workers all engrossed in their own work. One of them had
leaned over to switch on the radio. Ray swiftly slid the shoebox under
his flannel shirt, tucked it under his suspender strap and hunched
around it protectively.

"Just gonna lie down for a spell," he muttered over his shoulder as
he retreated quickly to the sleeping quarters.

He made his way to his cot, grateful for a rare moment of privacy.

Once seated, facing the wall, he opened the old box again, pulling out the contents with incredulity. He frantically sifted through each paper in the box, pulling out page after page of the music and lyrics he had penned five decades earlier. It was nothing short of a miracle—here were their songs, their history. How could his own songs have been delivered to the Mission of Hope donation center? Who had brought this? Where had the box been for all these years? Did this mean that Sally was nearby? His heart pounded with excitement.

He sorted through the verses, the jewelry, until his hands seized upon the pencil sketch of his love posing by the window, her dark hair in a bun. He held the portrait up to the light, crying out like a wounded animal to see her face once again. He pictured their sanctuary in the deep forest, the oranges and reds of fall and the blooming red bush and rhododendron of spring. Ray could still smell the sweet blooms of the Appalachian spring, feel the warmth of the sun on Doris's soft skin, hear the lilting melody of her voice, and swoon in the luscious deep brown of her eyes. He wiped his eyes, shaking his head, unable to believe what he was holding in his hands. "My darling, my darling. I'm so sorry, my darling," he murmured, rocking back and forth.

Doris.

"I'm so sorry, my darling. I know I've got to find our girl."

Sally.

***

"It's a shoebox, just a small brown one," Ellie explained at the front desk. "I was here Wednesday; someone helped me unload my car. It must have gotten mixed in with the giveaways."

"Was there anything valuable in the box?" asked the front desk clerk, who did not look up from her newspaper and was clearly bored with the whole thing.

"Well... some old jewelry. Some writings."

The clerk finally looked up and studied Ellie, taking in her tailored suit and Michael Kors bag. "What *kind* of writings?"

"Um, it was poetry, actually."

She snorted out a laugh. "Uh huh, I see, you lost some poetry at the Mission of Hope Holiday Resort for the Homeless. Now that's priceless. Someone should write a song about that. Lady, you can fill out an incident report if you like, and we can put a search out in our donation center. But most of our stuff gets processed through pretty quickly. People need boots, coats, socks, sweaters, so they can keep warm on the streets. They need a presentable outfit to look for work or to wear to a job interview. They need clothes that fit their little ones. Baby blankets and booties. Hats and gloves. Jeans without holes. You get where I'm going with this. My guess is the jewelry was at the pawn shop within an hour, and the rest of your box got thrown out in the trash. 'Cause I can tell you for sure—if there's one thing homeless folks don't need, it's poetry."

Ray rose from a nearby chair and approached, studying Ellie curiously. He cleared his throat.

"Excuse me," he said, in a gentle, deep voice, "but that's where you're wrong."

"So you need some poetry today, Ray?" asked the clerk teasingly, softening. Even she couldn't be nasty to the sad old man who sang them through the day.

"Yes, ma'am, we all need it. We need it desperately. Except what this young lady is inquiring about ain't poetry—it's song lyrics."

"Oh," said Ellie, turning to study the sad, smiling hazel eyes of the tall elderly gentleman in tattered suspenders. "But how would you know that?"

He looked her in the eye, hesitating as if deciding how much to share.

"Because I wrote them." He gave a little bow. "May I ask, miss, how did you come upon the box?"

***

Ellie and Ray moved to the lounge, an uninspiring common area with institutional vinyl furniture, dingy overhead fluorescent lights and motivational posters on the walls. The television spouted mindless daytime talk shows, and a few people sat silently staring at the screen or at the floor, passing time with no purpose, nothing and no one to look forward to.

Ellie offered her hand. "I'm Ellie Sanders. It's nice to meet you."

"Ray. Ray Jones. Pleased to make your acquaintance."

"I'm sorry; you must think I'm crazy. The thing is, the other day I was going through my bedroom closet and I came across a shoebox on the top shelf. I'd never seen it before and didn't know it was there. When I opened it, I realized it must have been left behind by the previous owner. You see, we bought the house about five years ago. So this box, it must have been left behind."

"Left behind? Y'all don't know who had the box before y'uns found it?" Ray asked, his face falling.

"No, I'm afraid I don't know," Ellie answered, shaking her head. "I'm sorry. I intended to call the realtor to return the box, but it got mixed in with my donations and unloaded here the other day."

Ray shifted in his seat and looked at his hands. "It gave me a great shock to see those songs again," he said softly. "I was unloading all the bags that came in. I just couldn't believe it when I opened that old box."

"So all that poetry is really lyrics to music? And you wrote all of it?"

"I did. I wrote it. Must be hard to believe an old feller like me could write down all those lyrics, but I wrote those down many, many years ago. Put it all to song. Put down lots of words to song over the years."

"And the old jewelry, the sketches?"

"Family memories," Ray replied. "From a very long time ago," he added with sadness.

"Well, I wonder how it ended up in my closet."

Ray regarded Ellie, his expression transforming from serious to playful. "So you're telling me you haven't cleaned out your closet for five years?"

"Okay, I'm not big on housecleaning." She laughed, surprised and appreciative of his sense of humor. "Mr. Jones, I'm glad the forces of destiny or coincidence returned your family memories to you, but how could your songs be in my house? Did you ever live up on the West Side?"

"No, ma'am, I never lived in that part of town. I really have no idea."

"Where did you used to live before you, uh, came to live here?" Ellie was careful to avoid using the word homeless. "Did you have a home? Any family?"

Ray thought of the little clapboard house in the holler with the flowered curtains, the dogwood tree in the back, the gravel driveway. Lying in bed listening to the call of the Mourning Doves in the thick summer heat. His guitar on the porch. Doris in the kitchen, sweeping the floors with the straw broom. Sally's tricycle in the yard, all ready for her to ride when she got a little bigger. Memories too painful and too private to talk about with this well-heeled young stranger. He shifted again, closed his eyes and sang in a deep rich voice:

"No family, no family, no one waits for me,
I'm all alone in this world, as alone as a man can be."

"Ahh. I'm sorry to hear that. You have a wonderful voice. And such a talent with words. I would love to hear how those lyrics sound with the melody. Can you sing any of it? Or do you play a musical instrument?"

"Well, I reckon I can sing all of it. And I can play whatever you put in my hands."

"You can play any musical instrument?" Ellie inquired, gently, wondering if perhaps the old man was confused.

He sat up straight and nodded solemnly. "Yes, ma'am, I do indeed believe I can play any instrument you put in my hands: fiddle, mandolin, acoustic guitar, upright string bass, electric bass, electric guitar, banjo, accordion, spoons, jug, horn, drums. And I can tickle the ivories too," he added, holding his hands out, fingers dancing over his air keyboard. "No instruments to play here, in this place. But I got my voice, got all the songs in my head. That's really all a soul needs."

***

Later at home, Ellie tried to describe the scene to Mike. "You should have seen it," she told her husband. "I've never met anyone like him. He sings all of his words. He has an incredible voice. He's intelligent and sad and sweet. I don't understand why he's in there."

"You know people have all sorts of stories," cautioned Mike. "You can't assume anything about anyone."

"He told me he could play any instrument that I could put in his hands. And then he sang some of the songs from the papers in the box. It was wonderful stuff, Mike. This guy should be famous."

Mike's old guitar from college was sitting in their basement and hadn't been used in years. Ellie paused to consider how to approach the idea with her husband, but she didn't have to. He said, "If you go back to visit again, take my old guitar along. See what he can do."

He smiled at her and they both laughed. "Are we getting to the point where we finish each other's thoughts?" she teased.

"I sure hope so," he answered, pulling her close.

***

Ellie's thoughts frequently turned to Ray over the next few days and how much she was looking forward to bringing him Mike's guitar and hearing him play. Her own father had passed away when she was younger, and Ray would be about the same age as her father, had he lived. How awful that an elderly person was living in a homeless shelter. If he could compose page after page of lyrics and had such musical talent, what had transpired over his lifetime?

She decided to take a peek into his background. "Ray Jones" was a common name, and she could only guess he must be around eighty years old. She played with this for a while on her laptop but found nothing. There was no mention of him in the criminal corrections databases. When she Googled him, many hits came up, but they were obviously not the same Ray Jones she had just met at the Mission of Hope. Finally, on page fourteen, she found a short blurb about a

Ray Jones playing the rhythm guitar with a band in the South in the 1950s and 1960s.

"The Gulch Jumpers..." she mused, reading aloud.

There was no photo to verify that this was the right man, but at least the story seemed to fit what she knew of him. Nothing else came close to matching the man with the sad, smiling eyes and the honey voice.

Finally, Saturday arrived. The snow had melted and it was a crisp spring day, the kind of day that required boots to be kicked on and off in her mud room by the garage door. Gracie looked at her quizzically, hoping for a walk. "Maybe later, girl—we'll walk when I get home." She pulled on her coat and grabbed the guitar case.

Suddenly unsure about just showing up unannounced with the guitar, she stopped on the way and picked up two dozen donuts. It was always easier to arrive bearing donuts. Donuts could open any door.

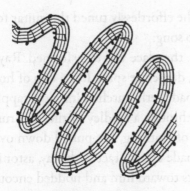

CHAPTER THREE

The Old Man Who Sings

When Ellie arrived at the Mission of Hope, she checked in at the front desk and asked for Ray. The man nodded toward the day room where a few people were milling about. She set the donuts on the coffee table, inviting everyone to help themselves.

"Well, well," said Ray as he walked over, obviously happy to see her. "I wasn't sure you would come back, West Side."

Ellie was glad that she had. "We still haven't solved the mystery of how your song lyrics ended up in my bedroom closet, Mr. Jones, and I have not yet had the pleasure of hearing you strum a guitar."

"Oh, my," Ray cried out as he noticed the guitar case. "Well, *well.*"

He popped the rest of his jelly donut into his mouth, carefully wiped his hands, and opened the case. He lifted out Mike's guitar, held it to the light and turned it over a few times. Ray studied the strings and frets and gingerly gave a few strums. Ellie watched as he shifted and then summoned memories embedded in his psyche like the wood carvings on the body of the instrument. No longer tentative, he took command of the instrument and began to tune.

There was nothing for him to tune the strings to, no piano at the shelter, no pitch pipe, no point of reference. But Ray didn't have any difficulty at all; he effortlessly tuned the guitar to perfect pitch and moved right into song.

In an instant, the place was transformed. Ray's soothing chords filled the empty, desperate space like a cup of hope, warm and real. A woman with bad teeth watched intently, tapping her feet as Ray worked his way through a medley of rifts and runs. A man wearing too many layers of clothing, hat pulled down over his face, shifted in his seat and made eye contact with Ray, astonished. Ellie pushed the box of donuts toward him and nodded encouragingly. The man quickly grabbed a chocolate donut and retreated, turning his back to the room while mumbling excitedly to himself.

Ray sang "Bright Lights, Big City" in a folksy bass voice, tapping his foot as he strummed to the relaxed walking beat. Ellie and the small crowd that was gathering listened appreciatively. Ray was simply wonderful on the guitar, and his voice was golden.

"Jimmy Reed wrote that song," he informed Ellie with a nod after he finished.

A few staff members came from other areas of the shelter and stood in doorways to the common room, listening to Ray play. It felt a bit like a special holiday at the Mission of Hope, with live music from a master musician bringing everyone out of themselves. There was some clapping, but he moved right into his next song, "In the Summertime."

He nodded to Ellie at the conclusion, tipping his imaginary hat in a gentlemanly fashion. "And that was Mr. Roger Miller."

Watching Ray transform was almost as wonderful as the songs themselves. He unfolded and blossomed as he warmed up and became acquainted with Mike's old guitar, sounding better and more confident as he went along. His face glowed and his eyes shined. He had come to life.

Ellie marveled that Ray knew so much off the top of his head. All the notes. All the words. Songs she knew and songs she had never heard before. He moved masterfully through folk, bluegrass, country, jazz, blues and early rock and roll, but seemed most at home with bluegrass—the mountain ballads. "Y'all surely know these old timey songs," he told Ellie. His fingers flew as he picked with precision, producing a banjo-like percussive beat for the refrain of "She'll Be Coming Around the Mountain," which he sang with a country twang.

"And let's not forget the great Monroe and Flatt." He segued into "Little Cabin Home on the Hill," slowing his tempo to croon the ballad with tenderness.

Ray went on and on and more than one hundred people—the homeless and hopeless, as well as those volunteering or employed to help—all stopped whatever they were doing to listen. Many in the group sang along, clapping their hands, and a few even got up and danced. Others hung back, but watched all the same. People arriving back after a day of searching for work, meeting with probation officers, or attending treatment stopped on their way through the day room to see where the otherworldly music was coming from. They poked their heads around doorways and craned their necks around the shoulders of those in front to get a better look.

It had been a long time since Ellie had heard live music. Her mind wandered back to her college days, frequenting concerts and clubs, wearing her ridiculous "hippie in the wrong decade" outfit: hot-pink peasant skirt, flat-heeled high riding boots and a tight, low-cut black knit top. Dressing like that in the late 80s, when the rest of the Reagan-youth girls were prepped out with ugly short haircuts and green and pink collared shirts adorned with strawberries or lady bugs; that was the younger, gutsier version of Ellie.

Ray let up to take a drink of water and looked around, surprised to see the crowd that had gathered. "Oh goodness, you got me going here, Ellie, with this guitar and I think I lost track of myself..."

"Please, don't stop," Ellie begged. "It's just wonderful hearing you play. May I make a request?"

"I dare you to name a song I can't play," Ray responded playfully. "Unless it's new, of course. Don't got no radio or record player anymore. Don't bother with television. Don't hear much new music these days.

Just keep the old-time music in my head."

"Well I'm sure you know this one," said Ellie as she pulled a folded piece of paper from her purse. "After all, you wrote it."

She started to read her favorite lyric from the shoebox to Ray:

"Baby child, baby o' mine,
We rock softly under the elms, the wind keeping time.
Come evening I'll strike out to earn me a dime,
Making music to bring home treats so fine..."

But Ray put his hand over the paper and shook his head no. His face darkened and closed. "Thank you for bringing me a guitar to play today, Miss Ellie," he said, strangely formal.

A bell started to ring. "That's our dinner bell here. I'm done with singing for today. We can't be late for supper." He stood abruptly, gave a little bow to Ellie and walked out.

Ellie stood in confusion, the paper hanging in her hand. Obviously, she had said or done something very wrong. The room was emptying—everyone was moving toward the dining hall. The guitar lay on the coffee table, abandoned. She scrambled to put it in the case, hoping to catch up with Ray and leave it with him for a few weeks.

A shelter counselor stopped her as she hurried behind him, guitar case in tow. "He won't be able to hang on to that here. The residents can't store possessions that don't fit in their bins. Otherwise, we'd be deluged trying to store households of possessions after people are evicted or foreclosed upon. I'm sorry, it's just too large."

Ellie murmured understanding and took her leave. Space constraints aside, it seemed unfair that a person with such talent could only play a borrowed guitar. She resolved to return and, when she did, three days later, she brought Ray something smaller he could hang on to—a harmonica.

Ray was pleased to see her and there was no mention of the lyric that had shut down the show last time. He blew the harp with gusto, tapping his foot along to the boogie woogie. He paused only to quiz her with a riddle: "How does one get that fat sound out of a harmonica?"

She confessed she had no idea. He laughed. "Ha! You don't. You use an accordion."

But his chuckling turned into a cough—a painful, rattling cough with no end. Ellie jumped up and ran to the kitchen to fetch a glass of water. A few residents were cutting up vegetables, cleaning pots and getting ready to lay out food for the day's meal.

A thin woman with wild dishwater blond hair turned and gave Ellie an accusatory stare. A sharp thrill of recognition froze Ellie to the spot. She allowed herself to soak up her old friend's appearance in silence: sunken face, bony arms covered in bruises, pockmarked skin and darkened teeth. Ellie's gaze faltered and hung over the woman's arms in dismay: *were those track marks*? The woman put her hands on her hips and looked Ellie up and down with fury. It was apparent to Ellie that Brandy wasn't as surprised to see her as she was to see Brandy.

"Brandy...?" Ellie ventured tentatively.

"Look at this snotty rich bitch, slumming with us today," Brandy announced loudly.

Everyone in the kitchen stopped their chores and watched the two women. The air grew dense, charged with tension.

Ellie's mind raced. What was Brandy Sarendesh doing here, in a homeless shelter? *My God, I haven't thought of her for years.* Ellie was suddenly conscious of her own appearance, her diamond-stud earrings, her two hundred dollar designer shoes. She snapped into action. "Sorry, just need some water." She pushed past her old friend, grabbed a cup, filled it and fled the room. Only afterward did she realize Brandy was wearing a blue button-down blouse donated from her own closet.

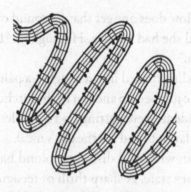

CHAPTER FOUR

PARTNERS IN CRIME

Over the next few weeks, Ellie found time to stop in for visits with Ray. Her face became familiar to the woman at the front desk, who would now look up and give an approving nod. Each time Ellie tried to bring something to help in a small way, knowing she couldn't give Ray more than he could store in his bin: nice-smelling aftershave, a pair of new socks, a batch of homemade cookies to share. Once she tried to give him money, but he politely refused. Always she brought the guitar.

She often tried to steer their conversation away from music and toward more personal topics such as his past, how long he had been at the shelter, and how he came to be there, but he deftly dodged her questions. Music was common ground they could meet on—he played snippets and phrases and paused to talk about the chords, the time signature (6/8 was his favorite), who wrote it and who had performed it.

"So who were The Gulch Jumpers, Ray?" she asked casually one day.

"Now how in tarnation would you know about The Gulch Jumpers, Ellie?"

"I found an article on the internet. On my computer," she clarified, seeing his perplexed expression. "I Googled you."

Ray shook his head in wonderment. "*Computer*," he muttered to himself, trying to get his head around such a concept. "*Googled me? Humph.*"

"Well," he went on, "to answer your question, The Gulch Jumpers was a little bluegrass band, but more importantly, they were the best friends a man could ever have."

"Tell me about them," she begged. "Please, Ray."

"It was fifty years ago, Ellie, a lifetime ago. Down in West Virginia. Owen, Charles and I, we wrote our own songs and played in a little honky-tonk. Best time of my life."

She leaned in, eager for Ray to share more. "And the portrait of the woman in your shoebox with the song lyrics—was she involved with The Gulch Jumpers too?"

Ray immediately retreated from his digression into personal topics and returned to the more comfortable subject of music, simply refusing to answer her question.

"So now, Miss Ellie, here's the thing: when a sculptor creates a statue, he thinks about it in his head, what it's going to look like, how tall it's going to be, how the lines are going to curve. He sculpts it and, while he's creating it, while he's working on it and chiseling away, he's in that magic zone. He's found that sweet spot. But then, once it's done, it's done. Folks can look at it and admire it. They can even put it in a museum, if it's good enough and they can find space for it. But just like our problem here at the Mission, it becomes one more thing that you got to find room to store. And it doesn't change from that point forward in time. People looking at it can bring their own attitudes, history, and assumptions to it. But the sculpture is done; it doesn't change. It just decomposes over time."

"Creating music is different. Instead of just making it one time and it's done, the composer writes down the *instructions* for how to make the music, which can be followed over and over again. Like a recipe. People can follow the instructions exactly, or they can change it. They might play it softer, or change the tempo, or sing it differently. Each musician brings a little of himself to it. That way the song is new each time. Not just for the musician, but for the listener too."

"And you don't need to own a home or have space to store it," he finished and pointed to his head. "You can store it up here."

Ellie nodded. "Environmentally sound," she said. The clutter filling her own home was just things requiring space to be stored. If she had to come to live at the Mission of Hope and fit all of her personal possessions into a plastic bin, what would she choose to bring? A pair of comfy slippers? A familiar blanket? A few favorite books? The most impractical things would be any of the artwork on her walls or knick-knacks adorning her shelves. That kind of art would have to be left behind.

She appreciated Ray's concept of music evolving and changing each time a musician played a song someone else had written. One day she brought her iPad, downloaded with covers that contemporary musicians had done of older songs. They each shared an ear bud of her headphones so they could listen together. *This is Amy Winehouse singing Frank Sinatra. This is Blues Traveler singing Try and Catch the Wind. This is Jack White singing with Loretta Lynn. Here is Mark Knopfler and Emmylou Harris.*

He marveled at the new takes on these old songs, and marveled at the technology that allowed recorded music to be carried around in the palm of one's hand. She told him about the satellite radio she subscribed to that allowed her to listen to every genre of music from all around the world in her car. "They've got one channel that plays nothing but bluegrass music. One that has only classical. A Bruce Springsteen channel. All sorts of different rock stations. Jazz, blues, country."

The last two decades had simply passed Ray by.

"It's mighty fine," he declared, staring down at her iPad. "But it makes it too easy for everyone just to listen to music. Music is not just about the listening; it's about the making. Before TV and radio, people had to entertain themselves. That meant learning how to make music on your own. It didn't have to be perfect; if you were playing it or singing it, you were a musician. How about you, Ellie? You need to make some music, girl. Anyone can find that sweet spot."

"I took some clarinet lessons as a child," Ellie said. "But honestly, I was kind of awful and I haven't played in years."

"Well then, how do you connect with music besides listening to that fancy radio coming through the satellite into your car?"

"I used to go hear bands, go dancing with my friends, back when I was in college, but I haven't done that type of thing in a long time. Actually," she went on, "one of my old clubbing friends seems to be living here now. At the Mission of Hope."

"Really?" Ray raised his eyebrow and stopped picking at the guitar. "One of your old friends stays here? Who is it?"

Ellie felt strangely embarrassed. "Her name is Brandy. Thin, blonde, about my age. I was so shocked to run into her I didn't know what to say, so I haven't talked to her yet."

Ray looked thoughtful. "Sounds like your old friend might be Miss 23. I'm not surprised you couldn't find anything to say to her, West Side. That young gal's always in trouble for skipping out and not doing her chores. I've not spoken to her either, but I can tell you one thing: that young gal's a heap of trouble."

***

After her lunchtime visit with Ray, Ellie headed back to the office. She had an appointment with a new client, a woman trying to leave an abusive husband. Jessica had warmly greeted the woman, who was very emotional, and ushered her into their conference room to meet with Ellie.

Framed posters depicting the scales of justice and famous court cases adorned the conference room walls: Gideon v. Wainwright, Brown v. Board of Education, Moore v. City of East Cleveland. Moore was one of Ellie's personal favorites—a grandmother ran afoul of local zoning laws in the 1970's by allowing too many extended family members to join her household. Faced with the choice of submitting to a criminal offense or putting her own five-year old grandson out of her home, Ms. Moore appealed her conviction, taking it all the way up to the United States Supreme Court—and won.

Good for her, Ellie had always thought. In other parts of the world, it was perfectly normal for large families to live together. Perhaps there would be fewer homeless if extended families continued to live together.

Ellie spent the next hour interviewing the new client and taking notes. She spent the remainder of the day getting the documentation rolling. First, she drafted the petition for divorce, division of marital assets and custody of the three children from the marriage. Next, she drafted a motion for a protection order. This was important. The woman believed she and her children had a safe place to stay for the night, but Ellie wanted to get the restraining order filed as soon as possible. She finished around 4 PM, with just enough time to send Jessica over to the Clerk of Court to get everything filed by the end of the business day.

Ellie enjoyed a sense of satisfaction doing something concrete and immediate to help her new client. One of her favorite law professors taught that when faced with any problem, always return to the basics: *Never forget you're a lawyer. Don't forget to think like a lawyer*. In the legal arena, at least, Ellie understood the rules and had the skills to make things happen. Conflict was easier within the confines of a trial where everyone had to play by the rules of evidence. The judge made calls on admissibility, there was a clear winner and loser and the right to appeal. Sometimes things got heated, of course, but she could maintain professional distance and put it all behind her at the end of the day.

But conflict in her personal life was much trickier. She was aware each time she went to the shelter that she may run into Brandy again. It was so awkward seeing her old friend in such circumstances. Ellie didn't know what to say, and until she had that figured out, she took pains to avoid running into her.

Her most pressing issue was trying to figure out how to help Ray. While Ray seemed to enjoy her visits, when she would offer to take him out for a restaurant meal, or drive him to the drug store, or give him money, he would always decline. "You know I'm a lawyer," she told him. "Is there any kind of legal help I can offer you?"

This was her thinly veiled way of repeating the same question, of trying to draw out more information. Why was he staying in a shelter and apparently alone in the world? Who was that woman in the sketch? The Google article about The Gulch Jumpers mentioned a show at the West Virginia State Fair. What had happened to The Gulch Jumpers? Why wasn't Ray playing in a band or reaping royalties from a brilliant musical career? And didn't he need to see a doctor for all of that coughing?

But Ray only seemed amused by her profession, and ignored her offer. "Well, young lady, there's many a ballad I could sing about lawyers..."

Ellie cut him off. "Yeah, yeah. I've heard them all before. 'Lawyers, Guns and Money.' That's Warren Zevon," she added, thinking she finally knew a song that Ray didn't.

"Hank Williams, Jr. did that song too," he quipped, having the last word.

She turned off her computer, shut off the lights and locked up the office to head home for the evening. Her cell rang and Mike asked if she wanted to have dinner at home or go out. They agreed to meet at their favorite Italian restaurant where they relaxed with good wine and easy conversation, confined to safe topics.

When they returned home, Gracie greeted them at the door as always, but as they walked into the kitchen, Mike stopped abruptly. "What the hell!" he exclaimed.

"What's going on?" asked Ellie, following from behind.

"*Look* at the place! Someone's been in the house!"

Food spread across the counter, a carton of melting ice cream sat open by the sink. Empty beer bottles. An empty box of chocolates with the lid discarded casually onto the floor.

"Stay back," cautioned Mike, as he moved gingerly through to the living room. The flat screen TV was untouched, but small vases and ornaments were missing from the shelves.

"Check your jewelry box," he said.

They went upstairs and, sure enough, the jewelry box was turned upside-down on the floor and had been emptied. Gone were some of Ellie's most treasured items: the turquoise pin from a trip to Santa Fe, a necklace Mike had surprised her with when she passed the bar exam, her mother's pearls presented to Ellie on her wedding day. A wet bath towel lay on the floor. The mirrored bathroom cabinet door hung open. Ellie stared quizzically at her toiletries strewn about, lids open. Clothing lay on the floor. She shivered at the feeling of invasion into her most private of things.

Wordlessly, she proceeded to the second bedroom, opened the door with shaking hands and stood in the silent nursery. The crib was arranged with brightly colored bedding—a teddy bear theme. The cheerful mobile hung silent and still. The rocking chair, changing table, diaper bin, wall hangings and large stuffed teddy bear sat unused. Tiny outfits, onesies, were folded neatly on top of the dresser. The thieves had not disturbed anything in this room. Mike came up behind her and awkwardly put his arm around her shoulder, but she shook her head and drew him back to the hallway, shutting the door again.

"Our vacation stash..." she said. They moved into the study and opened the desk drawer. The envelope where they had been squirreling away extra cash for their dream trip out west was empty.

"Call the police," Mike said. "We've been robbed."

***

The police officer compiled the incident report and list of missing property. He inquired about suspects. Could they think of anyone who had threatened them recently? Had they noticed any suspicious people around the neighborhood?

"Ellie," prompted Mike, "tell him about your visits to the homeless shelter. What about Ray?"

"Ray wouldn't rob us," Ellie said, shaking her head. "He's not that kind of person, and he won't even accept the cash I offer. Besides, I don't think he gets out much. And he doesn't know where we live. Maybe this is just one of those random things. Maybe it was a neighborhood kid."

She tried to appear nonchalant and shrug off the incident, but the enormity of it shook her to the core. Someone had invaded her home, used the shower, gone through her toiletries and clothing. It was too personal to be a random robbery.

"Well, if you think of anything else, call me," said the officer, leaving them with his card. "And you really should change your locks and fix that basement window so you can secure the latch."

They cleaned up and sat down on the porch. "Ellie, are you sure about this Ray fellow?" asked Mike. "I mean, what do you really know about him? You said he won't talk about his past. You've gone over there, what, five or six times? All you guys do is sit around while he plays the guitar and talks about chord structure? Don't you think that's a little *odd*?"

"We're still just getting to know each other," Ellie replied. "A lot of the homeless are ashamed of their situation. I know he's got a story, but he's not ready to tell it yet, and I don't want to press him."

"What if he's a criminal? Sex offender? Ax-murderer?"

"I just don't think he is. I think he's a sad old man without a home who needs a friend. Really. You've got to trust me about this."

"Well, perhaps you should go see him tomorrow," suggested Mike. "If he is the one who robbed us, he probably packed up and left. Got himself a hotel room. Or a one-way bus ticket out of town. I'll go with you."

***

After picking up the obligatory donuts, Ellie and Mike pulled into

the shelter parking lot late the next morning. Though the Mission of
Hope was located near the industrial area of the city, planters along
the main avenue overflowed with petunias, the result of a well-in-
tentioned downtown beautification project. Ellie had been to a local
music store earlier that morning to pick out a special gift for Ray—a
ukulele. Small and inexpensive, she hoped he could keep it amongst
his meager personal possessions in his bin. Several dozen people milled
about outside, enjoying the warmth of the day. With a sinking sensation in her stomach, Ellie spotted Brandy among a group standing
by a picnic table under a tree. She hadn't told Mike about Brandy
yet. She was sure Brandy saw her arrive, but she averted her eyes and
ushered Mike inside.

Ray wasn't in the day room.

Ellie peeked into the courtyard, but Ray wasn't there either. "Maybe
he's on chore duty," she said to Mike. "Let's check the kitchen." A few
familiar faces greeted Ellie, but Ray was nowhere to be found.

Her face flushed. Was Mike right? Had she just bought a ukulele
for the man who had invaded their home and robbed them?

Ellie returned to the check-in desk and inquired about her friend.

The volunteer checked the sign-out book, but there was no notation
indicating Ray had left the premises. "Hold on," she said as she leaned
back in her chair to call to the social worker whose office was stationed
behind the desk. "Alice, did you process a move-out for a Ray Jones?"

Alice peered up from her desk. "Who is inquiring about Mr. Jones?"

"We're the Sanders." Ellie extended her hand. "Ellie and Mike. I'm
an acquaintance of Ray's. I've been coming several times a week to
visit and bring him a guitar to play."

"Oh yes, of course," said Alice. "I have seen you here. And I've heard
Ray's wonderful little concerts with the guitar and the harmonica. It's
good of you to take an interest in him; he's had no other visitors while
he's been here. Do you know how his family can be reached?"

Ellie frowned and shook her head. "I don't even know if he has
family, let alone how to reach them. Did something happen?"

"Mr. Jones is in the hospital. He went into a coughing fit last night, passed out and hit his head on the floor when he fell. The hospital admitted him to run some tests. But I don't know if they'll give you any information since you're not family," Alice added.

"We have to try," said Ellie. "If he doesn't have any family, he needs to know someone cares about him."

"And *you* know all about caring for people, right, Ellie?"

Ellie and Mike turned to the accusatory voice from behind. Mike looked back and forth in confusion between his wife and the scrawny blond woman, each regarding the other with intensity. Brandy's eyes were smug and challenging.

"Have some donuts, Brandy." Ellie thrust the box of donuts into Brandy's arms while she grabbed Mike's hand and pulled him toward the door. "You know they were always good for a hangover," she called out behind her.

"Ellie, who is that woman?" Mike asked as Ellie tugged him to the car.

But she just shook her head. "No one important."

***

Ellie went home that night and read through her favorite of Ray's lyrics, the one that sounded like a lullaby. She wondered about the melody it would be set to. He still refused to sing it to her. Like so much about her new friend, it was a mystery. She fired up her laptop, miraculously not stolen in the robbery, and returned to the Google page about Ray Jones and his rhythm guitar. *West Virginia*. Where were the other guys in the band? And how did he end up north, homeless in Cleveland?

On a whim, she decided to Google Brandy Sarendesh—a fairly unusual name; perhaps there would be a clue here about what her old friend had been up to. A hit came up for a police blotter in a local paper:

Brandy Sarendesh, 31, was arrested on the near west side on July 14, 2002, with cocaine on her person, following execution of a warrant at a known drug premises. Ms. Sarendesh was arrested and charged with Possession of Cocaine and booked into the Cuyahoga County Jail.

Ellie was stunned. She knew her friend liked to drink and smoke pot, but cocaine? When did that start? How did things progress from pitchers of beer and Alabama Slammers at the clubs to an arrest at a "known drug premises?" She moved from the police blotter to the online court docket and a search under Brandy's name pulled up the subsequent conviction and one-year prison sentence. Brandy had done time. That explained a lot.

She sat back, stretched her legs onto the ottoman, and tried to imagine Brandy in prison. Brandy, dressed to the nines to go out, with her short skirt, heels and jeans jacket. They used to crank up AC/DC on the turntable as they were getting ready, dancing as they shared a curling iron, mascara and hairspray. Teasing for height, it took a lot of work to achieve the signature 1980s' big hair. Back in Black. Hells Bells.

The cocaine had led to other drugs, if the track marks on Brandy's arms were any indication. Ellie thought back to the others who were among their crowd. The old boyfriends, Doug and Jim. Other girls who hung out. Joanna. Angel. Michelle. She wondered if any of them had borne witness to Brandy's decline into hard-core drug addiction, or even facilitated it. Ellie was out of touch with her old college crowd. She hadn't thought about any of them for so long. Really, most of the other kids were on the periphery, hangers-on. She and Brandy were the ones who called the shots: which bar they were going to that night, which party, which concert, which band. Best friends. "Partners in crime," they used to joke.

Suddenly that expression was no longer so funny.

While Ellie had been trying cases in court, drafting legal briefs and making oral arguments, Brandy had been a defendant, standing up with her public defender to take her verdict, learning she had been found guilty beyond a reasonable doubt. While Ellie had been walking down the aisle, raising a glass of champagne for a wedding toast, and enjoying her first dance with Mike ("Follow You Follow Me," Genesis), Brandy had been visiting her dealer, going to drug houses, shooting up. While Ellie had been picking out flooring, lighting, and counter-tops for her kitchen makeover, Brandy had been in prison, wearing the standard-issue orange jumpsuit Ellie had seen so many prisoners come to court in. She had probably been *handcuffed* at some point, Ellie realized with a shudder.

Perhaps if she had stayed in touch, she could have helped Brandy. She could have represented her, testified on her behalf as a character witness, referred her to a colleague for a stronger criminal defense. Why hadn't she tried harder to find her to invite her to her wedding? Was she ashamed of Brandy and their clubbing days? No, she decided, it was more that she had just outgrown it. For Ellie, the party days were a kind of developmental stage she had moved through in her early twenties, but Brandy had somehow gotten stuck there, and fallen into a darker place. Ellie had moved on, and her old party friend didn't fit into her new life. There was some guilt in admitting that, but it was a fact.

Was it really worth getting in any deeper with Brandy at this point? People changed, and she really didn't know Brandy at all anymore.

For now, Ellie needed to focus on Ray. Ray was much older and he was having some kind of health crisis. Ray wasn't a convicted felon or a drug user. Ray was an extraordinary musician with a warm folksy voice; he was funny and wise and kind. And he needed help.

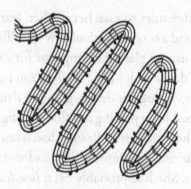

CHAPTER FIVE

BLACK LUNG

Ellie walked eagerly toward the elevator that led to the patient floors. Monday afternoon was a busy time at the hospital, and the nurses and doctors didn't give Ellie a second glance as her heels clicked importantly along the polished hallways. Ray was on the eighth floor. She rounded a corner and stopped in the doorway to his room, suddenly unsure. He lay in a bed by the window, head propped up on pillows, dozing.

"Hi there," said a nurse approaching with a tray of medications. "Can I help you?"

"Ray Jones?" said Ellie helplessly, gesturing to Ray's room. "Is he all right?"

"Oh, you're here for Mr. Jones. You must be Sally. So glad you've come, Sally. He had a bad night last night, kept asking for you. Calling 'Sally' even in his sleep. I'm sure he'll be so relieved to see you." She stopped. "You *are* Sally, right?"

"Uh, yes, I'm Sally," Ellie replied quickly, astonished at how smoothly the lie flew from her own lips. She followed the nurse into Ray's room.

Ray stirred as they entered. "Mr. Jones," sang the nurse. "How are we feeling? Time for a few pills." She set the medications out on his tray next to the water pitcher and cup. "And you've got a visitor today." She nodded brightly to Ellie, who prayed that the woman would not call her Sally in front of Ray.

"Maybe you can help him call down to the kitchen with his menu selections for dinner," she told Ellie. The nurse breezed out to answer a page from another room.

Relieved, Ellie pulled a chair up next to Ray's bed. "Ray... I've been so worried. They said you passed out and hit your head? What's going on?"

"Ah Ellie, I'm just taking a little rest here," said Ray, tired and withdrawn. "You don't need to go worrying 'bout old Ray."

"Well, of course I'm worried." She took his hand. "Did they tell you what's wrong?" Ray was hooked up to an IV line, blood pressure and heart rate monitor.

"Not a thing wrong with me," he drawled. "Just taking a rest here, and when I'm back on my feet, I'll show you some more tunes on the guitar. Not today, though, girl. Just taking a rest for now..." His eyelids sunk to half-mast and his head nodded back as he drifted off, snoring softly.

Ellie sat back, uncertainly, waiting. She picked up the menu for the hospital cafeteria by his bedside phone. She didn't even know Ray's favorite foods.

She jumped when a doctor walked in unannounced. "Family for Ray Jones?" he said briskly. Ellie nodded stupidly. "Looks like your father is asleep," said the doctor. "Let's talk in the hallway and I'll examine him later when he's awake. I understand he had a rough night last night, so if he's not in any pain right now, he could probably use the sleep."

Ellie followed the doctor to the hallway. "Let's sit a moment," he suggested. "I was becoming concerned there was no family to explain Mr. Jones' condition to, so I am glad to see he has a visitor. I understand he was transported here from a homeless shelter?"

Ellie heard the accusation in his question. Time to think fast. "I live on the west coast; I came as soon as I could."

The doctor waited, expecting more. Ellie was wearing a business suit, pearl earrings and professional pumps. How could she allow her father to live in a homeless shelter, wearing hand-me-downs and tattered suspenders? But Ellie remained silent, poker-faced, not offering anything more. If there was anything she had learned from cross-examination, it was to stop talking and wait out the other person.

"Okay, well then. I'm Dr. Stuart. I'm a pulmonologist and I've been treating your dad since he's been in here for problems with his lungs. His coughing and emphysema have decreased his lung capacity, which is why he's been tired and getting dizzy when he stands up quickly. We did X-rays, blood tests, a CT scan. His lungs are black, probably from smoking. Or mining, perhaps?"

Hmmm. Ellie nodded, uncommitted.

"So we need to biopsy some of that lung tissue and see exactly what's going on." Now it was his turn to stop talking and wait Ellie out.

"I see," said Ellie. "And in the meantime? Should he stay in the hospital?"

"Yes." Dr. Stuart nodded. "We can keep him on oxygen and make him comfortable. I think that's best for now. When we have more information we can talk again and decide a course of action."

Black Lung. Biopsy. Ellie wondered how long the coughing had been going on. Wouldn't the shelter social worker or any of the counselors have noticed? She should have spoken up about it the first time he went into a coughing fit during one of her visits. A tear welled in her eye.

"I'm sorry, Sally," said Dr. Stuart. "I'm sure it's a lot to take in, especially if it's been awhile since you've seen your father. Do you have any questions?"

She thought for a moment. "Two questions. Any restrictions on what he can eat?"

"No, he can eat whatever he likes. In fact, a healthy diet and good nutrition can be very helpful. He doesn't have to worry about his

weight and his blood pressure is within normal limits. I say encourage
him to eat a variety of healthy foods."

Ellie nodded, the wheels in her head turning.

"What is the second question?" the doctor asked.

"Can I bring in some music for him?"

***

While Ray was sleeping, Ellie returned home to round up her little
compact stereo, thinking about a playlist that would be upbeat and
positive, but also help Ray rest and relax. She left a note for Mike and
headed back out.

She would see what Ray thought about the food from the hospital
cafeteria. If he didn't like it, she could cook and bring something in, or
pick up takeout. No one sick should have to suffer mediocre food, and
life at the shelter had surely not included top of the line fare. Not that
she blamed anyone there. It was impressive how efficiently they turned
out three meals a day for hundreds of people, all on a meager budget
and reliance upon donations. Where would the Rays and Brandys of
the world eat, shower and lay their heads, if not for the Mission of
Hope? She wondered if Brandy still liked burritos. How many burritos
had they eaten together, laughing and running over to the food truck
after the bars closed? Did they even serve burritos at the shelter?

She pulled into the visitor parking lot and got out, walking with
renewed purpose. After all, she was "Sally," Ray's daughter who had
flown in from the west coast as soon as she heard the news. She had
been oh-so-busy with her own life but was here now at his bedside,
appropriately concerned, ready to do whatever was necessary for her
dad. Even though "Sally" had allowed her father to live in a homeless
shelter. Even though "Sally" had never visited and no one at the shelter knew whether he had any family. Even though "Sally" didn't even
know what kind of food he liked to eat. *Damn you, Sally*. But then
again, how did she even know if Sally was a daughter? Maybe Sally
was a long lost love or his wife. His mother. His sister. Maybe Sally

was no longer living. Or maybe Ray had just been dreaming and was confused when he said the name.

Ray was still dozing. She plugged in the boom box and set the volume to low. Ellie had brought along her laptop. She settled into a chair in the corner and spread her paperwork out. She set her coffee on the table nearby.

Ray stirred. He opened his eyes and looked at Ellie, the boom box. He listened a moment. "Good choice, Miss Ellie," he said and then closed his eyes once more.

The jazz was contemplative, all instrumental. The string bass deftly moved the rhythm along. There was no need to talk. Charlie Parker's sophisticated saxophone playfully weaved in and out around corners, making their conversation for them.

Ellie continued to work, thinking Ray was asleep, but soon he opened his eyes again.

"Ellie." He looked at her for a long moment.

"What is it, Ray?"

"Please don't leave."

"I'm not going anywhere."

The saxophone wailed like a baby. He nodded and drifted back to sleep.

***

Ellie spent the night and woke around six, stiff in her chair and wishing she had a toothbrush. She pulled the extra blanket up around her shoulders and looked over at her patient. It had been a fitful night until she rang the nurse and got Ray set up with some pain medication. The noises of the hospital were intrusive; she was nervous about Ray and had not slept well. She spent some time looking at her emails and checking various news apps until Ray's breakfast tray arrived. He sat up, rubbing his eyes and yawning, and looked over at Ellie.

"You look awful," he said.

"Good morning to you too, mister," she replied. "What have you got for breakfast there? And how are you feeling?"

"I feel just like I always do," he said. "Don't even know why I'm in here."

They looked over the breakfast tray, fussing over the food with comfortable familiarity. He insisted on sharing some of his pastry and yogurt with her. She in turn insisted that he eat everything on the tray. He refused until she finally relented and took a half piece of toast just to get him to eat.

"I think you're scheduled for a test later this morning, Ray," Ellie said. "I'm going to wait here with you until it's time for that. I believe the doctor is going to biopsy some lung tissue to see why you're coughing."

"You talked to the doctor?" he said, frowning. "Is he coming back this morning? I want to talk to him myself."

"I don't know, Ray, probably. I'll wait here with you. You can rest or read the paper. I brought some work along, so I'll be quiet and you won't even know I'm here."

She started to review research notes for a brief. Out of the corner of her eye, she watched Ray pick up the morning newspaper from his breakfast tray. He looked at it and frowned, moving the paper closer and then further from his eyes. He started flipping through the pages quickly, scanning but not reading. Finally he tossed it to the side.

"Nothing interesting?" she asked.

"Type is too small," he said. "Can't read the darn thing."

Ellie checked the clock. She wondered if the gift shop on the first floor would be open yet. "I'll be back," she told him.

She made a quick trip to the cafeteria for a spinach egg white sandwich and some coffee. Ellie wouldn't dream of eating Ray's food, but truth was that she loved breakfast and she was starving. She packed up the food to go, and then followed the signs down the hallway to the gift shop. She bought a toothbrush, toothpaste, some Chapstick for Ray and then looked at the reading glasses. She had to guess at what magnification he needed. She couldn't imagine not being able to read. She needed to read every day and would lose her mind if she couldn't.

Back upstairs, she asked Ray if he wanted to listen to music. They chose Glen Campbell, "Gentle on My Mind," and kept it turned low in the background.

Ray put on the reading glasses and picked up the paper again. "Well, *well*. Now that is just the ticket, Miss Ellie." He became absorbed with reading the news.

Dr. Stuart walked in a half-hour later. "Mr. Jones, glad to see you're awake. How are you feeling this morning?"

Ray put the newspaper aside and set the reading glasses on the bedside stand. "Everyone's taking real good care of me here, doctor, but I suppose I don't even know why I've got to be in the hospital."

Dr. Stuart explained to Ray about his coughing, passing out, hitting his head, the lung x-rays. He listened to his heart and held the stethoscope to his lungs, listening to the rattle as Ray attempted to take long deep breaths without dissolving into coughing fits. "Okay, let's put this oxygen back on." The doctor gently set the oxygen plugs back into Ray's nostrils and Ray lay back, gray in pallor, grateful for breath. Ellie hung back and watched helplessly.

"Mr. Jones, the scans we took show there is a large dark spot on your lungs, actually one on each lung. I'm pretty sure that's why you've been coughing so much and having trouble breathing. Are you a smoker, by any chance?"

"Not anymore," said Ray. "I don't have any spending money to waste buying cigarettes. I suppose I smoked as a younger man, lots of folks did."

"It appears there is a lot of damage to your lung tissue, which is what we would expect to see from a very heavy smoker, or perhaps someone who worked in a coal mine. Miners can develop black lung from long time exposure to coal dust."

Ray nodded. "Well, doctor, I did do some mining back in the day when I lived down home. I know about black lung. Other men I knew suffered with it. But I don't think I've got it that bad. After all, I can still raise my voice in song every day. Can still breathe well enough to sing."

"He sings all the time," Ellie interjected, "and it's wonderful. But you do get a lot of those coughing fits, Ray." She turned to the doctor. "What can be done to help?"

Dr. Stuart outlined his recommendation to biopsy some of Ray's lung tissue. If cancer was found, they would determine if it was operable. If it wasn't operable, or if it had spread, they may need to talk about radiation or chemotherapy. Whatever the outcome, the first step was the biopsy. "We need to know for sure what we're dealing with," he explained.

Ray listened to the grim news, not speaking. Ellie asked a few questions. If it was operable, how long would the surgery be? Were there any risks to the biopsy procedure? Dr. Stuart and Ellie became engrossed in conversation.

Finally Ray cleared his voice. "Y'all got it all figured out over there?"

"I'm sorry," said Ellie. "Just trying to get information. We need to have all our questions answered so you can make some informed decisions, Ray."

"Well, I've already made my decision," he announced. Ellie and Dr. Stuart turned to him curiously.

"It's nice having this comfy bed and a private room. The food's not bad. I don't ask for much and I get along just fine at the Mission of Hope. I do my work every day. If I have to chop vegetables or wash pots and pans, I do it. If I have laundry duty, I wash the bedding. I mop the floors. I give thanks for the food. I sing to the people like me who don't have a home to go to. When Ellie here brings me a guitar, I get my kicks playing some old time music. I don't have much and I don't ask for much. This here oxygen is helping with my coughing, and I appreciate it, but I'm not going to stay here and have tests and all those procedures. I'm too old. There's no point to it."

"Okay," said Dr. Stuart, looking in confusion from Ellie to Ray. "Maybe if I can answer some questions for you about the procedure? And you don't have to decide all of it today—surgery, chemotherapy, those things can wait. All we're really talking about today is a biopsy.

Can I tell you more about what will happen during the biopsy?"

But Ray shook his head. "No biopsy. I do thank you, doctor, for trying to help me. My mind is made up."

Dr. Stuart spoke again—this time to Ellie. "Maybe some time to digest all of this information and think it over? I can come back later. We can reschedule the test. And I'm sorry, but I'm confused," he went on. "Why do you call your dad by his first name? Why does he call you Ellie—I thought your name was Sally? And he said you've been bringing him a guitar to play at the shelter but you said you just flew in to town?"

Ellie faltered and gave a sideways glance at Ray who gave a long low whistle and raised his eyebrow at her.

"Dr. Stuart," Ray said. "Leave us in peace for a while. I'd like to talk to my *daughter* in private."

"That's fine, you should talk. I'm going to do the rest of my rounds." The doctor picked up his clipboard. "Sally, Ellie, whoever you are, please try to talk to him about the biopsy. It's not a difficult procedure and there's a lot that can be done. If it is malignant, the sooner we start treating, the better." He shook Ray's hand, nodded to Ellie and left.

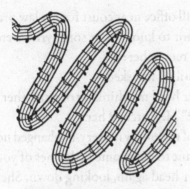

CHAPTER SIX

THE GULCH JUMPERS

Once alone, Ray and Ellie contemplated one another in silence, waiting to see who would speak first. The question could be put off no longer.

"Ray, who is Sally? *Do* you have a daughter?"

He turned away from her. "You told them you were my family to get that doctor to talk to you."

"Okay, yes. I'm sorry, I shouldn't have presumed to butt into your business, and I'll leave if you want me to." She hovered by the side of his bed. "I care about you, I like visiting you, I enjoy learning about music with you. You're sick and it seems that you can use a friend. I just want to help. But if you want me to leave, I will."

He folded his hands and sighed.

"Why me? Why do you have so much time on your hands to sit with an old homeless man in the hospital? To come visit me at the shelter?" he wondered aloud. "Pretending to be my family. Where's your own family?"

"I have a husband, Ray, his name is Mike. He came along to the shelter a few days ago so he could meet you. That's his guitar you've been playing. We have a house on the west side of town, we have a dog, I have a small office near court for my law practice. I don't know what else you want to know. Your song lyrics were in the back of my bedroom closet, remember?"

"No other family?" he asked.

She shook her head no, thinking of her father.

"No children?" He watched her.

She thought of the empty nursery, unchanged now for three seasons.

"Don't you want to have some little ones of your own?"

She shook her head again, looking down. She fought back a tear but said nothing.

He considered her thoughtfully for a moment. "Well, you're always asking questions about me and my past, but I can see I'm not the only one in this room with secrets."

Ray leaned forward, grasped both her hands and looked into her face imploringly. "Ellie, have you ever met a woman named Sally Jones? She'd be about your age. She's biracial. Do you know her? Is that why you let the doctor call you Sally? Is that how you got the shoebox with my song lyrics?"

Ellie grabbed a tissue, wiped her eyes and blew her nose. "I don't know a Sally Jones. The nurse said you were calling the name Sally in your sleep. She assumed I was Sally and I didn't correct her... same thing with the doctor... I'm sorry, Ray."

"All right then, Ellie. Don't cry, now. I'm laid up here in this hospital bed and my time in this world is running down. And you're right, I do need your help. So today I'm going to answer some of your questions. It's high time I tell ye my story."

She pulled up her chair close to his bedside.

"And I reckon the place to start with a story is at the beginning, so I'll tell ya that my given name is Raymond Virgil Jones, and I grew up in the hills of West Virginia, the Mountain State."

He paused and closed his eyes for so long Ellie thought he had drifted off to sleep. He opened his eyes and went on. "Ya have to understand, when I was just a kid, there was no hook-up for electricity in the hills. No indoor plumbing; you had to use the outhouse. And we had a hand pump where me and my folks pumped our well water, which we heated on the potbelly stove."

Ray described how he carried his lunch pail and walked to the one room country school where the teacher stood by the window and read poetry in the afternoon light, after it was too dark for the children to see their schoolwork. Ray liked school and loved listening to the teacher read Walt Whitman, Ogden Nash, Emily Dickinson, Langston Hughes. "That's where I learned to turn a phrase," he told Ellie. "Learned the melody of the words, the rhythm of the words, the soft sounds and the hard sounds. How it all sounded together.

"Aunt Mary Lou and Uncle Horace lived in a nearby holler, so I used to run to their house after school to hear my aunt sing and my uncle play the guitar. Uncle Horace taught me all the different chords in different keys. He pulled the fiddle down from the mantle by the fireplace and let me try out notes and bowings, just play around with it. Aunt Mary Lou sang while she was hanging up the wash or working in the kitchen. I learned all the words to her hymns and ballads. Each one told a story. 'Course I already knew a lot of the gospel songs and hymns from going to church with my parents, but my aunt and uncle, they were just so good to me, Ellie, so patient with me."

Young Ray sang along with his aunt and clomped his foot to the beat, as the cloggers would do. His aunt and uncle eventually hooked into the power lines. They had a radio and listened to the Grand Ole Opry, or Wilma Lee and Stoney Cooper and their Wheeling Jamboree. They listened to Bill Monroe, Earl Scruggs, The Foggy Mountain Boys. They listened to Red Foley, Bob Wills, Hank Williams. Grandpa Jones. Hawkshaw Hawkins, Mel Tillis, Ernest Tubb. And most of all, they listened to WWVA, the radio station out of Wheeling. Everyone listened to WWVA.

Everyone, that was, except for Ray's father. Ray's father was a coal miner. "He worked hard and he worked long hours," Ray told Ellie. "I respect that about him. When I came up and was old enough, they pulled me out of school and he got me a job in the mine, and I worked down there with him every day. Got paid in scrip. But my daddy thought the radio station was an evil influence on the family, and he forbade music in the home."

Ray recalled how it was torture to listen to the songs at his aunt and uncle's house but not be able to play a radio at home. He hummed under his breath as he walked to and from the mines, always composing songs in his head and moving his fingers to imaginary fiddle fingerings and positions on the fret of the guitar or piano keyboard. But he went silent if his father came up next to him.

"As a young man, I kept track of all the concerts and shows coming through Wheeling. The Virginia Theatre in downtown Wheeling played host to all the traveling bands and musical reviews, and the Jamboree was live every Saturday night. Once I began making a little money at my mining job, I could afford to head up there to see the shows, and I didn't miss a one of them. I tell you, it was worth it to travel into town to see those live shows even if it meant getting up at five o'clock the next morning, worn out and dog-tired."

Ellie pictured Ray as a young man, putting in his time in the mines but living for the moments he could watch The Osborne Brothers or Merle Haggard perform live at the Jamboree.

"The other boys worked in the mine too, including my best buddies, Charlie and Owen. Spent our days in the dark. It was hard, hard work. Thinking about the music, learning the songs, practicing at night—the music is what kept us going. I worked out the harmonies with Charlie and we practiced our singing down below the earth, so long as daddy wasn't around. It sure helped pass the time while we were working, I can tell you that."

"Is that how The Gulch Jumpers got started, Ray, with Charles and Owen? Is that how you guys learned to play?" Ellie asked.

"Yes, ma'am, trial and error, just by watching other musicians. So many folks played the fiddle or the banjo or the washboard, or anything," he said. "It's just the way it was back then. People made their own music. A feller at the hardware store had an upright piano and he would let me go over there and bang away until I figured it out. Used to try out the organ at church too, if I could get access to it without getting into trouble. There wasn't any right or wrong, it was just playing by ear and sounding it out.

"We were young men looking for a way to have a life. We were dirt poor, but we didn't know any different. We could see the mining was going to come to an end, though. We had strikes, union troubles with management. Lots of folk left Appalachia and moved north to get factory work. The mines were a dying proposition, but the music was our salvation. We were excited by the bands we saw coming through town; those guys seemed like movie stars to us."

The three friends lived and breathed old time music, bluegrass and country, the music of the hills. "But we were aware of other music too. We knew about Elvis. We were excited about Elvis. And the blues—I loved the blues. Johnny Lee Hooker. Elmore James."

"And, of course," he told Ellie with a shy smile, "we saw how the girls chased the musicians. We were *very* interested in finding us some girlfriends."

Ellie smiled and pictured Ray as a lanky, handsome young stud with his rhythm guitar. He must have been quite a catch to the young girls, with his deep bass voice, good nature and smiling eyes.

"So did The Gulch Jumpers make it big?" she asked. It didn't seem possible that Ray would *not* have landed a record contract or concert tour or at least been asked to sit in with some of the big names coming through town. His talent was so obvious. It was unlikely he would remain undiscovered.

"Now, Ellie," he chided. "You know how this story ends. Have you ever bought a Ray Jones album? Have you ever heard of The Gulch Jumpers?"

Ellie conceded that she had not. "Did you at least get some gigs around town?" she asked.

"Yes, ma'am, we sure did that," he nodded. He told her about the local honky-tonk dive with the small dance floor and room for the band to set up next to the bar. "The young people came and drank beer and whiskey and danced. The Gulch Jumpers played a few evenings each week and we managed to attract a small local following.

"And, actually, things started going very well for us after we got to play one of our songs on the radio. That was very, very big for us boys. The WWVA was everything; it was the voice of Appalachia all through the Mountain State and all the way to the East Coast. My daddy was furious, but I still maintained my daytime job, so what could he do? And like I said, I was a young man and I had to stand up and make my own way."

Ellie nodded. "It must have been hard living under his roof with your life taking a direction he didn't approve of."

"Oh, that's just the beginning of what daddy didn't approve of," said Ray. "The music versus the coal mining thing was nothing compared to what was to come. He thought I was wasting my time, but I showed up to work on time and earned my keep. Never called off sick. Daddy could put up with the music, even if he didn't like it. What really set things over the edge was Doris."

"Doris?" Ellie leaned forward, intrigued. "Was Doris your girlfriend?"

Ray coughed and rubbed his eyes and reached for a drink of water. A tear ran down his cheek.

"Ray, do you need to take a break and rest for a while? We can do this later. Or should I ring the nurse for more pain medication?"

He composed himself and shook his head emphatically. "No. I never told nobody my story. Now that I've started, I've got to keep going till it's finished. Then you'll understand." He finished his coughing and Ellie wet a washcloth by the sink and placed a compress on his forehead.

Ray's face had changed as he said Doris's name, his eyes shining. Ellie finally understood. "*Doris* is the woman in the portrait. You were in love with her."

Ray nodded, his eyes far away. "Aw, Ellie, I was just head over heels in love with Doris. There was no turning back. I was as gone as a young boy can be gone. The best thing of all, the best thing in the world, is that she felt the same way about me."

"So why didn't your father approve of Doris?"

"I'm afraid t'was all just as simple as black and white: Doris was black. I'm white."

Ray scratched his chin and looked thoughtful. When he went on, he talked the black musicians who came through Wheeling as part of a traveling blues show. "You've probably heard of the Chitlin' Circuit. On the Circuit, black musicians could perform and no one would bother them; they could be safe. As safe as things could be in the segregated South, anyways." After wandering into the honky-tonk one evening and hearing how hot the sound was, Ray convinced his friends to come along. "Those guys were just fan-tas-tic," he drawled. "I mean, smoking hot blues, the real stuff. It just didn't get any better."

Soon, The Gulch Jumper boys were at the blues show every night they didn't have their own gig. Ray, Owen and Charles would emerge from under the earth, clock out at the end of the workday, and agree to meet up an hour later after supper and wash up. "Don't y'all take too long," Ray always told his buddies, "or I'll head over to Marvin's place without ya." Charles and Owen just laughed. Everyone knew why Ray was in such a hurry.

Ray would scrub the coal dust from his face and hands, humming happily, as he daydreamed about seeing the girl who read poetry in the juke joint. She was there every afternoon and into the early evening, until her father made her go upstairs to their room in the boarding house before the moonshine really started flowing. For days he watched her from a nearby stool, trying not to stare too obviously, trying to get his courage up to talk to her. He noticed how her foot would start tapping as soon as her father's band started its twelve-bar signature blues chord progressions. She kept the time with her hand strumming on the table, as she turned the pages of her book. He longed to ask her to dance, but didn't want to call more attention to the fact that he, a white kid, really had no business in a black juke joint, and besides, there was the girl's father just a few feet away, keeping an eye on everything.

"But one Saturday afternoon there she was," he told Ellie, "downtown at the record store. I knew I had to grab my chance."

Ray had nervously combed his hands through his sandy brown hair. "Hello, miss," he ventured with a shy smile.

"So you finally got up your nerve to talk to me!" she said with a laugh, twirling and giving her skirt a little swirl for the tall boy with the deep voice. "Doris. My name is Doris. I knew you wanted to ask me what my name is," she added, as Ray had stood and stared, momentarily tongue-tied now that he was finally alone in her presence.

"Yes'm, Miss Doris, I know your name. I asked around." Ray recalled how he pulled himself together, gathering courage from his musical heroes as he and Doris began strolling up and down the aisles of the record store. He picked up a few of his favorite albums. "Do ya like listening to Loretta Lynn? And look here, the Osborne Brothers—'Ruby,' best guitar and banjo picking you want to hear. You can hear those boys on the radio, and sometimes they play the Jamboree up in Wheeling."

"That sure is fine," Doris had agreed, "and how about Sam Cook? Darlene Love? Or The Staple Singers? Have you heard that sound coming out of Motown? I dunno if they play it around here on the WWVA but, if you travel down to Little Rock or Memphis, you can hear that and the Chicago blues, the Delta blues too."

Ray smiled, his eyes far away. "Doris's daddy was Sammy Brown," Ray told Ellie. "He was a backup musician. Their family traveled through the south and he got jobs playing with various groups. When they reached the Wheeling area, Sammy landed a semi-permanent gig, so they settled down for a while."

Ray described how Mr. Brown enrolled Doris into her senior year of high school at the local school, desegregated a decade earlier. Doris's mother, Frances, had found the life of a traveling musician's wife wasn't for her. Trying to raise children on the road, with uncertain income and nowhere to set up housekeeping, was too much. She got fed up and took the other children away with her, but Doris wanted to stay with her father and follow the music. Sammy slowed his traveling to attempt to entice his wife to come back, but it didn't work. Doris was old enough to take care of herself, for the most part. She was interested in the grand dames of the Blues: Etta James, Ruth Brown, Mavis Staples. It was the cusp of the golden era when the great girl groups of Motown were forming in Detroit. Doris listened to her father's band, listened to the radio and shopped at the record store in town. She dreamed of becoming a singer.

Ray saved as much money as he could, hoping to move out of his daddy's house and set up his own home with the woman he loved.

"Did you get married?" asked Ellie.

"Married?" Ray looked at her incredulously. "No, Ellie, we didn't get married. We *couldn't* get married. That was our problem. There was nothing I wanted more than to ask Doris to marry me; it was what we both wanted. But it wasn't allowed. The State of West Virginia said an interracial marriage was illegal, a criminal offense even. There was nothing we could do."

Ellie understood very well. Until the Supreme Court settled the matter in 1967, West Virginia was one of sixteen States that prohibited marriage based on racial classification. The framed poster from *Loving v. Virginia* hung amongst the gallery on the wall of Ellie's office conference room. Just like Ray and Doris, in 1958 Mildred Jeter, a black woman, and Richard Loving, a white man, were married in the District of Columbia and then attempted to return to Virginia, only to be arrested. The Judge sentenced the couple to one year in jail, suspended on the condition that they leave and not return to Virginia for twenty-five years. The Judge wrote his opinion to reflect the prejudices of the day:

"Almighty God created the races white, black, yellow, malay and red,

*and he placed them on separate continents. And but for the interference
with his arrangement there would be no cause for such marriages. The
fact that he separated the races shows that he did not intend for the races
to mix."*

Ray and Doris were in an impossible situation at that juncture in
history.

"So what did you do?" Ellie asked.

"Life went on. I wasn't gonna wait around for somebody to come
and tell me what I already knew—we were a family. Eventually we
found out we were expecting our own beautiful little child."

"Sally!"

"Yes, our sweet baby Sally. When I found out Doris was expecting,
I took the money that I had and packed up what little I owned from
my daddy's house. Got my own little clapboard home, in our special
spot in the holler. The boys in the band helped me cut down the trees
and build it. We built our own damn house with our own damn hands.

"I was angry I couldn't do things the way they ought to have been
done. But no one could stop me from standing up as a man to provide
a home for my wife and child. I couldn't marry her in the eyes of the
government of my own country. She may not have been my legal wife
on paper but she was my legal wife before God. There was no question."
Ray slammed his shaking hand onto the hospital tray.

"Doris's father was furious, but my Doris, now she had some pluck
to her." Ray recalled with pride how Doris displayed the brave deter-
mination of a new mother, adamant on raising her baby with Ray, as
a family. She pieced together scraps and sewed a layette for the baby,
making her preparations with dignity.

"And how did your father react when he learned about your plan?"
asked Ellie.

"Well, he told me he was ashamed of me. He turned his back on
me. Wouldn't allow my own mama to talk to me anymore if they saw
us in town. Wouldn't acknowledge their own baby granddaughter. It
was very, very hard, Ellie, a rough time for us. But also, a happy time.

We were in love."

Ray and Doris found disapproval from both of their families and from most everyone else as well. "Not everyone was awful, though," he explained. His fellow bandmates had seen Roy pining after Doris at the black juke joint for all those months, and his heartsickness for her was obvious. They admired her father's musicianship. They didn't carry the deep prejudices of the older generation, and didn't object to their union. Doris was also able to find a friend in the local midwife, who mothered the young girl a bit and helped her through the delivery when the time came.

"I paced back and forth outside our little house, hearing her cries, and I was just beside myself," he said, "until the midwife came out and told me I was a father. And then I was just as proud as could be. It didn't matter we were poor, it didn't matter we were hillbillies, it didn't matter we were mixing the races and breaking the law. We were a real family.

"Things are so different now, Ellie, it's probably hard for you to understand. Black and white folks couldn't even be laid to rest next to each other in the same cemetery."

"You know we still live in one of the poorest and most racially segregated cities in the United States," she said.

"Well, maybe things are segregated up in your part of town, Ellie, but we got all kinds living at the shelter. Things ain't perfect, for sure, but they're a lot better than they used to be." Ray scratched his chin. "That's how I see Cleveland, anyway."

Ray went on. "But what was true then is still pretty much true now. If people had hate in their heart, they were blind and deaf to anything else and they weren't going to change. If they were sympathetic and tolerant and could live and let live, well then, they were kind to us. Uncle Horace helped me with the woodwork and lent me tools and nails to build the house. Aunt Mary Lou talked to Doris about little Sally's colic, taught her how to burp the baby and rub her tummy to ease her gas pains. Sometimes she left a freshly baked pie on our windowsill; she knew we didn't have much.

"And, of course, we shared music. Doris, Sally and I would head up to my aunt and uncle's home for evenings of down home music. I played the guitar, Uncle Horace played the fiddle, Aunt Mary Lou plucked the mandolin and Doris sang along, bouncing the baby in her lap.

"It was different than playing with the band—relaxed, just family. One of us would say 'key of C' and start a rift, and the rest joined in, making it up as we went along. If we happened upon a tune that worked, I wrote down the words and the chords, so we could play it again another evening. If Sally cried, we sang her lullabies in four-part harmony. I danced that little gal around on my shoulder and comforted her with the vibration of my voice."

"Were those songs some of the lyrics you wrote down that I found in my closet?" Ellie asked.

"Yes, I believe so. I wrote down so many lyrics over the years from the band and from just playing with the family. I wrote down those lullabies that got my little colicky Sally to stop her crying. If the song brought out a smile on that little face, well then that song was a keeper."

Ellie pictured the smiling baby, the center of attention, serenaded by her adoring mother and father. Her heart ached. "Did you keep your job in the mine, Ray?"

"Yes, I kept the job, we went on like that for a year or so, but then we all ended up going out on strike. Union and management were always arguing about something. It was a relief to catch a break from having to go underground every day, doing that hard, dangerous, dirty work. But, Lord, I needed the money. I had mouths to feed. So it really wasn't good for me to be out of work while that strike just dragged on."

Once again, music came to the rescue. The Gulch Jumpers still played the local juke joint a few nights a week, earning a small percentage of the take from the regulars who sauntered in to drink whiskey and listen to the band. "And then," Ray said, "our big break came along." The boys received an invitation to perform at the West Virginia State

Fair. "The State Fair! Can you imagine that? It was the big time for us—a chance for The Gulch Jumpers to finally be discovered. It was too big to turn down."

The problem, Ray explained, was the logistics of travel. The State Fair took place every August in the town of Fairlea, a five-hour drive away. The boys were to play at noon on Saturday and again early Sunday afternoon on one of the smaller stages near the grandstand. They decided to sleep in Owen's car to save money. The instruments would be jammed into the trunk, or in the case of the large upright string bass, lie across laps in the back seat. Amps and microphones provided by the Fair would be set up on stage for them.

"My buddies and I were so excited—so many big musical names performed at the West Virginia State Fair over the years."

Doris held Sally in the clearing outside their little clapboard house, holding the little toddler's hand as they waved goodbye, hopeful and trusting. Ray lingered over the treasured image in his mind, the memory like a snapshot now faded from being handled over and over.

"And that was the last time I saw my family," he said with finality. "I should never, ever have left them. It was the worst decision I made in my life. It was the decision that ended Doris's life, all of our lives. It's all my fault." Ray hung his head and cried out, and then fell into another coughing fit.

A nurse stuck her head into the room. "Is everything okay in here? Mr. Jones, you need to *rest*." The nurse adjusted his oxygen and pillows then checked his vitals. "You can't be yelling and crying and getting all agitated and upset in the hospital." She looked at Ellie pointedly.

"Yes," Ellie agreed. "This is too much for you, Ray. Let's take a break; we can listen to some music." The nurse nodded with satisfaction and left the room.

Ray took a few breaths and wiped his face with a tissue. "I'm okay... just had to catch my breath. I don't want to take a break. I don't want to listen to music. Music is what took my family away from me."

"What?" Ellie cried. "You *love* music. Tell me what happened, Ray."

He took a drink of water and, when he was ready, went on with the story.

"The State Fair was like nothing I'd seen," he told Ellie. "Livestock of all kinds, long rows of stables and barns. Exhibit buildings showcasing needlework, quilts, woodcarvings, paintings. Carnival rides. The big wheel, that Ferris Wheel, went so high into the sky. And the food: pies, cakes, cobblers, barbecue. The best in the state.

"When we arrived we spent several hours just walking through the grounds, trying to figure out where we were supposed to set up for the next day's show. There were several stages, and a grandstand for the main acts." Ray remembered how all the families visiting the Fair made him miss his own family even more. Ray, Owen and Charles found the schedule for all the musical acts and went to each show to listen to the other groups at the Fair. They were impressed with the musicianship, the harmonies, the guitar and banjo picking. There were groups made up of singers who were all from the same families. There were solo crooners. There were old men yodeling. There were square dancers and callers who played the fiddle and double-talked as they yelled to the dancers to swing their partners and do-si-do.

The boys felt intimidated, but when the next day arrived and it was their turn, all their years of playing together made it feel natural. Once they started, the music took on a life of its own and their awkwardness faded away. A crowd gathered and people moved closer to the stage to hear the new group. Folks nodded their head, clapped their hands and yelled out encouragement. The Gulch Jumpers finished their set with the song that had received radio play. They were rewarded with a standing ovation.

"Sometimes you just know you hit a home run," Ray said. "Everyone has off nights and on nights. But we knew we played well. We were a hit."

The boys were on top of the world as they watched the fireworks that night. The show the following afternoon went just as well. They had turned out two successful performances. The young miners from the holler were the talk of the Fair.

A man from a record company approached them after the Sunday performance. He thought The Gulch Jumpers had a sweet sound and gushed over their original songs. Ray had introduced the boys to some of the lyrics and music he, Doris, Uncle Horace and Aunt Mary Lou had improvised. The silly and sweet lullabies for Sally sounded even better with the young men's instrumentation and harmonies. Their songs spoke to the simple joys of life folks could relate to. The man was interested in signing them on to cut a record.

"It was exactly what we were hoping for," Ray said. "A record deal! Really, it just couldn't have gone any better for us. I was starting to see there might be hope for me to make my way in the world through music, doing what I loved, instead of working in a coal mine. And maybe music could be a way for Doris and me to move beyond all the small-minded prejudice and find us a place in the world where people wouldn't judge us."

Ray explained that the boys had an offer to go to Charleston the next month to start working in a recording studio. If all went well, they would lay down enough tracks to put out a record. Then, the record would be promoted: radio play, interviews and photo shoots, shows in different towns and concert venues. If they made it big, they might get to go to Nashville, perhaps play at the Ryman Theater. They might make it onto television.

"I had visions of fame and fortune, big dreams: a fine home for my family, a shiny Cadillac in my driveway. And I wanted to get Doris out there too, singing with us. She had such a beautiful voice," he said wistfully. "It was all part of her dream too."

"That day—" Ray turned to Ellie, speaking deliberately and slowly. "—was one of the happiest days of my life. It was *the last* happy day of my life."

He went on, almost mechanically, stepping outside of himself. "I couldn't wait to get home and tell Doris the news. The drive home seemed to take forever. We were excited, talking the whole way back.

Owen was going to ask his steady girlfriend to marry him. Charlie was just happy about not having to worry if the strike was going to settle, if he should move north for work. As we traveled along, absorbed in all our reveries, I thought I noticed what looked like Sammy's truck, heading in the other direction. I didn't get a good look, and it went by so fast. I sure didn't want to rain on the parade, so I didn't say anything about what I thought I saw to the boys. But I just got this funny feeling in the pit of my stomach. It was like I felt it before I knew it.... something was off, something was wrong."

When they arrived back in the holler, Owen swung by Ray's house to drop him off. "I could tell as soon as we rounded the bend, and I can tell you I just had a sense of dread.... I had the car door open and I was jumping out before we even rolled to a stop. I ran through the clearing up to the house. Yelling for Doris. Banging open the front door. Running through an empty house. No wife. No baby daughter." Ray found their meager possessions strewn about, clothes lying limply on the floor. "It was as if she had up and left me, but I knew she would never, ever do that of her own volition. Someone had taken them from me. It looked like there had been a struggle."

Ray yelled and screamed, and Charles and Owen ran after him, trying to figure out what had happened. Suddenly, Uncle Horace was there. "Now, Ray, listen to me!" he yelled, grabbing his nephew by the shoulders. "I ran over here as soon as I heard what was happening, and I can see I didn't get here fast enough. Listen to me!"

Doris's mama, Frances, had returned to town, enraged to learn of Doris's new familial arrangements. Frances and Sammy waited until Ray left for the Fair, then forced Doris and Sally into the truck.

"We didn't hear about the crash until later that night in town," said Ray. "I had run everywhere I knew to look for them. The juke joint where Sammy's band played, the boarding house—all vacated. I was desperate. I went to the police to try to file a missing person's report. The State Highway Patrol man sat me down and told me there had been a bad accident on Old McCracken Road."

From what they could gather, Sammy's truck went off the side of the road and flipped upside-down.

"It was in a remote area," Ray said. "We're not sure what time the accident happened. But by the time the authorities came upon the scene, only Doris was left behind in the vehicle." Ray started crying and shaking his head back and forth. "She didn't make it, Ellie. She didn't make it. They killed her and then they just left her behind."

Doris's parents had fled the accident scene on foot, taking their granddaughter and abandoning the truck and their daughter's body. The State Highway Patrol had searched the area but could turn up no sign of Sammy, Frances or baby Sally.

"I believe they may have walked out to the main road and hitch-hiked out of there," said Ray. "We never knew. I don't know why they ran like that and I don't know how they could just leave Doris like that, not even sticking around to say a proper goodbye to their daughter and make sure she had a proper burial."

Ray took a deep breath and wiped his brow, steadying himself before going on with his story. "I didn't want her in a cemetery; they were all segregated and none of those churches ever welcomed us as a family anyways. I built a pine box and laid her to rest in a grave the boys helped me dig by our little house. I laid wildflowers on the pine box. It was the best I could do for her."

"Oh Ray." Ellie reached over and squeezed his hand. It was awful and she searched for the right words. "I'm so sorry. And little Sally? She survived the car crash?"

"No one ever found Sally or the other two," he said. "There was a search of the area to see if the baby was thrown from the vehicle, but nothing was found. I never saw her again, Ellie." He put his hand over his chest. "But I know in my heart that she made it, she survived. I like to think that her mama threw her body over her to protect her and took the brunt of the crash all upon herself."

"I'm sure she did," Ellie reassured him. "A mother will do anything to protect her child."

"A father should do anything to protect his child too," Ray lamented. "But I went off after fame and fortune and wasn't there to protect my family. I never should have left them alone like that. It's my fault."

Ray wept freely now, the release from telling his story churning up decades of heartache and hurt still as fresh today as that August day in 1966. Ellie waited respectfully, letting him have his cry, not wishing to disrupt the delicate balance of trust he placed in her by finally opening up.

After a time she carefully spoke. "I'm so, so sorry about what happened. But, Ray, it's *not* your fault. It sounds like you were a great husband and a wonderful father. It was a horrible, tragic accident. Did you ever find out why Doris's parents had them in the truck, or where they were going?"

"Rumor was that Frances heard through the grapevine 'bout how Doris took up with me and had a child, so she came back up to West Virginia and they waited, they waited and plotted till they knew I was out of town. I don't know where they were heading, Ellie, but I know her parents wanted her away from me."

"Ray, let's take a break." Ellie sat back in her chair, feeling she needed to recover as well. "You're getting upset and I think this is wearing you out."

As if on cue, a man popped in with Ray's lunch tray, setting it on the bedside table.

"Let's take a look." Ellie pulled off the lid to find grilled cheese and tomato soup, sliced melon, coleslaw and a brownie. "It looks good, Ray. How about you eat some lunch? Then maybe nap a little while. We can finish the story later."

He closed his eyes and his warm bass voice rang out in song:

Got all the time in the world for sleeping
Later, when my work is done,
No time for sleeping now
Gotta keep plowing on....

Ellie watched Ray with concern. She tried to imagine the awful tragedy he'd endured and lived with all of these years. The injustice of Doris kidnapped and then left for dead by her own parents. The guilt Ray felt, blaming himself for the horrific loss of the love of his life, and on top of that, the unspeakable loss of his child. She wondered how he had ever managed to go on. He just held it all inside, an approach Ellie understood all too well. She and her new friend had more in common than she had first realized.

He took a few bites of food, looked at the soup and set his spoon down. "I'm not really hungry... I look for Sally's beautiful brown eyes in every face I see."

Ellie nodded, stricken and silent.

Ellie's cell phone went off and she stepped into the hallway. It was Jessica, calling from the office. "You got a call from a Detective Lawson," she informed Ellie. *Lawson... Lawson...* Ellie racked her brain, trying to place the name. A witness she had subpoenaed for a trial, perhaps? She took down the number and returned the call.

"Ms. Sanders? Thanks for calling back. I want to let you know that we've made an arrest pertaining to the break-in at your home."

"Oh!" Ellie cried. She had been so absorbed in Ray's story and the tragic events that unfolded fifty years ago that she had forgotten about the break-in to her own home. "Who did it? Did you recover any of our things?"

"Well, we've recovered a few of your items. As to who did it, I can tell you it's someone who says she knows you and is sure that you won't want to press any charges." Ellie knew the name before he said it, but got a heavy feeling in the pit of her stomach all the same: Brandy Sarendesh.

"Can you come over to the Mission of Hope Shelter?" Detective Lawson asked. "We should talk before I write it up and turn my case over to the prosecutor."

Ellie agreed to meet him in an hour and hung up, shaking. Even though deep down she had known the truth, hearing the detective say it aloud made it all more real, impossible to deny any longer. She pictured Brandy rifling through her possessions, using her shower, looking in her jewelry box, her desk drawers. Had Brandy gone into the nursery? This made Ellie angriest of all. It was the most private of places, and Brandy had waltzed in out of the past and trespassed where she most certainly did not belong.

When she returned, Ray had finished half of his lunch and was breathing comfortably. "I'm going to run out in a little while, Ray, but I'll come back this evening to see how you're doing. We need to talk more about the biopsy procedure. Dr. Stuart is going to want to know the plan. I can also bring you anything you may need from the Mission since I have to stop by there this afternoon."

He looked at her curiously, but she did not elaborate.

"How soon do you need to leave, Ellie?"

"I can stay till three o'clock," she said. "Is there something I can do for you, Ray?"

"Yes, Miss Ellie. You're always asking if there is something you can do for me, and today I'm going to tell you 'yes.' I may not be long for this world, which is why I decided to tell my story. If you truly want to help a sad old man who is probably dying, I do have a request and I'm ready to name it."

Ellie sat back down in the chair near his bedside. "Good. It's about time you trust me enough to allow me to help you. Does this have something to do with finding Sally?" She was wondering what happened after the accident and eager to hear the rest of Ray's story.

"Yes, it has everything to do with finding Sally. That's the only thing I want—to find my child. And I have a plan for how to do it."

"Tell me," said Ellie, enthusiastically. This was something she could do; she was at her best when she was helping people.

"Okay. Here's the thing: I'd like for you to take me down to the crossroads."

"Excuse me?"

"Before I die—" Ray put his hand on his heart. "—I want to travel down to the crossroads. You've heard of the crossroads, right? It's a mighty powerful intersection down in Mississippi. Do you know who Robert Johnson is, Ellie? Blues musician. Robert Johnson made his famous deal there. Legend has it that Mr. Johnson went down to the crossroads at midnight and sold his soul in exchange for his musical talent. That's how he came about to be one of the most gifted blues men of all time."

Ray was sitting up now, his face animated. Ellie regarded him with puzzlement, her mouth hanging open as she tried to formulate a question.

Ray saw Ellie's confusion, cleared his throat, and sang a few lines of the infamous "Cross Road Blues." "So you see," he went on excitedly, "Mr. Johnson traded his soul away to become a great musician. I *already* have musical talent. And what has it gotten me? *Nothing*. In fact, it's a curse that caused me to lose the people I love. Music is useless to me. What I would like to do, Ellie, is get down south to them crossroads and make a different kind of deal. Since I already possess the currency of what is traded in those parts, I want to trade in my musical talent in exchange for finding Sally. I don't want to trade in music for my soul. My soul's already lost. I want to trade in music for Sally."

"Umm, but Ray," she started slowly, "does that really make any sense? Aren't there more practical things we can do? Have you tried to look for Sally over the years?"

He hung his head. "I did what I could. I went to the sheriff for help. They took down the information and were sympathetic about the crash, but couldn't do anything. I wasn't able to establish paternity over Sally under the eyes of the law since I couldn't marry Doris. I went back to the black juke joint and asked around, but nobody was talking. Sammy took off and wasn't seen around those parts again. I packed up and started traveling to different musical venues in the south, looking for Sammy and asking around for information from every musician and performer I met, but it was as if they just disappeared off the face of the earth. Finally made my way up north to look for work in steel, got laid off, lost everything… lost everything important to me. I didn't do enough," he confessed, his face full of shame.

"No, Ray, I'm not judging you. You did what you could. But the world is so different now. It is so much easier to track down lost people. I'm just wondering if we shouldn't try some more practical things first. Perhaps we could hire a private detective?" she suggested.

He shook his head. "I want to put my faith in the power of music. I need the most powerful magic that music has to offer; I need a miracle. And the only place in the world I know to get that kind of musical miracle is at the crossroads. This is the last hand I have to play and I'm throwing in all my chips. Will you help me? I won't blame you if you say no. I know I'm a crazy old man and, Lord knows, it's a crazy request I'm putting here before you today."

She regarded him thoughtfully.

"Please, West Side. Please. Please take me down to the crossroads."

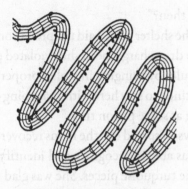

CHAPTER SEVEN

THIEF

Ellie arrived at the Mission of Hope to find Brandy's probation officer, social worker and the police detective waiting for her. "I understand you found my stolen property?" she said.

"Let's sit in this side room to talk," suggested Detective Lawson.

"We did find jewelry that matched the description of your lost property. A woman was over by the projects and the cruiser saw her jumped and beaten by a man, some thug, who then fled the scene. It's a good thing they got over there or she may have been badly hurt. She's on probation and ordered to live here at the shelter and attend treatment. They arrested her for drug paraphernalia, heroin residue. She said she knows you?"

Ellie sighed. "We were friends many years ago, in my college days." She paused and thought. "Actually, we were pretty good friends. Just fell out of touch over the years. I have another friend staying here at the Mission of Hope and Brandy sees me coming here to visit him. She must have followed me or something to find out where I live. Is she hurt badly?"

"She has a black eye and a busted lip. Wouldn't let us take her to the ER to get checked out."

"Where is she then?"

"She's here at the shelter now," said the probation officer. "Of course, the theft and new drug charge mean she's violated probation. And she violated shelter rules by bringing in stolen property and drugs. They won't let her continue to stay here with that going on. Your old friend might be looking at some prison time."

Detective Lawson spread out the items recovered from Brandy on the table. Ellie was able to recognize and identify Mike's watch, the pearl necklace, the turquoise pieces. She was glad to have the jewelry returned, but sick with the confirmation that Brandy was indeed the robber. How could Brandy have done that to her? But then again, how could she have repeatedly visited the shelter for Ray, knowing Brandy was homeless and staying here, and not seek her out and talk to her? Ellie was not free of blame. She had taken the easy route and avoided confrontation.

"Brandy was sure you wouldn't want to press charges on account of you two being old friends," said Detective Lawson.

Ellie thought for a moment. "Can I talk to her alone for a few minutes?"

The social worker left to retrieve Brandy while Detective Lawson and the probation officer filed out of the small conference room. Ellie was not prepared for Brandy's face when she walked in. Her eye was swollen shut and turning purple. Her lips were also swollen and bruised. "Jesus, Brandy," she cried out.

"Hey, Ellie, what's up, long time no see, how's your old man, and all that shit," Brandy drawled tiredly. She slouched into the chair, off balance and slurring her words.

"Brandy..." Ellie was truly shocked and worried about how badly Brandy had been beaten. It certainly wasn't the reunion conversation she had imagined they would have. Brandy started to nod off. Was she coming down off a drug high? Or was she slipping into unconsciousness due to the blows to her head? What if she had a concussion?

"I really think we need to get you to a doctor."

Brandy regarded Ellie wearily. "No, no doctor. You gonna send me to prison, Ellie?"

"Listen, let's not worry about that now. I'm pissed you broke into my house but it's just stuff, things. You're suffering enough. What you need is some help."

"What I need is some peace," Brandy said. "I'm just looking for some peace, Ellie."

"What's happened to you? It sure doesn't look like you're leading a peaceful life to me. You used to be the best dancer on the floor, telling jokes, full of life. I don't know your story, but they're saying you're going to have to leave the shelter for breaking the rules and you might get sent back to prison. It's like you're hitting rock bottom here."

"Ah, I'm very familiar with the rocky bottom, El. You have no idea how low I can go. I'm like a freaking limbo game."

"Brandy, come on, this is serious. Do you have any kind of plan? If you don't get sent to prison, where will you live?"

But Brandy had dozed off.

***

Ellie needed to think more about Ray's request and return to the hospital but, first, she had to do something for Brandy. She still remembered the way to Brandy's parents' house. It was a working-class neighborhood that had slipped into disrepair. Gang insignia was spray-painted on a bridge abutment. Aging duplex bungalows lined the street, each set out on a tiny lot. A few sat empty, foreclosed, and yet some were well-tended, with flower boxes and basketball hoops. She slowed and peered at the homes. The tree in front jogged her memory and she parked on the street and walked up to the side door.

Despite the years, Ellie instantly recognized Brandy's mother when she answered the door. The woman looked at Ellie inquisitively through the screen door, trying to place her.

"Hello, Mrs. Sarendesh? It's Ellie Sanders. I'm an old friend of Brandy's. Brandy used to have me over to your house years ago—do you remember me?"

"Brandy." The woman's face darkened. "Brandy doesn't live here anymore," she barked.

"I'm sorry," Ellie faltered. "Yes, I know she isn't living with you anymore. I came because I'm worried about her."

Mrs. Sarendesh softened as she focused on Ellie, seeing her anew. "Oh Ellie, my dear, pardon my bad manners. Brandy's a sore subject for me." She opened the door and beckoned. "Of course I remember you. Come on in."

The cluttered living room had not changed much in twenty-some years: frayed recliner, musty couch covered with an afghan, tiny television sitting on a metal tray. A faint smell of cat urine hung stale in the air.

"So, Mrs. Sarendesh, I really haven't kept in touch with Brandy over the years but I did run into her recently. I'm concerned about her—she needs help. I thought I'd come to you."

Brandy's mom shook her head emphatically. "If you haven't kept in touch with her then you don't know everything going on, Ellie. Brandy is beyond any help I can offer her. And I'm not offering anything anymore. She's worn out her welcome here."

"If you don't mind me asking, what *has* been going on?" asked Ellie. "Do you know she's been staying in a homeless shelter?"

"Well, that doesn't surprise me," she said bitterly. "In fact, a homeless shelter is probably a step up for her. Better than prison or some flop drug house."

"She's going to be asked to leave the shelter. She broke some rules, broke into my own house actually and stole some things. But she also was beaten this morning, badly. She was jumped by some man who punched her in the face. Her face is black and blue, black eye, swollen lip. It might have been much worse if the police hadn't come along and scared the man off before he hurt her worse. She doesn't have a place to stay now and wouldn't let anyone take her to the doctor. She needs help."

Mrs. Sarendesh listened, her face flinching imperceptibly when Ellie described Brandy's injuries.

"She's stolen from me too, Ellie. She's brought those same violent people into my home. She's brought drugs into my home. And she's turned her back on her children. I get no kind of financial help from her at all, nothing. She chose drugs over her own children."

Ellie's jaw dropped open. "Her *children*?"

"You didn't know?"

"No," Ellie replied slowly, "I had no idea. I had no idea Brandy is a mother."

"Well the term 'mother' is a bit of a stretch." She snorted haughtily. "She gave birth to them all right, but she don't mother them. I raised my own kids and now I got custody of grandchildren I gotta raise with no help at all. She doesn't buy them shoes. She doesn't come to see them, help out with their homework, take them anywhere to give me a break. I'm too old for this. I'm doing the best I can, but I'm too old for this and it's not right."

"How many children does she have?"

"She has three—now *I've* got three—two boys and a girl. Well, here's Brandy's daughter, Nevaeh, right here."

A small girl, perhaps five or six years old, walked in and sat on the couch with her feet dangling, looking at Ellie shyly. She had a sweet, sad little face with big eyes and shiny long hair. The resemblance to the younger version of Brandy was startling. "Say hello to Miss Ellie, Nevaeh."

"Hello, miss," Nevaeh said obediently.

Ellie was charmed. "Well hello, Nevaeh. It's nice to meet you. I'm an old friend of your family. Is that a Panda bear on your shirt? It's so cute."

The little girl smiled and nodded, pleased.

How could Brandy have turned her back on all this? It was simply unthinkable.

"The boys are over at a friend's house, or I'd introduce you to them too," said Mrs. Sarendesh, jerking her head in a direction down the street. "They're good kids, Ellie. I got to protect them; I'm all they've got. So you see, I'm sorry to hear what you're telling me, but I'm tapped out. She always bounces back on her feet. She's like a cat with nine lives. But she can't come here."

"I understand. I didn't know the extent of the situation. I'm going to try to find somewhere else she can go. Maybe if she had the right kind of help, she could get back to her old self and take back some of her, um, responsibilities." Ellie attempted to talk cryptically with the child listening. "Do you have any recommendations or ideas about what I should try?"

"No, dear—" she shook her head sadly. "I'm all out of ideas. As for recommendations, I would just recommend that you keep her away from your valuables. That daughter of mine has sticky fingers. She'll rob you so fast it'll make your head spin."

Ellie nodded and thanked Brandy's mom for talking to her, patted Nevaeh on the head, and got up to leave. Mrs. Sarendesh stopped her on the porch. "Wait." She went into the kitchen and pulled a photograph off the refrigerator. "If you can get her clean from those drugs, get her away from those dealers and criminals, if you think you can find the real Brandy underneath all that, then give her this. Maybe it will give her something to shoot for."

Ellie tucked the photograph of Brandy's three beautiful children, arms linked around each other, into her purse.

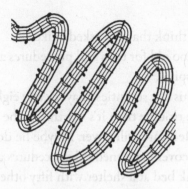

CHAPTER EIGHT

ROAD TRIP

It was an ideal July evening, close enough to the summer equinox that daylight persisted well into the night. The brutal winter was a distant memory as Ellie and Mike packed a simple picnic supper, loaded their bicycle panniers, and rode to the park by the Lake Erie shore. A brass band was setting up in the pavilion as families spread out blankets on the lawn. Mike and Ellie claimed a picnic table on the ridge overlooking the lake, and set out their chicken salad sandwiches, pickles, potato chips and fruit.

They ate slowly, enjoying the peaceful sunset, watching children running by the playground and seagulls swooping down by the water. The Cleveland skyline rose in the distance. The smell of hot dogs and hamburgers smoking on the grill permeated the evening air, festive and tantalizing.

"Okay," said Ellie as they finished their supper.

Mike reached over and brushed a strand of hair off her cheek. "Talk to me, El. What's going on."

Ellie told Mike about her morning with Ray, the doctor's recommendation, how Ray wouldn't agree to the biopsy. "He's on oxygen, he has emphysema, he coughs all the time. But he won't listen to common sense."

"Why do you think that is?" asked Mike.

"He says he's too old for tests and procedures and he doesn't want to stay in the hospital."

"Well, he's in his late seventies, maybe early eighties, right? Maybe he feels it's more trouble than it's worth. Maybe he's scared. Maybe it's more than Medicare will cover. Maybe he doesn't want to deal with trying to recover from medical procedures and stuff when he's sleeping in a bunk bed at a shelter with fifty other guys in the room. It could be a thousand things, El. Does he just want you to take him back to the shelter?"

"No, no, he doesn't want me to take him back to the shelter. Mike, he made a really strange request of me. Kind of like a bucket-list, last request."

"What's he asking for?"

Ellie watched a young girl in a sun dress and sandals near the playground retrieve a ball and throw it back to her mother, squealing in delight. Ellie paused a moment, and then spoke. "He asked me to take him down to the crossroads. In Mississippi. Like the Robert Johnson song. He says he wants to go down to the crossroads and make a deal where he trades in his musical talent to find his long lost daughter, Sally."

Mike's face was incredulous. "What? Are you kidding me? He asked you to take him to Mississippi?" Mike struggled to comprehend. "So, instead of selling his soul in exchange for talent, he wants to trade in the talent he already has? That's the opposite of what Robert Johnson did. That's more like a Reverse-Robert Johnson."

"I know, I know," said Ellie, shaking her head.

"It's like a movie or something. And what does he think is going to happen once he gets to the crossroads? Is the devil going to come along wearing a black suit, carrying a suitcase? Is the ghost of Robert Johnson going to appear and bust out some smoking hot blues guitar? What is he going to do once he gets there?"

"I haven't a clue," said Ellie.

"And he's looking for a long lost daughter named Sally," Mike went on. "I'll hand it to him; he certainly gave the girl a good musical name. Just think: you've got your 'Lay Down, Sally.' 'Ride, Sally, Ride.' 'Sneaking Down the Alley with Sally.' 'Mustang Sally.' This just doesn't get any better. How old is this Sally anyway, and how does he think Robert Johnson's ghost is going to help him find her?"

"She's got to be going on fifty years old," Ellie said. "He lost her almost fifty years ago, when she was barely a toddler. In West Virginia."

"How does one lose a baby?" asked Mike. Ellie caught her breath. They both hesitated, not meeting each other's eyes. "I'm sorry," Mike started, but Ellie shushed him. This was about Ray, not them.

Ellie proceeded to tell Mike the story Ray had shared about the love of his life, the interracial backlash from his relationship with Doris, the little house in the holler, the mining, the bluegrass band, and the ill-fated kidnapping of Doris and Sally, who was left a motherless child by her own maternal grandparents.

Mike shook his head. "That's just horrific. Poor guy, he lost everything. And so unbelievable it was against the law for them to marry. It wasn't even that long ago, in the grand scheme of things. What a different world."

Ellie agreed. Basic freedoms, taken for granted now, were so hard fought for by those denied. Ray's story was undeniably tragic, but his plan was equally unbelievable. It was a fairy tale; completely unrealistic.

"El, he wants you to take him on a road trip four states away so he can stand at an intersection and pawn his musical talent based upon some hokey superstitious nonsense. It makes no sense. He's been spending too much time daydreaming about this pipe dream story instead of doing something real."

"I know, I know," Ellie said. "I tried to suggest doing something real, like hiring a private detective, but this is what he's pleading for. To him it's not hokey superstition; I think he sees it as some kind of miracle."

"First of all, modern day miracles don't occur," Mike said. "And second, how is selling your soul supposed to be a miracle?"

Ellie pondered, thinking back to Ray's words. "What he said was he wants to make a deal with *the devil, with God, with the patron saint of music, or whoever*—some fill-in-the-blank higher power, I guess—and he said he didn't want to bargain with his soul, just with his talent. I think he believes there is some magical spot where a person can go to receive or give up talent, and there's an element of miracle tied to that, somehow. It is hard to understand," she admitted.

"It's just plain crazy if you ask me. And why put all your faith in a miracle and ignore real, concrete things you can do to solve your problem?" Mike said.

"So you don't think modern day miracles can occur?"

"Do *you*?"

"I don't know," she conceded. "I see awful things in my clients' lives. I see Ray, losing Doris and Sally. I see our story." She looked Mike in the eyes. "No doubt, bad things happen, life can be unfair, people can be just plain rotten. But good things happen too. No one ever questions whether true evil exists. Why are we so skeptical that good, spectacularly wonderful things can happen?" She took a swig of water from her water bottle. "So, yeah, sure, why not? What have I got to lose by believing in an old man's wish? He may have some wisdom from walking this earth for eight decades that you and I can't imagine."

"So you're thinking of actually taking him?" asked Mike.

Ellie realized she had already made her decision, even though she hadn't acknowledged it yet to herself or to her husband. "I suppose I am," she said with some surprise. "It's not like me to do something like this, is it?"

"Well, you're always the practical one. More inclined to solve problems with reason, not magic—my law and order kinda gal."

"Yep, that gal is still here," she said. "If I do it, if I take him down there, it's going to be the Ellie-way."

"And I'm assuming the Ellie-way means you're going to take him to Mississippi via a little detour through West Virginia," Mike said, thinking.

"Right," said Ellie. "What I really want to do is take him back to his hometown, or holler, or wherever he's from. It sounds like he took off looking for his daughter after the accident and never returned. I bet we can find some clues there. Look for his old house. Check local police records from the car crash. See if there is anyone still living there who remembers something and may have a clue to what happened to Sally. An old friend, a relative. There must be people who know what happened, and I would think back in those times a mixed race couple and biracial child would have attracted some attention. Maybe seeing the place will jog something important in Ray's memory."

"I think that makes a little more sense," Mike agreed. "At least you would have a solid destination in West Virginia. Do you even know where these Mississippi crossroads are?"

Ellie wasn't sure if the locale of the Robert Johnson legend was a fictive place or a real place Ray would know how to find. Perhaps it didn't matter. "I'll research it. But we may be able to solve the puzzle right in West Virginia. What do you think?"

Mike cocked his head. "I think not doing it would be like the Tin Man taking Dorothy to Oz to meet the Wizard, while bypassing a clearly-marked exit to Kansas along the yellow brick road."

"So you think it's a good idea?" she pressed.

"No," he said with a laugh. "I think it's a spectacularly bad idea. The whole thing is just as crazy as can be. But I think you should do it anyway."

Ellie looked at her husband curiously, and he leaned closer to give her a hug. "It's been a rough year for us. This is the happiest and most interested in anything I've seen you for a while. You're at your best when you're helping someone, and you needed a project. So, yes, I think it's the craziest thing I've ever heard, but if you want to do it and it's making you happy, then I say go for it, my little Tin Man. Take Dorothy to the Wizard."

Ellie smiled. "You are amazing," she said. "And now let me tell you the rest of the plan." She pulled Mike's stolen wrist watch out of her bicycle pannier and handed it to him. "The police recovered our things today, and I'm pretty sure the person who robbed us will need a place to stay for the next two weeks or she'll go to jail. So I think there's going to be one more person coming along on the trip, even though the person doesn't know it yet."

"Huh? What? ... Ellie—"

"Let me tell you about my old friend Brandy."

***

"All rise," said the bailiff as the judge walked into the courtroom. The judge settled himself on the bench and looked over the small gathering at Brandy's arraignment for her probation violation.

"Let me see who we've got in the courtroom," he muttered. He read off the names of the prosecutor, the probation officer, and the defendant, Brandy Sarendesh. The judge then paused as he looked from the public defender to Ellie.

"Ms. Sanders? Are you here to represent the defendant?"

"I'm not here as her attorney, Your Honor," Ellie said. "The defendant is an old acquaintance—well, actually, an old friend. So I'm here in a personal capacity."

"I see," said the judge. "Of course, all we're doing today is taking her plea and deciding if she'll wait out her next hearing in jail or out on bond. Now let's see. Arrest was for Theft and Possession of Drug Paraphernalia?"

The prosecutor confirmed the charges and stood to address the court. "In light of Ms. Sarendesh's prior felony drug conviction, her minimal, cursory compliance with treatment, her violation of the rules of the Mission of Hope Shelter, and the new Possession charge, the State requests the defendant be remanded to the county jail pending the next hearing."

"Your Honor," said the public defender, "she's been going to treatment. She had a slip up, but she was also the victim of a violent beating on the street. Her injuries are obvious. She was a victim; she doesn't need to be sent to prison."

Brandy looked down at her hands, not meeting the eyes of anyone else in the room. Her black eye said it all. The judge regarded her thoughtfully.

The probation officer spoke up. "The problem is that she can't stay at the shelter. She broke the rules bringing in drug paraphernalia. They're very strict about that."

"So if I release you until the next hearing, miss, you have nowhere to go, nowhere to live?" the judge addressed Brandy directly.

She continued to look down at her hands on the table and did not respond.

"Ms. Sarendesh?" asked the judge again.

"You have to answer him," the public defender whispered to Brandy.

Ellie jumped to her feet. "Your Honor, excuse me, please, but I have a proposal. Release Ms. Sarendesh to me. I have a trip planned and can take her along and assume responsibility."

Brandy turned and gave Ellie a sideways, curious look.

"Give me some details, please," said the judge.

"I'm helping another resident of the shelter find some lost family. I'm taking him down to Mississippi to try to find a lost relative. I know Brandy, and I believe she's met Mr. Jones since they stay at the same shelter. I can bring her along. I'll watch over her and get her back for the next hearing."

There was a pause as everyone gave consideration. "It's cheaper than making the taxpayers pay for a prison stay," Ellie added.

"Well, it's certainly unusual," said the judge. "I suppose it's similar to releasing her on her own recognizance though, of course, as a well-esteemed attorney with a solid reputation in this court, Ms. Sanders, you make an interesting argument here. Thoughts?"

"I'm okay with it, so long as we have restrictions," said the probation officer. "And I can probably have the shelter let her stay one more night until Ms. Sanders here picks her up to leave on this trip."

"The state has no objection," said the prosecutor with a shrug.

"Okay, I'm going to allow it," said the judge. He turned to Brandy. "No drugs. No drinking. No violation of any laws, whatsoever. You have two weeks," he said to Ellie. "I understand trying to help out an old friend. Just be careful. Good luck and court is adjourned."

Ellie walked over to Brandy.

"Ellie, you're taking me on vacation?" Brandy asked in wonderment.

"I guess I am, Brandy. Get your bags packed. I'm picking you up at nine o'clock tomorrow morning."

"Where did you say we're going?" Brandy asked.

"We're headed down south to find Sally, Ray's daughter."

"Ray? The old man who sings?"

"Right."

"His daughter lives in Mississippi?"

Ellie noticed the probation officer standing nearby, listening. "Actually, we're just going south to visit some places Ray's been singing about for years. That's really all it is."

A slight smile formed on Brandy's bruised face.

***

Ellie spent the rest of her day working to clear her schedule. She filed motions to continue hearings that could wait and called in favors from colleagues where coverage was needed.

Far from disapproving or critical, Jessica was excited to see her boss do something impulsive. "It's so refreshing to see you doing something that makes no sense," she told her earnestly. "I think this will be very cathartic for you, Ellie."

Jessica, an internet junkie, pulled up some pages about the history of Robert Johnson and the crossroads legend. "I emailed you the links, El. Take a look when you have time. It's pretty interesting stuff."

Ellie made arrangements with the hospital and stopped by late afternoon to bust out Ray.

Predictably, Dr. Stuart was not pleased. "I'm disappointed that you were unable to talk him into the biopsy," he told Ellie. "Of course, it has to be his decision, but I'm afraid I am going to have to discharge him against medical advice."

Ellie understood the need for the biopsy, but it was Ray's decision—it was Ray's life.

"I'll keep working on him about it," she promised the doctor.

Ray was going to be discharged with an oxygen tank. This took Ellie aback. Could she travel with Ray with an oxygen tank? Would it be a problem in hotels, restaurants? What if someone lit up a cigarette? The nurse explained the discharge instructions and how to safely use and travel with the tank. The hospital had also already been in communication with the social worker at the shelter. Ray would return to the Mission of Hope for one more night. Then, in the morning, Ray, Brandy and Ellie would set out.

Ray signed off on his discharge papers against medical advice. "I feel like I just got a dishonorable discharge from the military or something," he grumbled.

Dr. Stuart shook both of their hands and had a final word with Ellie. "It's good to see how you are trying to honor your father's wishes," he said. "I respect what you're trying to do, even if I don't agree with it. Not many people would take an ill, elderly parent on a trip, putting up with an oxygen tank and all that." He paused a moment, waiting for Ellie to correct him. Finally he added, "He's not really your father, is he?"

Ellie regarded the doctor for a moment.

"No, he's not family," she admitted. "He's my friend."

To herself she privately vowed: *And I'm taking my friend to the crossroads.*

PART TWO

"The freedom to marry has long been recognized as one of the vital personal rights essential to the orderly pursuit of happiness by free men. The Fourteenth Amendment requires that the freedom of choice to marry not be restricted by invidious racial discriminations. Under our Constitution, the freedom to marry, or not marry, a person of another race resides with the individual and cannot be infringed by the State."

-Justice Warren, writing for the majority, Loving v. Virginia, United States Supreme Court, 1967

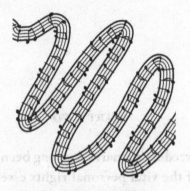

CHAPTER NINE

WE EMBARK

Ray woke at dawn and lay in his bunk at the Mission, listening to the snoring, rustling, and sleep noises of his fifty or so roommates. Today would be his last morning with these sounds. His heart filled with gratitude for the place that had housed and fed him when no one else would, the closest thing he could call a home for years. But he had already decided he wasn't coming back.

Last night, after Ellie had dropped him off, the shelter supervisor had explained the impossibility of holding a bed open. People came and went at the Mission. New arrivals were accommodated on a space-available basis and nothing was guaranteed, even for a long-time resident such as Ray. This was the trip of his lifetime. If it ended poorly, he would ask Ellie to leave him by the side of the road. Returning, even if possible, would be unbearable.

But he was sure, deep in his bones, that it wouldn't end badly. Re-discovering his music, with Ellie's help, had awakened something deep inside of him. Something he had forgotten, or tried to deny about himself. Whether it was a gift or a curse didn't matter, because now he understood. By giving it away, all would be revealed.

At peace with his decision, Ray was giddy with excitement to set out on the road. When it was finally time for lights on, he rose and quickly prepared. He neatly folded his few items of clothing and meager toiletry items, and then set the shoebox with the song lyrics he had written for Sally on top of his modest pile of worldly possessions. His oxygen tank sat beside him. Ray was ready. He hummed softly, waiting for Ellie.

Meanwhile, in the Sanders home in the west side suburbs, Ellie started her morning with twenty minutes on the elliptical trainer, cereal, coffee and her morning news show. She had laid everything for the trip on her bed to pack, and her suitcase now bulged with clothing, shoes, jewelry, toiletries, hair appliances. To this she added a cooler with snacks for the drive, a couple bottles of red wine for relaxing at the hotel in the evenings, and of course her briefcase. She had given Mike a kiss earlier that morning and promised to keep him updated. She loaded and started the dishwasher, filled Gracie's dish, and gave her a final pat before heading out the door.

Ellie hoped they could make a coffee-donut stop on the way out of town. She hadn't mentioned to Ray that she planned to take him to the crossroads by way of West Virginia. She would find a way to work that into the conversation later. Donuts were definitely in order prior to *that* conversation.

Alice, the social worker, was particularly animated as she greeted Ellie in the parking lot. "We are all *so* excited for Mr. Jones," Alice said, trotting along next to Ellie. "He's so hopeful about traveling to Mississippi, and I don't think he's gone anywhere in all the time I've worked here."

Ellie was startled to hear Alice knew of their destination. "Oh, he told you about what he has planned for the trip?"

"Well, no dear, Ray doesn't share too much personal information with anyone here," Alice said. "It was actually the other one's probation officer. You know, that Brandy character. Now, that is someone we will be glad to see gone. Her probation officer told us what you're going down South for. What a fascinating story. So, yes, we are all very happy for Ray and hopeful he'll find his daughter. And as for Brandy ... well, all I can say is good luck."

Ellie nodded uncertainly, and walked into the day room. Ray sat quietly, patient and stoic as he waited for Ellie. Brandy sat next to him, puffy-eyed and sullen. Brandy had the ever-present backpack, and the rest of her things were wadded in a pile on the floor by her feet.

Ray and Brandy didn't have anything to pack their possessions in. The numbered plastic bins that were dispensed to each resident belonged to the shelter. "Hold on, I'll get some garbage bags from the kitchen," Alice offered, but Ellie stopped her. For the next two weeks, at least, Ellie was determined that her friends would not feel homeless, and she wasn't going to allow them to carry their things in garbage bags.

"I'll be right back," she told them. Ray nodded, unquestioning.

"Whatever," Brandy yawned.

She drove to the nearest department store, bought two duffel bags, and presented them to Brandy and Ray upon returning to the Mission of Hope. "Here: a duffel bag for each of you. This will be much better for packing your things."

"Ah now, Miss Ellie, that's not necessary," said Ray. "I don't want you to go buying us things. You're already doing enough with this trip falling on your dime."

"Ray, it's no big deal. We want to do this right."

"Well, maybe it's a good time to discuss some rules for the road, before we set out down South," Ray announced. "I am deeply grateful, Miss Ellie, that you are accommodating an old man's dying wish. But I can't abide by allowing this to put too much of a hurt on your pocketbook. We got to keep this as cheap as possible. Cheap motels. Cheap diners and truck stops. Hell, I can even sleep in the back seat and you gals can share yourself a motel room."

"I wouldn't have agreed to take you on the trip if I couldn't afford it. I don't do cheap motels, Ray. Actually, I hate motels period. I prefer bed and breakfasts. You don't need to give another thought to the cost."

But Ray insisted. "No." He shook his head. "We've got to get this straight between us before we set out. I can't abide by you spending any more of your hard-earned money than absolutely necessary. We got to go on the cheap. We got to do this the Ray-way."

"Ray, can't we give the Ellie-way a try?" Ellie pleaded. "You'll be more comfortable staying in a nice place. Good food will help you feel better. After all, you just got out of the hospital and we want to keep you healthy." This was as much for herself as for the other two. She didn't care if they thought she was spoiled; there were things she couldn't compromise on.

Brandy watched the exchange, squinting her eyes to regard Ray and Ellie with contempt and amusement. "Well, I for one vote for the Ellie-way," she said, running her hand over the new duffel bag. "You go right ahead and spend whatever you like on me, Ellie."

Ray glared at Brandy disapprovingly. He sat back down. The old man had a stubborn side. The morning was wearing on and Ellie wanted to get going. Thoughts of donuts and coffee beckoned. As the driver, and holder of the credit cards, she could revisit this argument with Ray later, or just pull rank on him. "Okay," she relented. "You win. We'll do it the Ray-way. Can we leave now?"

Ray clapped his hands with excitement, stomped his foot emphatically and stood up. "All righty then! We are settled on it and ready to ramble on down the hillbilly highway." He chuckled with delight, breaking into "King of the Road."

Brandy made a face. "Oh, Jesus. Dumb mountain music for the next two weeks. Just put me in jail already."

"Come on, come on." Ellie ushered them to her SUV. But the spat continued when she pulled through the drive-thru and tried to order donuts and coffee for all of them.

"Don't need it," declared Ray.

"Well, I do," Ellie retorted. "The car needs fuel, the driver needs coffee. And donuts. And happy passengers." She proceeded to order for all of them, not even bothering to check with Ray and Brandy to find out how they took their coffee or if they preferred glazed, jelly-filled, or chocolate.

Brandy sat in the backseat. Ellie glanced in the rearview mirror and caught Brandy studying the reclining leather seats, the dashboard with rear backup camera, satellite radio, navigation screen. Brandy gazed up through the sunroof, her face full of wonder. Ellie thought she detected a hint of a grin, Brandy riding like a queen through the city, safe behind the tinted windows of their moving middle-class fortress. She wondered how long it had been since Brandy had been in a car.

"How's that coffee?" Ellie asked her.

Brandy's face instantly retreated to bored contempt. She shrugged. "Beats prison coffee. Beats shelter coffee."

Soon they cleared the city limits and Ellie set the cruise control once they were on open highway. She showed Ray her satellite radio, the bluegrass channel. A tear welled in his eye as Bill Monroe and his bluegrass mandolin sang out. "They're playing the music of my day, here, fifty years later, in the big city up north," he marveled.

"It plays all over the country," Ellie informed him. "And people like the music of your day. You know, there are current-day bluegrass musicians; young people play bluegrass."

"Guess I've been kind of out of what's going on these days in the world," Ray admitted. "Can't stand television, and I wasn't looking at any magazines or newspapers, at least until you got me those fine reading glasses."

Despite the shelter's location in the midst of a bustling downtown, within close proximity to universities, art galleries, corporations, major league sports and one of the best orchestras in the world, the homeless were on their own island of social isolation. It was a different Cleveland that co-existed invisibly with the world Ellie moved in. More than anything, the homeless suffered information isolation. They didn't even know what they didn't know.

Ellie considered Ray and Brandy's few possessions, and resolved to find an opportunity to take them shopping. Surely there would be a chance to take a break from the Sally search. She glanced again in the rearview mirror at Brandy, who was nodding off. What had Brandy done with the money she'd stolen? She must have spent it on drugs, Ellie thought. She sighed, wondering with trepidation how she was going to keep her promise to the judge to keep Brandy out of trouble for the next two weeks. The Brandy project in addition to the Ray project might be too much. She also suspected that Brandy and Ray were not particularly fond of each other. While waiting at the shelter, they were sitting next to each other but not talking. That wasn't a good sign. Ellie could always predict if a case in her practice was going to be difficult when the opposing parties refused to sit next to each other or make small talk in the court waiting area. If there was at least some conversation going on, there was room to negotiate a solution; but if people were sitting stone-faced and silent, you were going to trial.

Ellie's attention was drawn back to the road. The traffic grew heavier and she attempted to avoid getting boxed in between several trucks. She tried to keep her breathing steady. Her hands became clammy with sweat as she clutched the wheel, concentrating.

Ellie hated trucks on the highway. She hated getting stuck behind trucks when they couldn't accelerate on the entrance ramps. She hated trying to pass trucks. She hated when she couldn't see road signs around trucks, and she hated when snow swirled around trucks, blizzarding other drivers. She hated when rain blew off trucks, blinding drivers trying to pass. And most of all, she hated when trucks tried to pass other trucks, clogging all the available lanes.

Ray watched Ellie, silently registering the fact that she was a very nervous driver indeed, surprised to see some show of human weakness in his friend who usually presented as so polished and put-together.

"Sorry I can't help you with the driving, West Side," he said kindly. "I sure do appreciate you taking me on down South."

"It's okay, Ray," Ellie said, relaxing a bit. She glanced over at her friend and paused. "Ray, can I ask you a question? Have you thought about what exactly you're going to do when we get to the crossroads?"

"Well, Ellie, I reckon I'll know just what to do when I arrive at the place," he replied brightly. "It's a magical place. I'll probably say a little prayer and I'm quite sure the answer will just come to me there."

"But say a little prayer to who, Ray?" Ellie asked. "It sounds like some kind of scary black magic to me—it doesn't sound like you. Do you even believe in such things?"

Ray scratched his chin, thinking. "Well, I was raised in the church, and despite everything that's happened to me, I still believe. Not sure what I think about the other one, but don't reckon I have to deal directly with that character, do I, since I ain't selling my soul, right? I'm just trading in my music. Just need to stand at the crossroads to do it since it's such a powerful place. I sure heard the tales about Robert Johnson over the years, and everyone knows how talented the man was, so something must have happened. I'm willing to do whatever it takes for Sally."

But music *is* your soul, Ellie thought, checking herself before saying it aloud. She didn't understand Ray's reasoning, but he was so hopeful and determined. Paralyzed by heartache for the past fifty years, the man was finally mobilized by blind faith and beyond any reason.

She nodded reassuringly and gave Ray a weak little smile. She was going to have to let him know about the detour to West Virginia. For now, she enjoyed his happiness as he tapped his hand affably, keeping the beat to the Oakridge Boys on the radio.

Soon, however, Ray was coughing. "Let's get you in the back seat so you can hook up to that portable oxygen tank," Ellie said. "We'll take a little rest stop at the next exit. You can switch places with Brandy."

Brandy woke up and settled in the front seat after their stop.

"Good," Ellie said. "I need you to ride shotgun, so you can help me with the navigation."

"I don't know how to work any of your gadgets up here," Brandy said as she pushed the various radio buttons. "But before we do anything else, you're going to show me how to work this freakin' car radio. I can't take any more of this bluegrass shit."

"What do you want to listen to?" asked Ellie.

"Metallica."

Ellie and Brandy's eyes met and, despite herself, Ellie burst out laughing. "Now that is certainly a blast from *our* past."

"Remember that metal bar we used to go to?" Brandy asked.

"Sure. Remember how they had hair dryers and cans of hairspray in the bathroom so you could tease up?"

"Oh, yeah. They had it all there. Stage for the bands. Big dance floor with the wood floors. Nice long bar, top shelf stuff. Lots of pool tables. Pinball machines. Pac-Man. Remember how we used to play Pole Position to see who was in the best shape to drive home?"

"Oh, come on! I always drove home. You were always too wasted to drive."

Brandy laughed and kicked her bare feet up on to the dashboard. "You were always the responsible one. I always knew you'd get me home, Ellie. And looks like you're still doing the driving, after all these years. I was there for the dancing and the guys, and you were there to scoop up my leftovers."

"What?" Ellie demanded. "What do you mean by that? I wasn't scooping up anyone's leftovers."

"Come on, El. You were always too shy to talk to a guy. I'd meet the guys, and then my little tag-along boring friend would be right next to me, and I'd introduce you. You've always been into getting your vicarious thrills through me."

Ellie smarted at the jabs. "I'm *not* a boring person," she insisted.

"Right," Brandy laughed sarcastically. Ellie's anxiety behind the wheel had not gone unnoticed. Brandy dug into the cooler and picked out a bag of M & M's from the snack bag Ellie had packed. She was hitting her opiate peak from this morning and the buzz rendered the trip almost enjoyable. On some level, it was good to be talking to Ellie again, even though Ellie had changed a lot. Ellie was smart. She knew things. She dressed well, she looked good. She had money, the house, the husband. She was a lawyer. But Ellie was still Ellie. And Brandy was pretty sure that she could recall some stories about Old Ellie that would make Current Ellie blush.

"Here, why don't you help me with some navigation," Ellie said, pushing her smartphone into Brandy's hands.

"I told you, I don't know how to work all your gadgets."

"Then it's high time you learn. Time to join the twenty-first century, Brandy."

Ellie showed Brandy how to open apps on the smartphone. "First, we're going to look for cheap gas." She showed Brandy how to pull up the gasoline apps to search for the nearest gasoline and compare prices between the stations. "Each one on the list will show you how many miles away it is from our current location," she explained.

Brandy looked it over. "And then how do you know how to get to it?"

"You can hit the map right there in the app to pull up directions," said Ellie. "It will link to Google Earth or MapQuest or something. Or we can program the address into the GPS." She showed Brandy how to pick the gas station and then punch the address into the GPS. "Now hit *Go*," she directed. Brandy did, waited for the GPS to calculate, and watched it come back with the route and estimated time of arrival.

"Okay, that's good, I think you've got basic GPS mastered," Ellie said. "Now let's look at some other apps."

"What else is there?" asked Brandy.

"What *isn't* there?" Ellie replied. She showed Brandy how to check the local weather forecast, news, music, shopping, movies, stock market, calorie counters, videos, travel information, police scanner, encyclopedia.

"I think you're getting the hang of it," she commented.

"Huh?" Brandy asked, distractedly, already playing games on the device.

"Ahem, excuse me," Ray spoke up from the back seat, clearing his throat. "I'm not a student of geography," he began, "but from what I can recall from the subject, it seems to me that the way down to Mississippi lies through Cincinnati and down yonder through Louisville. I don't know much about these interstate highway systems, Ellie. I'd wandered up North by the time they were done building them. But it seems to me perhaps we are veering too far to the east?"

Ellie glanced nervously at Ray in the rearview mirror. "Well, Ray, I did promise you I'd take you to the crossroads. And I'm going to keep that promise. But on the way, I'd like to take you through West Virginia." She waited for his reaction.

"Well...." Ray said.

"I know you want to put all your faith in the deal you're going to make, but I think we should at least try to return to the last place you saw Sally. We may be able to find a lead there. When is the last time you were in your hometown, Ray?"

"I told you," he said, "I left that place. There was nothing for me there. I buried my Doris, and then I took to the road trying to track down Sammy and his band, so I could find Sally."

"So it seems that it would make sense to at least drive through that area, see what we can find. It's logical to at least *try* it."

Ray shook his head. "Logic can't find a person who's been missing for this long, Ellie. There was nothing logical about the way I lost my daughter. There's nothing logical about the way I'm going to find her. It's gotta be faith."

"Ray, there are practical things we can try. We can visit your old house, see if there are any clues there. We can try to track down some folks who may remember the incident. See if there are any witnesses. Police records. A birth certificate for Sally."

"Heck, I don't even know where my own birth certificate is," Ray said.

"Me neither," Brandy chimed in.

Ellie looked over in surprise at her traveling companions. How could they not know where their own birth certificates were? Surely they must have needed some kind of documentation over the years— to apply for government benefits, food stamps, apply for subsidized housing. "You know you can apply for a copy of that online, right?"

"Whatever." Brandy looked out the window, unconcerned. "Registering to vote hasn't exactly been high on my priority list lately. And for your information, in case you haven't already used this smarty pants phone to look me up, I'm a convicted felon." She gave Ellie a challenging look, daring her to deny that she had already researched their backgrounds. Ellie shifted her glance, maneuvering the conversation back to Ray.

"We've got the same goal here, just different ways of approaching it. Can't we try both methods, Ray? Can't we go through Wheeling and then further south to your hometown, try to track down some leads, see if we can find Sally? And then, if that isn't successful, we'll proceed directly across Kentucky, Tennessee... well, wherever the GPS tells us is the best route." She waved her hand at the GPS on the dashboard. "Just head directly to the crossroads from there and then try the Reverse-Robert Johnson and see if that works...."

"Doesn't anyone use a map anymore?" Ray grumbled. "Go wherever the machine tells us to go? Whoever heard of such a thing?"

"So we don't even know where we're going," Brandy piped in cheerfully, munching on her M & M's. "Not that I give a shit."

Ellie gave her an annoyed glance.

"Come on, Ray," Ellie pleaded. "Can you please trust me on this one?"

"Well, I reckon I don't have a choice," he said, resigned. "It's your car, Miss Ellie, and you're the one driving and you're the one paying the bills. Don't get me wrong, I am grateful. I am a guest in this car and if you want to go to Mississippi through West Virginia, then I'm not going to argue with you."

"Good," Ellie declared, relieved.

"There's just one condition," Ray went on. "Let me pick out the motel when we stop for the night. Like I told you before, we gotta do this on the cheap."

"Okay, okay," Ellie relented. "I know that's important to you. We have a deal."

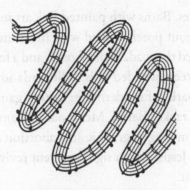

CHAPTER TEN

WHEELING, WEST VIRGINIA

Wheeling was the first stop Ellie planned. It was a haphazard, needle in a haystack approach; but could a blind visit to Wheeling, West Virginia be any worse than a last ditch plea at an intersection? Ray had described attending concerts at the Wheeling Jamboree, and the Wheeling radio station used to play a Gulch Jumpers song. Ray might recall or see something that would trigger a memory.

Guilty over tricking Ray into the detour she planned, Ellie decided to hold her tongue and go along with Ray's wishes about their meals and lodging. They took their dinner at a truck stop diner. "Separate checks?" the waitress asked, trying to figure out the improbable trio. Ellie figured "breakfast for dinner" may be the safest menu choice. She was rewarded with runny eggs, burnt toast and undercooked bacon. *How can anyone ruin bacon and eggs?* she wondered. Brandy ordered a burger, fries and a milkshake, but didn't eat much. Again, Ellie wondered about the drug use. Brandy was so skinny. The bruising on her face was progressing through a rainbow of colors. Her fingernails were chewed down, choppy and ragged. Earlier she had slurred her words.

They moved into hilly farmland as they approached the foothills of the Alleghenies. Barns with painted folk art murals and Red Man Tobacco signs, front porches filled with furniture and yards stacked with old tires lined the road. Trailer homes and a few log cabins dotted up the sides of steep, wooded hills. Billboards advertised the ubiquitous ugly landmarks of modern life: lottery games, car dealerships, Waffle House, Cracker Barrel, McDonald's. Some of the billboards touted religious messages; graphic anti-abortion ads, stern warnings about following Jesus, even a sign for a tent revival coming through on Saturday night.

Strip mining operations left huge swatches of earth scalped off the tops of the hills. Coal trucks, their black dust filling the hot humid air, struggled to wind their way up switchbacks.

It was a land of rural poverty and high unemployment and, yet, breathtaking beauty: stunning mountains, deep gorges, white water rafting, the Appalachian Trail. They exclaimed over the massive suspension bridge spanning the Ohio River, pontoon boats docked along its banks, while smokestacks from the steel plants rose in the distance.

And, of course, the music. The ballads and hymns of the hills, transplanted from the British Isles, since so many who originally settled in Appalachia came from Wales, Scotland, Ireland, and England. Their instruments: the hammered dulcimer, washboard, steel guitar, bluegrass mandolin, fiddles playing their own dialect of Irish jigs. Porch-picking roots musicians put their mountain spin on these old-time songs, and bluegrass was born.

Ray eagerly took it all in, craning his neck to see everything they passed. He sporadically muttered, "oh my goodness," or "will you look at that," but otherwise sat silent, lost in his thoughts. He was unprepared for the drastic shift of his feelings as they neared the hills of his youth. The air smelled different. It was so unlike the city, the concrete and tall buildings. It was easier to breathe here. Ray relaxed. He was going home, to his hills and his people. Maybe Ellie had been right for them to return here first.

Ellie honked the horn cheerfully as they passed into West Virginia.

"Welcome to West Virginia!" read the sign at the state line. Brandy muttered that she had never crossed the state line before, never left Ohio. Wheeling was no small town, and had modern office buildings and a beautiful restored historic district.

Ray was incensed to see the new location of the Jamboree, attached to what was essentially a hotel complex. "What happened to the beautiful old theater?" he said.

Ellie cruised hopefully past a Holiday Inn and other chain hotels in a reputable area, but Ray refused. "Too expensive there," he declared.

"Maybe you should let me be the judge of what's too expensive," Ellie said. When was the last time Ray had stayed in a hotel? What did Ray know about the cost of a hotel room, or the cost of anything having to do with modern life?

"Keep going," he directed Ellie.

They made their way into a shadier part of town. Ellie cringed as Ray pointed out a decrepit motel with blinking neon lights announcing "Vacancy." *No surprise there*, she thought. There were no interior hallways; the rooms opened directly to the parking lot. She reluctantly pulled up by the screen door of the tiny office.

"Now, I don't need a room," Ray said. "You ladies go ahead. I'm happy to sleep right here in the car."

"No, Ray, I can't have you doing that." Ellie shook her head. "We've got to keep you safe. And don't forget you just got out of the hospital, against doctor's orders. You've got to use your oxygen tank while you sleep. We are all going to have our own room. It's okay, really." She knew she could share a room with Brandy, if need be, but Ellie preferred her privacy. She wasn't a college kid anymore. She was too old to have a roommate.

She booked three rooms and handed them each a card. "No key?" asked Ray, looking at the card.

"Just swipe that card to unlock your door," Ellie explained. "Put it in your pocket and hold on to it."

Brandy seemed delighted with the idea of her own room. "Gonna turn on *all* the lights, take a *long* shower, pick my *own* TV channel," she sang, swishing her hips and waving her hands. She paused, noticing a shopping center across the road and a bar next to the motel. "Hey now. I'm going to run a few errands," she told the other two.

What kind of errands could she possibly have? Ellie wondered, but just nodded and turned her attention to a thorough bed bug inspection of her own room, wrinkling her nose in disgust at the dingy light in the bathroom and the musty odor. She would humor Ray for a night, but there was no way she was going to stay in this place longer than that.

She settled into her room with her bags and tried to relax with a glass of wine as she checked her emails.

She had forgotten about the links Jessica had sent about the crossroads and clicked on the first, reading curiously. She examined a photo of a young Robert Johnson from the early 1930s, holding his guitar, elegant and slim in his black suit and tie and black hat. She watched videos of his recordings. "Kindhearted Woman Blues." "Me and the Devil Blues." And, of course, the "Cross Road Blues" song itself. Johnson's recording was much slower than the later rocking Cream cover version. The original acoustic vocal and guitar was personal and intimate.

There were many articles and theories about the crossroads legend. One version speculated that Johnson was simply standing at the crossroads looking for a ride home, since it was so dangerous for a black man to be alone and out at night in the South. He was in Mississippi in the 1930s, when the Klan reigned terror with lynching and unchecked racial violence.

As a talented musician, he may have faced additional mistrust and hostility. Ellie read about how suspicion grew when Johnson progressed so rapidly from an unremarkable musician to a master blues guitarist and vocalist. She pondered how people were mystified by exceptional musical talent and sought ways to explain it. It was easier to attribute the difference between mediocrity and extraordinary accomplishment to magic. The alternative would be to acknowledge that the only true way to develop natural talent is through hard work and practice. If the latter was true, then shouldn't anyone be able to accomplish such feats? But then again, how was Ray able to remember how to play with such mastery when he hadn't touched a guitar in so many years?

Some theories drew links to African and European mythology depicting mystical events happening at crossroads, where believers sought wisdom, knowledge, power or earthly pleasures: the Faustian bargain. But these stories differed from Ray's quest. Most of those seekers were motivated by ambition, greed, or lust for fame and fortune.

Poor Ray, Ellie thought. The return of a lost child certainly was not so much to ask.

Ellie opened another webpage—this one expounded upon possible locations of the crossroads. She was shocked to discover this was not a settled matter. There were quite a few places in the State of Mississippi where two roads came together at right angles. According to the website, the likely crossroads location most visited by tourists was the intersection of Highway 61 and Highway 49, in Clarksdale. But some believed that Robert Johnson made his deal at the intersection of Highway 1 and Highway 8, in Rosedale. Ellie had never considered the possibility that the location of the crossroads could be up for debate. How would she even know where to take them? What address would she use to program her GPS? Would it just be a tourist trap? And what on earth would Ray do when he got there, assuming they even found the right place? The legend described Robert Johnson handing his guitar to a large black man—the devil? Mephistopheles?—at midnight, who tuned the guitar and turned it back over to Johnson, thus bestowing the musical gifts. Would Ray bring a *tuned* guitar and hope some magical force would *un-tune* it, take away his musical talent, and somehow in the process reveal the whereabouts of Sally?

Still, as unbelievable as it was, Ellie was glad the trip was underway. A crossroads is, by definition, a spot where a decision must be made: which way to turn? It was good for Ray to make any choice at this point; he was finally mobilized. She didn't know how or where, but surely this was some form of progress. And she was going to work the West Virginia angle as hard as she could. There had to be a lead.

There was a knock at her door. Brandy burst into Ellie's room, backpack in hand. "Okay, I got you a few things, El," she announced. "The sign at that bar over there says 'Live Band' tonight. Thought it might be fun for us to dress up like the old days and go dancing." She was busy taking items out of her backpack and laying them out on Ellie's bed.

Ellie watched her in astonishment. "You went shopping? How? With what money?"

But Brandy was flying high and didn't answer Ellie's question. "What do you think of this?" she asked brightly, holding up a very short skirt and a low, tight purple top. "I thought these colors may look good on you." She was very proud of herself. "Try them on, El."

Ray appeared in the open doorway, leaning up against the frame with his arms crossed, watching the exchange.

"What?" Ellie exclaimed, looking at the clothes Brandy was holding up. "That's way too short for me. I don't dress like that, Brandy." She noticed that Brandy was in her own new outfit—short skirt, skimpy hot pink top. "How did you pay for all this? Where are the bags, where are the receipts? Brandy, did you shoplift this stuff?"

"Don't worry about that, Ellie. Come on, let's go dancing," Brandy pleaded.

Ellie's gaze fell onto Brandy's feet. "And are those my Jimmy Choo shoes you're wearing? *My* shoes that you stole out of *my* closet?" She put her hands on her hips, gearing up for a fight with her old friend. Did Brandy have any idea how much those shoes had cost?

"Oh, whatever," she relented, seeing Brandy's disappointed face. Brandy had at least tried to put herself together. "Go ahead and keep them; they look good on you. But you can't be out shoplifting. It's a violation of your probation. We promised the judge no trouble, and if you get in trouble down here you are on your own—I'm not licensed to practice in West Virginia."

"Great, El, now try your stuff on so we can go out. You got to get into some heels too!"

"I'm not wearing that outfit," Ellie declared. "I'm not going out dancing in stolen clothes. And they're too short and too tight."

"Oh my God, you are the most uptight person I know," Brandy complained.

"What do you mean? I'm not uptight."

"Well, you are wound a little tight, West Side," Ray piped in kindly, smiling. "It might be good for y'all to go out on the town and kick your heels up a bit."

"We're not here for me," Ellie protested. "I want to work on our plan for tomorrow. My heels don't need kicking up. I don't need to unwind."

"Oh yeah, I can see that," said Brandy, gesturing to the open bottle of wine on Ellie's dresser. "You know you get all over me for my habits. You're such a hypocrite."

"Now, now, ladies, enough already," said Ray. "Ellie, you did all the driving today and we could see how you tense up when you get out on the busy road. Your old friend here went to the trouble of picking out some fancy new duds for you. What harm can it do to walk over and sip a little whiskey and hear some live music?"

They both think I'm too uptight to go dancing, Ellie thought, irritated. She, judged by an old man who believed in a fairy tale and a woman who shot heroin into her veins and left her own kids to be raised by their grandmother. Neither had to work long hours every day, make car payments, house payments. *Sure I'm uptight*, Ellie thought. *Someone in this group has to be responsible*. And the last thing she needed was to get arrested in another state for Theft or Receiving Stolen Property, thanks to Brandy's little shoplifting expedition.

She looked at their faces. Brandy was staring her down, challenging, rocking those expensive Jimmy Choo's with attitude and no remorse. The girl was just plain nuts, Ellie decided. Ray was relaxed and amused, trying to fight back a smile. Ellie's traveling companions had not a care in the world.

"Oh, what the hell," Ellie declared. She grabbed the stolen clothes and went into the dingy bathroom to change.

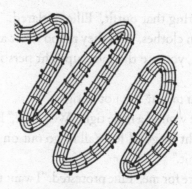

CHAPTER ELEVEN

MASTER OF THE FIDDLE

For Ellie, the walk from the motel to the bar was akin to walking the plank. Her stomach tightened into knots. The sun had set for the night and neon lights blinked in the moonlight. The booming bass and drum beat from the band and the voices of the crowd echoed from the tavern. Pickup trucks and motorcycles filled the parking lot. Ellie was self-conscious in her skimpy outfit, tottering slightly in her outrageous heels.

Ellie had insisted that Ray come along, and he had affably agreed. "Don't mind if I do come along," he had told them. "I haven't heard a band play a live set in many, many years. And look at me, stepping out on the town with two beautiful ladies, all dolled up."

Brandy excitedly charged ahead, oblivious to Ellie's anxiety. "I'm not so sure this is a good idea," Ellie tried to tell them. Brandy grabbed her arm and pulled her through the door and into the bar. Ellie, Brandy and Ray paused in the doorway. Everyone in the bar stopped what they were doing to turn and stare.

The crowd looked to be made up of regulars who all knew each other well. *We may as well have "out of town" stuck on our foreheads,* Ellie thought. She tugged at her skirt.

Brandy charged up to the bar and ordered a round of drinks. "Umm, I really can't do shots anymore," Ellie tried to tell her. "I'll get sick..."

Brandy would hear none of it. "Down the hatch," she ordered. She, Ray and Ellie all did a shot of Jim Beam, and Ellie reeled at the burn as the drink went down. She set the empty shot glass on the counter, gasping.

"Hit us again," Brandy told the bartender.

"Y'all from around here?" the bartender asked, trying to figure how the old man and the two women went together.

"My sister and I are taking our dad on vacation to visit some relatives," Ellie answered quickly.

"You two are sisters?" asked the bartender, looking at the scrawny, rough blonde with the bruised face, next to the pretty, nervous brunette who looked healthy and professional despite her tawdry outfit.

"Oh yeah, she's my soul sister," cried Brandy, putting her arm around Ellie and swinging her hips. The men at the bar were watching.

"You don't look like sisters," one of the men yelled out, "and y'all look like you're too far from home."

"I think he's right," Ellie said to Ray and Brandy. "Let's just head back to the motel and turn on our air conditioning and see what's on TV."

But Ray was not listening. He was studying the stage and looking over the night's entertainment. Five young men made up the band, and they had an array of instruments set up on the stage: an electric guitar, acoustic guitar, and fiddle were perched on stands, at the ready. A harmonica was secured to one of the microphone stands. They had a saxophone. There was an electric keyboard, slide guitar, bass, drum set with snare, bass, tenor drums and Zildjian cymbals. A five-string banjo and stand-up string bass leaned against the back wall. Large amplifiers and a mixer sat to the side.

The lead singer took a few swigs from a beer as they rested in between songs. He said a few words to one of the others, the drummer counted out "three-four" and they all came in, sounding solid. A few people got up and started dancing on the small dance floor in front of the band. Ellie recognized the Rascal Flatts song. The singer had a nice twang and they were pleasantly loud.

Ray was transfixed. No detail escaped his notice. He studied each musician, watching their fingerings, their movements, the nonverbal cues and communication between the band mates. He was not familiar with the song they were playing, but he registered the moments they pulled off as well as their mistakes. He was excited about the whole show, even their mistakes—it made them more accessible. There was nothing in the world like live music. He couldn't remember when he had last heard a live band play for people, the way he used to with his buddies.

Brandy didn't delay in enthusiastically joining the crowd on the dance floor. Ellie watched her a moment, admiring how she could dance with abandon, tossing her hair and moving her arms up in the air, not caring what anyone thought of her. Ellie remembered how she always used to be one of the best dancers on the floor.

"Maybe we should get a table," Ellie said to Ray. She was eager to find a corner where they could sit out of the way, where she wouldn't feel people staring at them.

Ray nodded and coughed a few times.

"It's too smoky in here for you," Ellie told him. She walked back over to the bartender. "Can you open the back door to let some air in for my dad?" she yelled over the music. "It's kind of smoky in here, and there's not a lot of fresh air, and he's got emphysema; we've got an oxygen tank for him back at the motel, but I don't want him going into a coughing fit in here, and if you could just prop open that back door..."

The bartender ignored her. The man next to her on the barstool gave her a scowl. "Umm, excuse me!" Ellie tried again, yelling to the bartender.

He turned around and looked Ellie up and down. "It's my bar. Back door stays closed. You want to order another round of shots?"

Ellie glanced at the other guys at the bar, who were now collectively looking her up and down. "Uh, yeah, sure, another round..." She retreated with the drinks back to their table. "Sorry, Ray, he wasn't too interested in letting some fresh air in the place."

"Look at Miss Ellie Sanders, letting her hair down," Ray chuckled, gesturing at the drinks she had set on the table.

Brandy appeared and downed her shot quickly. "Come on, El, do your shot and come dance with me. Just like the old days."

Ellie did her shot and followed Brandy out to the floor. The band was now playing Stevie Ray Vaughan, "Tightrope," one of Ellie's favorites. She had always been partial to the blues.

The alcohol was taking effect and Ellie started to relax. Brandy was laughing, grinding and twirling next to Ellie. A couple of guys were suddenly next to them on the dance floor, and Ellie wasn't sure if she was still dancing with Brandy or with these strangers.

One of the men leaned in to yell in Ellie's ear. "What's your name?"

She told him her name and he introduced himself. "I'm Bob. And this here is Johnny. You and your friend are good dancers."

"Sisters," Ellie corrected him, deciding to stick with this white lie for the sake of consistency.

Ellie was buzzing from the alcohol and realized it was fun to be out dancing again. *Look at me*, she thought. *Out on the dance floor in West Virginia, with Brandy Sarendesh of all people, wearing a stolen skirt and dancing with some Jim-Bob stranger.*

The band was rocking some Stray Cats rockabilly swing and the crowd was thick on the dance floor. When the band took their break before the next set, Ellie headed back to the table to check on Ray. "I'm just fine," he told her. "It's not all that different from the old honky-tonks I used to play in; some things never change. Good whiskey and good music, that's what people like."

Ellie scanned the bar for Brandy. "I'll be right back," she told Ray. She made her way through the crowd toward the back of the building, looking for the Ladies Room. She pushed open the door to the restroom. Brandy and one of the musicians from the band stood hunched over the sink. On the counter was a syringe and white powder, laid out in a two lines.

"Brandy, what's going on in here!"

Brandy and the man regarded Ellie, nonchalantly. "Just keeping the party going, El. You want to do a line?"

"No, I don't. Brandy you can't be doing that—you're going to get busted. Don't you remember what the judge said? Come on, let's get out of here."

"Ahh, go on now and get outta here, *you* are a *buzzkill*," said the man, kicking the door shut in Ellie's face.

Ellie waited, not sure what to do. Brandy was completely out of control. The girl was a total addict. She tried the bathroom door again, but this time it was locked. Ellie struggled for balance and tried to think clearly. The crowd was swimming in front of her eyes. It was going to be hard to walk in a straight line.

Suddenly, Ray was next to her. "You okay, West Side?"

"Brandy's locked in there with some guy, doing drugs," she told Ray.

"Let's sit back down." He grabbed Ellie's arm and led her back to her seat. "Ellie, I know you want to save everyone, but Brandy's a big girl. She's gonna do, what she's gonna do."

"You don't understand, Ray. She had a syringe, so she was probably shooting up heroin. And there were lines of what I think was cocaine. You can't mix that shit. She's going to kill herself. And she's had a lot to drink."

"Ellie," Ray said seriously, "I lived at the Mission of Hope for a long time. I watch people, and I watched Brandy before I met you and before I knew her name and before I knew she was an old friend of yours. I'm sorry to tell you, but she's been using right along. She may have been going to the counseling sessions, but she never quit using the drugs. I could tell. She's got a bad habit, a bad addiction there. I know you want to help her, but the truth of the matter is you're probably not going to be able to. Something's broken on the inside, and it won't get fixed until *she* makes the decision. There's not a thing you can do about it, Ellie."

"But I'm responsible for her. I promised the judge I'd keep her out of trouble."

"No one can do that for Brandy, except Brandy," Ray said.

The lead singer was suddenly standing at their table. "Hey," he said. "Your friend, or sister, or whoever she is, got my buddy high in the bathroom. Now he's too messed up to play. We can't go on now with our next set."

"Um, I'm sorry about that," Ellie said, exchanging a nervous glance with Ray. "I'm worried about her. Do you know what they were doing?"

"Well, I think they crushed up some Percocet or Oxy that Fred had and shot it up," said the lead singer. "And maybe she had some shit on her too, I don't know. All I know is we're supposed to go back on to do our bluegrass set, and now I don't have a fiddle player. The man can't even stand up."

The eyes of the crowd were upon Ellie and Ray, and people were talking and whispering. The drummer and bass player shuffled about on stage, shooting dirty looks their way. The bartender had a towel in his hand and was drying off some glasses, but he was also looking over and frowning, watching, wondering what was going on with the next set for the band.

Ray stood up. "I'll sit in for your fiddle player." He turned and coughed to the side, putting his hand over his mouth.

The lead singer looked at the old man, raising his eyebrows. "You?" he said, incredulous. "Thanks all the same, but I don't think so."

"Y'all don't think I can play the fiddle?" Ray asked him.

"No offense, mister, but no, I don't. And even if you can, we've never played with you. And you don't know our play list."

"Well, why don't we give it a try? I can set up there with you and listen to a few bars, and once I got the feel of what y'all are doing, I'll come in."

The lead singer listened to Ray, considering. The other guys on the stage were pacing, impatient. The bartender was watching, looking angry.

"What have you got to lose?" Ray pressed. "If I can't get the feel of what you boys are doing, I'll just sit it out. If I come in, and you don't like it, then we'll call it a day. But I can tell you, son, I do know my way around the strings of a bluegrass fiddle."

"Oh geez, okay," said the lead singer. Brandy and Fred had disappeared again. Ellie was wringing her hands. The band had already been on break for over half an hour and the crowd was going to move on if they didn't start playing again soon. "All right, we'll give it a try."

Ellie sat back on her stool and watched Ray head up to the stage. He picked up the fiddle, rosined up the bow and began tuning the violin. He sounded the strings together: A-D, D-G, A-E, turning the pegs, adjusting the pitch of each open string. He adjusted the chin rest. "It's a mighty fine instrument you got here," he commented to the fellow next to him, who had switched out his guitar for a banjo. The electric bass had also been traded for the upright string bass. Then he nodded to the band. "I'm ready."

"Okay," the lead singer said. "You know 'Modern Day Bonnie and Clyde'? We don't do it like Travis Tritt did, we do a bluegrass version."

Ray shook his head no.

"What key is it in?" the lead singer asked the banjo player.

"Don't worry about that," Ray told them. "Just start the song, I'll listen a few moments and then I'll come in if I get the hang of it. I don't need to know what key it's in. I can play the bluegrass fiddle. I was raised on bluegrass, boys."

The guys looked at each other and shrugged. "Let's do it."

The lead singer walked up to the microphone. "It's time for our nod to bluegrass," he told the crowd. "So we're welcoming this fine gentleman here who's going to sit in and maybe play a little fiddle if the spirit so moves him. What's your name, sir?"

"Ray. Ray Jones."

"Ray Jones!" the lead singer declared to the crowd, waving his arm toward Ray. The crowd clapped, and the band started the song.

Ray sat on his stool, tapping his foot, nodding and watching the others. He listened, learning the song instantaneously. And then, when he was ready, he put the fiddle to his chin and took bow to string.

Ellie had heard Ray sing. She had heard him play the guitar, the harmonica, the ukulele. But she had never heard anything like this. He was not just good, he was *out of this world*. His fingers danced across the fingerboard with mastery and precision. His bow arm moved fast and tight, near the bridge, with total control over the sound, hitting several strings together to produce twangy, juicy chords, with a commanding vibrato that seared over the room, sweet and high.

People stopped talking, looked up from their conversations and stared at Ray Jones. There were exclamations of astonishment from nearby tables. A few held up cell phones to take photos or to videotape a few minutes of the action. Ellie had no doubt that Ray would be all over social media within minutes.

Folks on the dance floor were going crazy. "Whooo," they hollered, clapping and encouraging Ray.

Ellie was dumbfounded. She knew Ray was very talented, but even she was surprised by what she was witnessing. The man truly was some kind of musical genius. And none of it made any sense. If he had the ability to just walk into a bar and play like this out of the blue—with a band he's never played with before, playing a song he didn't even know—then how was it he had been living homeless and destitute? Why hadn't he just walked into any bar in Cleveland and done this?

Bob and Johnny sat down at her table. "Your dad is amazing on that fiddle!" Bob yelled. "Holy smokes. Who *is* your dad? He's someone famous, right? Should we be trying to get his autograph?"

The bartender sent over another round of drinks, on the house. When Ellie looked over, he tipped his hat to her. "Hey," she heard him yell to the other bartender. "Open up that back door so the old man can get some fresh air in here."

The fresh air was a relief. Soon Ellie was engrossed in conversation with Bob and Johnny. She told them all about meeting Ray at the homeless shelter, running into her old college friend Brandy, Ray wanting to find his long lost daughter Sally. The alcohol had loosened her tongue and her inhibitions, prompting her to pour out her whole life story to these strangers.

"So we're on a road trip down to the crossroads," she shouted to them above the music. "Ray's going to trade in his musical talent in exchange for finding Sally. It's going to be a Reverse-Robert Johnson."

The men burst into laughter. "Reverse-Robert Johnson! Sounds like a sexual position!"

Ellie dissolved into laughter with them, gasping for breath. They did another round of shots. The room continued to swim before her eyes. The band had progressed on to a full bluegrass set: Bill Monroe, Doc Watson, Special Consensus, Alison Kraus & Union Station.

"Now, let's see," Bob said, getting more serious. "You gotta think this thing through, Ellie. You're trying to find Sally who was kidnapped by her grandparents from Ray's home down here in the holler. And it sounds like the only thing that made it out of that home, besides Doris and Sally, was that shoebox you found in your closet."

"So, what's your point?" asked Ellie. "I'm not following."

"Right, you're *not* following," yelled Bob. "You gotta follow the leads. And right now the biggest lead you have is what you found in your own closet. Right under your nose. In *Ohio*. If that box somehow made it into Ohio, the people who were carrying that box with them made it into Ohio. I'll bet you any amount of money you're going to find Sally in Ohio."

Ellie tried to concentrate. Could it be possible Jim-Bob here was making some sense?

"Let's head back to the dance floor," Bob suggested hopefully.

Ellie waved her hand and her wedding ring in front of his face. "Married," she told him.

"I don't see any husband here tonight."

"He's home in Ohio."

"Yeah, right, Ohio—that would be the same Ohio where your friend Ray, or your dad, or whoever he is, is going to find his daughter Sally."

"Hey, Ellie," Brandy ran up to her excitedly. "Ray's the star of the band. Come on. Let's get up and dance on one of these tables."

"Yeah, I'm not really the dancing-on-tables-type. You go right ahead, though, just don't break your neck." The crowd yelled encouragement as Brandy jumped onto a table and proceeded to stomp and dance to the bluegrass, putting on as much of a show as Ray was.

The band finished their song and, as they paused to take drinks of beer, Ray asked if they minded if he did a song. "Play whatever you like, Ray," they told him gratefully. "You just come in and we'll try to follow your lead. Who are you going to play?"

"It's an original," Ray told them.

They tilted the microphone over to Ray so he could introduce the song to the crowd. As the applause finally quieted, Ray said, "So now we're going to try an original song from back in my day, folks. This here is a Gulch Jumpers song." He strummed the acoustic guitar and sang, while the band offered soft backup to the sweet and simple ballad. The mood in the room was nothing short of hushed rapture.

When Ray finished his grand finale, the members of the band shook his hand, thanking him profusely. "You come play with us anytime," they told him. "In fact, we'll come to you, if you tell us where you live. We could make it big with you in the band." Fred the Freebasing Fiddler had been demoted and was all but forgotten.

The bartender approached. "You come play in my bar any night of the week, drinks on the house," he told Ray.

Ellie staggered over. It was time to try to gather up Ray and Brandy and get back to the motel. A young man stood to the side, waiting for his turn to talk to Ray. He had his cell phone pressed to his ear. He approached Ray and Ellie, nodding into his phone. "Yes, Grandma, okay, I'll tell him. Yes, Grandma."

"Excuse me, sir," the young man addressed Ray. "May I please speak to you a moment? My name is Evan McTaggert. I heard you say just now that song you were playing was a Gulch Jumpers song."

"Yes, The Gulch Jumpers, that's an old band that's not around anymore and never amounted to anything." Ray waved his hand dismissively.

"Well, sir, my Grandpa Owen used to talk about playing in a band called The Gulch Jumpers when he was a young man."

Ellie gasped.

"Your Grandpa *Owen*?" Ray asked excitedly. "*Owen*? What did you say your name was?"

"I'm Evan McTaggert. My granddaddy was Owen McTaggert."

"Sweet Jesus!" Ray cried out.

"And I've got my Grandma Dottie on the phone with me now..."

"Dottie Davis, Owen's steady girl, the prettiest girl in our high school class," Ray declared with excitement. "I can't believe it! Did you tell Dottie you found your granddaddy's old band mate and mining buddy, Ray Jones?"

"Yes, sir." Evan nodded. "I've got her here on the phone with me now, and she wants me to pass along a message." He turned his attention back to his phone for a moment. "Yes, Grandma. I'll tell him exactly what you said." He turned back to Ray, smiling. "Grandma Dottie says to tell you: 'Lord Almighty, I never thought I'd live to see the day that Ray Jones came home, and if ole' Ray Jones and his kin don't come up to the farm for supper tomorrow night, he better not ever step foot in this county again.'"

Ellie clasped her hands together in excitement and let out a whoop. She and Ray shared a joyful hug. Into their laps had dropped a lead, just as she had been hoping.

Ray beamed and shook Evan's hand. "Tell Dottie we'd be pleased to join y'all for supper tomorrow night. Nothing would make me happier. I just can't believe it," he exclaimed, shaking his head happily and pumping Evan's hand with joy. "Nothing would make me happier."

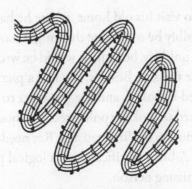

CHAPTER TWELVE

GRASPING FOR CLUES

Ellie lay in bed the next morning, battling to peel her eyelids open and struggling to determine if the room was going to stop spinning. Her mouth was bone dry and her head hurt all over. The air conditioning must have quit in the night. It was sticky and humid, even this early in the day. Miserable, she considered the depressing and dank motel room.

She stumbled to the bathroom and retrieved her Tylenol. The bottled water was in her car. She stepped out to the parking lot for the water, and then plunked down in one of the lawn chairs lining the walkway that faced out toward the road. She sipped her water, looking out over the hills that rose in the distance, engulfed in fog.

It was definitely going to be a hot day. Her sweat stunk of alcohol. *How much did I have to drink last night?* She thought back over last night's events, trying to put together everything that had happened: the shock of seeing Brandy using heroin and cocaine, Ray's thrilling debut on the fiddle, and the marvelous, fortuitous luck of running into Owen's grandson. Who could have predicted they would be that lucky, on their very first night in West Virginia?

What would be the best use of their time today? She hoped to take

Ray for a drive to visit his old home, where he had lived with Doris. Could there possibly be some clue that might have been missed fifty years ago? It was unlikely, but still, it would be wrong to come all this way and not visit the site. Besides, she had a picture in her mind of how she imagined it looked, and she was eager to see the place.

She also wanted to look for police records about the car crash and pay a visit to the Bureau of Vital statistics. Ray needed to request Sally's birth certificate. A birth certificate was a logical place to start when searching for a missing person.

The door to Brandy's room opened and Fred, the guy from the band, emerged, disheveled and hung over. "Mornin'," he said casually to Ellie as he strolled toward the bar parking lot. Ellie scowled and did not return his greeting. *What was Brandy thinking, allowing some stranger to spend the night?*

He paused several feet away. "You two ain't really sisters, are you?" he called out over his shoulder. Ellie didn't answer him, rubbing her aching head. Fred shrugged, ambled along to his car and drove away.

She walked over to Brandy's room, where Fred had left the door ajar. Brandy was still in bed, dead to the world. Ellie gave her a little shake. "Go way..." Brandy mumbled. Satisfied that Brandy was still breathing and just coming down off her high from last night, Ellie retreated and pulled the door shut. Better to let her sleep it off.

Ray emerged from his room, stretched and tucked his thumbs under his suspender straps. He nodded happily toward the view. "Good morning, Ellie. How do you like our foggy mountain mornings in West Virginia?"

"It's sure not the view I'm used to at home," she admitted. The mist hung heavy in the hills, casting a magical juncture where heaven and earth met.

He sat in the lawn chair next to her. "And where's our other friend this morning?"

"I don't think we're going to see Brandy for a while. She's still sleeping off our wild night on the town. And judging by how I'm feeling, just from the drinking, she's better off asleep. Even without working air conditioning."

"Ah now, we never had air conditioning back when I was coming up. You just get used to it after awhile. I guess that was one good thing about the mining; one could cool off a bit underground."

Ellie groaned and hung her head, wondering if she would feel better if she just got sick.

"You're gonna feel better after a cool shower and some breakfast," Ray told her. "We'll go and get us some grits and coffee. Fix you right up like new."

"I don't think I could stomach that right now," said Ellie. "And I don't eat grits."

"When in the South, do as the Southerners do. You may be surprised. Some nice grits will settle your stomach and soak up the rest of that alcohol. A good down home southern breakfast will put you right."

Ray didn't complain at all of being tired or hung over from the smoky bar, the drinking, or the exertion from playing his extended set. One would never guess from looking at him that he had been in the hospital just two days earlier. "Did you hook up to your oxygen tank last night, Ray?" Ellie asked.

"Uhmm hummm," he nodded dreamily, gazing up at the hills and humming.

"I'm so glad we ran into Owen's grandson last night, Ray." She gently put her hand on his arm.

Ray grasped her hand and held it tightly. "Yes, Ellie, I owe you an apology for squawking about coming through West Virginia first. I just can't wait until supper time when we head up to Dottie and Owen's place. I haven't talked to anyone from my old life in so long; it's just amazing to come back down here and find someone who remembers me. It's good for the soul to be back in these hills again, I tell you, just plain good for the soul."

She nodded. "Well, we've made some real progress already. It's an encouraging sign. I'm hoping you and I can head out and go exploring today, maybe make even more progress. What do you say?"

"I'm up for it," he agreed.

Ellie attempted to pull herself together, despite the anemic water pressure in the shower and the texture of the grits at the diner ("You gotta put some honey in it," Ray had advised). With the help of the Tylenol and two cups of coffee, she managed to rally.

They settled into the front seat after breakfast and Ellie pulled up the local road map on the GPS. "Okay, Ray. Here we go. Let's see if we can find your old house. Do you remember your address, by any chance?" She waited, poised to enter the information and pull up directions.

"Address? No, no, there wasn't any address, Ellie. It wasn't like living in the city. Doris and I just picked a spot in the hills and that's where Charlie and Owen helped me cut wood to put up the house."

Ellie struggled to absorb the "no address" concept. Had Ray and Doris purchased the land they built on, or had someone deeded it over to them? Had they rented, or just squatted and built without permission? Perhaps they built on land not owned by anyone. She wondered if there was land left anywhere in the United States simply not owned by anyone. Was there any land that fit that description in rural West Virginia in the early 1960s?

"Umm, I'm not sure how to set out without an address."

Ray waved his hand toward the GPS. "We don't need that contraption, Ellie. Just head out down the road, head down south from here. I'll remember it when I see it."

"Well, do you at least remember which county you lived in?" Ellie asked.

"Well, now, I used to drive up to Wheeling to see the live Jamboree show, but we lived down in Wetzel County."

Ellie decided they needed a paper map for an overview of the area. She retrieved her road atlas from the trunk.

"Now that's more like it," Ray said approvingly as she spread the map out over the dashboard. They both studied the State of West Virginia

for a few moments. South of Ohio County lay Marshall County, and
below that lay Wetzel County. New Martinsville was the county seat.
Perhaps the Office of Vital Statistics could be found there. That type
of information could be answered from Ellie's smartphone, assuming
she could even get cell reception deep in these hills. But she couldn't
Google or MapQuest or GPS the location for 'little-clapboard-house-
in-the-holler-that-we-built-with-our-own-damn-hands-and-I'll-rec-
ognize-it-when-I-see-it.'

Ellie saw these counties bordered the Ohio River. "We could just
follow the river," she suggested. "Do you remember, Ray, if you lived
close to the river?"

"Beautiful Ohio. But, nah, not in that area. Further inland. In the
hills."

She sighed. "Let's just head down that way and see what
happens, then."

The drive was scenic if nothing else. They wound along the river,
crossed below the Mason-Dixon Line, and then cut east, traversing the
Allegheny Plateau. State and county routes that were marked would
somehow inexplicably become unmarked, and then branch off onto
confusing smaller rural roads that meandered through rolling hills,
valleys and ridges.

The fog cleared and the sun burned high in the sky, revealing
sweeping vistas: family farmsteads nestled on hillsides, livestock
grazing in cleared meadowland, tobacco farms, and nurseries. Pretty
Victorian-style houses alternated with dilapidated shacks. Glassworks
and steel mills along the river gave way to mining operations as they
wandered further south and east into the bowels of the mountain state.

Ellie had lost track of their exact location long ago, but the compass
on her dashboard at least confirmed their direction. The narrow rural
roads that veered up and down the steep hills of the Alleghenies had
her hands sweating on the steering wheel. She was not accustomed
to these steep grades, and despite the impressive views, the driving
was terrifying.

"Well, I sure don't remember this road being here," Ray would occasionally comment. He tapped his hand along to the radio. Occasionally the radio cut out altogether, unable to permeate the dense mountain rock. Ray wasn't too bothered by the fact that he wasn't recognizing any landmarks. Ellie, on the other hand, grew increasingly frustrated. The air conditioning in her car was a godsend, but her headache had returned. She suspected they were starting to drive in circles.

"Do you remember the name of the road heading up to your hollow, Ray?"

"Well, I believe we used to head up Old Pigeon Pass to get to our clearing," he said thoughtfully, rubbing his chin. "Just can't recall if that fed in to one of these county routes. A lot of these roads must have come through after my time here. And I sure don't recall power lines coming all the way back into the hills. It was pretty rustic living for us."

She pulled into a gas station with old-fashioned style pumps with big levers that she remembered from her childhood days. No credit card swipe on these machines. Inside the convenience store, Ellie grabbed a Pepsi from the cooler. "Do you have any idea where Old Pigeon Pass Road is?" she asked the cashier.

The young man shook his head. "Sorry, never heard of it."

The heat was oppressive. "Ray, let's head over to the county seat. I don't feel like we're making any progress wandering up and down these hills."

They made their way west, back over to New Martinsville, another river town. Ellie located the courthouse and county buildings with ease—all open since it was a weekday. She parked right on the square, marveling at the ease of free parking. The only spot not available was the one reserved for the sheriff. The courthouse and county offices were housed in an old building with impressive architecture and a shiny dome.

They stood and stretched, looking around the town square. Next to the courthouse was a library, a red brick, federal-style building. "Let's try the library before we get Sally's birth certificate. Maybe we can find a newspaper clipping about the accident."

It was quiet and cool in the old building that was all but deserted except for an aging librarian who looked up hopefully from her desk when Ray and Ellie entered. "Can I help you folks?"

Ellie explained they were searching for a local newspaper clipping from the mid-1960s. The librarian importantly directed them to the microfiche machine. Ellie hadn't realized such things were still in existence, but after twenty minutes or so, she was able to retrieve the local gazette published on the dates following Ray's fateful State Fair weekend. She turned the knobs, flipping through articles about striking miners, high school football games and church bake sales. She finally found the small article and winced as she read the hurtful language:

Young Negro Woman Killed in Crash on Old McCracken Road: The body of Miss Doris Brown, an unmarried mother, was found deserted in a crashed truck in a ditch off of Old McCracken Road. The other occupants of the vehicle were missing from the scene. The vehicle is registered to Miss Brown's father, Mr. Sammy Brown. Mr. Ray Jones, who was away performing at the West Virginia State Fair with his band The Gulch Jumpers on the date of the accident, filed a Missing Person Report for his illegitimate daughter, Sally Jones. The child remains missing.

Ray, who was reading over Ellie's shoulder, fumed. "Unmarried, illegitimate," he began rumbling angrily.

Ellie quickly hit Print and shut off the machine. "Don't let that get to you. You know your own family; no one else gets to define you. Let's get over to the courthouse."

They walked down the long corridor in the County Building, perusing the signs on the doors: Clerk's Office, Marriage Licenses, Building Permits, Cashier's office. Finally Ellie spotted the Office of Vital Statistics.

A sign on the wall posted the requirements to request a birth certificate. Paperwork could be completed to request a birth certificate from the West Virginia Vital Registration Office, which was located in Charleston. A birth certificate could only be requested by oneself, as the registrant, or by a parent of the registrant.

"Okay, Ray." Ellie sat him down with the form and a pencil. "You are Sally's father. That makes you a parent of the registrant. You have standing to fill out this form and put in the request."

"Not sure how this will help, Ellie, but we can try," he said.

Ray carefully printed out "Sally Eugenia Jones." He listed Sally's date of birth: October 14, 1964. He listed Doris's name under Mother, his name under Father, and after pausing over Location of Birth for a few moments, wrote in "Wetzel County." Ellie couldn't help but peer over his shoulder as he completed the form, interested to see details such as Sally's middle name and date of birth. It was a relief that Ray was able to recall this information, especially given his poor performance that day in recalling the geography of his youth.

"We'll pull it up in the state database," the clerk informed them after they submitted the form. "Everything was scanned in a few years ago. If we can match the information on the request to the birth certificate, you can submit your fee and then the certified copy can be mailed to you from Charleston or you can go there and pick it up in person. We can print out an unofficial uncertified copy for you here, but we can't provide the certified copy from this office."

Ray and Ellie nodded. They waited nervously as the Clerk entered Ray's information into the computer. Ellie couldn't help but feel that something substantial and concrete would be achieved if they could hold the official state recognition of Sally's birth and life in their hands.

But the clerk frowned, hitting the keys, his eyes scanning up and down. "You sure you have everything spelled correctly here?" he asked. "Sure you have the right date of birth?"

"I'm sure of it," Ray answered.

"And you're the child's father?" the clerk asked.

"I'm her father." But Ray and Ellie exchanged worried glances. They knew there may be a paternity problem. Ray was unable to benefit from the presumption of paternity that marriage would have bestowed, had he and Doris been legally able to marry before the Supreme Court settled the matter in 1967.

The clerk finally looked up. "I'm sorry, but I'm not finding Sally Eugenia Jones in our database. I can't provide that birth certificate for you."

"What if there was a paternity issue?" Ellie inquired.

"I tried the search under the child's name and under the mother's name, not just under your name." He looked at Ray. "So if the other information was correct, it should have pulled up that way, even if no legal father was listed."

"How could there be no birth certificate for Sally?" Ellie asked. "Mr. Jones here is sure of the information we've provided on the form."

"Do you remember anything more specific about the location of the birth? What hospital was the child born at, sir?"

"No hospital, son," Ray answered. "My daughter's birth was at home, attended by the local midwife."

"Well, that may explain it," answered the clerk. "Sometimes rural births and deaths went unreported long ago in these parts. It was just like you say—a local midwife, a remote location, isolated or uneducated folks,"—he gave Ray an apologetic glance—"and the birth might have just gone unreported and unregistered."

"Ray, do you remember if the midwife registered Sally's birth?" Ellie asked him.

"I honestly do not recall," Ray answered helplessly.

They considered the situation for a moment. "Of course, there could be another possible explanation," offered the clerk, "if you are sure you have all the other information correct on the form."

"What is the other possible explanation?" Ellie asked.

But she knew the answer before he even said it. Adoption was one of the few legal circumstances that permitted a birth certificate to be amended. Except with adoption, it wasn't just a simple amendment such as correcting transposed numbers or the spelling of a name. When a child was adopted, a new birth certificate was substituted for the original one. With an adoption, history was rewritten.

"Adoption?" Ray gasped, sputtering. He reeled as if he had been punched in the stomach. Ellie grabbed his shoulders, worried he was going to fall to the floor.

"Ellie!" Ray cried, turning toward her, "how could my child be adopted? Without my permission? How could it be possible?" His hands flew up and clutched the sides of his head to keep his mind from exploding from such cruel and impossible information. "It just can't be." He collapsed, weeping, into a chair in the waiting area. "Sally, Sally, Sally," he cried, his shoulders heaving.

"I'm sorry," the clerk offered genuinely. "Certainly don't mean to be the bearer of bad news to you folks. And we don't know for sure she was adopted. It could have just been an unregistered rural birth."

Ellie nodded to the clerk gratefully as she comforted Ray, putting her arms around him and walking him out of the office. She had meant for Ray to request a copy of his own birth certificate as well, but now was not the time to bring this up. Ray was too upset.

The mood from last night's joyful celebration had come crashing down. And the downward spiral continued upon their return to the fleabag motel.

Brandy was finally awake, still looking drunk and about twenty years older than her true age. Heavy dark circles and bags under her eyes, she was dressed, but shaking and sloppy.

Ellie snapped. Perhaps it was the frustration from the day, or the emotion from the visit to the Vital Statistics Office, but without really meaning to, she went on the attack.

"You know, Brandy, this is not some kind of altered-state, expense-free, drug-binge vacation for you to do whatever the hell you want."

"What's your problem?" Brandy shot back.

"*My* problem? My problem is you. And *my* problem, *our* problem, the whole reason we are here, is supposed to be *Ray* and figuring out what happened to *his* daughter. And what we don't need is you going out and shoplifting, and you doing drugs in the bathroom of a bar, and you bringing home some stranger you don't even know and sleeping with him.

"You know," she went on, trying to tug up the top of Brandy's neckline to cover up some cleavage, "just because you can do something doesn't mean you should. Just because you think something doesn't mean you should say it. We're not kids anymore. Haven't you learned any kind of self-restraint? It's not always all about you."

"Oh, I can see what this is about, Ellie," Brandy retorted. "You're all worked up because you saw Fred walking out of here this morning. You think you know how everyone else should behave, all the time. You can't stand anything that doesn't fit into those perfectly drawn lines."

Ellie's mouth flew open, but Brandy wasn't done. "You're just judging me again, the way you've always judged me." She moved closer so she was directly in front of Ellie, right in her face. "You just can't stand it that I got laid last night. When's the last time that *you* got any loving from a man, Ellie?"

"My relationship with my husband is my business," Ellie yelled. "And I didn't come down here to cheat on my husband. You think *I'm* jealous of *you*?"

Brandy flinched, hurt, and gathered herself up. "I think you're a snob. I think you know you're better than me and you always have. You want to fix people because it makes you feel better about yourself. I bet you think you're better than Ray, too."

"I don't even know what you're talking about," Ellie said. "You aren't making any sense. All I'm trying to do is help Ray the way he asked me to, so he can find Sally."

"You're not helping him the way he asked you to. He asked you to take him to Mississippi, to the crossroads. What do you do? You take him to West Virginia instead, without even telling him what you're doing. Why? Because you're a know-it-all. And, I'd like to point out to *both* of you, that for all your Ray-way versus Ellie-way bickering, the only thing that has worked so far was us running into Ray's old friend's grandson at the bar—and why did we go to the bar? Because we did things the *Brandy*-way." She looked triumphant.

Ellie fumed, not wanting to admit that Brandy had a point on that one. "That was just dumb luck, that's all."

"Of course you would say that. You've always got to be right. You can't even see where you need help. You've got a full view to everyone else's problems, but you keep your own problems out of sight, in your blind spot. I saw that room in your house, that nursery."

"What?" Ellie cried.

"I saw how you keep it like a shrine," Brandy went on. "There's no baby in there. You keep the door closed. You just shut it off and shut it out, and don't deal with it."

Ellie was shaking, furious. Ray looked at Ellie, confused. "Nursery? Baby? What's she talking about, Ellie?"

"You had no right to go in there," Ellie screamed. "You broke into my house!"

Brandy crossed her arms, and shifted her weight, staring Ellie down.

"You've gone too far, Brandy," Ellie warned. "I don't need this. Not from you—the mother of three children, who leaves their grand-mother to try and raise them, while you're in prison, or doing drugs, or breaking into people's houses, or getting beat up on the street—"

The slap came fast and hard, stinging Ellie's cheek. Without think-ing, she returned the blow, landing a sound smack onto Brandy's cheek.

The two women paused, stunned, and then were on top of each other, struggling, falling to the ground. "You—you saw my children," Brandy screamed. "How dare you? You had no right."

Ray was on top of both of them now, pulling them apart. He pushed Brandy into one corner of the motel room and pushed Ellie into the other. "Enough," he declared, coughing and gasping for breath. "What y'all doing!"

The women stared at each other, not responding. Ellie put her hand to her cheek, smarting from the smack. Ray stood in between, arms outstretched, looking back and forth from Brandy to Ellie.

"Ladies," said Ray. "We're a team here. Life is too short for saying things you're gonna regret later. Go on now and apologize. So we can go on."

Ellie looked at the two of them. "Brandy's behavior is too much, she's just gonna get us all in trouble. I made a mistake bringing you along, Brandy. I made a promise to Ray and I have to see that out."

"Well, you made a promise to the judge and you made a promise to Brandy, too," Ray pointed out.

"And you...." Ray turned to Brandy. "Ellie's just trying to help you. It wouldn't hurt to be more gracious about it." Then, without waiting for a response from either of them, Ray started singing in his deep comforting bass. He chose a hymn, "Drifting Too Far From the Shore," one he remembered singing in church as a boy.

As he sang, Ray thought of Bill Monroe covering the song. But Ellie and Brandy's eyes also met with a flash of recognition. They remembered The Grateful Dead's cover of the song from their tie-dye days.

Leave it to Ray to scold them through a song.

"Now," he said sternly when it was over, "we're going to retreat to our own rooms and rest up for a while. And we'll be ready to head out for our dinner invitation at 4:30. Good afternoon, ladies."

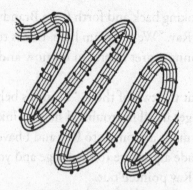

CHAPTER THIRTEEN

OWEN AND DOTTIE'S FARM

Evan stood by the mailbox at the end of the driveway to the McTaggert place. When he saw Ellie, Brandy and Ray approaching, he flagged down their car. Ellie was grateful for his signal. She easily would have missed the driveway, as the turn came right after cresting a steep hill and a turn in the road.

She rolled down her window.

"Howdy again!" Evan greeted them cheerfully. "It's easy to miss this driveway, so I figured I'd just walk ole Molasses here and we might see you come up the road." The black Labrador Retriever at his feet waited patiently, excited to see newcomers.

"Where's the house?" Ellie asked, looking up the long gravel driveway.

"About a half mile up. You can see it beyond those trees. If you all want to head up, I'm going to finish my walk with Molasses and check on the animals, then I'll join you at suppertime. Grandma Dottie baked a pie this morning. She's so excited you're coming."

"Beautiful property the family has here," Ray said. "We are just delighted to be invited." Ray was mindful of his manners and ready to be good company. An invitation for a home-cooked meal was not something he had enjoyed in many, many years. He couldn't wait to see Owen and Dottie and talk about the old days with someone who knew him, who remembered him, Doris and Sally, living as a family. It was so good to be remembered.

Ellie and Brandy, on the other hand, were nervous in each other's company. There had been palpable tension and not much conversation on the ride over. Ellie had rested a bit in her room after the fight, and now she was more embarrassed than angry. Fighting with Brandy wasn't getting them any closer to their goal.

"I'll walk the dog with you," Brandy volunteered, jumping quickly out of the car and joining Evan.

Good, Ellie thought with relief.

Ellie and Ray proceeded slowly up the narrow gravel driveway, passing cleared farmland, split rail fencing, grazing cattle and a pond, with geese and ducks on the water. Cannas and sunflowers, over six feet tall, stretched to the sun. The house came into view, with a large wrap-a-round front porch and a row of carved wooden rocking chairs that beckoned. Wind chimes twinkled merrily in the light summer breeze. Morning Glory and Old English Ivy crept up the lattice of the veranda. A rope tire swing hung on a massive poplar tree in the front yard.

Dottie burst out the front door in her apron, running up to greet them as Ellie parked the car.

"Oh, Ray," she cried. "I just can't believe it's really you."

"Dottie," Ray cried happily. They looked each other over and enveloped one another in a long hug. Ray wiped away a tear. "You look as beautiful as you always did. My, my, my, just can't believe I'm here." He looked behind her, searching for his old friend.

"Owen would have been so happy to see you again. He was always talking about old Ray and Charlie and The Gulch Jumpers doing this or that...." She saw Ray's inquisitive face. "I'm sorry to have to tell you, Ray, he passed on five years ago. I sure wish he could be here today."

Shock and pain passed across Ray's face and his shoulders sagged.

Another person lost to him forever. "Oh Dottie... I'm very, very sorry to hear that, I truly wish he could be here too."

Ellie stepped forward tentatively, extending her hand to Dottie. "And Dottie, this is my good friend, Ellie," Ray introduced her.

Ellie smiled. "Thank you for having us, Dottie, good to meet you."

"Ellie's helping me look for my lost girl," Ray explained. "Ellie and her friend, Brandy, who's walking up the driveway with your grandson."

"Oh my," exclaimed Dottie.

***

Molasses trotted alongside Evan and Brandy. "The dogs I see in the city are usually strays roaming in packs or they're chained up," Brandy commented.

"We don't need to put him on a leash out here in the country," Evan said. "He knows this property like I know the back of my hand. He comes along every day when I do the chores, feed the animals. He can even herd the cows back into the barn."

They approached the water, surrounded by tall grasses and meadow. "You wanna see a trick?" Evan offered. "Molasses and I like to race each other around the lake. Watch this."

Evan crouched down and spoke softly into Molasses's ear for a moment. The dog stopped, listening to his master, waiting to run. Evan bent into a sprinter's take-off position.

"Go!" Molasses took off to the left and Evan took off to the right. Brandy watched them race around the perimeter of the lake, man and dog looking across the water at each other as they ran. The sunlight twinkled on the water and the geese honked. There was a ruffle of feathers as ducks flew up from the bank, disrupted by the barking, running dog. When they reached the other side, they passed each other, crisscrossing as they circled back to where Brandy waited.

Evan ran up panting, laughing. Molasses was ears-up and tail-wagging, barking with excitement. Brandy squatted and petted him, hugging him with both arms. "Good boy," she told him.

"Why don't you try it? It's fun."

Without waiting for her response, Evan got Molasses back into his ready-set-go position and started the dog off running again. "He's got a head start on you, you better run," Evan told her.

Without thinking, Brandy took off running. She ran as hard as she could. She planted her feet firmly on the earth, swung her arms, and sucked deep breaths of air into her heaving lungs. Her hair swung behind her. Her heart pounded in her chest. It was crazy and free. She was running because *she* wanted to run—not because some drug-dealing thug was chasing her to beat her up, not because some cop was chasing her to throw her in jail. She was running for the simple joy of running. She was shaky from last night's partying and the fight with Ellie, but each step took her further out of all her stress, aches and pains. She looked across the lake at the dog, who was watching her with happy, smiling puppy eyes. As they circled past each other at the far end of the lake, Brandy yelled encouragement to Molasses, who easily beat her back to where Evan was waiting.

She ran to him and bent over, heaving to catch her breath. "I think I must be sweating all the impurities out of my body."

Evan laughed, pleased with Brandy's delight. "You wanna race him again?"

"Yes!"

***

Dottie gave Ray and Ellie a tour of the farmhouse. The wood burning stove in the sitting room was homey and comforting, but not needed on a hot day such as this. A big wooden table in the center of the large farm kitchen was all set for supper. Lovely smells wafted from the oven and pots on the stove. Upstairs in the bedrooms there were large antique dressers, patchwork quilts on the beds, and shelves full of books.

"Your home has a real down-home feel to it, Dottie. I feel like I'm really home again," said Ray.

"I want to show you something, Ray," Dottie told them, as she led them to one of the upstairs closets. She opened the door and, reaching around some old hanging coats, pulled out an upright string bass.

"Oh my goodness," Ray exclaimed. "Our old bass fiddle."

He ran his hands over the wood, the strings. The bridge had collapsed and looked a bit warped, but other than that, the instrument was in good condition. "I haven't seen this in almost fifty years."

"Well, Owen knew you would have wanted it if you ever came back through here. He took care of it for you. We've still got the old guitar and mandolin from the band too."

"Did Owen keep playing?" Ray asked.

"No, honey, when ya'll took off and left town, that was it for The Gulch Jumpers. Owen and Charlie didn't keep it going. Charlie went up north to see if he could find a better job, and I honestly am not sure where ole Charlie ended up. Owen kept up his work in the mine, we got married and got this place, did some farming. I think Owen would have loved to find some new fellows to make music with, but he never did find a new crowd. Nothing would have been able to top what the three of you were doing, anyways.

"They were really good," she informed Ellie. "I wish you could have heard them. Had a song on the radio and everything."

Ray sat still, quietly digesting the news. He had been so focused on finding his daughter and wild with grief over Doris, that he hadn't given a thought as to how leaving town would affect anyone else. He was heartbroken to learn his departure marked not only the end of The Gulch Jumpers, but the end of music in general for his friends. Charlie and Owen had been true friends, sticking by him when others did not. They helped him build his house and didn't pass judgment about his love for Doris. He wondered what became of Charlie, and was filled with regret that Owen wasn't here to thank. And he was touched beyond belief that his old buddy had held on to the band instruments, keeping them here at his home, in case his fellow Gulch Jumpers ever came back.

"Dottie," Ray began, but his voice trailed off into a muffled sob.

"It's all right," she told him. "It's all right. We all understood why you had to leave. It was just a tragic, tragic thing that happened to y'uns. The boys understood you had other business to attend to and couldn't keep up The Gulch Jumpers."

He shook his head and wiped a tear from his cheek. "I loved playing with Owen and Charlie. I just loved it. But when we went to the Fair to play that show, it cost me the love of my life. And it cost me my little girl. Robbed of her mama and then robbed of her papa too when they ran off with her. There was just too much pain in my heart to keep anything going with the music, with the band. I am sorry, though, Dottie."

"Ray, goodness. All that happened a long time ago. Don't beat yourself up over it. Owen and I, we had a good life. And now I've got this beautiful farm up here on top of the hill—well, you know—up on the hill, almost like heaven on earth. Do you remember Louis Bromfield's writings about living on a farm?"

Ray nodded, smiling wistfully. "'I Live on the Edge of Paradise.' Malabar Farm. Yes, I sure do remember. Before I had to leave school, I loved hearing those stories, loved listening to the poetry."

"Well, it *is* paradise. When the sun comes up in the morning and the rooster crows, when the fog sinks low over the mountain, when the trees go orange and red in the fall and then the frost comes and paints all the branches crisp white, just like ivory lace. And I'm lucky enough to have my grandson to help me keep the place up, tend to the animals. He's a very fine young man."

As if on cue, they turned together to look out the upstairs window over the property, looking for Evan. Ellie did a double-take and squinted: was Brandy running in circles around the lake? *What on earth?*

Ray twirled the upright bass absent-mindedly. He righted the collapsed bridge and began gently plucking the strings and turning the big pegs, tuning. "I'm on a quest, Dottie," he said softly, looking down at the bass. "I traveled all over the South, going to clubs and honky-tonks, trying to find that blues band that Sammy used to play with. Kentucky, Tennessee, Georgia. I talked to musicians. I asked around. Kept looking for my little girl. Nobody knew nothing. I gave up and went north like everybody else was doing."

"Ray, word around these parts was that Sammy and his folk headed into Ohio, not further south. Rumor was that they took your baby Sally up to Ohio so she could be raised by some kin they had up that way," Dottie said.

Ray stopped fiddling with the string bass and looked at up sharply. "Why didn't anyone tell me?"

"We didn't know how to find you. You took off and no one ever heard from you again. You didn't come back when your papa passed on; you didn't come back when your mama passed on. It was like you fell off the face of the earth."

Ray and Ellie looked at each other, processing this important new piece of information. Ohio again, Ellie thought. Just like Bob from the bar had told her. Now they had two leads pointing back toward Ohio: the shoebox with the song lyrics, and Dottie's gossip about Sammy and Frances taking Sally to be raised by relatives in Ohio. But Ray was upset.

"It's good, Ray," Ellie reassured him. "This is a step in the right direction. We're getting news, and news is what we wanted."

"Well, where are my manners," Dottie exclaimed. "We're up here going through this old closet and I should be checking on supper. Will you come downstairs and ring the dinner bell, dear?" she said to Ellie. "Let Evan and your friend Brandy know it's time to come on in for supper?"

The group trooped back downstairs, and Ellie found the brass dinner bell mounted to the wall by the back screen porch. She pulled the cord and the bell sang out across the fields. Evan and Brandy were by the barn; Brandy was holding a pail and tossing food out to the chickens. Molasses trailed behind Evan, who had closed the gate and pen after the last of the cows were herded inside for the night. They walked up past the tire swing to the house. Brandy's cheeks were flushed, sweat on her brow. Her eyes were bright and shining. Though still fairly roughed-up and hung over, she was better and more-focused somehow. Ellie watched her cautiously. She wanted to apologize for going after her earlier, but couldn't find the words. Instead, she leaned toward her as she came through the screen door and whispered, "We should help Dottie set the food out on the table."

"Yeah, all right, whatever. I can set a table. I'd like to wash my hands first. I just milked a cow for the first time in my life."

"The facilities are down the hall to your left, honey," Dottie cried out.

Brandy made her way down the knotty-pine hallway and found the powder room with gingham-checked curtains and a tiny vase of wildflowers on the sink. She looked at herself in the mirror and splashed cold water on her face. She took a deep breath. She liked the farm, the animals, the smell of the country air. She was impressed by how Evan went through his evening chores, checking on all the animals, feeding them, cleaning up after them. She wished she could have a dog like Molasses. It must feel wonderful to have a loyal friend like that who followed you everywhere, protecting you. Never alone. And what would it be like to live somewhere beautiful and open like this with her children? But, then again, this wasn't her life. She would soon be returning to the city, the shelter, maybe prison. She opened the medicine cabinet and looked over the jars of lotion, aspirin, band aids, Epsom salts. Her eyes fell upon a prescription bottle. She picked it up, looking it over and decided they would do nicely. She emptied the contents into her pocket, flushed the toilet, shut the medicine cabinet and finished by washing her hands with the lavender-primrose soap in the dish.

When she opened the bathroom door, she found Evan sitting on the bottom step of the stairway in the darkened hallway near the bathroom, watching her. "I know what you're up to," he said accusingly. "I heard you going through the medicine cabinet and opening up those pill bottles."

"I don't know what you're talking about."

"Hey, I'm not going to say anything. I'm not going to rat you out. But I know what you're up to. Lots of folks down here are addicted to painkillers. We've got pill mills up and down the Ohio River—they'll write anyone a prescription for anything, no questions asked. People my age get addicted. Older people too. My mom and dad struggle with that stuff. That's why I live with my grandmother."

Brandy looked at him, turning red. He had taught her how to milk a cow and feed pigs and let her run with his dog, and here she was, stealing medication from his grandmother.

She spoke slowly and deliberately, determined not to slur her words or appear glib. "I'm sorry about your mom and dad. I bet they think about you every day and feel really bad that they got too messed up to raise you. You have to understand; it's really, really hard once you get addicted. It's really hard. This is not how I want to live. I'm sure it's not how your parents want to live either. Please don't think badly of me."

He got up and shrugged. "I don't think badly of you. I've seen it all before."

She sheepishly reached into her pocket and handed the pills over to Evan, who restored them to Dottie's prescription bottle. "Come on, supper's on." He headed back to the kitchen.

Evan had not counted the pills to make sure they were all there. Brandy's fingers ran over the four pills she had kept for herself, still in her pocket. She gathered herself up and followed.

Dottie had laid out a wonderful spread of food—a feast, really, with fried oysters, collard greens, creamy mashed potatoes, biscuits, and coleslaw. The country-fried chicken was battered and deep-fried to a perfect golden crisp. Lemonade twinkled invitingly in a large pitcher filled with ice. "If it's too hot to eat in the kitchen, I could put a plastic tablecloth on the picnic table out under the front tree," she offered.

"There's no need," said Ray as he took a seat at the table. "This is just perfect. A wonderful, home-cooked meal, and we are deeply,

deeply grateful."

"Well, it's a happy day for me to welcome back an old friend from our childhood. I would be honored, Ray, if you would say Grace."

Brandy grimaced. Did the lecturing never end?

Everyone looked at Ray, who was sitting in silence, contemplating the food spread before them. "There's so much to be grateful for," he began, "even when it appears there's nothing to be grateful for. I'm grateful to Dottie for this wonderful meal. I'm grateful for Owen and Charlie; we made wonderful music together and we had a lot of fun together. I miss them. I'm grateful for the songs that give our lives meaning, and I'm grateful that for some reason, God chose to bestow me with some musical talent. I'm grateful to my new friends, Ellie and Brandy, for helping me get to a place where I can put that talent to some good, to find Sally." He looked at everyone a bit sheepishly. "And, it may sound kinda silly to y'all, but I'm grateful to Mr. Robert Johnson too. He went first; he's gonna show me how to do it."

They all smiled and nodded politely to Ray and each other. No one shared their private views about Ray's plan or the soundness of his judgment. He looked at them, sensing their doubt. "Well, what are all of *you* thankful for?"

"I'm thankful for my grandmother," Evan offered quickly, squeezing Dottie's hand. "I'm thankful for you too, honey," said Dottie.

Ellie looked over the wonderful meal, inhaling the melt-in-your-mouth aroma from the homemade yeast-risen biscuits. Suddenly, she missed Mike very much. "I'm thankful for my husband. I wish he was here so you all could meet him."

"That's good, Ellie," said Ray. "Don't ever take one day together for granted." He turned to look at Brandy.

Just like another group counseling session, Brandy thought. She thought about each of her three children and her own mother. She didn't need anyone to remind her that she wasn't taking care of them the way she should be. She didn't need anyone to remind her that she had nothing. But now everyone was looking at her, waiting, and the food was getting cold. She sighed.

"I'm grateful for Molasses."

Evan chuckled a bit.

"Well, I am," Brandy insisted. "I'm thankful I got to spend a little time with him this afternoon. He's a really good dog."

"Yes, he is," Dottie agreed. "Okay, folks, help yourselves and don't be shy about taking a second helping. Let's eat."

***

Ellie and Brandy offered to wash the dishes after dinner so Ray and Dottie could have a chance to talk. Ellie filled the sink with hot soapy water and started working through the pots and pans while Brandy grabbed a hand towel and dried, stacking the clean dishes on the table. Coffee was brewing and Dottie's apple pie was proudly displayed on a sideboard. It was pleasant working in the homey kitchen, which spanned the entire back of the house, with panoramic views of the barn, birdfeeders, and the setting sun glowing orange over the hills.

"What a meal," Ellie said. "She's an amazing cook."

Brandy flipped her hair as she dried a platter. "Sure beats prison food."

Ellie looked at her cautiously, trying to discern if Brandy was being sarcastic or looking to provoke another argument.

Brandy set her towel on the counter and turned to face Ellie, speaking calmly. "Do you know what they fed us in prison, Ellie?"

"Guess all I know is you get your three-squares a day. I don't know too much about the food, no."

"Well, you ever hear of Nutraloaf? It's this god-awful patty, like a loaf of different foods all stuck together. It's the most disgusting thing you can imagine. But you gotta eat it 'cause you're hungry, and that's all you're getting."

"I can't imagine..."

"Most people wouldn't even want to try," Brandy said. "When you're in prison, you're invisible. Out of sight, out of mind. I'm telling you, people on the inside would kill for a meal like this."

"Oh, you know what? I think I have heard of that Nutraloaf after all. I think I recall talking about it in law school. There were some cases—the ACLU was trying to prove it constituted cruel and unusual punishment."

Brandy bristled. "So while I was eating it, you were studying it."

The contrast was embarrassing and Ellie regretted her insensitive comment. "Do you like to cook?" she ventured.

"I dunno. I don't cook. I don't have a place to cook. I may chop up vegetables at the shelter, but I don't choose the menu or anything like that... What about you?"

Ellie did like to cook. She told Brandy about some of her favorite recipes, what she liked to make for holidays or family gatherings. Roasted turkey, pot roasts or pork tenderloin, soups, cookies, desserts. Brandy listened, not saying much. She had seen the updated modern kitchen in Ellie's home. Ellie paused, not knowing what else to say. It was awkward trying to find common ground. "I like using my slow cooker," she offered again.

"You used to hate anything domestic like that," Brandy reminded her. "We were all about ten cent wing night, burritos, nachos with cheese, beer nuts, pizza. You never cooked."

"Oh, damn, remember how good the pizza was from Rocko's?"

"Oh yeah—it was good cold the next day for breakfast too. Now *that* is something I definitely miss."

***

Ray, Dottie and Evan were enjoying the rocking chairs and the cool evening breeze on the front porch. Evan softly strummed the guitar while Ray plucked the upright string bass. Dottie tapped her foot and rocked along, humming or singing when she knew the words. Fireflies glowed out on the lawn.

Ellie and Brandy pulled up their own rocking chairs and joined the group. Everyone gladly accepted a slice of Dottie's apple pie, and they savored the cinnamon and tartness of the apples.

"Did your grandfather teach you how to play?" Ray asked Evan.

"He taught me a bit... I just fool around on the guitar on my own. I'm not a musician like you and Grandpa Owen."

"If you're playing it, you're a musician," Ray told him. "Don't wait for somebody to come along and tell you that you're a musician. Do you know 'Ring of Fire'?"

"I think so," said Evan. "Is it just chord changes from D to C to G?"

"That sounds right." Ray started plucking the bass line and offered up his deep bass voice, and Evan came in with the chords.

Dottie and Ellie joined in, and Brandy joined in as well after she heard them go through the refrain once. Before they knew it, all five of them were singing at the top of their voices, and laughing with enjoyment as they finished the song.

"Let's keep that Johnny Cash thing going with some traveling music." Ray jumped right into a quick moving bass line for "I've Been Everywhere Man." He was able to sing the next part fast, running through all the cities just like Johnny. Everyone else had stopped, unable to keep up. "Come on," Ray laughed. "Y'all can learn it." He went through the cities more slowly, pausing for the others to repeat after him until they had it memorized. "Now say them all together," he directed. "Good... now do it faster." They ran through it a few times. "Okay, folks, now up to tempo and loud!"

When they finished the song, Ray had a wide grin on his face. "This is how we used to do it back in my day, with my aunt and uncle. We'd just relax in the evenings together and pick out some notes or chords and play around with it. Everyone would chime in, throw out some silly lyric and we'd try to harmonize. We'd steal bits of songs we knew from other folks and we'd add our own nonsense that we made up to it. Some of the happiest days of my life, making music like that with the folks."

"And with your granddaddy too," he told Evan. "He was a good man and I can see you're growing up that way too. He'd be proud of you."

"Well, when you folks get ready to head out, I want you to take that bass fiddle with you," Dottie told Ray firmly. "Owen would want it that way. It belonged to The Gulch Jumpers and it's a marvelous thing to finally be able to restore it to a rightful owner."

Ray looked to Ellie. She was attempting to calculate the height of the instrument and how it could fit in her SUV. The back of the car was full of luggage, mostly her stuff, she realized with some shame. Perhaps they could fold down one of the seats and lay the bass the long way from front to back. Or perhaps it would have to lie sideways across someone's lap in the backseat, the way Ray had described The Gulch Jumpers transporting it to the State Fair. It was not going to be a very practical thing to transport, and they already had Mike's guitar in the car, in addition to Ray's traveling oxygen tank. But seeing the way Ray's face lit up when he played, there was just no way she could say no.

Ray was looking at Brandy now. They both had a playful grin on their faces.

"What do you gotta say about that, Blondie?"

"It's so...." Brandy searched for the right word. "*Large.*"

"Yes, that's it. It's really, really large," Ray agreed happily. "And what do y'uns think about that?"

"I think there's no freakin' way it would ever fit in Bin #23 at the Mission of Hope. I say here's to owning something way too large to ever fit in a plastic bin ever again. I raise my cup in a hippie, hillbilly toast to you, Ray Jones, and I raise my middle finger in a solemn hippie, hillbilly salute to the Mission of Hope Homeless Shelter."

"Oh my stars," exclaimed Dottie under her breath, rocking her chair vigorously in a show of indignation at Brandy's language. But she quickly recovered. "Don't forget the bow."

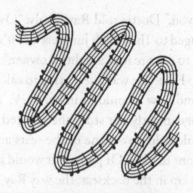

CHAPTER FOURTEEN

We Built with Our Own Damn Hands

Ellie, Ray, and Brandy agreed to meet Dottie and Evan the next morning. Dottie was going to lead the way to the location of the infamous "little clapboard house in the holler."

Ellie was unhappy about spending a second night at the same motel. The musty smell intensified with the lack of air conditioning, and she slept fitfully in the dank humidity. The blinking neon "Vacancy" light glared into her window, torturing her second by second as she tossed and turned with insomnia. Apparently, she had been too drunk the prior night to be bothered by it.

She managed to pull herself together slightly with the air conditioning in the car running full blast, but on the way back to Dottie's, Brandy kept rolling down her window.

"You can't have the window down with the air conditioning on," she repeatedly told Brandy, hitting the switch to roll up her window. A few minutes later Brandy would have the window down again, enjoying the warm breeze and the fresh air billowing through her hair. Back and forth they would bicker—window up, window down.

"It's not like you're going to have a high electric bill from running air conditioning in your car," Brandy groused. "Doesn't seem like a big deal to me."

It's my car, Ellie thought, but didn't say more. She didn't want things to escalate the way they had yesterday. Today, they needed to stay focused on the search. She was optimistic for Ray's return to his old home. Perhaps the current owners would give them permission to come inside the house, look around. She hoped for some kind of clue that would lead them to the next step.

She followed Dottie and Evan in the car ahead of them as their little caravan wound through many of the same hills she had covered with Ray yesterday. Even so, Ellie was still lost and confused. She was grateful they now had local guides to show them the way. Her ears popped with the altitude changes.

"Ahh, yes, here is the turn," Ray nodded with excitement, finally recognizing some of the landmarks as they drew closer. "Old Pigeon Pass."

"What?" Ellie said, watching Evan turn off onto a dirt road overgrown with brush and barely passable. "Is this a road?"

"Well, sure, it's a kind of a road, or a pass, I suppose," said Ray. "Looks like no one goes through this way much anymore."

The two cars wound their way up the path, over roots and branches, until a downed tree blocked the way completely. Evan pulled over to the right and gestured for Ellie to pull up next to him. "Can't go any further by car," he said.

"Are we sure this is the right way?" Ellie called over to Dottie.

But Ray nodded his head enthusiastically. "This is the way. We can leave the cars here and hike the rest of the way. It's just a bit further up."

The heavily forested hillside had encroached upon the dirt road, but they were still able to see enough remnants of the path to follow. Ellie walked next to Ray, steadying him when he faltered. The last thing they needed was for him to turn his ankle, and an uphill hike without the oxygen tank probably wasn't one of their smarter moves. Evan helped his grandmother along, while Brandy hiked on her own, quietly taking in the forest canopy.

They crested a ridge, turned a corner and came upon a clearing. They stopped at once and gazed. "This is it," said Ray. "Home."

"Home?" asked Ellie with surprise, looking at the small, dilapidated structure that leaned precariously to one side. Shingles peeled from the roof, part of which had fully collapsed into the shell of the lean-to. The boards of the walls had separated and vines and vegetation grew freely into the crevices. Windowpanes were broken or missing altogether.

Ray walked up to the abandoned shack and stuck his head into what used to be a front door.

"Looks hazardous to enter, Mr. Jones," Evan warned. "We don't want that to collapse on you."

Ellie approached tentatively, peering through a hole where the windowpane was missing. Inside were a coal-fed stove, washboard, and a lantern on the floor. She could also make out the rotting remains of a wooden table and bed frame. It had never occurred to her that they would find the site untouched after all these years. "Ray, are these your things?"

"Yes, ma'am, they sure are."

"But, when you left... you didn't pack up? You didn't store your things somewhere else? You didn't sell off your property?"

"I packed up what little I needed and left and didn't look back. Every minute I delayed was them getting further away from me. I just flew out of here." Ray reached up to knock on the side of the house. There was a flurry from above and a wave of bats came screeching down. Ellie and Brandy screamed. Ray ducked and shielded his head.

"Come on out of there." Evan grabbed Ray and led him back into the sunshine in the clearing.

The bats screeched and swarmed up through the trees. "What the hell!" Brandy cried, shaking her hands through her hair. "Do you think there's a wasp nest in there too?"

"Very well could be," said Evan. "Let's stand off a bit. We don't want the whole place to come crashing down on us."

Ellie was trying to process the turn of events. She thought about Bob's words. *Ohio.* "Ray, this is important and I need you to concentrate and think and remember: when you left this house, did you walk out of here with that box in your hands? The shoebox that I found in my closet? Your songs? Doris's jewelry? Any of it?"

"No, Ellie, no. If I had taken it, I would have kept it with me. Even when I was on the street or in the shelter. I would have held on to those things. Any little thing to remember Doris by.... to remember Sally. But it was all lost to me."

"Then we have to assume Doris carried that box out of here with her. That's the only explanation, because it sure appears no one else ever came along and gathered up your left-behind belongings. And when Doris was killed in the crash, the box somehow followed Sally, Sammy and Frances. And then it ended up in the back of my closet in Cleveland. Ray, we've got to go back to Ohio. I think that's where we're going to find her. I've got to get a hold of that realtor and talk to the prior owner of my house."

But Ray was looking off toward a crab apple tree, his eyes far away.

Ellie followed his gaze and tried to read his face. Of course. Doris was here. This was her final resting place.

She glanced at the others as they hung back and let Ray walk on ahead.

"What's going on?" asked Brandy.

"He was too upset about how they were treated by the town-folk to lay her to rest in the cemetery," Dottie whispered. "Back then we had cemeteries for white and cemeteries for black. Ray wanted her laid to rest right here, at their home. Owen and Charles helped him build a pine coffin and dig deep enough in the ground to make it right."

Make it right? Ellie couldn't help but wonder if such a burial was legal. It probably wasn't, but then again, so much of Ray's story was outside the boundaries of what was just and right: A man and woman, parents of a child, unable to marry. Living in a shack in a remote clearing on land they didn't lease or own. A baby born and named, but possibly not given a birth certificate. Kidnapping. Abandoning the scene of an accident and leaving a body behind. A possible adoption with no notice to the child's father. A broken man, living homeless

among strangers, hundreds of miles away. Legality was an inconse-
quential afterthought.

But perhaps something could be done to make a small part of
it right.

"Was there any kind of service after Doris died?" Ellie asked Dottie.

"No, I don't recall anything like that. Ray was heartbroken and
almost wild with fury. He was in a hurry to get on the road and find
his baby. There wasn't time."

"Well, maybe we should do something here, now, with us. Say a few
words, or a little prayer, in her honor?"

"That would be nice, honey, if you think it might be comforting
to Ray."

Ellie thought it might. And she thought it might help her as well—
she had grown a curious fondness for this woman whose child they
sought. Doris's little box of precious keepsakes had somehow ended
up in her own home, meaning Ellie was linked to Doris too, in a
mysterious way. Her presence was strong in this clearing. Surely this
was just as magical a place as any crossroads would be.

"What can we do?" asked Evan. "A song, maybe?"

"That's a good idea; music will comfort Ray the most. Is there something we can sing?"

They looked at each other blankly, each waiting for another to make
a suggestion. Brandy sighed. "I can't sing. I can't think of anything—
Journey, maybe? 'Don't Stop Believin''?"

"Ray's not going to know that song." Ellie shook her head. "It's not
really his genre, if you know what I mean."

"Well, I don't know any old-timey hillbilly mountain songs, if you
know what *I* mean."

"Okay," said Evan. "Here's a suggestion: how about John Denver?
'Take Me Home, Country Roads'? It's corny as heck, but he may like
it. Do you know that one?"

Brandy shrugged. "Guess it fits."

They agreed to give it a try. Evan counted them off and the four of them came in, sounding more than a little rough around the edges.

Ray looked up in surprise at the group as they sang, moving slowly over to circle around him. A smile formed on his face and he put his hands on his hips and cocked his head, listening. Ellie patted Ray on the back as she sang. Brandy leaned over to pick some wild Queen Anne's Lace and Goldenrod, assembling a bouquet that she presented to Ray. Evan and Dottie stood, arm in arm, Evan with his hand casually in his jeans pocket.

As they finished they looked at each other, pleased. It wasn't a horrible effort. A flock of Canada Geese honked and passed overhead, in formation, offering a salutary flyby in Doris's honor. Dottie went ahead and said the "Lord's Prayer," as they joined hands.

Then they turned to Ray. He cleared his throat and coughed a few times. When he was ready, he closed his eyes, lifted his face upwards and gently hummed "Amazing Grace," slowly and with reverence. When the last note traveled upward in the wind, Ellie squeezed his hand. Ray's eyes and voice were full of gratitude. "Thank you, Ellie. It means a lot to be back here."

"You know we're going to find her. It's going to happen."

He nodded earnestly. "It's going to happen at the crossroads. Everything will lead to Sally."

Ray simply could not be deterred from his crossroads wish. Ellie decided the time had come to get serious. "Can we all pull up a tree stump and have a little conference about our next step?" she asked Brandy and Ray.

Brandy wiped the sweat from her brow. "Can we go somewhere with air conditioning?"

After a last long look at the shack, Ray placed the flowers Brandy had gathered by the tree where Doris lay beneath the ground. They trooped back down the hill and bid a heartfelt farewell to Dottie and Evan, who had helped them so much. "Don't be a stranger," Dottie said, hugging Ray. "Any of y'all. You're all welcome back up to the farm next time you come through here."

"Take care of Molasses," Brandy told Evan. "Give him a pat for me."

They had asked Dottie if she could recall any further details of the gossip about Sally: where in Ohio had Sammy and Frances headed? Who was the relative they delivered Sally to? But Dottie knew nothing more. She promised to call Ellie if anything else came to mind.

They piled into the SUV, and Ray took up the backseat with the big string bass. Ellie followed the winding hill back down and cruised along until she spotted a restaurant. "Let's get some lunch and talk about where we're going next."

Her cell rang and she was pleased to see Mike's face displayed on her screen. She excused herself from the other two and strolled several feet away to talk in private. She told Mike about Ray's old house in the clearing, the impromptu memorial service for Doris, and most importantly, Dottie's revelation. "The local gossip according to Dottie was that Sally's grandparents sent her up to Ohio to be raised by a relative. I think we've got to narrow the search to Ohio."

"Sounds logical to me," said Mike. "But what about your promise to Ray? What if he insists on going to the crossroads instead?"

"Well, I suppose if that's the case it won't hurt anything to go down there first. But honestly, Mike, I'm starting to feel like I can solve this thing on my own if I can just sit down and mine the internet for a few hours."

"Possibly," Mike mused. "Too bad Sally's got such a common last name."

"I know. We've got a 'Jones' and a 'Brown.' They sure aren't making it easy for us."

"And how's your old college friend doing? She get you arrested yet?"

Ellie decided not to mention the fistfight. "She's okay... we're still getting reacquainted, and I suppose you can say we don't have a lot in common anymore. Anyway, I miss you."

"I miss you too. Gracie misses you. We want you to come home soon. Oh, that reminds me, almost forgot: the realtor called back. She got in touch with the prior owner."

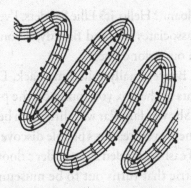

CHAPTER FIFTEEN

GATLINBURG, TENNESSEE

They found a comfortable booth with a plastic red checked tablecloth and good lighting. Following a hearty lunch of salads and a shared appetizer sampler—boneless wings, potato skins, jalapeño cheese poppers and artichoke-spinach dip, with plenty of ice tea—"*unsweetened*, please," Ellie directed the waitress—they were ready to spread out and work.

"We need a work session. We need to put our heads together," Ellie told the other two.

She had brought in her laptop, a map and three legal pads, two of which she distributed to Ray and Brandy. The haphazard approach to the search was bothering Ellie. They were floundering. The words of her law professor rang in her head: *Don't forget to think like a lawyer.*

"We need to list what we know so far, what we don't know, and how we're going to go about finding the missing pieces of information." She handed her iPad to Brandy. "And I need you both to help." Brandy began to doze off. "Keep the ice tea coming," Ellie asked the waitress.

They had the corner of the restaurant to themselves. Ray was breathing comfortably with his oxygen tank, and the air conditioning was a welcome relief. Ellie set her phone to speaker and dialed the realtor's phone number. "Joann? Hello, it's Ellie Sanders. I've got you on speaker phone with my associates Ray and Brandy, if you don't mind. Were you able to reach our prior owner?"

"Yes, the son, Bruce, finally called me back. Ellie, he's inquiring about the contents of the box you found on the property."

Ellie winced. She was familiar with litigation between current and former homeowners over treasures people discovered hidden in their houses: stashes of cash squirreled away under a floorboard, abandoned artwork in the attic that turns out to be museum-worthy. She had been worried that opening this door with the prior owner may lead to this type of thing.

"There was nothing of value in the box," she said.

"I guess they're wondering why you're asking about it then," the realtor gently countered.

"Well, it has sentimental value, Joann. The box contained some handwritten song lyrics that were actually written by my friend Ray here, a long time ago. He last saw those papers almost fifty years ago and we're trying to use it as a lead to find a family member."

She decided not to mention the few pieces of jewelry. They were nothing fancy, they had belonged to Doris, and their rightful place was now with Ray.

"Okay, I'll let them know that. No cash, nothing of value. Bruce didn't recall any shoebox when they cleaned the house out. The home actually belonged to his mother, who passed away. That's why they sold the home. He said she used to love going to garage sales, flea markets, picking up quirky antiques or curiosities. Other than that, he really had no idea. Mostly he just wanted to figure out if you found something valuable."

Ellie thanked her and hung up.

"Okay, okay, so that wasn't the lead we were hoping for. Maybe it was just some odd coincidence."

"The nerve of that fellow trying to get my box from us," Ray said.

"Okay. Start the list. Two columns: What We Know; What We

Don't Know. How the box ended up in my closet goes under Don't Know. But how the box left Ray's house—we can put that in the Know column. Doris must have carried it out of there, right?"

"Yes, I think we know that's a fact," Ray agreed. "When they dragged her out of there with the baby, they wouldn't have known she kept that little box with her things underneath the bed. She must have grabbed it at the last minute."

"So how did those songs travel from your house in the holler to my bedroom closet in the suburbs of Cleveland? Doris didn't make it, so she didn't carry the box to Cleveland. Sally was just a baby; she was too little to carry the box. So what do we know?"

She shot a look to Brandy, who was yawning. "Okay, I'll play along, El. We know Doris's parents carried the box."

Ellie wrote it down under the Know column.

"We don't know where Sammy and Frances went next, if they gave the box to Sally when she got older, or if they gave it to someone else," said Ray. Ellie put that under Don't Know.

"Sammy and Frances Brown..." Ellie mused. "Ray, do you know Frances's maiden name? Maybe we can go onto some relative search sites, see if any of Doris's younger brothers and sisters are still alive. Ancestry search sites."

"Didn't Dottie tell you they sent Sally to be raised by relatives in Ohio?" Brandy asked. "Seems to me you need to be searching out the Brown clan, in Ohio."

"Can you get on the iPad there and start working that angle—see if you can trace back to the marriage of Sammy and Frances Brown and the family tree of their children, their brothers and sisters, aunts and uncles. Just go to some family ancestry search sites. Work it, Brandy."

"Sammy," Brandy muttered, hitting keys.

"Short for Samuel," Ray told her.

"Or maybe my prior owner was somehow related to the Browns?" Ellie threw out. "Why don't we search out her relatives too? Her name was Gladys Goodworth."

"That name's going to be a lot easier than Jones," said Brandy.

"Was she African American?" asked Ray. "Don't forget Sally's bira-cial; her maternal relatives are black. And I highly doubt, *West Side*, that a black family was living on your side of town. You know how segregated all the different Cleveland neighborhoods are."

Ellie realized he had a point. Historically, white Clevelanders tended to go west and black Clevelanders tended to go east, but the law prevented any kind of inquiry into the racial makeup of a buyer or seller of real estate, and she had never met Mrs. Goodworth face-to-face. "It all goes under Unknown, unless you can get some hits there, Brandy, with the ancestry research."

Ellie decided it was time to pull in reinforcements. She contacted Jessica, and got her on the cell speakerphone on the table. Jessica's internet skills were unparalleled. She provided Jessica with the names they were looking for and everything else Ray could remember Doris telling him about Sammy and Frances: where they were born, their birthdays, anything he could recall about other relatives Doris might have mentioned.

"I'll work on it," Jessica promised. "Give me some time. There are plenty of sites I can use to search for relatives."

"There must be web sites for adoptees looking for their birth parents," Ellie mused.

"I'm on it," said Jessica. "We'll search to see if a Sally Jones has put anything on the internet seeking her birth parents." Jessica took down Sally's date of birth, the county she was born in, anything else Ray could remember.

"Little gal had a birthmark on the back of her left calf," Ray offered up.

"Good, Ray, good. Any details like that are helpful. We're getting focused here. I feel like we're narrowing in on our goal."

"I'm glad we are, Miss Ellie, and I'm eager to get back on the road and start cutting south to the crossroads."

Ellie could not believe how determined Ray was to go to the cross-roads and she was dismayed he had brought it up again. They had solid, viable leads pointing to Ohio, and the most powerful tools imaginable right here in their hands—her laptop, iPad, cell phone, and free wireless internet. If Sally truly had been adopted, Ellie wanted time to research adoption law in Ohio and West Virginia to see if records for a child born in 1964 might be opened. But she couldn't do the internet legwork and legal research she needed to do and drive the car at the same time. What was to be accomplished by going down to Mississippi? And where exactly were they going to go in Mississippi?

"Yeah, about that Ray..." She explained that there were multiple possible locations for the crossroads. "It could be Rosedale, it could be the Dockery Plantation, but Clarksdale is the location most people believe it to be."

"Hey," said Brandy, perking up. "I know that tune. Cream!" She played a little air guitar. "The song mentions Rosedale."

Ellie pulled out the notes she had taken from her crossroads research. "There's a variation in the lyrics. The Cream/Clapton version mentions Rosedale, but the original Robert Johnson version does not mention Rosedale."

"And"—she looked at Ray—"it's also believed the crossroads legend was not really about Robert Johnson at all; there are theories it was actually blues musician Tommy Johnson who sold his soul. Somehow, the legend became mistakenly associated with Robert Johnson rather than Tommy Johnson over the years. So knowing all that, Ray—that we're not sure it's about Robert after all—that we're not sure which crossroads to go to—does it really make sense...."

Ray had been listening with his eyes closed. He opened them and spoke definitively. "We follow the music. Follow the lyrics. Mr. Johnson didn't mention Rosedale in the Crossroads song, but he sang about Rosedale in 'Traveling Riverside Blues.' We go to Rosedale."

Ellie nodded with resignation. The whole point of the trip was to accommodate Ray's wish, the only thing he had really ever asked of her. She could not imagine anything was to be found in Rosedale, Mississippi, but so be it. She pulled out a map and spread it out across the table. Rosedale was all the way to the Mississippi River, too far to drive in a day. She looked at her friends, enjoying their meals. Brandy was wearing her shoplifted top again, and there was Ray in his tattered suspenders. She hadn't had a chance to take them shopping yet. If they were going to Mississippi, it would be fun to take them somewhere enjoyable on the way.

"How about Gatlinburg? I've never been, but I hear it's beautiful. Little mountain town up in The Smoky Mountain National Park, right along the Appalachian Trail? Supposed to be quite the vacation spot."

"Cool," Brandy said, thinking about the drugs she could probably score in such a touristy destination.

But Ray was skeptical. "Sounds expensive... We gotta do this on the cheap, Ellie."

"Ray, I can't take doing it that way anymore. I can't take another night with broken air conditioning, a crappy mattress digging into my back, dingy lighting, lousy water pressure, blinking neon lights in my eyes all night, the smell of urine and God knows what else: fleas, bedbugs. I can't take it! You can call me a materialistic hypocrite"— Ellie was looking at Brandy now—"so yes, you'd be right: I like nice things, I'm spoiled, I admit it. But everyone's got their limit and this is mine. We are going to stay in a nice place, hopefully a cute little cabin or a hotel suite with a Jacuzzi, or a bed and breakfast that serves up scones and wine and cheese, and maybe has a spa where I can get a pedicure or a massage, and maybe has some nice live acoustic music in the evenings, and where they leave the daily newspaper outside your door, and there's a plush bathrobe and potpourri in the bathroom, and cable television on a big flat screen TV, and turn-down service with chocolates or mints on your pillow at night..."

Ray watched Ellie with amused astonishment. "Well, okay now, Miss Ellie, that was quite a speech. I can see it's important to you. All righty then, it's settled: we're off to Gatlinburg, with Miss Ellie to choose where we lay our heads at night. Don't worry, Ellie, I don't think you're spoiled."

Brandy smirked. "Don't worry, Ellie. I always knew you were a materialistic hypocrite."

***

Ellie became absorbed with the ear-popping ascents and crashing descents as they worked their way further south into West Virginia and Kentucky. Long tunnels blasted through massive rocky mountains. Patches of fog limited visibility at the higher elevations. Glancing occasionally at her cell phone and GPS, drinking coffee throughout, she tried to concentrate on the road and keep her breathing steady.

Ray took the backseat so he could use his portable oxygen, and they arranged the upright string bass from back to front, the scroll of the neck peeking up over the back seat near Ray's head.

Brandy and Ellie were still on shaky ground, so Ellie wasn't surprised when Brandy elected to sit in the backseat with Ray rather than join her up front. Brandy slept for a long while, and stirred as Ray began softly strumming the guitar next to her. She started itching and picking at her skin, telltale habits of an addict. "Would you like to learn some chords, Blondie?" Ray asked her.

"Nah, I can't learn to play a guitar," she told him, flushing with embarrassment and sweating amidst her opiate struggle. "I'm not good at that kinda thing like you are. I'm no good at anything."

"Everyone's good at something, Blondie," Ray told her.

"Not me."

"You're good with animals," he said, after a moment. "You understand animals and you get along with 'em."

Ellie had been wallowing in a private anxiety-ridden reverie, imagining the latch springing open on the horse trailer in front of them and the horse flying through her windshield, but she looked in the rearview mirror at Brandy's face when Ray mentioned animals. Brandy's eyes flashed with recognition. He was right, they all realized. Ray had seen something true in Brandy and named it. Ellie also registered the fact that Ray had bestowed Brandy with a nickname—surely a sign they were getting along better now.

"Animals." Brandy slurred the word, struggling to put a thought together. "Any mother in the wild knows to take care of her young. Even animals know that. I'm not fit to hang out with the animals."

Ellie had carefully avoided the subject of Brandy's children since their fistfight. Some subjects were simply off-limits, for Brandy as well as for herself. But Ray was nonplussed.

"Naw, honey, y'all still got that instinct. Of course you do. That's why you're in so much pain. I understand that kind of pain." Ray continued to strum softly. "Don't be so hard on yourself, Blondie."

Brandy sniffled a bit and swiped a tear from her cheek.

"And I'm telling you," he went on, "you got some kind of natural talent there, some kinda gift for connecting with our four-legged friends. You should work with animals."

Brandy snorted. "Can't do anything like that when you got a felony on your record."

"I dunno about that," Ray admitted. "But seems to me if you can set a goal, come up with a dream for yourself in your head, that's the first step to making it happen in the real world."

Brandy fell silent and drifted back to sleep. Probably for the best, Ellie thought. Ellie worried about the drug use; the last thing they needed was for Brandy to get herself arrested down here at some roadside rest area.

The traffic was manageable until they approached the town of Gatlinburg. As multitudes of vacationers approached their destination, traffic began to resemble rush hour. Brandy sat up and rubbed her eyes, staring dumbly at cars, campers and motor homes, full of families and loaded down with bicycles on racks or big roof top carriers, some pulling trailers that toted four-wheelers. There were license plates from all over. She struggled with the concept of a family vacation. She had trouble even affording the bus across town and certainly didn't take her children anywhere. But people drove from all over the country to vacation here—a place Brandy could not have imagined even two weeks ago.

As they approached the little town, there were even more sights to gawk at. Gondola cars swung on a heavy cable all the way to the top of the mountain. Tourists waited in line at zip-line attractions. Signs pointed the way to trailheads, scenic overlook pull-offs, campgrounds and bridle trails. National Park rangers patrolled in cars and on horseback.

The downtown area was nestled between the mountains. It bustled with trolley cars, traffic and tourists. Gift shops touting arts and crafts, restaurants, mini-golf, go-karts, ice-cream parlors and even amusement park rides lined the main drag. They passed by open-air plazas, filled with the sounds of street musicians playing guitars or banjos.

The cool mountain air smelled crisp and fresh. Brandy needed to swallow to get her ears to pop. She imagined she was in a Swiss mountain village rather than Tennessee. Ellie had put Brandy on the task of using her smartphone to book lodgings for them several hours earlier. She had made Brandy read the online reviews aloud and had discriminatingly rejected anything that garnered any negative feedback. Now the address for the log cabin Ellie had booked was programmed into the GPS, and Ellie watched for their turn. It was amazing what could be accomplished with a car, a smartphone and a credit card.

When they finally arrived, there was even more to stagger the imagination. "This place is called a cabin?" Ray asked in wonder, looking around the foyer of their private lodge as he set his small duffel bag onto the gleaming hardwood floor.

The A-frame log chalet boasted floor-to-ceiling windows that overlooked a spectacular mountain view. Large plush leather chairs and sofas gathered around a cozy stone fireplace that reached all the way to the ceiling. Sliding glass doors opened to a wooden deck with big rocking chairs and a hot tub. They stepped out onto the deck that loomed over the winding, bubbling river, and admired the view from the railing.

Brandy, Ray and Ellie each had their own room, with giant log beds and plush rugs on the floor. There was a small kitchen area and a Jacuzzi tub in the bathroom.

Ellie had probably over-corrected from their meager digs in West Virginia. It was indeed expensive, but she wanted her friends to enjoy some luxury, some beauty, something very different from the shelter and the city. She could see Brandy was impressed by the area when they had entered the Smokies and driven through the National Park. Ray, on the other hand, was baffled by the commercialism of Gatlinburg and its characterization of mountain culture. "Dottie's place.... now that's the *real* South," he said.

Ellie treated to dinner at a steakhouse: crisp salads, succulent steaks, plump baked potatoes with sour cream and butter, family-style creamed spinach and melt-in-your-mouth sourdough and pumpernickel bread. It was a good dinner, and everyone ate heartily after the long hours in the car.

A boy paused by their table and pointed to Ray. "Look, Mommy, it's the old man who plays the fiddle."

His mother took his hand and pulled him along. "Don't stare, Cam, it's not polite."

What was that all about? Brandy, Ellie and Ray wondered, shrugging to each other.

After dinner, Ellie ran into a small convenience grocery and picked up breakfast supplies. She'd put the cabin kitchen to use and make the crew French toast in the morning. Brandy pulled her baseball cap over her head, grabbed her backpack, and jumped out of the car as well. "I'll see you back at the cabin," she told the other two. "Don't wait up."

Ellie opened her mouth to protest, but Ray put his hand on her arm and stopped her. "She's a big girl, remember; she's gonna do what she's gonna do."

Later, in her room, Ellie hunkered down for a work session, laptop and legal pads strewn across the country quilt on the bed. At this point all leads pointed to Ohio. And with the absence of a birth certificate, the possibility of adoption could not be ignored.

She logged onto her legal research search engine and read about adoption law, eager to learn how Ray could petition to open up any records that may exist for an adoption of Sally Eugenia Jones. She was shocked and dismayed to learn that access to Ohio adoption records was based upon a three-tier system. Adoptees born before 1964 could freely access records. For adoptees born after 1997, there was a similar process, whereby adult adoptees and birth parents could seek to have records opened. But for people born between 1964 and 1997, the records were sealed. How could such a system be fair? She learned there was legislation pending to remove this disparity, but it had not yet cleared the Ohio Legislature.

She sat back on her pillow, thinking. Ray, Doris and Sally had certainly drawn a poor hand by coming together in the mid-60s. If Doris had survived, she and Ray would have had to wait only a few more years before they could have legally married in 1967. Ray could have been legally established as Sally's father. Even if paternity could not have been established, had Sally been born before 1964 and adopted in Ohio, Ray would be able to unseal her adoption record now and find her.

All of these *what ifs* weren't getting them anywhere. She hoped Jessica was having better luck with her online search for relatives. If law and technology couldn't carry the day, the crossroads might be their only hope.

***

The next morning Ellie woke to the sound of Ray softly plucking the string bass. She found him on the deck, looking out over a gentle mist in the hills. His hands flew deftly up and down the fingerboard as he rocked back and forth, scatting softly in his golden voice, "Doo dat... bee bop..."

His back was to Ellie, but he sensed her presence. He paused and said over his shoulder, "Good morning, and I know, Ellie, you don't have to say it. You're thinking how the deal at the crossroads isn't going to work."

"Actually," she said, "I was thinking what a shame it would be if it *did* work. What a loss it would be if you *did* lose your music."

Ray carefully leaned the bass up against one of the Adirondack chairs. "Anything's worth it if I can find my daughter."

"Music is who you are, Ray. I can't imagine you without it, and I can't imagine you thinking it's something you should ever give up. Talent like yours is a gift, not a bargaining chip. I think you've got your father's voice in your head, telling you that music is something bad."

He thought for a moment. "It's the only thing I've got that makes me different from everyone else. And I turned my back on it for many, many years. Until that old box with my songs appeared and you came along, learned my name, brought me that guitar and all... It's like something just woke up inside me again and I remembered who I was. And I know I didn't try hard enough to find her; I just gave up. Except I don't know how to go about it. Don't got no money, don't know how to work the computer like you do. It may sound silly to y'all, but it's the only thing I understand—it's the only way I know to try to find my family, to try to find someone who will know about me once my hundred years are past..."

Ellie was going to ask Ray what he meant by this, but was interrupted by her ringing cell phone. It was Jessica. She stepped back inside the lodge living room to take the call.

"El, I've got news."

"Were you able to trace Sammy and Frances's descendants? Did you find any relatives?"

"Yes and yes, but that's not the biggest piece of news I have to tell you. Are you ready for this? Are you sitting down? Grab your laptop: Ray's on YouTube."

"What? What are you talking about? How?"

"I don't know, but there's a video of him playing in a bar that's gone viral all over the internet. Just type in 'Old Man Playing the Fiddle.'"

"Hold on, I'm logging into it." Ellie fumbled with her tablet, pulling up YouTube. There it was. Someone at the bar must have posted a video of Ray up on stage with the band. She watched close-ups of his fingers flying across the fingerboard, bow arm drawing the bow across the fiddle, the astonished expressions on the faces of the other musicians, the crowd yelling and clapping. There was Brandy, dancing up on a table. "Oh my God," she exclaimed.

Brandy came up behind her, looking over her shoulder. "Hey, it's Ray. Does this mean he's famous now?"

"Do you see how many people have already liked this video?" Jessica asked. "I tell you, it's spreading like wildfire. People are pasting it up onto their Facebook pages. Look at the comments people are posting."

Ellie clicked on and read a few:

Nice suspenders—not—but the old man sure can play!

Like Old McDonald and The Charlie Daniels Band all in one.

This guy should be on the Grand Ole Opry...

"Oh yeah, he's famous," Brandy said. "Cool." She went out to talk to Ray.

"Well that explains this kid at the restaurant recognizing Ray last night," Ellie told Jessica. "I better call you back, Jessica. Brandy's out on the deck telling Ray there's a video of him all over the internet; he's not going to understand any of this. I better get out there and talk to him."

"Wait, El—there's more. I have to tell you. I found a relative."

"You did? Oh my God, that's fantastic! Tell me."

"Doris has a younger brother who is still living. His name is Albert. And I was able to use search engines to find what just might be a current address for him."

Ellie's heart quickened. Sally's maternal uncle was still alive. Surely he would know what had become of baby Sally. "Jessica, that's fantastic. You're a lifesaver."

"Yes, I know, I'm pretty good," she said with a laugh.

Ray and Brandy came inside from the deck, Ray's face a question mark. "Ellie... Brandy said I've gone viral. I got emphysema but it's not contagious. What does she mean I've got a virus?"

Ellie put her hand over the phone. "No, not a virus, Ray—*viral*. It means people all over the world are watching a video of you playing the fiddle.

"Jessica? I've gotta go, I'll call you back. Can you just tell me really quick where he is?"

"Sure can. Albert lives in Memphis."

***

Ray, Brandy and Ellie chatted excitedly while Ellie fixed breakfast. Brandy read the comments to the video aloud, shrieking with laughter at the more outrageous ones. Ray grew increasingly agitated. "All those people can see and hear me? How can that even happen without my permission?"

Ellie explained to Ray that he had entered the public domain by stepping onto the stage of a public bar and playing before an audience. But while Ray enjoyed performing, he was essentially a private person. This unwelcome spotlight was an uncomfortable place.

"So that's what that little boy was talking about at the restaurant last night," he fretted, pacing back and forth and coughing. "Reckon I don't want to go out in public again till this commotion blows over."

"Are you kidding?" Ellie said excitedly. "Don't you see what you've got here? Ray, you're looking for a missing person and now *you're* famous—this is the best thing that could have happened to you. All you gotta do now is wait for her to come to you. The last thing you want to do is hide away." She flipped the French toast and set the maple syrup on the counter next to the powdered sugar.

"Ray, come on and sit down, have some breakfast. And let's get your tank hooked up for you."

"How can we get that video erased, Ellie?" he asked, accepting his breakfast plate.

She took a bite, thinking. This unexpected fame was a window of opportunity.

"I don't want you to erase it, Ray. In fact, I'd like you to help me make another video. Everyone knows who you are now, they're going to care about your story and listen to what you have to say. *This* is how we are going to find Sally."

For once, Brandy was in full agreement. Ray was unsure, but the women were able to cajole him into their plan. After breakfast, they staged Ray in a rocking chair on the cabin deck, with the Smoky Mountains in the background. They leaned the upright string bass against the table next to him and propped the guitar onto one of the empty Adirondack chairs to his side. Ellie got Jessica back on the phone and they set up a new email account for the sole purpose of receiving contact from the long lost Sally Eugenia Jones. Ellie wrote down the email account address for Ray to read when they filmed the video. She positioned Brandy with the smartphone set to record and film, after confirming that Brandy's hands weren't shaking too badly.

It required several takes. Ray was nervous and unsure what to say. "Just speak from your heart," Ellie advised. "Don't look at the phone. Just look at Brandy."

Ray, as to be expected, was his naïve and trusting folksy-self. Just as he had started his story with Ellie, he began with "My given name is Ray Virgil Jones, and I come from West Virginia, the Mountain State."

"Give the abbreviated version—not the whole story!" Ellie whispered to him.

Ray proceeded to explain his search for his long lost daughter, but at Ellie's advice, he left out the part about going to the crossroads. "There's nothing more I want from this life than to see my little girl again, my long lost daughter, my Sally. Sally, if you're out there," he finished, "please, please get in touch. Y'uns can send me a message at..." Ellie pushed the paper in front of him and Ray dutifully read the email address. He paused at the @ symbol.

"At," Ellie helped him. She nodded when he finished. This was going to work, she was sure of it. The number of "likes" to Ray's video was growing by the minute, and the second video would be a compelling follow-up.

Ray retreated to his room to rest after they were done filming the video, which Ellie promptly posted online.

Ellie had not yet broken the news about locating Doris's brother Albert. She figured she wouldn't overwhelm Ray with too much at once.

While Ray rested, Brandy and Ellie decided to walk into town. They wandered into little gift shops, looking at the ceramic pottery, quilts, and woodcarvings. Brandy was drawn to a miniature replica of a log home, picking it up to peer inside the windows at the interior rooms filled with miniature rustic furniture and an antique stove. A pine tree nestled near the front porch. Ellie walked up next to her, admiring the little log cabin. "It looks like a doll house. Do you think Nevaeh would like playing with that?"

Brandy set it down, shaking her head. "I don't have money to get them a gift," she said.

You seem to find a way to buy drugs on a regular basis, Ellie thought, but held her tongue. "Do you ever send them clothes or anything to help out your mom?"

"Um, I'm a homeless junkie, remember? I sit through useless treatment programs and go see my probation officer and pee in a cup. I don't have a job."

"Let's shop for some things for the kids, my treat," Ellie suggested. "We can send them some t-shirts."

"I'm not even sure what sizes they're in these days. It's gotten kind of awkward with my mom. I haven't kept up with my visiting and phone calls, 'cause I'm ashamed. So when I want to call, I feel like I can't. I don't know what to say. And Mom's so angry she just chews me out, so I just gave up trying."

More giving up, Ellie thought. "Well, you've got to start somewhere. The longer you let that go on, the harder it's going to be. Send the log cabin to Nevaeh and pick out something for the boys—how about these?" Ellie picked up a carved wooden kaleidoscope and held it to the light, turning the cylinder to watch the pattern turn inside the viewfinder. "This is pretty neat."

Brandy looked at the kaleidoscope and agreed. They chose one for each of the boys, and Ellie also had Brandy pick out a touristy t-shirt for herself. She added a t-shirt that appeared to be Ray's size. The clerk boxed the toys and Ellie paid to have it shipped to Brandy's mother's house.

Back out on the street, they paused to watch a group of street musicians: acoustic guitar, banjo, upright string bass and fiddle. Thanks to Ray's bluegrass tutorials, Ellie recognized the Jim & Jesse tune they were playing. She gave particular attention to the woman playing the fiddle. While the woman certainly could play, Ellie now understood the wide gulf between this and Ray's performance in the bar in West Virginia. No wonder he had become an internet sensation.

She turned her head as several hikers joined the crowd. Shell-shocked and ripe with body odor, they'd emerged in town after days in the wilderness. She retrieved some mini-packs of peanut M&M's from her purse and passed them out to the hikers, who gratefully received the candy as if they were pieces of gold.

"What's their story?" Brandy asked Ellie, curiously staring at the men's beaten hiking boots and large metal-framed backpacks.

"They're hikers. They carry all their supplies with them. They're coming into town off the Appalachian Trail," Ellie told Brandy. "Probably going all the way from Georgia to Maine."

Brandy looked at the men, thinking. "Do women do that kind of hiking too?"

"Sure. Of course."

They walked back up to the lodge, and Brandy stretched on the big leather couch for a nap. Ellie grabbed her map and a cup of coffee and settled into a rocking chair on the deck. It was good to relax in the sunshine, listening to the water rushing in the river below. Ray joined her, and they sat quietly for a few moments, admiring the mountains and gazing up through the trees, watching the birds.

"Ray, I've got some news for you—*good* news." She told him how

Jessica had researched ancestry sites and found the recorded marriage of Sammy and Frances, then traced the children born of their marriage, including Doris. "Doris has a younger brother who is still living, Ray. His name is Albert."

"Albert—yes! I remember her mentioning him. Goodness." He started rocking his chair vigorously in his excitement.

"Did you ever meet him?" Ellie asked.

"Naw, never did meet any of her kin except for her daddy. Her brother and sisters were living with their mama. They weren't around. Don't expect I would have been well-received by her kin, anyhow. They all disapproved of me because I'm white."

"Well, a lot of time has passed since then. He may not hold those old prejudices against you. And you know he's got to know what happened with Sally. What do you think?"

Ray readily agreed as Ellie spread out the map. "Jessica says Albert's living in Memphis. Looks like it's on the way to where we're heading anyways. It's right along the route to Mississippi."

"That's joyful news," Ray said happily. "Your law office gal found an address for him and everything?"

"Yes, I've got it written down right here." Ellie showed him.

Ray shook his head in amazement. "Can't believe a person can find all of that knowledge from a computer."

"We'll head to Memphis tomorrow," Ellie declared. She took a sip of her coffee, breathing the fresh mountain air and rocking in contentment. She was starting to believe, for the first time, they might find Sally after all. Ray's dream just might come true. She wanted to call Mike to share the good news, but her cell was already ringing as she reached for it. Jessica's face flitted across the screen.

"Hi," Ellie sang out. "Ray's so excited about finding Albert, Jess. You done good."

"And I want ya to know that I thank ya deeply," Ray called out, toward the phone. "Much obliged for your help."

"My pleasure," Jessica replied. "But it gets even better. I've got more news for you."

Ellie set her cell to speaker phone so Ray could hear too. "Ray and I are both here, Jessica. We're listening."

"We already received a response to the email account from this morning's video." She paused a moment, and Ray and Ellie's eyes locked, listening with anticipation.

"Ellie, Ray, I think we have found Sally."

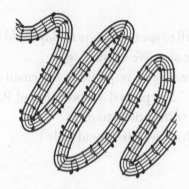

CHAPTER SIXTEEN

WRONG SALLY

Ellie and Ray sipped coffee in the Sunrise Café the next morning, anxiously watching the door, scrutinizing each woman who came through. The intoxicating aroma of fresh-brewed coffee and baking pastries permeated the charming coffee house, filled with plants and colorful macramé wall hangings.

Ray always felt he would instantly recognize Sally, but now he wasn't so sure. Of course a person wouldn't look the same as they did as a toddler, with so many years passed. Would she be disappointed if he didn't recognize her immediately? Would she be disappointed with him in general? It would be heartbreaking to find her, only to be rejected and cursed for a life trajectory forever thrown off course by tragedy. His stomach churned and he fidgeted, hardly able to sit still.

The email had not provided much information:

"I saw your video and think you are my birth father. I've wanted all of my life to find you but didn't know how. I can see from the Smoky Mountains in the background of your video that you're not too far from where I'm at. Can we meet tomorrow morning at the Sunrise Café on Moonshine Road? 10 AM? Can't wait to meet you! Love, Sally"

Ray had been abuzz with excitement after the receiving the message. Ellie was cautiously optimistic, while Brandy was outright dismissive. "How do you know the person who sent this is your daughter? This could have been sent by anybody."

"How do I know it *wasn't* sent by my daughter," he countered. "My Sally's gonna be drawn to music, with all the music sung to her as a young'un. And she's got music in her blood, from both sides of her family. So it makes sense she would be looking at videos of folks playing music on a computer."

"She probably just looked at that video since it's hot right now and everyone's looking at it. And don't you think it's a little too convenient that she just happens to be in the same area we are right now?" Brandy went on. "And how can anyone tell from a picture which mountain range it is?"

Ray was confused and upset. "Reckon I don't know what to believe, Brandy, but I sure am hoping, I sure am hoping."

"And hope is a good thing, Ray," Ellie reassured him. "It's wonderful to have hope. I'm excited and happy for you—this may be the real deal. Just think: you may be hugging your daughter tomorrow."

"Getting your hopes up in life is how you get your dreams shattered," Brandy said matter-of-factly.

Ellie gave Brandy a sharp look. "The only way to find out for sure is to go meet her tomorrow morning," said Ellie. "It's not like we have to go out of our way for this meeting. We have nothing to lose by seeing what it's all about."

They agreed to find an activity to pass the time and keep Ray calm. Ellie suggested a walk into town to listen to music, but Brandy offered a different idea.

"How about a walk on a nature trail? Like those hikers?"

Ellie was unsure about Ray's physical stamina for a hike, but he perked up as well at Brandy's suggestion. "A hike in the mountains; now that sure is something we could never do back in the city."

They agreed to find an easy, shorter trail that would not be too taxing for Ray. Ellie parked at a trailhead by a scenic overlook and they walked to the wooden railing to admire the view, a visual feast of Mountain Ash, Scarlet Oak, Red Maple, Yellow Birch and pine. "Think how stunning it must be in the fall when the colors change." Ellie paused to take a picture with her cell phone.

She had Ray and Brandy pose for a picture, and then Brandy took one of Ray and Ellie. "Not sure I know how to take a picture of you two gals," Ray said, looking at the device. Ellie showed him how to line up the shot and where to press to take the photo. When was the last time she and Brandy had appeared in a photo together? It had to be going on twenty years.

She reviewed the photo Ray had snapped. The two women stood, arm in arm—Ellie trim and healthy in shorts and an athletic running shirt, brown hair pulled into a pony tail, smiling confidently into the camera with white perfectly aligned teeth, and Brandy weathered beyond her years, staring defiantly at the camera, hair and eyes as wild as always, blackened teeth and bruises, too skinny in her new Gatlinburg t-shirt and that same pair of jeans. Ellie's eyes lingered on the condition of Brandy's teeth in the photo. *When we get back to Cleveland, I'm going to get her some dental care.*

They proceeded to the trail and set out at a relaxed, leisurely pace. Ray was chatting hopefully about Sally, pausing every few steps to take a few deep breaths and enjoy the view. "Seems like a good sign Sally signed off on her message with 'love, Sally', don't ya'll think?"

"Sure, definitely," Ellie replied encouragingly.

"Seems suspicious to me," said Brandy. "How does she know she loves you? She can't remember you. She doesn't even know you."

"Wouldn't you hope your children loved you, even if they didn't know and couldn't remember you?" Ellie retorted. Brandy turned her head away. Ellie instantly regretted it. There was certainly enough guilt and blame to go around, and she didn't need to make it worse.

They made their way along the dirt path, following the ridge. Brandy kept one eye on the ground to circumvent tripping over rocks or large roots, but paused frequently to look up through the trees and over the drop off to their right. They didn't come across any other hikers on the trail, and it was wonderfully quiet: no honking cars, no train whistles, no sirens, no booming radios. Just the sounds of the birds. Ellie pointed upwards as a hawk circled and soared.

They rounded the next bend in the trail and came to a screeching halt. "Oh my stars!" Ray whispered under his breath.

"Aaauughhh," Ellie cried out softly.

A large black bear ambled down the middle of the trail, on all fours, coming toward them. Ellie froze in fear. Her mind raced, trying to recall everything she had ever learned about bears. She tried to remember the difference between a black bear and a grizzly bear. Was it the coloring of the coat? The size of the animal? Was it true that one could climb trees while the other couldn't? Could black bears be aggressive? Did grizzlies venture this far east? Did it make a difference if it was a male or a female? Was it possible to outrun the bear? Would Ray be able to run? She turned her head slowly to Ray, who was very still next to her, staring at the animal in shock.

Ray began humming softly. The bear paused at the sound and cocked its head, considering the three hikers. He rose on his hind legs for a moment and then dropped back to all fours, resuming his walk in their direction. He was coming right at them.

Brandy, standing on Ellie's other side, snapped into action. "Yawwww!!! Go away!!!!!!" she screamed, raising both arms over her head and jumping up and down, creating as much commotion as she could. Ellie watched in confusion for a moment, and then joined in, holding her arms to the side to appear larger, yelling at the top of her lungs. Ray saw what the tactic was and added his own screaming yodels to the mix.

The bear stopped again, watched them in puzzlement for a moment, and then turned and resumed walking nonchalantly in the other direction. "Lord Almighty!" Ray declared. They quickly retreated to the car, laughing with excitement now that the danger had passed.

Ellie tried to describe the scene to Mike later that evening. He let out a long whistle. "Now that is quite a story."

"Black bears are pretty common in this area, we should have been better prepared," Ellie said.

"Yeah, but what's funny is how you guys handled it," Mike said. "You just stood there trying to reason the whole thing out, Ray tried singing to it, and Brandy just went nuts and scared it off."

"I think she was high."

"Perhaps, but she's the one who did the right thing."

Ellie had to agree. "We're quite a combination, aren't we?"

"With your brains, Ray's faith and Brandy's chutzpah, I don't see how you can lose."

And now, sitting in the cheery little café, Ellie hoped Mike was right. Could it be true they had so quickly found Sally by posting the video? She imagined how wonderful it would be for Ray to find his family, to get to know his daughter again. She prayed the reunion would go well.

A young girl paused by their table, hovering. "No more coffee, thanks, we're good here." Ellie waved her hand dismissively. The girl was blocking their view of the door, and Ellie leaned sideways to see around her.

But the girl didn't move. She was staring at Ray.

"No, I don't work here," she mumbled.

Ellie looked at her again, curiously. "Can we help you?"

"'Old Man Playing the Fiddle.'" She looked at Ray. "It's *you*. *I'm Sally*. Mister, I think you're my father."

Ray's mouth fell open in surprise. The girl wore a White Stripes t-shirt, dirty jeans and flip flops. Her long hair hung in two braids down her back. She didn't appear to be biracial, but more importantly, she could not have been a day over eighteen years old.

"Oh my goodness." Ray began.

The girl plunked into the empty chair at their table. "Are you the one who sent the email suggesting we meet here this morning?" Ellie demanded.

The girl hiccupped. "Excuse me." She looked at her hands, hiccupped again, and started crying. Soon her shoulders were heaving and shaking, and people at nearby tables started to glance their way.

"Have a drink of water, missy." Ray slid his glass over. Ellie grabbed some napkins and pushed them toward the girl to dry her eyes and blow her nose.

"I'm sorry—hic—I'm making a scene—hic—I get the hiccups when I get nervous," she sputtered.

"Take a deep breath," Ray said kindly.

Ellie waited for the girl to compose herself. The real waitress came by. "Another coffee here, please," Ellie said with resignation. She turned to the young girl. "Look, I don't want to be mean, whoever you are, but what the hell are you trying to pull here? There's no way you're the Sally we're looking for. Who are you, really?"

The girl looked frightened and started hiccupping again. Ray frowned at Ellie. "I'm sure there's an explanation. Take your time, missy."

The girl took a sip of coffee and wiped her eyes with a napkin. "I seen your video on the YouTube, mister—Old Man Playing the Fiddle—and then the other one, y'all talking about finding your long lost daughter, Sally. Well, you see, I'm adopted. I'm out on the road, took off from home, trying to find my own birth mother and father. I kinda got stuck here in this area, not sure where to go next... you seemed like a perfect match for me: you're a daddy, looking for his daughter, and I'm a daughter, looking for her daddy."

"No, you're not the perfect match," Ellie told her. "The Sally we're looking for was born in 1964. She's in her late forties. You're the *wrong Sally*. If your name is even Sally."

The girl just looked down, sniffing.

Ray started singing. Ellie and Wrong Sally looked to him curiously. "It's The Louvin Brothers, ladies. Song from my younger days about mistaken identity."

"You can sing too," Wrong Sally exclaimed appreciatively. "When I saw how you could play that fiddle, I just hoped that somehow you were my real daddy..."

"Well, you're young enough to be my granddaughter, not my daughter, I'm afraid," said Ray.

The girl hung her head. "I'm sorry, mister. I didn't mean no harm. I was just hoping so bad."

Ray nodded. "That I certainly do understand. Been doing a lot of hoping myself. Where is home?"

The girl shifted in her seat. "You mean my adoptive parents? They live in Memphis. That's where I grew up. But they don't care about me. That's why I'm trying to find my birth family."

Ellie and Ray looked at each other. "They're probably worried sick about ya. We can give y'all a lift home," Ray offered. "We're headed that way, ourselves."

"Now wait a minute," Ellie said. "I'm not sure that's such a good idea, Ray. I'm all for helping people out, but we don't even know her."

"Ah, Ellie, she's just a young, little upset thing who got in over her head and needs a ride home. What more do we need to know about her?"

"Well, for starters, we need to know how old she is. I'm not transporting a minor across state lines."

Ray hooted. "Miss Ellie, you rely on that contraption in your car so much to tell you where you're going that you forget to look at maps. I don't know much geography, but I do know that we are *not* going to cross any state line from here to Memphis. It's all just more Tennessee Waltzing."

"I'm eighteen," the girl insisted.

Ellie looked at her doubtfully. Even if it didn't violate the Mann Act, there were a multitude of reasons not to pick up this vagrant and give her a ride. What if the girl was some kind of scam artist? What could anyone possibly think they had to gain by pretending to be the lost daughter of a man known for playing the fiddle on the internet?

She excused herself and stepped out to check in with her paralegal.

"She's the wrong Sally, Jessica," Ellie said into her phone, leaning on the railing of a bridge overlooking a small waterfall near the coffee shop. "She's a teenager. Not even close to the right age. Said she's adopted and was hoping Ray might be her birth father since she was impressed by how he plays the fiddle. And now Ray's gone and offered her a ride back to her family in Memphis."

"What? That's crazy. How's Ray taking it? Where's Brandy?"

"Brandy's back at the lodge, sleeping. She'll be all over us with the *I told you so*s. She knew it was too good to be true. Ray, I don't know. He thinks we should help her. Why would someone intentionally pose as someone they're not?"

"El, brace yourself. She's not the only one. We're getting more emails now, from all over the country—women who are claiming to be Sally."

"What? Have you opened them?"

"I've gone through some of them. Some have photos attached."

"Do any sound like real prospects?"

"Not judging from their photos, at least. We've got a redhead. We've got an Asian woman. We've got more women too young to be Sally; we've even got one with white hair who's probably the same age as Ray—maybe she got mixed up and thought Ray was looking for his sister."

Ellie groaned. The video was such an exciting idea yesterday—concrete and real, a logical way to solve the mystery. But it was just another dead end. Ray had achieved some notoriety from the fiddling video, but his virtual world fame was only attracting imposters looking to exploit him.

"Some people will do anything to be around someone famous," Jessica said. "They must think he has money. And of course you have your crazies too—we also got nasty responses, even some death threats. There are just a lot of very disturbed people out there."

"So did any of the responses seem plausible?" Ellie asked.

"I don't know. I haven't gone through all of them carefully yet. I'll sort them and weed out the *definitely not*s. Then you can read what's left. Maybe you can come up with some way to further cull out the Wrong Sallys."

Ellie said goodbye to Jessica and turned her attention back to the coffee shop, where Ray and the first Wrong Sally were deep in conversation, like old friends. Ray looked up and waved to Ellie when she walked back in. "Don't worry, Ellie. It'll all get sorted out when we get to the crossroads. We're going to find my Sally. But in the meantime, the good thing that came out of us making that video plea is we now have the opportunity to help this young lady."

Ellie looked at Wrong Sally.

"I'd be ever grateful, miss," Wrong Sally said. She gave Ellie a weak, apologetic grin and hiccupped.

***

Against her better judgment and without any modicum of common sense, a short time later Ellie found herself back at the wheel, Ray seated next to her, a grumpy, sleepy Brandy in the back seat, a nervous Wrong Sally next to her, and the bags, suitcases, guitar, oxygen tank and upright string bass crammed into the back. The neck of the bass hung over the top of the seat between Wrong Sally and Brandy.

Ellie glanced into her rearview mirror at the young girl. She was traveling light, adding only a small duffel bag to their collection of belongings.

"So, you're sure you're eighteen years old?"

The girl assured Ellie that she was.

"Can you give me your home address to program into my GPS? It's a long drive, but I think we may be able to knock it down in a day. And maybe you want to borrow my phone to call your parents and let them know you're okay and you're on your way home?"

The girl paused a moment. "Address... address is...sorry, I've got it now: 3717 Elvis Presley Boulevard. In Memphis."

Ellie rolled her eyes and glanced over at Ray, who raised an eyebrow but said nothing.

"Okay. And your real name?"

"My name is Mattie. Sorry I lied to you. You probably think I'm an awful person."

"Ah, we've seen lots worse than the likes of you," Brandy interjected, propping her sweatshirt behind her head, pulling her baseball cap down over her eyes, and drifting back to sleep.

"So, Mattie, do you want to call your parents?"

"Maybe later, thank you."

Ellie wanted to ask a lot more questions. Had Wrong Sally run away? Had she gotten to Gatlinburg on her own or had someone brought her there? Was she a victim of some type?

Ray passed the cooler into the back seat. "Let's get into these snacks. Help yourself, Mattie." The girl eagerly dug in.

Brandy started singing a few lines from Tom Petty's "Runaway Train" from the back seat. Her eyes were closed but she was still awake. Ellie stole another glance in the rearview mirror to see Wrong Sally's reaction, but the girl remained silent.

They wound their way through the Smoky Mountains, linked to the interstate and headed west. When Brandy rolled the window down, they could smell Honeysuckle and Goldenrod. Eventually, the mountains gave way to rolling hills and sprawling, spectacular horse farms. It was all downhill elevation from here to the Mississippi River, Ellie figured.

A few hours later, she pulled off the highway into a small town, hoping for a bathroom break and a good lunch spot. They chose a main street diner that served sandwiches and soups, and settled into a booth. Wrong Sally ate with gusto, and Ellie was glad to provide the girl with a meal. "Have you been getting enough to eat?" she inquired gently.

"When I can... sometimes it's tough going from place to place, being on the road... I was hoping to find me a job somewhere."

"Where were you sleeping at night? Did you have a place to stay?"

"Here and there," Wrong Sally answered evasively.

"This is what *here and there* will get you," said Brandy, turning her arms to show the girl her track marks. "You'll get mixed up with the wrong people, if you haven't already. You'll get beat up, pimped out."

The girl looked uncomfortable.

"Has someone hurt you, Mattie?" Ellie asked.

The girl excused herself to go to the bathroom.

Ray, Ellie and Brandy conferred. "Y'all can't push her too hard with your questions," Ray advised. "You're gonna scare her off."

"Well, I'd like more information, and I'd like to get her help if she's been some kind of victim," said Ellie.

"What other information do you need?" Ray asked. "She's young, she's scared and nervous, and she's very hungry. So, we make her feel safe. We give her food. It's not that complicated."

"Yeah, like at the shelter," said Brandy. "Everybody's got a story. It would be better if they just gave us food and a place to sleep. Instead they make us go to treatment. Counseling. It's just a bunch of crap. People see *homeless* and they think they're gonna dig deep and fix what's wrong with you. All that's wrong is you need a place to stay."

"They've got to dig deep, though," said Ellie. "It's the only way to get to the root of the problem to figure out *why* the person is homeless or *why* the person is addicted or *why* the person can't hold a job."

"Oh, so you think it's the homeless person's fault that they're homeless; that it's because something is wrong with *them*?" Brandy's voice was starting to rise. "Sometimes crappy things happen to people, and it's not their fault!"

"It's not a matter of fault," said Ellie matter-of-factly. "It's a matter of finding the cause of the problem so you can find out the best way to help someone, to truly help them."

"You know, Ellie," said Ray with deliberation, as he looked at her thoughtfully, "sometimes it's easier to be the one *giving* the help than to be the one *receiving* the help."

Chastised, Ellie momentarily allowed herself to consider her own situation. When she worked with a client to solve a legal problem, donated clothes to the shelter, cooked food for her friends—she was powerful, in control. Even in this: taking Ray on this trip, helping him find Sally, standing up in court to take responsibility for Brandy. Ray was right—it was easier to be the helper. If she talked about last November, if she acknowledged she needed help, she would be surrendering control. She did not intend to lay herself open like that for more pain. Who was she to be prodding this young girl to open up to them, to strangers, when she herself was unable to open up to her own husband, or to her own friends?

Still, as an attorney, Ellie knew about women who were victimized—whether it was domestic violence, child abuse, sexual exploitation, emotional abuse—and she knew there were legal avenues available for help. If she didn't push with these questions, they might miss something critical. Brandy and Ray had a point about giving the girl some space, feeding her and making her feel safe, waiting until she was comfortable enough to talk. But too many people were doomed because other people didn't take notice, didn't keep asking questions, didn't dig deeper to find out what was really going on. She decided she would call the police and make a report, see if at least there was a missing persons report on file for someone matching the description of their young Wrong Sally. She would just step outside the diner and make the call.

The waitress came by and refilled their water glasses.

"Hey, where *is* Wrong Sally? Hasn't she been in the bathroom a long time?" Ellie looked to the other side of the restaurant, toward the restrooms. Brandy got up to go check, but returned to their table a moment later, shaking her head.

"Too late. Wrong Sally's gone. She took off."

***

Before leaving the little town, they checked everywhere—stores, the post office, the library, the playground by the school. "Mattie!" they yelled, asking around about her. "Have you seen a young girl with two long braids going down her back?" They returned to the diner and checked the bathroom again. They waited by their car for an hour in case she changed her mind.

"How does a person just disappear into thin air like that?" Ellie wondered. "Especially in such a small town where she doesn't know anyone?"

"When a person wants to be gone, there are all sorts of ways to do it," said Brandy. "She's lying low until we clear out. She doesn't want to be found. I bet she's watching us right now, waiting for us to leave."

"Is there any way we can leave her a message in case she changes her mind?" asked Ray.

"Good idea," said Ellie. She got out a legal pad and wrote:

Mattie: if you change your mind and you need help, or a way to Memphis, or want to come along on the Sally search, call my cell phone. 555-555-1428. Hope everything is all right. Ellie

She retrieved some snacks from the cooler and set them by a tree in the town square, with the note propped up against the tree.

"Whoa, she took off without her duffel bag," Brandy remembered. They retrieved it from the trunk and added it to the little message center at the base of the tree. "Should we look inside?"

The three looked at each other, unsure. Ellie didn't want to invade Mattie's privacy and go through her things, but who was this person, really? Why had she posed as Sally, and why was she so easily spooked by their questions? "Let her things be," said Ray. "Like I said before, she's just a hungry, scared young girl, and the rest of it ain't our business to be getting into."

"But, Ray, what if your Sally was in some kind of situation like that? Wouldn't you hope someone would do everything they could to save her?"

The possibility that Sally had been adopted but felt so unloved and unwanted by her adoptive family that she would run away, be mistreated and on the street with no one to help her—it was Ray's worst nightmare. He couldn't stand to imagine such a scenario... to think that his daughter might have become homeless like himself. And what if she was so damaged by everything she had gone through that she would hate him and blame him when they did find her? What if she was bitter and strung out on drugs like Brandy? Had anyone gone out of their way to help Brandy, to try to alter the path she was on? "All right," he conceded. "Open it up; let's have a look."

"She left it behind, fair game," Brandy agreed.

Ellie tentatively unzipped the bag and reached in to sift through the contents. The girl's things were nothing remarkable: a few t-shirts, underwear, socks, a toothbrush. The only thing of real value was an earphone headset and an iPod. Ellie picked it up and listened a few moments. "She's got a lot of music on here...sounds like country. Lady Antebellum, Keith Urban, The Dixie Chicks, Willie Nelson."

"Doesn't anyone listen to metal anymore?" Brandy scoffed.

"Okay, then, zip it back up," said Ray. "She'll be okay. She's got something there to soothe her soul."

"Well, I'm going to add something to soothe her hunger pangs." Ellie pulled out a wad of cash and tucked it into the bag.

Brandy watched in surprise. "Aren't you worried someone will just come along here and steal that, and it won't get to the right person? Hell, if I was coming through this park, I'd steal it in two seconds."

"Well, I guess whoever needs to do that needs it more than I do." Ellie shrugged. "I don't know what else to do for her. And you're right; she's probably watching us right now. So that's it." She set the bag next to the snacks and note and stood up. "I'm sorry, Ray, that she wasn't your Sally, and I hope she will be okay. Do we push on?"

They agreed nothing more could be done and, with last glances around the town square, returned to the SUV and started back on the road to Memphis.

Ray sat up front with Ellie, and Ellie turned her radio to the old time country station broadcast live out of Nashville. "Speaking of old Willie, huh," she commented, as they listened to Ray Price, Willie Nelson and George Jones. Ray coughed a bit but didn't say anything.

Ellie stole a nervous glance at him. She wondered if the toll of the trip was wearing him down. She had been foolish to take Ray to meet with the very first person who had responded to their video. It was too hard on him to get his hopes up and then be let down. She resolved not to put him through that again until any other potential Right Sallys were properly vetted.

Ray finished his coughing spell and composed himself. "We go right by Nashville on the way down to Memphis, don't we?"

"Sure do, have you ever been there?"

"So long ago... when I was trying to find Sammy and his band. I went everywhere I could think they might be playing. I'm sure it's changed a lot since then."

The highway bypass circled the outskirts of Nashville. Traffic grew heavier as they approached the city, and Ellie became absorbed. However, she did notice the sign for an exit for the Grand Ole Opry. It would be fun for Ray to have a look, she thought, and the exit was right there. She pulled off and followed the signs, pulling into a mammoth parking lot near a huge shopping mall and hotel complex.

"What is this business?" Ray was indignant as he looked around. "This isn't the Ryman. I don't know why folks just can't leave the beautiful old theaters alone. Whoever heard of the Opry sitting next to a shopping mall?"

"Times do change," Ellie offered.

"Seems this city has changed too much. Let's keep heading on. I'm looking forward to talking to Albert and finally making my plea at the crossroads. Time's a-wasting. I want to find my daughter."

"Okay, let's do it." She glanced into the backseat. "Are you awake, Brandy? I need some navigation assistance. Let's figure out where we're going to stay in Memphis."

"You know what I'll recommend," Ray started, but Ellie shut him down with a wave of her hand.

"Sorry. We've already had that discussion. We're not doing it on the cheap. We're doing things the Ray-way by going to the crossroads, but where we stay tonight is going to be the Ellie-way."

"What do you have in mind?" Brandy asked, reaching for Ellie's smartphone. "Luxury hotel or something?"

"Eh. I really don't like hotels. How about a bed and breakfast? Some of them are really nice, and that way you get more local character. Perhaps if we can find something toward the south end of town it will cut down the distance to Rosedale and we can just use it as our home base for the final launch to the crossroads."

Brandy got to work searching, checking availability and dates, reading out the descriptions and online reviews. "Some of these places are kind of small; they seem to be set up more for couples."

"Keep looking," Ellie advised.

"Okay, here, what about this: Gracious Victorian painted lady with generous, well-appointed private rooms (each with private bath), antiques, piano in formal sitting area, and enchanting courtyard near a tranquil pond. Hearty southern breakfast served in the dining room each morning—Eggs Benedict, country sausage, grits, scones & muffins, fresh-squeezed orange juice, fruit, coffee and tea. Complimentary wine & cheese happy hour in the sitting room or courtyard late afternoons. Located in a historic, walkable neighborhood yet close to downtown attractions. Come relax, unwind, and reconnect at this charming southern hideaway."

"Hey, sounds pretty good—happy hour. We might even make it there in time for a glass of wine," Ellie said, perking up.

"Yeah, happy hour, cool," Brandy agreed, "I'm liking the sound of that. Remember how we used to get our meals at happy hour, El? Ten cent wing night and one dollar draft beers."

Ray was shaking his head, balking at the expense. But Ellie wanted to treat her friends to beautiful surroundings, good food, privacy. She wanted a comforting home-like location where they could rest and recharge before searching for Albert and going to Rosedale. What if Albert had bad news about Sally? What if Ray had some kind of breakdown at the crossroads? It would be too depressing to have to retreat to a fleabag motel. And she really needed to keep an eye on his health.

Brandy programmed the address into the GPS. As Ellie drove, she realized the GPS was taking her to the bed and breakfast by way of the address they had programmed in for Wrong Sally. As she followed the directions the GPS was providing and saw the signs, she soon realized what was happening. She looked over at Ray and as their eyes met, they burst out laughing.

"You see where she was taking us?"

"I kind of had an inkling," he laughed. "Graceland."

"That girl was scamming us for sure."

"Nah, Ellie, she was just making things up 'cause she didn't want to go home. She had some sad story about herself that she just wasn't ready to face yet. My, my, my, Graceland. Well, at least she had a sense of humor and some musical knowledge. The home of the King. And, you know, it's not just Elvis who came from Memphis. Johnny Cash, Carl Perkins, Jerry Lee Lewis, Muddy Waters, Howlin' Wolf. They all came from Memphis. And do y'all know who else used to romp around Memphis, Tennessee?"

"Santa Claus?" Brandy sarcastically interjected.

"Oh, we give up, Ray, tell us," Ellie responded, enjoying Ray's excitement.

"None other than THE Mr. Robert Johnson himself. The man who led the way, the man who's going to show me how to do it."

He grinned and looked out the window, humming. "Pass me up that guitar from the back, Blondie, if y'uns can reach it. I'm feeling inspired as we approach the hallowed ground of all these great musicians who came here before me. And in case you didn't know, Memphis was smack in the middle of the civil rights movement, even if it was where Dr. King was slain. All those who fought so that Doris and I could become a recognized, legitimate family, no matter what color we are. I can just feel it. Everything's gonna come together for me here: music, racial relations, family, and the bargain I'm going to strike. This is where I'm finally going to become a father again. Yes, siree, it's all gonna come together for me here." Ray settled in with the guitar, and broke into a heart-felt rendition of Robert Johnson's "Crossroad Blues." Hearing Ray sing Johnson's song, knowing the stakes of all Ray hoped to discover at the crossroads himself, sent a thrill through Ellie's heart. He seemed very pleased as he finished the song, and continued picking and playing with chords. Within moments, he settled upon "Key to the Highway," strumming through a bluesy chord progression.

Ellie's grip on the steering wheel relaxed with relief. Ray was recovering. Losing Mattie had rattled them all. She truly hoped Wrong Sally would be all right and prayed she hadn't made things worse for the girl.

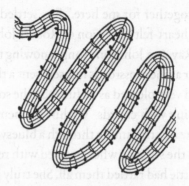

CHAPTER SEVENTEEN

A Family-run Business

Three hours later Ellie, Ray and Brandy stepped stiffly out of the car, stretching their limbs by the gravel driveway of the bed & breakfast. The Victorian home resembled a gingerbread house, with blue and violet trim and lace curtains framing the windows. A white picket fence encircled rose bushes, peonies and a spectacular perennial garden. A trellis led the way to the backyard.

"Must be the way to the courtyard in the back," Ellie said. "Come on; let's see if we can get checked in. It's like an oven out here. If it's not air-conditioned we're on to the next place."

She led the way up the steps to the front porch and knocked at the door, then pushed it open when she found it unlocked. The foyer was set up as a reception area with an antique cherry secretary, Tiffany lamp and oriental rugs. Ellie rang the bell. "Hello?"

"Oh...!" A middle-aged man came through French doors from the backyard, glass of red wine in his hand. "Didn't realize anyone had pulled up to the front."

Well-dressed people mingled in the back courtyard, enjoying their happy hour. "Hi," said Ellie. "We'd like to check in for a few nights, if you have rooms available."

The man regarded the two women and the older man. The bruises from Ellie and Brandy's fistfight rose on their cheeks, showing telltale handprint marks from their slaps to each other. He frowned at the track marks on Brandy's arm and her drug addict, skin-and-bones frame. He sniffed disapprovingly at Ray in his tattered suspenders and beat up shoes, duffel bag in hand and oxygen tank trailing behind him. He peered around them and raised his eyebrow at the upright string bass leaning up against the side of Ellie's car.

"Well," he started, "we're a family-run business; we try to serve a certain clientele here, perhaps out of your price range."

"My sister and I brought our father to Memphis to visit family." Ellie quickly proffered the familiar cover story, sensing the man struggling to calculate how she, Ray and Brandy went together. She rummaged through her purse for her credit card, but Ray had pushed past them into the parlor of the home. "Is that a piano I see there?"

"Sir, the piano is for the guests, if you don't mind."

Ray waved his hand dismissively. "Y'all don't mind if I just tickle the ivories for a few moments while you and Miss Ellie work out the logistics, now do ya?" Without waiting for a response, he seated himself at the spinet keyboard and struck the opening chords of the "Maple Leaf Rag," deftly going into the song with as much mastery as Scott Joplin ever did.

A woman in a sundress, hair piled in a high up-do, poked her head in through the French doors and smiled broadly at the sight of Ray at the piano. "Well goodness, what a surprise. Had to see where that wonderful music was coming from."

She extended her hand to Ellie, looking at Brandy curiously. "I'm Maxine; I can see you've met my husband, Greg." She turned again to Ray. His fingers danced across the keyboard, striking each note with just the right force to produce a clear, perfectly balanced sound. "We usually just use that piano for show; decorate it with fresh greens at the holidays. Can't remember the last time someone played it who actually knew what they were doing."

A few guests moved inside to better hear Ray. He had finished his instrumental Joplin tune and transitioned to a song with vocals: "Sing Me Back Home." Ray's folksy voice was as much a treat as the piano accompaniment, and was perfectly suited to Haggard's wayward melody.

Brandy had also pushed past the foyer into the parlor, heading for the bar where several wine bottles sat open next to a cheese board. She poured herself a generous glass and drank it down quickly.

Greg watched Brandy in distaste and gave his wife a look. "*Hon*, aren't we filled to capacity tonight?"

Ray finished his song, and the guests who had congregated around the piano broke into spontaneous applause. "Marvelous," a man leaned over and commented to his wife.

"Do you take requests? Can you play any Ray Charles?"

"Sure, my given name is Ray too," Ray chuckled, rocking back and forth with a grin on his face as he accommodated the man's request.

"Wait a minute!" the man cried out to the other guests. "Do you know who this is? Isn't this gentleman the internet sensation everyone's talking about this week—Old Man Playing the Fiddle? He's all over the internet: YouTube, Facebook. Yes, it's you, isn't it?"

"Oh yes," his wife agreed with excitement. "It *is* him. We have a celebrity in our midst."

Brandy had refilled her wine glass and raised it from across the room in a toast, shouting to Ellie. "Come on, El! Happy hour, girlfriend!"

Ellie could see Greg weighing what to do. She waved her American Express card in his face. "Three rooms, please?"

"Certainly, three rooms," agreed Maxine, brushing past her husband. She accepted Ellie's card and started booking them in. "We're happy to have you stay with us. Greg and I started this place up twelve years ago. Started with the original Victorian house and then built the addition so we could offer more rooms. We love meeting folks traveling from all over. Breakfast is served at eight each morning and, as you can see, we serve a complimentary wine and cheese hour in the afternoons.

We like to give our guests an opportunity to mingle and socialize, try to offer some southern hospitality."

"Some *civilized* southern hospitality," Greg interjected. "The social hour is part of the bed & breakfast experience. But we keep things on a civilized level. Two drink limit. You might want to let your sister know." He regarded Brandy dubiously. "...And you said you are here to visit family?"

"Yes, we're from Cleveland, we're down South to visit family. I'm an attorney," she added, hoping to change the subject.

"And your sister," Greg asked, looking across the room, "what does she do?" Brandy had started dancing and swaying to Ray's music, eyes closed, wine glass balanced sloppily in her hand.

"Oh, Brandy?" Ellie's mind raced for a presentable way to spin Brandy's back story. "She's a consultant," she declared. "And our dad, as you can hear, is a gifted musician. Excuse me, if it's all right, perhaps you can show us to our rooms after the social hour? We've had such a long drive today and I'd love a cocktail." She slid past Greg and winked at Brandy as she poured her own glass of wine.

Ray looked up from the piano and nodded to Ellie and Brandy, winking and grinning as he played. He called across the room to them: "Welcome to Memphis, ladies."

***

The following morning Ellie chose a light cotton sundress with Coach gladiator-style sandals and gave a few minutes of extra attention to her hair and makeup. She would try to dress up a little for the breakfast hour at the inn, try to smooth things over and fit in a little better with the beautiful people.

When she went downstairs to the dining room, she found Ray at the piano again, entertaining the guests while they ate. Ray had indeed elevated the mood of the affair with some wonderful song choices, the poignant "Hard Times Come around No More," followed directly by cheery ragtime piano as he banged out Asleep at the Wheel's

"Roly Poly."

A dozen or so guests were enjoying breakfast, and they clapped appreciatively. Ellie stole up next to the piano. "Ray, have you eaten yet?"

"Nah, Ellie, I'm happy to play some music for these fine folks," he replied.

"That's nice of you, Ray, and you sound wonderful, but you're not a hired performer—we are *guests*, we are *paying* to stay here. You come sit down and have some breakfast." She shot Greg an annoyed look for taking advantage of Ray. Greg avoided her gaze and scurried back into the kitchen.

Ray pulled the top down over the keyboard and gladly accepted a cup of coffee, filling his plate with fresh fruit, a spinach omelet, country sausage and a blueberry scone. He pulled up a chair at the massive dining room table, set with white tablecloth, quaint mismatched pieces of antique china and vases of fresh flowers. Ellie helped herself to fresh cream for her coffee from a small pewter sugar and creamer set. The couple who had recognized Ray from the internet sat across from them, and the man extended his hand to Ray and Ellie.

"I'm Steve Mason and this is my wife, Rose. We're from Chicago."

Ellie introduced herself and Ray.

"Stephen Foster, you were just playing, before the western swing." Steve nodded to Ray. "Wonderful songs; pure Americana. Have you visited the outdoor musical about his life in Kentucky?"

"No, sir," Ray replied, "but I sure enjoy his music."

"Don't know if I'm familiar with his music," Ellie commented.

"Sure you are," Steve told her. "Everyone knows Stephen Foster; everyone's heard his songs; you probably just didn't realize who the composer was. 'My Old Kentucky Home.' 'Oh Susannah.' 'Camptown Races.'"

"Beautiful Dreamer," Ray added.

"Yes," the man agreed. "An American treasure, though the poor man died broke, only thirty-eight cents in his pocket. Only thirty-seven years old. How long have you been playing the piano, Ray, and where did you study? Who did you study with?"

Ray chuckled. "Well, I taught myself, just banging around on the keys. But I haven't had a piano to play in years and years. It's a treat to sit down at that fine keyboard."

"You remember all those songs? You played them perfectly, without any music."

Ray blushed, shaking his head. "Don't read music, sir. Just keep it all up here." He pointed to his head.

"Ray can play any instrument you put in his hands," Ellie offered. "He's wonderful on the guitar, stand up string bass, harmonica. As you can hear, he can sing like nobody's business. And you saw how he plays the fiddle on the internet video."

"Really." Steve was transfixed. "So you're considered what we call a multi-instrumentalist. And you never learned how to read music?"

"Where I grew up, there was music going all the time, and lots of folks played the old-timey instruments. My aunt and uncle sang the old songs and ballads to me as a boy, and we'd make up songs, trying little chords or melodies from here or there and seeing how they sounded when we put it together. Had a little bluegrass band with my old buddies and we did the same, just put it together till we got that sweet sound."

"So you composed too. That's fascinating. Sorry, don't mean to bombard you with nosy questions. I'm a musicologist," Steve explained.

"A whatchamacallit?" Ray asked.

"A musicologist. I'm a professor at the University of Chicago. I'm not a performer, like you, but I study music—the history of music, different genres of music. Rose and I are down here to follow the Blues Trail. I've been pretty excited to travel into the history of Delta blues, but now I'm starting to think I've stumbled upon a musical phenomenon right under our noses here at this inn."

"Nah, sir, not me." Ray shook his head modestly. "I just do what comes natural to me. Nothing worth studying about in ole Ray Jones."

"Well, maybe it comes natural to you since you were exposed to it from an early age with your aunt and uncle while you were growing up. You know, there's a lot of research about how children learn and remember music. Even before they can speak or read and write. Early music is imprinted onto the brain of a young child."

Ray and Ellie looked at each other, thinking of Sally.

"Would a young child remember music sung to them as a toddler?" Ray asked.

"Yes, it stays with them, even if they don't remember on a conscious level. People learn language by ear, and they learn music by ear. You listen to people speak to you, even before you understand the meaning of the words. You learn the meaning of the words, then you learn to talk, then you learn to read, then you learn to write. Same with music. And early memories of music are so powerful. That's why little children learn their alphabet by singing their A-B-Cs. It stays with you."

"Music is so good for the growing brain," Rose commented. "It's the best education you can give a child."

Ray sat up a bit taller, looking proud, remembering how he had sung to baby Sally.

"So you didn't study music formally at all, Ray?" Steve asked.

"I ain't even got a high school diploma. But I got all the musical knowledge I need to get by, yessir."

"You seem to have perfect pitch too—what we call absolute pitch," Steve offered. "It's a real treat to meet you folks. What brings you to Memphis?"

The conversation was interrupted as Brandy clunked noisily down the stairs, wearing her too-short-stolen skirt and the Gatlinburg t-shirt. She sprawled down at the table and put her head in her hands, holding her head. "Too early..." she grumbled.

"Coffee? Tea?" Ellie asked her. Brandy just grunted.

They set off with hope after breakfast, the address for Albert Brown programmed into Ellie's GPS. It was going to be another very hot, humid day. Memphis was the biggest city they had visited since leaving Cleveland, and it perched on a bluff overlooking the Mississippi River.

"Never figured I see the Mississippi River," Brandy yawned.

"Mississippi River makes me think of Mr. Mark Twain," Ray commented. "My old teacher used to read us some of his writings. And the City of Memphis—well, it's just all music here, plain and simple."

Albert's place was on the other side of town. With no phone number, they had no choice but to show up unannounced. This was going to be awkward. Ray fidgeted distractedly, having the same worries as Ellie.

"Let's stop and pick up some donuts on the way," she suggested. "So we don't arrive empty-handed."

They picked up a dozen donuts in a variety of flavors and, a short time later, pulled into a trailer park. Ellie slowed to a crawl and cruised along rows of trailers, trying to see numbers. Each trailer was identified by lot number, but Jessica had not included Albert's lot number as part of the address. "How are we going to know which place is Albert's?"

A barefoot boy played by a stack of tires. Ellie rolled down her window. "Hi there, do you know of a man named Albert? Do you know which trailer he lives in?"

The child shook his head and ran off.

An older man stepped out of a nearby trailer, wearing a t-shirt and smoking a cigarette. "Who's looking for Albert? No one's called me by that name for a long time."

"Albert Brown?" Ellie asked through her open window. She parked and shut off the engine. They got out and the man looked them over, guardedly.

"What, y'all with the IRS or something? I swear I declared all my income from my gigs last year. Don't know why you people don't quit hasslin' me."

"No, we're not from the IRS. I'm Ellie, this is Brandy, and this is Ray."

The man extended his hand. "Everyone knows me by Alligator Joe, not Albert. I'm a blues man, like my daddy."

"Like your daddy, Sammy," agreed Ray, shaking his hand. "He was a master blues man."

"You knew my daddy?" Albert did a double-take, looking at Ray more closely. "Who did y'all say you were?"

"I'm a musician too. I used to listen to your daddy on his bass guitar, playing the blues in the juke joints in West Virginia."

"A white boy going into the black juke joints over there? Why'd you wanna go and do that?"

"For the music. I loved his music." Ray paused and took a deep breath. "And I loved his daughter too. Your sister, Doris. I'm Doris's common law husband, her widower." He extended his hand again and looked Alligator Joe in the eye. "I can't tell you what a pleasure it is to meet you, Albert. I'm Ray Jones."

Albert looked at Ray in astonishment, his face contorting as he struggled to comprehend. He did not take Ray's extended hand.

"*Ray Jones*? Doris's common-law husband?" Albert's face closed up, and he spat on the ground.

"You gotta lot of nerve showing your face here, Ray Jones. You ain't nobody's widower—there was never no legal marriage between you and my sister. And you took off, left her on her own to raise that young'un, and then wrecked your car drivin' too fast, killed my sister, left her body behind."

Albert started pacing back and forth angrily, his eyes flashing. Brandy and Ellie looked at each other with alarm and took a few steps back. Ellie wondered if he might have a gun. Brandy clutched the box of donuts.

"Sir, that is not what happened," Ray protested. "I never left Doris alone to raise the baby. Please let me explain. I was with her every step of the way, built a house for us to live in and tried to support the family even after the mine went on strike. I wanted to marry her more than anything, but you know as well as me it was against the law back then for white and black to marry."

Albert shook his head. "Naw... my mama and daddy told us exactly what happened with our big sister. You gotta lot of nerve showing up here on my property and lying to me."

"I swear to you I mean no disrespect to you or your family and I'm telling you the truth. I never left her alone to raise the baby. Only time I was gone was when my band played a weekend show at the State Fair. That's when your parents came and got her and Sally and tried to run 'em out of town, except your daddy crashed his truck and Doris was killed."

"My *daddy* crashed *his* truck? That's not how it happened. Y'all left my sister in a bad way, didn't take no responsibility for the young'un, then *you* crashed *your* vehicle and killed her!"

Ray took a deep breath, raising his hand to Albert to stop. "I know that must be how your parents told you it happened. But I'm not lying to you here today. Your daddy was driving his own truck when Doris was killed. I wasn't there. They went off the road, crashed. Left Doris behind. Your mama and daddy walked away with Sally and must have hitchhiked out of there. I came home to an empty house. I never saw my daughter again. I lost the woman that I loved and I lost my baby girl."

Ellie stepped back to the car and opened the back to go through her briefcase and retrieve her notes. "We can prove it to you, if you give me a minute here!" she called over her shoulder. She rummaged through her papers until she found the copy of the newspaper article about the crash. But when she turned around, Albert was heading up the step back into his trailer.

"I ain't got nothing to say to you. Y'all can go ahead and get off my property now." He slammed the door.

Ellie, Brandy and Ray looked at each other, Ray's face stricken.

Ellie took the box of donuts out of Brandy's hands and set it on the stoop to the trailer, with the copy of the newspaper article. "Here's an article that ran in the local paper in 1966 explaining what happened with that car crash," she yelled through the trailer door. "There's a copy of the state highway patrol report too. Please read it! We've come a long way to talk to you; you're the only living relative we could find. Ray hasn't seen his daughter in almost fifty years. He's sick; he wasn't even supposed to leave the hospital. We've traveled all the way down from Cleveland. Please read the article. Please help him."

There was no response from inside the trailer.

"I'm leaving you a box of donuts here too..." Ellie yelled out. "Let's see, we've got chocolate, we've got jelly, we've got glazed, we've got cream-filled...and I'm gonna write my phone number on the box so you can call us if you change your mind. We'll be in town for a few days."

Brandy approached the trailer and helped herself to one of the donuts out of the box. Ellie gave her a look. "*What?*" Brandy whispered. "What's one donut?"

"So yeah, no chocolate frosted donut left anymore, sorry," Brandy called awkwardly to the closed door. "But you still got eleven perfectly good donuts here...so cool, right?"

They shuffled about for a moment, watching the trailer, but Alligator Joe was truly done with them. Ellie put her hands around Ray's sagging shoulder and led him back to the car. "I'm sorry, Ray. Let's go."

"What a waste of good donuts," Brandy mumbled as they pulled away.

But a few minutes later Ellie's cell phone rang.

"Come on down to Beale Street this afternoon: The Hot Sauce Café. I'm playing a gig. I'll talk to you between sets."

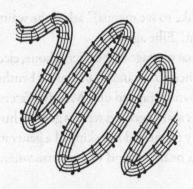

CHAPTER EIGHTEEN

ALLIGATOR JOE

Beale Street was teeming with people, and live music rang out from dozens of clubs and restaurants. Ellie found parking near the Mississippi River, and they walked up the strip from there. "Home of the Blues," announced a sign as they entered the historic district. There was indeed Delta blues, in addition to gospel, rock & roll, jazz, R & B—a musical mecca of roots music, as well as a melting pot where all ages and races came together to enjoy good music and good food. Ellie enjoyed the vibe on the street, the energy of the place. Brandy looked around with interest, taking in the bars, the shops, the people, the sounds. It was the kind of place one could sit and people-watch for hours without getting bored.

"Here's the place," said Ray. They stopped outside of The Hot Sauce Café, peering in the window low by the ground, framed by red and white checked curtains. A sign boasted the barbecue specials: ribs, pulled pork, pulled chicken, baked beans, cornbread. They descended a few steps below street level to the entrance.

The bar was dark and cool, a welcome relief from the sun and humidity of the street. They found a table, ordered cold beers and turned their attention to the stage.

"Would you like to see menus?" asked the waitress.

"Sure, we'll eat," Ellie agreed.

Alligator Joe sat on stage at the microphone, electric guitar in hand, harmonica fastened to a stand. A drummer brushed the drums for a soft beat as the band wrapped up a Muddy Waters tune.

Albert's vocals and fingerings were as good as his father's, Ray recognized. The family talent had not skipped a generation. The band was rewarded with a hearty round of applause when they finally went on break.

Albert nodded and set down his guitar, making his way over to their table and pulling up a chair.

"Y'all sound fantastic, as good as I remember Sammy did," Ray told him. "He taught y'uns how to play?"

"Sure, a bit," Albert nodded. "When he was around, he schooled me a bit on the guitar. I saw him play in some of the clubs, at least when he and my mama were together. They had a habit of getting together, breaking up, getting back together, breaking up again... you know how that goes."

"I remember it. When I first met your father and Doris, the rest of the family wasn't around. I never met your mama. I never met you, or the rest of her brothers and sisters."

Albert shuffled in his chair, looking down. "The last time I saw my sister I was fourteen years old. Mama and Daddy split for a while; Doris stayed with Daddy in West Virginia and we went to stay with my grandparents. When that happened, I never dreamed I would never see her again. What a horrible tragedy, such a young life. I remember her singing..."

Ray nodded sadly. "Yes, she had a beautiful voice. She loved music, and she was just crazy about our little girl, just the best mother."

Albert sat up straight and wiped a tear from his eye. "Well, I read that newspaper article and that police report you left. I want to say I owe you an apology. Things didn't happen the way my parents told us they happened, and we never knew. My parents..."—he searched to find the right words... —"didn't always make the best decisions."

Ellie was tempted to whistle under her breath at this massive under-statement. She was impressed how Ray delicately danced around the conversation, gaining Albert's trust in hopes of drawing out as much information as possible.

"You don't have to apologize to me. My family wouldn't give Doris the time of day either. Couldn't get past the interracial thing."

"Was she happy living with you, Ray?"

"Oh sure, yeah, we were happy. We were poor, we didn't have either of our families on our side, and most of the local folk disapproved of us too. But we loved each other and we loved our little Sal very much. Used to make up little songs for Sally and we'd sing to her."

"Is that right?" Albert looked thoughtful. "Did y'all write down those songs?"

Ray and Ellie looked at each other. "Are you aware of some writings, some song lyrics?" Ellie asked eagerly.

"I heard that there was a box with some keepsakes—some jewelry, some song lyrics—it was all there was left of Doris. It was all the little girl had to remember her mama by. Her little box of treasures."

Ray leaned forward eagerly in his seat. "That's right. Those were the songs we wrote for her, her lullabies. Did you meet Sally?" he pressed. "*Please*. What happened to her? I gotta know what happened to her."

"Well, I never did meet her, I'm sorry to say. Mama and Daddy took her up north and left her with some kin who agreed to raise her. It was all kept kinda hush-hush, you have to understand. Little gal born out of wedlock, biracial, her mama killed and her papa run off—at least that's how the story was told. I remember them telling us kids that she was a beautiful little golden-skinned toddler named Sally, she had her little box of treasures, and our kin up north was going to take her in and raise her. Little orphan girl."

Ray closed his eyes and started breathing hard, struggling to control his emotions. Sally was no orphan. She was a beloved daugh-ter, kidnapped from her father.

"Back then, it was a scandalous situation. I think people would be more accepting of things now," Albert pondered. "I'm sorry, Ray. I suppose we were what modern folk would call a dysfunctional family."

"Do you remember the name of the kin that raised her?" Ellie asked.

Albert shook his head, thinking.

"Or how they were related to you?" Ellie added.

"Reckon there's a high possibility they weren't technically related to us at all," Albert offered. "You know—folks got their 'play aunts,' their 'play cousins,' and so forth."

Ellie fell silent, shocked. Could this saga possibly get more unbelievable? Every lead they uncovered just turned out to be a dead end.

Ray looked at Ellie, his eyes wild with grief, and she was at a loss as to what to say to him. How could Sammy and Frances's deceitful plot remain so airtight, even after all of these years? They were no closer to knowing who had raised Sally, where she had been raised, how her shoebox ended up in the closet of Ellie's house, or where she was now, than when they had left Cleveland.

Brandy reached over and put her hand on Ray's arm in a surprising display of affection. "Ray, we haven't gotten to the crossroads yet. Don't give up hope. You still got your deal to make."

"Crossroads?" Albert asked curiously. "Headin' down to Mississippi, are ya?"

"Got nothing to lose by trying," said Ray. "Gonna throw myself on the mercy of the crossroads and hope for a miracle."

"You gonna sell your soul, brother, to find your little gal?"

"I'm gonna sell my musical talent to find my little gal," Ray told him.

"Reverse-Robert Johnson," Brandy added.

Albert nodded, not fazed in the least by this information. "Yeah, that's probably what I'd do too," he agreed, completely serious and without any hint of sarcasm. Ellie stared at him dumbly and downed the rest of her beer. Perhaps this utter faith in the crossroads legend was a generational thing. Still, she couldn't believe that they had come all this way, had located Doris's brother, and yet the man was unable to provide any useful information at all about Sally. Dysfunctional didn't begin to describe it.

"So y'all headed down to Clarksdale, then?" asked Albert.

"Nah, not Clarksdale. We're going to Rosedale."

"Some people believe the crossroads are in Clarksdale, some believe they're in Rosedale," Ellie informed him. "The original Johnson song doesn't mention Rosedale, but he sings about Rosedale in a different song, so Ray said we gotta follow the lyrics."

"Now that's a sound piece of advice," said Albert heartily. "For a musician or any person seeking a musical miracle. Follow the lyrics. Yesiree, I agree with your approach. Follow the lyrics."

Albert stood, stretched, and headed back to the stage. He settled into his chair and tipped the microphone to his mouth. "Welcome back, folks, and before we go into our next set, I want to say a few words to some special visitors here today. I want to welcome Mr. Ray Jones, a fine gentleman who is trying to put his family back together, trying to do the right thing, and his friends, Ellie and Brandy. I wish I could help him more, I truly do. But I'm grateful nonetheless to learn that he made my sister Doris happy, such a long time ago."

Ray composed himself and nodded to Albert. "The honor is all mine," Ray called out across the room.

"Well, I gotta invite you up here, Ray, to play with me. Gotta give you a proper musical send-off for your pilgrimage to the crossroads. Won't you sit up here with me and play some blues?"

Ray blushed, giving Ellie and Brandy a sheepish grimace, but he gamely rose from his chair and made his way over to the stage. Ellie wasn't surprised. As upset as Ray was, he still was never one to decline an invitation to make some music.

Alligator Joe pulled up a chair, and the back-up musicians produced another Fender Stratocaster. Ray seated himself and tuned for a moment, acquainting himself with the instrument.

It occurred to Ellie that something significant was about to happen. She turned her cell phone video recorder on and aimed the camera toward the stage, where the two men, white and black, sat next to each other with guitars in hand.

"Let's play some classic Delta blues. 'Dust My Broom.' In honor of Robert Johnson," Alligator Joe suggested.

"And don't forget Elmore James, king of the slide guitar. You bet."

"But before we start, folks,"—Alligator Joe turned his attention to the audience again—"I fear my introduction of Ray hasn't been complete. Not only is Ray a fine man trying to put his family back together and trying to do the right thing, but Ray is actually my brother-in-law, who I have just met today, for the first time in my life."

Ellie and Brandy smiled at each other, and Ellie continued to videotape.

Alligator Joe counted it out, and the two men started the song as if they had been playing together all of their lives. Ray tapped his foot and sang deep bass as Alligator Joe harmonized higher in the range over him.

Ellie listened, awestruck. The men sounded fantastic together. Brandy chugged her beer and joined several folks dancing near the band, shuffling her feet to the blues rhythm. She beckoned to Ellie to join her, but Ellie waved her off, remaining at the table with her video recorder trained on the two blues men. Even if Ray was unsuccessful in finding Sally, it was wonderful that Ray, who previously had no known relatives, had found a new relative, a contemporary and fellow-musician who was willing to welcome him as a friend.

Watching them together, it occurred to Ellie that both Alligator Joe and Ray would bear some physical resemblance to Sally. She zoomed in for close-up shots of their faces as they sang. She thought about the new information Albert had provided. Even though he didn't know the names of the people who had raised Sally, or exactly where she had been sent, he had confirmed she was raised "up north." Again, all leads pointed to Ohio. And he knew of Sally's song lyrics in her "box of treasures." Ellie thought about genetic testing, collecting samples from Ray and Albert. Could that be a way to rule out the Wrong Sallys and narrow down the list of Plausible Sallys? Or perhaps the video of Ray and Albert together could provide some visual confirmation, if a biracial woman of the right age showed a resemblance to both of them. Was there a way to narrow the search to Ohio and somehow circumvent the law that limited the ability of adoptees born between 1964 and 1997 to find their birth parents, and vice versa?

She tried to concentrate, wishing she had her legal pad with her notes and lists, so she could reason out what to do. *Don't forget to think like a lawyer.* Her mind wandered back to the box she had found in her closet. Ray had sung many of the songs, but still refused to sing Ellie's favorite lyric, the one that had somehow touched her heart and compelled her to find Ray. She didn't need her notes to remember the lyric:

> Baby child, baby o' mine,
> > We rock softly under the elms, the wind keeping time.
> Come evening I'll strike out, to earn me a dime,
> > Making music to bring home treats so fine.
> Catfish, cornbread, berries on the vine,
> > Common time with a walking beat,
> For sweet baby o' mine.

This must have been the most special of Ray's lullabies for Sally, the most personal. She wondered again what the melody would sound like. *Follow the lyrics.* She thought back to Steve's comments about how music imprints upon the brain of a young child. Hadn't he said that a person may be able to remember songs sung to them as a young child on some level?

A plan started to form in Ellie's mind. As the band continued to play, she retrieved her copies of the police report and newspaper article from her purse. She directed the camera from her video recorder to the papers, slowly panning down so the documents could be read. Right Sally must have heard the same family lies that Albert had been told about Ray and what happened to her mother. Right Sally might need as much proof that Ray was the real deal as Ray needed about her. When she completed filming the documents, she turned the recorder back to the musicians, as they finished up the song. She then set the video to pause. They were going to have to film one more segment later. Then she would post the third and final video to the internet.

***

"Come on, Ray, I promise, this will be the last video we post. We've got to weed out the imposters and find the Right Sally."

"Don't want to do it," Ray grumbled as Ellie led him into the courtyard of the bed & breakfast. "My daughter will be revealed to me when I conduct my transaction in Mississippi. You know darn well my plan to relinquish my musical talent, which has gotten me absolutely nothing in life."

Ellie was non-deterred. She knew she had a good plan. She was just going to have to give him a push.

"Now I sure don't believe that for a moment," she chided, sitting him down in a lawn chair. "It's provided enjoyment to so many people, as well as to you. I've seen how your face lights up, your passion when you explain how making music is creating art, over and over again, different each time. Music has gotten you *everything* in life. And it's going to help you find your daughter. *This song*, in particular, is going to help you find your daughter."

"That's just it, Ellie. I don't want to sing that song for millions of strangers to see on their computers and fancy pocket telephones. That song is special. It's Sally's song. It was meant just for her."

Ellie sat next to him and took his hand. "I know—that song is the special one. That's why it's the one we need to use. Do you remember what Steve said about young children and how they learn through music? How they retain music sung to them as babies? You and I have been around and around about whether to approach this thing through logic or through faith. I've tried to use the law, but that legislation is backed up in the Ohio Legislature. Even if it passes, we would have to hope Right Sally follows through the legal channels as an adoptee searching for a birth parent. My guess, if she heard the same family lies about you that Sammy and Frances told Albert, is that she won't. She was probably told that you ran off on her and her mom. So not only do we have to find her, we have to convince her that you are a good person, a good father, who never meant to lose her for even a moment. I can't help you through the law, as much as I want to. But I think I can help you through technology."

"Law, technology, I say fiddlesticks to all that nonsense, Ellie." He spat on the ground. "Do y'uns understand the power of the crossroads? Robert Johnson was a poor excuse for a musician—he was a hack. Couldn't play a lick. He disappeared for a spell, traveled on down the road, sold his soul to the devil and, when he returned just a few short months later, everyone saw the miraculous transformation. It *was* a miracle. A musical miracle. It can happen."

"But, Ray, for God's sake, you are not really wanting to make a deal with the devil, are you? Do you really, honestly think that can happen? Would you even want it to happen? You're one of the kindest people I've ever met, not an evil bone in your body. Why would you want to transact business with an evil entity, in fact with the most evil of entities there is?" She crossed her arms. "*And*, for your information, Robert Johnson only lived to be twenty-six years old. They think he was poisoned by a jealous husband. Do you really think things worked out that great for him?"

Ray looked at her suspiciously.

"I did my homework," Ellie informed him smugly. "I read about ole Robert."

"So you're not going to take me to the crossroads, then, is that it?"

Ellie softened. "I made you a promise, and I'm going to keep it. But, I guess, Ray, I gotta say what I'm wondering: do you really want to find her? It seems you argue about every practical idea we attempt. Shouldn't we be pulling out all the stops and trying everything we can think of? Every approach?"

"Of course I want to find her," Ray said, looking at the ground.

Ellie watched him, waiting.

Ray shook his head. "But what do I have to offer her? Look at me. I'm homeless. I live in a shelter; I live on handouts. Been living that way for years. Don't got no high school education. Don't got no family. Don't got nothing to offer her except an apology."

"Ray, you've been on your own. But not anymore. You're like family to me, and I bet Brandy would say the same thing. You're not alone anymore, no matter what happens. And as for a high school education? Well, maybe that's true, but there you are writing song lyrics, reciting poetry. And didn't Steve say you're a multi-instrumentalist, with perfect pitch? You're like some kind of prodigy; you can do things other people cannot. You have *so* much to offer. And if all you think you have to offer is an apology, well then, start with that. Everyone has to start somewhere."

Ray looked at Ellie, surprised.

He thought for a moment, then began slowly: "Ellie, no matter what happens, I want you to know that you've been the best friend anyone's ever been to me. Like a daughter, really."

Ellie beamed. Suddenly, the miles of heavy traffic, winding roads, trucks, dumpy motel, days away from work, nights away from her husband—even putting up with Brandy—were all worth it. It was one of the best things anyone had ever said to her.

"Sounds like no one could be a better friend to you than your buddies Charles and Owen were, sticking up for you back then," she said.

"They were the best," he agreed. "But you and Brandy, y'all are the real deal too, just as good. I just can't tell you how much it all means to me."

"So why *did* you call the band The Gulch Jumpers, Ray?" Ellie had been wondering about this for a while.

"Well, we dreamed of hitting it big and seeing the world, but seemed like all us country boys ever managed was just hopping from one gulch over to the next. So that was it for the three of us—good friends, with big dreams: The Gulch Jumpers."

"I get it," Ellie nodded. "I like it. So, Ray, it comes down to this: do you trust me?"

"Yes."

"Okay then. Listen up, this is what we're going to do. We're going to convince Right Sally that you did not kill her mama and run off and leave her. We're going to convince her that you, her true father, want her more than anything. We're going to convince her that you are the source of that little piece of music that floats around in the back of her head, that melody that she's seemed to know for as long as she can remember. She's got musical genes from both sides of her family. The first part of the video is going to show you and Alligator Joe next to each other, playing. Right Sally is gonna see how she resembles both of you—her father and her maternal uncle. She's gonna hear how good the music is, her family heritage. Then the video is going to show the newspaper article and the Highway Patrol report from the crash. She's going to read the name of her mother, her maternal grandparents. She's going to see the date, 1966. She's going to see the West Virginia location. She's going to read about how they crashed their truck, how you were out of town when it happened but returned and tried to find out what happened. She's going to read about how you tried to find her. And then, she's going to watch and listen as you sing the first verse of her lullaby. And it's going to trigger a subconscious memory—and she'll *know*. She'll just know."

Ray watched Ellie, impressed. "Damn girl, you are a smart one. Just sing the first verse, you say?"

"Right, Ray, just the first verse. That's how we're going to end the video. We have to convince her, but then she has to convince us too. Whoever can supply the next verse, whoever can tell us how the rest of the song goes, will be Right Sally. Follow the lyrics."

"Ellie, what if she doesn't remember the words to the second verse? She was just shy of two years old."

"She might not. I agree, it's a gamble." Ellie smiled. "Maybe that's where the crossroads miracle will need to come in."

Ray chuckled. "Okay, West Side, you've sold me. Let's do it. I'm ready for the camera. Start filming."

***

"That's a wrap, Ray!" Ellie called excitedly. Ray had talked earnestly to the camera, explaining to Sally how she had been taken from him and how he had traveled throughout the South, searching for her. He apologized, sincerely, but also held his head high and voiced his desire to find her now and be a dad, even at this late stage in the game.

He sang the first verse of the song, strumming along on the guitar. "Now, I know you remember it, Sally. I wrote the words down for ya. Your mama and I kept the songs we wrote for you in the little shoebox. It's right here, I have it now." He held up the shoebox, showing the writings within. "You had this growing up, your little box of treasures. Somehow, it got away from you and ended up back with me, but I know you remember it. There were Gulch Jumpers songs, but this was the most special song—because it was written just for you." He re-read the email address, with instructions for Sally to respond and share what she remembered of the next verse.

"You can remember it, Sally, I know you can. Don't think, just feel. Y'uns was raised on music. And that is always, always something to be proud of."

Ellie hit stop when he was done, and they reviewed the entire video together. "Good with it?"

"I am."

Ellie nodded with satisfaction, and the final chapter of the "Old Man Playing the Fiddle" video trilogy was posted online. She sat back in her lawn chair and raised her arms to the sky in a long stretch of glee. "That's it, Ray, we've done it. Fantastic. Now we just gotta sit back and wait, and monitor what comes back to us through the email account."

"*And*, we need to motor on down to a certain intersection in the

State of Mississippi," he added, "lest you forget, Miss Ellie."

"Yeah, cool, we sure will. We're pulling out all the stops. We're going down to the crossroads."

"Ah, so it's a crossroads visit you have planned, is it?" Ray and Ellie looked up as Steve, the musicologist, strolled over to join them in the courtyard, glass of pink lemonade in hand. "Sorry, couldn't help but overhear you talking." Steve pulled up a chair and joined them by the fountain.

"Ray's trying to find his long lost daughter. It's kind of a long story. He wants to make a plea at the crossroads for some kind of miraculous intervention. I know, pretty far-fetched, isn't it?"

"Actually, it might be more common than you think. Many blues aficionados are obsessed with the whole crossroads legend. It's a pretty popular tourist destination, and quite a few folks like to visit at midnight to log some kind of wish. I guess it's the Delta blues version of sending a letter to Santa, or throwing a coin in a fountain."

Ellie and Ray looked at each other. "Reckon I don't want to run into a lot of other folks trying to do the same thing when I get there," said Ray. "That's the kind of venture one needs privacy for."

Ellie agreed. They had come so far for Ray to have his wish, even risking his health. He deserved his own private moment at the crossroads, without other visitors or tourists with cameras or vendors hocking crossroads t-shirts, crossroads mugs and crossroads shot glasses.

"You going to Clarksdale?" asked Steve.

"Rosedale," Ellie told him. "Again, long story."

Steve nodded. "Well, that site should be less crowded than Clarksdale. A good drive from here, though—several hours. Will you go during the day or at night?"

Ellie looked to Ray. They hadn't even discussed it. What to Ray was the whole purpose for their journey was in fact the most poorly planned and least thought-out part of the trip so far. But the timing for their arrival was obvious, at least if they were to follow the legend of the song and the Johnson story.

"We will stand at the crossroads at midnight," Ray answered. "No other way to do it."

Steve looked at his watch. "Couple of hours… you could probably get to Rosedale before midnight tonight if you left now, but I'm not sure I'd advise traveling tonight. Weather report says there are big thunderstorms moving in. You don't want to kid around with that in this area. They get severe flooding, Mississippi River valley plain and all. Remember hearing about the big flood from a few years ago, when the water was waist-high up in Nashville at the Opry? And sometimes they see tornadoes moving through these parts. That can level a whole town. Maybe you better wait for that weather system to pass and then make your launch into Mississippi."

Ellie pictured squinting in the dark, windshield wipers furiously pumping as the defroster struggled to keep the windows from fogging. She pictured the car stalled in high water, rushing floodwaters rising around them. She pictured thunder striking big trees that might fall across the road, blocking their path, or even fall on their car, crushing them with a single blow. She pictured terrifying tornadoes roaring across the plain, destroying everything in their path, smashing them into millions of pieces. Her hands started to sweat and her heart raced.

Brandy had come downstairs and joined them, hands on her hips, listening.

Ellie looked at her traveling companions, her partners in crime. "What should we do?"

Brandy spoke without hesitation. "It's what we're here for, isn't it? What are we waiting for?"

"Woohoo, Blondie!" Ray yelled in excitement, stomping his foot. "Here we go!"

Ellie took a deep breath, trying to steel her nerves. The boring, logical, law-and-order-kinda-gal, wound too tight, always playing it safe, realized the time had finally come for bravery.

"Give me five minutes to change into my stolen skirt. Coffee and donuts on the way."

PART THREE

"A natural parent's desire for and right to the companionship, care, custody and management of his or her children is an interest far more precious than any property right."

Justice White, writing for the majority, Stanley v. Illinois, Supreme Court of the United States, 1972.

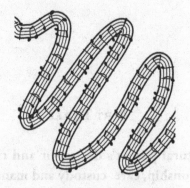

CHAPTER NINETEEN

The Crossroads

The mood in the car was joyous as they careened down Highway 61 south. Ray was hooked up to his oxygen in the back, strumming his guitar. Brandy helped Ellie with the navigation. After an initial minor glitch, they were finally enjoying decent coffee and donuts.

The sign had read "Dunkin Donuts" but when Ellie pulled off, it turned out to be just a donut kiosk inside a gas station convenience store. "What's wrong with these donuts?" Ray asked.

"I don't eat gas station donuts," Ellie declared. "We can do better. Brandy, get on that smartphone and pull up all the donut shops in this area so we can see what else is out there. I'm sure we can find better coffee too."

Ray grumbled under his breath, despairing about time lost on donuts when they were so close to their final destination. Brandy shook her head, snickering.

"What?" Ellie demanded.

"*You.* You are such a snob. *Ellie Sanders doesn't do gas station donuts.* I'll have to remember that."

Ellie looked at her defensively but couldn't help but crack up as well. "Okay. Whatever. Go ahead and make fun, but you're going to enjoy eating them as much as I am. Maybe we'll end up putting a little weight on you yet, girlfriend."

"You can spin any conversation back to the topic of fixing me," Brandy told her. "Maybe you can trade in your donut obsession for eternal healing powers at the crossroads, Ellie."

Ellie laughed good-naturedly, but Brandy's comment gave her pause. Steve had said the crossroads was a place to make a wish, like tossing a coin in a fountain. If such a thing was even possible, which she firmly believed it wasn't, what would she wish for? She quickly shrugged off these thoughts. If she had learned anything over the past year, it was to not go too deep into her own head. Keep moving, keep busy, and focus on others.

"What are you playing back there, Ray?"

"Miss Ellie, I'm playing the classic, golden, sweet melodies of The Everly Brothers. Course I'm singing their songs a few octaves lower than they did."

"It's beautiful." She wished she could have heard Ray harmonizing with The Gulch Jumpers.

When they crossed into Mississippi she honked the horn again—yet another state. Ellie couldn't believe she was actually here, together with Ray and Brandy on this unlikely journey. Her law practice, so far away, and the clients she was neglecting, inspired a pang of guilt. Thankfully, Jessica could handle so much while she was gone, but there was going to be a backlog of work when she returned. Even harder was being away from Mike. Ellie wondered what he was doing right now.

As if on cue, her phone rang.

"How do you always seem to know when I'm thinking about you?"

"Because I'm missing you," Mike said.

"I miss you too."

"Are you guys all right?"

"Sure, we actually just crossed into Mississippi and I would say we are about an hour or so away from the crossroads in Rosedale as we speak. So Ray, of course, is very excited. And you should hear how sweet he's making your guitar sound here in the car."

"I didn't know you were going to the crossroads tonight," Mike said, a frown in his voice. "What's the weather doing, El? There are severe storm warnings all through that area."

"We're fine, honey. We heard about the storms, but it's not even raining right now, just a little breezy." She perused the sky, which was churning and beginning to turn dark.

"Well, be careful. And call me if you need me to come down to help you."

Ellie was a little surprised at Mike's offer. Why would she need his help now? She had managed pretty well so far, despite hours on the road, hundreds of miles of driving, even the black bear encounter. Still, she was reassured to know he was there if she needed him. "I love you, thanks. I'm doing okay, though; I've got things under control."

"Ellie, you've always got things under control—that doesn't mean you don't ever need help. Just be careful. Maybe turn your radio on so you can get the local weather reports, okay?"

Ellie promised Mike that she would, and they said their goodbyes. Ray's strumming was too beautiful to interrupt with the radio, though. She could check the forecast later.

They followed the Mississippi River as it wound through farmland that stretched with endless rows of cotton, soybean and corn, until they finally spotted signs for the town of Rosedale. The flat delta was a sharp contrast to the steep mountains and deep valleys of West Virginia and Tennessee.

"This is it." Ellie slowed as they cruised past aging storefronts and run down houses with front porches, set out on neatly drawn blocks with tree-lined streets. The streets were mostly deserted this late on a weeknight. "We're looking for the intersection of Highway 1 and Highway 8," she reminded the others. The GPS directions led them near a state park by the river.

"We're very close, maybe I should park? We can walk from here. But perhaps we should wait; it's still a little while 'til midnight."

Ray agreed. "I'd rather have my private moment at the crossroads at midnight, if it's all right with the two of you."

Ellie parallel-parked along the street by the park and they got out, looking past picnic tables, public restrooms, grills and a playground, over to the Mississippi River. The water was still. Even though it was past eleven o'clock at night, it was still very warm, and moonlight briefly shone through peaks in the gathering storm clouds. Music and voices could be heard from a nearby riverboat gambling operation. Otherwise, the area was deserted. They strolled along the border of the park, guided by moonlight and streetlights. They came upon some storefronts, but most of the businesses were closed-down or vacant, with the exception of a convenience store and a tiny bar aptly named "Sell Your Soul."

"Sweet Jesus," Ray commented, shivering a bit despite the hot summer night. "Don't believe I care to have a drink in that establishment."

They bought a bag of chips in the convenience store and Ray and Ellie sat outside on the curb, munching while they waited for Brandy, who was using the restroom.

When Brandy emerged from the back room of the store, she paced nervously near the magazines and breath mints, watching the clerk out of the corner of her eye. She fidgeted and scratched at her skin; the craving was consuming and all she could think about was getting high. The clerk, a young man, looked over and gave a friendly nod. "What's up? How y'all doing tonight?"

Brandy weighed her options.

"I'd be doing better if I could get some dope," she confessed to the young man.

He nodded. "I've got some stuff you might be interested in. Real good stuff. It's the shit."

He showed her his stash under the counter, and Brandy quickly conducted her purchase, but before she could head back to the restroom to shoot up, Ellie stuck her head back into the little store. "Come on, time's getting close—we gotta start walking."

Brandy decided she would walk with them over to the crossroads, and then slip away into that park while Ray did his Reverse-Robert Johnson voodoo thing. She just needed to lose them for about five minutes. Then she could enjoy that warm rush and fly high in the back seat on the ride back to Memphis.

Ray fell quiet as they approached the intersection. Ellie and Brandy let him have his peace. It was momentous to finally close in on this hallowed ground. Was this truly where Robert Johnson had sold his soul? What had this site looked like in the 1930s? How many had come through here since then, trying to replicate Johnson's feat?

Ray paused a moment and coughed as they drew close to the intersection. He stood to catch his breath. Ellie sensed his hesitation.

She stopped and gently put her hand on his shoulder. "Are you afraid, Ray? You don't have to do this, you know."

Ray ran his hands through his hair, his eyes darting around as his mind reeled back through memories of hymns and sermons at church as a boy, the way sunlight felt like rebirth each time he emerged from the underground mine shaft, how lovingly his aunt and uncle had imparted everything they could teach him about music. He heard Doris's voice, saw Sally's sweet smile. His heart hardened as he pictured the flowers on Doris's grave, the abandoned little house, his child gone. How utterly he had failed them. This was the end of his journey, and nothing, *nothing* was too great to give up for his daughter. Right versus wrong, good versus evil, caution versus reckless abandon. None of it mattered.

"Yes, I do have to do this," he answered Ellie, his voice strangled with emotion.

The intersection itself was bare, with no cars or open businesses clouding the clarity of the spot where the two roads met, at perfect right angles. Perfect, Ellie thought. Good for Ray. He believed so fully in the magic; he deserved his best shot here.

"Ray," she said quietly. "I'll sit here and face this way and watch for cars. Brandy can sit over on 8 and watch for cars coming from that direction." He turned gratefully to them and nodded, his face full of emotion but far away. Ellie squeezed his hand. "Take as long as you need."

The trees rustled in the wind, and the breeze was hot and humid on Ellie's skin. She sat on the berm, glancing over her shoulder once to make sure Brandy was in her assigned spot. Satisfied all was well, she settled in. Her mind drifted. She should probably be checking work emails or reviewing incoming messages to the Sally email account, but she had left her phone in the car. Left with her own thoughts, she twiddled her fingers nervously. Recalling her breathing techniques from yoga class, she tried to steady her breaths and calm herself.

She wondered which direction she was facing. East, she thought. Yes, that must be right, since the big river was behind her. She tried to concentrate on her breathing. Breathe in. Breathe out. Wasn't it George Harrison who talked about meditation? Who has the patience for such things, anyway? She tried to quiet her mind. The breeze on the back of her neck indicated the wind was picking up, and the temperature had dropped. Must be the storm, rolling in from the west. She tried to stop intellectualizing it and just feel the wind on her skin.

She wondered if Brandy was thinking about her children. Her little girl had been so sweet, like a fresh, innocent version of Brandy. And what about Ray? Was he thinking about holding Sally as a baby, singing to her in the sunshine of the clearing near the little clapboard house in the holler? She thought of her own parents, how she had benefited from their unconditional love. She had always known they were there for her, encouraging her and caring for her, just the way her husband did. So much love, love to receive and love to give. She thought of Nevaeh's big innocent eyes and again pictured a younger Ray holding his daughter up to the sky and singing. She struggled to suppress a thought that had been with her all along, trying to bubble its way to the surface of her consciousness. She tried to push it back down. *I don't want to go there. Not now.* But the more she tried to ignore it, the louder it became in her head. Ray... Brandy... their children.

Ellie recognized that she, Ray and Brandy had something in common: They were all parents mourning the loss of children. Except for Ray and Brandy, there was at least a chance to reunite with their children. Brandy could just go to her mom's house and see her children—not one, not two, but three children. She didn't even understand how rich she was. And Ray, he had a chance, a shot at least, to find Sally—hopefully a more likely shot thanks to their search efforts, and perhaps some magic that was happening right now. It might be unlikely, but it was at least possible.

But not for Ellie. For her and Mike, it was not possible. Baby Michael. Big blue eyes, dark curly hair, dimple on his chin, who smelled so sweet after his baths. Baby Michael's cries, baby Michael's little hand curling around her finger, clinging tightly, Baby Michael's eyes following her, his face always attuned to hers as she would rock him to sleep, nurse him, change his diapers, push him in the stroller, start the mobile over his crib... the crib, the teddy bear-themed blanket... she had followed all the baby care books, her pediatrician's advice about not putting a baby to sleep on his tummy... she and Mike had always been careful to prop their son on his side or on his back, remove any kind of choke or smothering hazard from the crib... he had been healthy, a perfect little boy, and they had followed all the instructions. Crib death, SIDS, the doctor had told them. Why us? Why us? *Why my son?*

From far away Ellie heard someone screaming. She was somehow now lying on the road, rain pelting her. Arms encircled her but she didn't see, couldn't see. The night had gone pitch black, and a sudden, violent burst of thunder echoed in the darkness. Who was screaming? Who was pulling her to her feet? Why was that woman screaming, and why wouldn't she stop?

***

"Help me with her!" Ray yelled to Brandy. "She's having some kind of nervous breakdown. Grab her other arm, come on, see if you can lift her up. Let's see if we can get her back to the car."

Brandy stared at Ellie, dumbfounded, watching her old friend lying in the road, screaming with her arms around her head, not responding when they called her name. Lightning streaked across the sky and seconds later a crack of thunder shattered around them. Rain was coming down in sheets. Brandy sprang into action and grabbed Ellie, threw Ellie's arm around her neck and pulled her to her feet. Ray held on to Ellie's other side and together they struggled to pull her back to the car as fast as possible.

"Put her in the back seat," Ray said. "Lay her down across the back."

They managed to load Ellie into the backseat, and Ray grabbed a blanket from the back and threw it over her, but she continued to scream as if she was in some kind of trance. Ray tried to soothe her. "There, there now, Ellie, it's okay, ole Ray's here, you're all right, just let it go, just let it go."

Brandy backed away from the car, shocked. El, always so put together and in control, was coming completely unglued. Brandy put her hands over her ears to block Ellie's screams.

She needed to shoot up and she needed to do it immediately. She retreated from the car and ducked into the park, behind a bush. Her hands shook violently as she tried to find the syringe in her pocket and attempted to open the top to the vial. She couldn't see in the dark and hunched over to keep the rain from soaking her heroin. Brandy cursed to herself. She should have just used back in the bathroom at that store. Ellie's screams stopped. Another sound carried through the rain: the sound of Ray singing. She struggled to load the syringe. Ray's song reached her ears, and she recognized the tune from the lullaby he had written for his daughter. He sang the part she had overheard him sing before, when he and Ellie made the video, but this time Ray kept going. This time, Ray was singing the rest of the song:

"Baby child, baby o' mine,
We rock softly under the elms, the wind keeping time.
Come evening I'll strike out, to earn me a dime,

Making music to bring home treats so fine.
Catfish, cornbread, berries on the vine,
   Common time with a walking beat, for sweet baby o' mine.
With a song in your heart, and the sound of my voice,
   Sing it out, little girl, in our love we rejoice.
Sassafras, honey, huckleberry pie,
   Don't need no coal in the ground, don't need no cry.
Baby child, baby o' mine,
   You'll always remember, the wind keeping time.
Little house in the holler, where de sun always shine,
   Golden melodies from mama and daddy,
For sweet baby o' mine."

Brandy stopped. She turned her face upward, letting the rain wash across her eyes, her mouth. She saw Ray's house in the holler and the sunshine in the clearing, Ray holding Sally and singing the song to her. She saw the faces of her own three children. "What am I doing?" she screamed into the wind. "What am I doing!?"

Something seismic shifted within her, and with that, Brandy Sarendesh made a decision.

She threw the vial and the syringe as hard as she could, flinging them into the darkness of the bushes. The spark of bravery proved fleeting, however, and as the sound of Ray's voice trailed off, she immediately regretted it.

She dropped to her hands and knees and crawled through the wet grass and mud, trying to see in the dark. She ran her hands desperately across the ground, searching. Where was that vial? In which direction had she thrown it? She scrambled about, desperate. She crawled closer to a thicket of bushes. Her eyes stung with the rain and she stopped to rub them with muddy hands.

Lightning illuminated the night, and with the flash of light, she was horrified to find herself face to face with a pair of angry, red eyes, down on the ground at her own level. The wild boar stomped and snorted angrily. The huge beast must have weighed three hundred pounds, and she could feel its hot breath in her face.

"Eeeehhh!!" Brandy screeched in horror as the eyes of the beast flashed. She froze in fear as it grunted and appeared ready to charge. Suddenly, firm hands on her shoulder were pulling her to her feet and back away from the wild animal. Ray was there. As he pulled Brandy to safety, lightning flashed again and they both saw the vial on the ground, right in front of the wild boar.

"Let it go!" Ray yelled. "Back away, let it go, leave it there. Let it be. Come on, let's get out of here."

Brandy hung back, straining against Ray's grasp, her eyes lingering on the vial of drugs, now completely out of reach. She wanted it back, badly. With a final victorious snort, the feral pig snatched the vial into its teeth and swallowed it whole. It gloated at Brandy before giving a vicious, departing snort and charging away into the storm.

Ray tugged her toward the car. "Come on. Run."

He pushed her around to the driver's side of the front seat, but Brandy resisted. "Ray, what are you doing? I can't drive! I don't have a driver's license."

"I don't have a license either!" he screamed through the pouring rain. "But someone's got to get us out of here, and she can't do it." He pointed to Ellie under the blanket, lying down across the back. "You know how, right? It's been too long since I drove a car and my vision is too poor. You've gotta do it."

He pushed her into the driver's seat and then jumped into the passenger side.

Brandy was soaked to the skin and caked in mud, and she shivered violently as she stared fearfully at the controls on the dashboard. "Ray, in case you haven't noticed, I'm going through something here. I'm getting sick. I don't think I can do this."

"You can do it, Blondie. I'm gonna sit right up here and help. You know how to do it. Come on, you remember how to pull up the address for our place in Memphis on this doggone map contraption thing?"

Her hands shook as she fumbled with Ellie's GPS, but she was finally able to recall the last address programmed in for the bed & breakfast. "Good," said Ray.

There was another crack of thunder and a huge tree crashed down, no more than fifty feet in front of their car. "Back up," Ray yelled. "Go!"

Ellie heard the thunder and crash of the falling tree. She lifted her head dreamily, in a haze, and tried to register the fact that Ray and Brandy were in the front seat of her car and Brandy was at the wheel. She laid her head back on the seat and looked up through her sunroof window, watching in horror as the sky lit up. She closed her eyes and pulled the blanket over her face.

Something seismic shifted within her, and with that, Ellie Sanders finally accepted some help.

***

Ellie was vaguely aware of them helping her out of the car, walking her inside to her room and putting her to bed. She quickly sunk into blissful unconsciousness. To not think, to not feel—merciful nothingness. The blinds were pulled and it was mid-afternoon by the time she stirred from deep sleep. She opened her eyes a cautious slit and rested her gaze upon an oil painting of a horse over an antique dresser. She didn't want to think about last night. She didn't want to think about the crossroads. She didn't want to deal with being in Memphis with Brandy and Ray and trying to figure out what to do next. She missed Mike. She missed her son. She closed her eyes again and pulled the quilt up over her head, hoping to sink back into oblivion.

There was a knock at her bedroom door, which she ignored. *Go away, whoever you are. I don't care.*

"Miss? Hello?" The knocking continued.

She lay still a moment, trying to place the voice. It was Greg, the annoying innkeeper. Perhaps he would give up and leave her alone if she just ignored him, but the knocking went on.

"Sweet Jesus," she muttered as she finally jumped out of bed. She opened the door a crack. "Yes?"

Greg shuffled back and forth on the Oriental rug in the hallway. "So, y'all missed breakfast this morning, missed the complimentary breakfast which is part of the social hour of the bed & breakfast where we encourage our guests to mingle and socialize—part of the bed & breakfast experience and all..."

Ellie stared at him unhelpfully, waiting. "We had a late night last night."

"Yeah, okay, well your dad, or whoever he is, the musician, he came down this morning and sat at the piano like he was going to entertain the guests for breakfast, but he just played a few bars and then he slammed the lid down on the piano and stomped off. So he's just been sitting outside in the courtyard all day and not talking to anyone. And your sister, or whoever she is, the skinny blonde, she hasn't come out of her room all day long, but it sounds like she's in there vomiting. We keep hearing her retching and moaning and the toilet flushing, so I don't know if she's sick or what. And y'all know we are a family-run business here and we try to keep a certain southern charm ambience to the inn..."

Ellie ran her hands through her hair. "I'll check on Ray and Brandy, and I apologize if we've somehow bothered your other guests. Was there anything else?"

"Oh, well, no...."

"Okay, great, thanks." She closed the door in his face.

She opened the window blind to look down into the courtyard below. Last night's storm had passed. Ray sat by himself in the garden, hunched over, head in his hands. Ellie watched him, alone, in despair. She struggled to piece together the events of the past hours.

It was all her fault. Something had happened to her last night, when it should have been happening to Ray. She realized with shame that she had allowed the downward spiral to start, had failed to maintain control. Ray had been the one to save her and pull her to safety, but she had interrupted his magical time at the crossroads.

She realized why Ray had slammed the piano lid down. He had been checking to see if he still had his musical talent. He must have woken up this morning hoping that he could no longer carry a tune, strum chords on a guitar, make a violin sing. When he discovered that he could still play the piano just as well as he could play it yesterday, he realized it hadn't worked. The deal had not been transacted.

Ellie gulped with the awful realization of what she had done: she had ruined Ray's Reverse-Robert Johnson.

Someone was knocking on her door again. Why wouldn't Greg just leave her alone? She should have just checked them into a hotel.

She pulled the door open with exasperation, but this time she found Steve in the hallway.

"Hi," he said tentatively, looking her over in surprise. Ellie was still wearing yesterday's clothes, muddy and wrinkled from last night's storm. Her hair was wild and tangled.

"Ellie, I'm sorry to bother you, I get the impression you guys had a bad night last night, but I think something is seriously wrong with Brandy."

"What's going on?"

"Rose and I caught her coming out of our room this morning. We left the room unlocked when we went down to eat. I think she was rummaging through our toiletries looking to steal some medication."

Ellie looked down, embarrassed. "I'm so sorry. She's got a bad habit; you've probably figured that out. I will absolutely reimburse you for anything she stole from you."

"Nah, we don't have any prescription meds; we don't have anything she would want to steal. You don't need to reimburse us for anything. The point of why I'm telling you this is she looked bad. I mean *really* bad. She was all sweaty and shivering and clutching her stomach and staggering on her feet. She went back into her room. I think something is wrong. She might need a doctor."

Ellie tried to think, to pull herself together. "Oh my God," she mumbled as she pushed her feet into shoes and grabbed her purse, her keys and her cell phone. She glanced out her window again at Ray, still brooding in the courtyard below.

"I'm coming. I'll check on her; I'll take her to a doctor. Please... can you do me a huge, huge favor?"

"Certainly."

"Please keep an eye on Ray. Try to encourage him to eat. Tell him I'll be back."

Steve nodded as Ellie flew down the hallway toward Brandy's room.

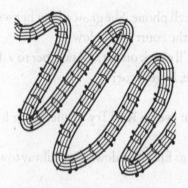

CHAPTER TWENTY

WITHDRAWAL

"Brandy! Brandy!" Ellie screamed as she pounded on Brandy's door.

"El, wait," Brandy cried weakly after a moment. There was a crash from the other side of the door and Ellie heard Brandy cursing. A moment later Brandy unlocked the latch on the door and flung it open, as she attempted to steady herself on the nightstand and then collapsed onto the bed.

Ellie rushed in and shut the door quickly behind her. Brandy lay in a fetal position, sweating and clutching her stomach. Her face contorted in pain. The room smelled of vomit. Ellie quickly opened the windows, trying not to gag.

"Ellie, Ellie," Brandy moaned.

"Brandy, what's going on? You're sick. What's happening?"

Brandy continued to moan, but she opened her eyes and grabbed Ellie's arm. "That devil-beast. It ate my stash. It growled at me, Ellie—it had red eyes."

"What?"

"It ate my stash."

"Okay, sista, you're not making any sense here. Your stash? You're not supposed to have a stash."

Brandy clutched Ellie's arm again, trying to make her understand. "I'm dope sick. I need to get high." She gagged, jumped up and ran toward the bathroom. Ellie followed and held her head as she vomited into the toilet.

"We've got to get you to a doctor. You're going through withdrawal. Probably really dehydrated. Can we get you down to my car? Can you let me put your shoes on?"

"Too sick to go anywhere," Brandy wailed. "Just need to get high. How come none of these rich people have any pills in their bags? It had red eyes, Ellie."

Ellie knew drug withdrawal needed to be medically monitored. Addicts could die going through withdrawal. Ellie wet a washcloth and blotted at Brandy's face.

"Okay, take a deep breath, I'm going to get you there. We *have* to go the hospital." She pulled Brandy off the floor and onto the edge of the bed. She guided her sandals onto her feet. "If you can't hold on to me and let me walk you out to the car then I'll have to call an ambulance. Can you do it?"

"I dunno, I dunno, I dunno." Brandy shook violently, looking around in confusion. "Ambulance gonna freak me out, car's better... it snorted and I could feel its breath in my face."

Ellie wrapped Brandy's arm around her shoulder and half-dragged her down the hallway, through the front door and out to the car. Mercifully, the other guests were not in sight to gawk. Ellie pushed her friend into the front passenger seat and ran around to the driver's side. She was momentarily perplexed to find her rear and side view mirrors had been adjusted, and then she remembered seeing Brandy at the wheel of the car last night. Brandy had driven them all the way back to Memphis, in that horrible storm, while going through drug withdrawal. Both Ray and Brandy had saved Ellie when she had so shamefully fallen apart. Ellie knew she had to pull herself together to return the favor for her friend. She tried to concentrate and think. Brandy needed fluids. Perhaps she could get her some Gatorade on the way to the hospital. She programmed "hospital" to navigate directions to the nearest emergency room.

Brandy had turned a pallid gray color and her eyes were rolling back in her head.

"Brandy!" Ellie called her name sharply. Brandy snapped back to attention and nodded weakly to Ellie. "Stay with me."

Ellie turned the radio on and hit the Grateful Dead channel, gunning the car out of the driveway. She turned the air conditioning up full blast and rolled the windows down, the way Brandy liked it.

The familiar cheerful reggae beat started up. "Come on Brandy, listen. It's the Dead! Remember our Deadhead days?"

Brandy responded a bit to the music. "Last time I heard this song I was trippin' on magic 'shrooms..."

"No, don't think about the drugs, think about the music. Focus; stay with me. Remember the live shows? The Grateful Dead, Tom Petty, Bob Dylan, Santana, Heart, Springsteen, Neil Young, Elton John, Stevie Nicks, James Taylor, Clapton..." Ellie chatted on nervously, trying to keep Brandy awake and engaged. "Remember those day-long outdoor Dead concerts? Remember how we danced in the middle of the Akron Rubber Bowl, wearing our tie-dye?"

Brandy groaned. "I remember trippin' at that concert. You weren't, but I was. You were always hanging around for the vicarious thrills. I was just more of the show for you to watch. So how do you like the show today?"

Ellie started to protest, but Brandy signaled she was going to be sick again. Ellie screeched the car over to the curb and jumped out to help Brandy, who had collapsed to her knees on the tree lawn by the street to vomit into the grass. Music from the radio spilled out from the open car door. Several schoolchildren in plaid uniforms, fresh from the school bus, stopped on the sidewalk and stared at the two mud-caked women.

"Wild pig ate my stash!" Brandy screamed as she retched.

The schoolchildren looked frightened. "Go on." Ellie shooed them off as she held Brandy's hair back out of her face.

"Okay, good, back in the car now. We're going to get you some Gatorade. What do you like? Lemon-lime? Mountain Berry? The white stuff? The green stuff? The blue stuff? Nice and cold. Stay with me, Brandy."

Brandy moaned and held her stomach. "Wild pig, wild pig...."

"Okay, wait here. DON'T get out of the car." Ellie ran into the convenience store. She didn't see any single bottles of Gatorade, so grabbed a whole case out of the cooler, threw a twenty dollar bill on the counter and yelled "Keep the change" as she flew back to Brandy. She ripped a bottle out of the case, giving it to Brandy as she threw the car in reverse to back out and continue to the hospital. "Drink."

Brandy scratched at herself, agitated, fingernails digging into her skin. "I know I could have taken that fucking pig. I should have fought him for it."

"Stay with me... we're almost there..."

"Wild pig! Wild pig!"

Ellie pulled up to the emergency room entrance, left the car parked where she probably should not have, and ran around to usher Brandy inside. "Heroin withdrawal," she announced breathlessly to the woman at the check-in desk, who nodded, unimpressed.

"Okay, have a seat." The woman gestured to the waiting area.

Brandy staggered over and collapsed into a chair in the waiting area.

"She'll probably be admitted into the three-day in-patient detox program," the woman told Ellie. "It will just be a short wait; try to keep her calm."

"Ellie," Brandy moaned, "think I'm gonna be sick again..."

The woman looked over in disgust as Brandy retched in the waiting area, effectively bumping herself to the head of the waiting list. The woman picked up the phone and called for a wheelchair. "Okay, we're going to get her into a room."

"Stay with me, El. Wild pig ate my stash! It had red eyes. *Do you understand?!?* WILD! PIG!"

A nurse appeared with a wheelchair, but stopped Ellie. "You won't be able to go back with her. We're going to work on her awhile and then admit her into the three-day program. You can come back Thursday morning to pick her up. We keep patients isolated from outside visitors while they're going through withdrawal, since it could be very dangerous for them if someone were to bring them narcotics while they're detoxing."

The woman handed Ellie a printout with information about the narcotics detoxification program. "Here's a number to call for a general status update on your friend, but you won't be able to talk to her until pick-up day."

Brandy looked at Ellie with terror in her eyes. "No, I need Ellie to stay with me. I can't do this alone."

"It's okay, we'll take good care of you," the nurse said as she started to wheel Brandy away.

"Wait," Ellie cried. She grabbed the Gatorade bottle out of Brandy's hand and pulled off the sticker. She rummaged through her purse until she produced the photograph of Brandy's children, arms linked and smiling sweetly into the camera. She stuck the photograph onto the sticky spot on the bottle where the label had been, and thrust the bottle back into Brandy's shaking hands.

"Be strong," she whispered into Brandy's ear, giving her arm a little squeeze.

Brandy held the bottle close to her face and tried to focus her terrified eyes upon the photograph. "Wild pig!" she screamed in a hoarse whisper. She clutched the Gatorade bottle with both hands as she was wheeled away.

Ellie watched until the wheelchair rounded a corner out of sight. She retreated in despair. Her friend was suffering, badly, and she wasn't going to be able to see her or talk to her for three days. *Oh Brandy. Please, please, come through this.* She hung her head, overwhelmingly tired again, and walked back to her car in slow motion. She opened another bottle of Gatorade and took a few sips, trying to calm her own shaking. She was empty. There was nothing to do but return to the bed and breakfast, where Ray was also suffering. *Oh Brandy. Oh Ray.* Everyone had come unhinged, herself included.

The Dead channel was now onto "Sugar Magnolia," but Ellie wasn't in the mood.

She shut the radio off. She couldn't do anything further, even return to the bed & breakfast, until she talked to her husband. She pulled the car into a real parking space and turned the ignition off again. She picked up her phone and dialed Mike.

"El?" he answered on the first ring. "Haven't you seen I've been trying to call you all day? Are you guys okay?"

Ellie tried to speak, but tears sprung up, closing her throat.

Ellie cried and cried, in the impersonal privacy of the hospital parking lot, alone in the car, yet connected to Mike and able to talk freely, with no one to overhear.

Mike waited patiently, making soothing noises every few moments. "I haven't heard you cry in a long time," he said softly. "Just let it go."

Many people lately were advising her to just "let it go." She finally composed herself, sniffling. "I'm sorry, just lost it a bit when I heard your voice."

"It's okay; you've got a lot on your shoulders. Was the storm bad last night?" he asked. "Did something happen?"

"Yes, yes, something happened. The storm was very bad, but that was the least of our problems."

"So what happened, my little Tin Man? Were you finally able to get Dorothy to the Wizard? What happened with Ray at the crossroads? Was he able to pull off his Reverse-Robert Johnson?"

She rubbed her forehead, trying to think. "I'm not sure what happened with Ray at the crossroads," she admitted slowly. "I lost track of what was going on with Ray, because something happened to me."

"Ellie, are you all right?"

"Yes—no—well, I guess I had some kind of breakdown. I remember sitting by the intersection, it was midnight, really hot out and no one else around, just the three of us. I was trying to give Ray some space to do his thing. My mind started wandering and... I started thinking about..."

"What?"

She drew in her breath. "I was thinking about last November. I was thinking about Michael. Our baby. What happened to him, what I should have done differently, how we'll never see him again. Everything. His smile, his dimple, his smell, his laugh, his cry. His funeral."

There were a few moments of silence on the other end. "El," he said in a strangled voice, "I thought we agreed things would be better if we didn't dwell on what we can't change."

"We did," she agreed. "That helped for a while. Just putting one foot in front of the other, getting up out of bed each day, burying myself in my work. But it's not working anymore. I can't keep it all bottled up inside. I miss him; I need to talk about him. I need to talk about him with you."

"I miss him too. I didn't want to say anything because I didn't want to upset you. I miss him all the time."

"I feel responsible. I keep going over it in my head."

"You can't do that to yourself. You have to remember what the doctors said. Sometimes it just happens, and there is no reason."

"Knowing doesn't stop me from feeling," she replied.

"I know," he admitted. "Sometimes I feel like it's my fault since we gave him my name. Like I wasn't able to make him strong enough somehow, like a part of me failed him because I'm not good enough."

"Oh Mike, you know that's not true—you were a great father."

Mike wept softly. "And people say 'you guys can try again, you can have another baby.' Well that might be true, but it doesn't change the fact that I miss *this* baby. I miss Michael."

They both cried openly then, time suspended, the phone and the distance making it possible to express what was too much to confront in person. Ellie felt closer to Mike than she ever had.

"I miss him so much. Every minute of every day."

After several minutes she shifted in her seat, blew her nose and took a sip of Gatorade. It was so good to be able to talk, even if the conversation was painful. "I guess holding all of this in finally caught up with me. It just all came pouring out, like a tidal wave I couldn't control. So I think I was screaming and I couldn't see. Ray and Brandy somehow got me into the backseat and Brandy drove all the way back here to Memphis. I just completely, totally, lost control."

"El, maybe that's a good thing. Sometimes it's a relief to acknowledge there are things way, way beyond our control, and we all need help. Your friend Ray, praying for his miracle at the crossroads. I respect him for wanting to surrender to some greater power like that, even if I don't understand it or agree with his approach. At least he has faith. And Lord knows I would be down there with you right now at that crossroads if I thought there was any chance in the world it could bring our son back."

"Ray did have faith," she agreed, "but I don't know what shape he's in today. The crossroads didn't work for him. He still has his musical talent and he doesn't know where his daughter is. He doesn't even know if she's still alive."

"I feel bad for him," Mike said, "and I also want to thank him—for helping you. And Brandy too, for getting you back safely. I guess I wasn't sure about either of them when you left on this trip; two homeless people, kind of flakey back stories, but it turns out they helped you get to a place where you can admit you need some help too. And they took care of you in that storm. Good friends."

Ellie looked at her surroundings. Her good friend was in the hospital, in bad shape. And it was absolutely remarkable she had been able to drive them all the way home last night. "Something else is going on," she told Mike. "It's Brandy. We're at the hospital."

"What?"

"I guess you could say the Wicked Witch of the West released the flying monkeys. She's in withdrawal."

"Oh my goodness. Wow. That is not good."

"No, it's not. She started getting sick last night, and then today she was in really bad shape: stomach cramps, shaking, sweating, vomiting. And I think she may have been hallucinating too. Kept talking about a wild pig. I just got her to the hospital about half an hour ago. She's going to have to stay for three days to detox, and she's not even allowed to have visitors."

Mike whistled. "You did the right thing getting her to the hospital. Maybe it's the start of getting clean for her. Do you know if she's ever tried to quit before?"

Ellie admitted that she didn't know. And truly, she wasn't sure if Brandy had purposefully decided to try to quit or if she had just run out of her supply. Perhaps it didn't matter what her motivation was, if the end result was the same. It would be a blessing if Brandy could get clean and be a mom to her children again. Ellie knew she loved them; she could see her friend's pain even if she didn't want to talk about it. Maybe Brandy could get a job, get out of the shelter. Selfishly, Ellie thought about how great it would be to have Brandy's friendship back—not stoned, sleeping, stealing, high-all-the-time Brandy, but Brandy from their old days: funny, energetic, eager to go to concerts, dancing. How fun it would be to hang out again with Old Brandy, back at home in Cleveland.

They could meet for coffee, go shopping, get their nails done together. They could head out to see a movie or hear a live band. They could chat on the phone, send funny text messages to each other. Brandy could come over to her house as an invited guest rather than breaking in through her basement window. Maybe she would bring her kids over and they could barbecue, play Frisbee in the backyard. Maybe Brandy would want to go cycling with her; she certainly seemed to enjoy the hiking trail. Ellie missed her old friend. Over the past few days, glimmers of Brandy's personality had come peeking through the drug haze, like rays of sunshine cutting through the clouds. Old Brandy was still there, somewhere inside. Ellie was sure of it.

She decided she would shop for Brandy while awaiting her release from the hospital and have fun surprising her with some new outfits. Ellie pictured a celebration of what Brandy's future could look like.

"I think it's a very good thing," she told Mike decidedly. "She just has to get through this rough patch, get through the withdrawal, and get on the road to recovery."

"I imagine that's a pretty rough road," Mike offered cautiously. "It takes some people years and years to get clean. They relapse, go into treatment, try again, relapse again."

Ellie knew this was true. She had seen plenty of drug cases in her practice. She would call Brandy's probation officer to see what treatment programs could be an option upon their return home. With the right treatment, and support from Ellie and her family, Brandy could do it. Brandy was strong. Hadn't she proven that last night, saving both her and Ray from the storm?

"And what about Ray?" Mike asked.

Ellie held her hand to her forehead. "I'm not sure. I've hit a brick wall; I just can't come up with any new ideas as to how to help him. I just feel so bad for him. He wanted this so desperately, and his health is poor... he really needs family."

"Ellie," Mike said, "do you want to ask Ray if he would like to move in with us? So he doesn't have to return to the shelter?"

Ellie had been thinking about the same thing for days. Ray was family now. She could not bear the thought of dropping him off at the shelter. But she needed to make sure her husband was truly okay with a new household member.

"Do you mean just temporarily?"

"I mean for the rest of his life. If he wants to and if that's what you want."

"Are you sure you're okay with that?"

"Yes," he said. "I'm sure. We have a big enough house. We have empty bedrooms..." They both thought about Michael's bedroom, the nursery.

"You don't have to change anything with Michael's room until you're ready to, Ellie," Mike went on, reading Ellie's thoughts. "We can put Ray in another bedroom. It's going to be all right. We can't have the family we envisioned, with Michael, but we can create a different kind of family. It's not what we planned, but it's still good. Things are going to be okay."

Ellie appreciated once again what a wonderful husband she had. Mike was willing to open their home and their family because he trusted her enough to believe in what she believed. They talked on, and husband and wife finally said their goodbyes an hour later, after they had worked out the details of their plan.

She would do her best over the next few days to make a plan for Brandy with the probation officer. She would pick out some new outfits for Brandy. She would be optimistic and cheer on her recovery. She would comfort Ray as best she could. They would hope for some response to the latest video. She would catch up on her caseload, writing motions and briefs, phoning clients. She would think about Michael every day, and talk about him with Mike, every day. And then, in three days, when Brandy was discharged, they would drive home and figure out how to pick up their lives.

It was the best she could do.

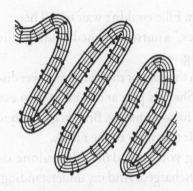

CHAPTER TWENTY-ONE

NEW BRANDY

Ellie reported to the hospital Thursday morning, nervous and unsure of what to expect. What would Sober Brandy be like? In a way, she would be meeting her old friend again for the very first time, after so many years.

She had been in communication with Brandy's probation officer as well as the doctor treating her withdrawal. Brandy was going to be discharged with Methadone. The daily dose would ward off cravings and help Brandy resist the urge to use again, but medication alone would not be enough. When they returned to Cleveland, Brandy would enter in-patient treatment. She would stay at least three months, ensuring a drug-free environment—the only way to give the counseling and group classes a real chance to work. Brandy would report every week on the drug court docket. She would submit frequent drug screens and be closely monitored. When she finished rehab, she would move into a halfway house and continue to work on her treatment and sobriety. She would also have to do community service, and the part Ellie was most excited about on her friend's behalf, was that Ellie had convinced the probation officer to allow Brandy to volunteer at an animal shelter. It was the perfect fit, and Ray was the one who had seen it in Brandy. Ellie couldn't wait to tell her.

"Come on back," a nurse beckoned, leading Ellie down the hallway to the detox wing.

Brandy sat on the edge of the bed, going over discharge instructions with the nurse. She was pale and thinner than ever. Ellie sat next to her and gave her hand a squeeze. Brandy gave a squeeze back, and they both turned their attention to the nurse.

"We're giving you your daily Methadone dose this morning, before you are discharged. And my understanding is you'll be leaving Memphis tomorrow morning to drive back to Cleveland?"

Brandy looked to Ellie. She nodded. "All right," the nurse went on, "so you'll return here tomorrow morning, before you leave, to get tomorrow's dose. And I don't suppose you can drive all that way in one day, can you?"

"Well, it would be a pretty long day in the car," Ellie pondered. "Doable, but perhaps too long for one day."

The nurse agreed. "Might be better to break it into two days. That way you won't arrive back home too late in the evening. We want our patient here to proceed directly into treatment. If you arrive in the afternoon, they can check her right in with no delay. So maybe tomorrow morning you can let us know where you want to take your overnight break. Louisville, or Cincinnati, perhaps? We'll call in the prescription to one of the clinics. That way you'll be covered until you can get into rehab, where the real work begins."

"You can't just give us the extra day's dose here?" Ellie inquired.

"No, it's highly regulated. Over time the dosage will be gradually decreased, which is how one is weaned from an opiate addiction. In the meantime, we administer it daily to prevent a person from having too much at any one time. We don't want Brandy to overdose."

Brandy looked out the window and said nothing. Her hands trembled.

Brandy signed her discharge papers and gave Ellie a deflated look. "Guess I'm ready."

"Wait," Ellie told her. She produced the shopping bags. "I got you a few things."

Ellie watched shyly as Brandy pulled the new clothes from the bags. Ellie was eager for her reaction and couldn't help but think back to West Virginia, where Brandy had been the one who tried to please her with new outfits, even if the gifts had been stolen. Brandy had been off the mark as far as Ellie's taste, but she had meant well. Ellie regretted criticizing Brandy's selections, especially when she recognized Brandy's lack of enthusiasm as she looked over Ellie's choices for her.

"Capri pants: good in the hot summer and in cold air conditioning," Ellie offered.

"Hmm, yeah," Brandy nodded, uncommitted. She unfolded a gauzy sundress and turned the new sandals over in her hands.

"It's okay," Ellie said quickly, putting the things back in their bag. "You can try these later, when you feel better."

"No, it's okay, I'll try 'em on now, before we leave. I've been in these same clothes for like four days now. I feel like crap. Maybe putting some new clothes on will make me feel like a new person, ha ha." Brandy's voice was tired and flat. She ran her fingers through her stringy dirty hair. Her fingernails were chewed down and ragged. There were dark circles under her eyes. They weren't leaving till the next morning. Brandy had been through hell over the past three days and there were plenty of tough days ahead in rehab.

Ellie thought for a moment. "Let's get out of here. I've got an idea."

***"We want the full spa day," Ellie told the receptionist, with a big smile. "Give us the works. But maybe not the deep tissue massage. My friend here is getting over an illness, so we're going to go gentle on her." She pushed Brandy forward, presenting her. "This special lady is to be treated like a queen today."

"Yes, ma'am," said the receptionist at the Memphis Rose Beauty Spa, nodding professionally.

She handed Ellie and Brandy a menu of salon services available:

steam sauna, massage with essential oils and acupressure, hot river rocks, apricot-mango body scrub, facial with exfoliating peel. There were also snacks: cheese, cracker and fruit plate with shrimp cocktail on ice, Greek yogurt with fresh fruit and granola, spinach quiche, chicken salad on mixed greens, champagne, mineral water, dark chocolate and strawberries.

Ellie looked it over. "Yes. All of it. Except for the champagne. We're going to be here all day. Do you have coffee?"

They were ushered into an elegant changing room and slipped on plush white robes and slippers. They pulled their hair into tight, high ponytails.

The massages were first. Ellie and Brandy laid on adjacent massage tables, with low lights and soothing new age music. The room was filled with fresh flowers and smelled wonderful.

"Ellie!" Brandy whispered. "I've never done anything like this before. I can't remember the last time I even went for a haircut."

"We never did anything this extravagant in our college days," Ellie giggled. "I guess we didn't need to back then—we were young. We didn't have body aches or age spots or baby-bump-mom-jean bodies."

"Uh yeah, no burnt fingertips, track marks, collapsed veins, bad teeth, thinning hair... I think my body issues go way beyond yours. And this place is way beyond what this homeless junkie is used to."

"Don't think of yourself that way anymore," Ellie whispered back with a frown, disturbed. "That's not you anymore."

Brandy gazed back at her and said nothing.

The massage therapists started working on their backs, arms, legs, rubbing in the oil and pressing out the knots and tense spots. Ellie surrendered. Her coffee sat and went cold as she lost track of time, peaceful and content. An hour later, after her massage was finished, she looked over and saw Brandy was in a similar state of deep relaxation. Brandy opened her eyes and blinked. "That was freaking amazing. I don't feel like my skin is crawling anymore."

"Get up slowly." Ellie held her hand and steadied her. "Drink some water. Are you up for some sauna time?"

They moved into the steam sauna and settled onto cedar benches, which they cushioned with thick white towels. The hot steam was marvelous and luxuriously relaxing.

"Ellie, I want to tell you something," Brandy spoke eventually. "I got to get this off my chest, 'cause I'm feeling really guilty." She cleared her throat. "Early in the trip, when we set out from Cleveland, Ray had some pain meds that were prescribed for him when he left the hospital. I stole them from him."

Ellie was stunned. Ray had never said a word, never indicated he was in any kind of untreated pain. He had just silently borne it.

"When?" Ellie demanded tersely.

"The first night," said Brandy. "I stole them from him the very first night. And Dottie—you should know—I took her pills too."

Ellie struggled with her emotions. Addiction was a disease. Brandy had come safely through detox and now she had a chance to get her children back, have a life again. But Brandy had stolen from Ray, so undemanding and kind, and from Dottie, who had done so much to help them.

"So why are you telling me now?"

"Because... I know you want things to go back to how they were when we were friends twenty years ago. But I'm not that person anymore. I want to be a better person, I really do, El. But you can't just rub your middle-class off on me and fix me. My mom probably warned you what a thief I am. Don't forget, I'm a convicted felon."

Ellie bristled, shaking her head. "Convicted felon, homeless junkie, thief—listen to you. Why don't you stop letting other people define you? Why don't you decide how you're going to define yourself? I get what you're trying to tell me: we don't have as much in common anymore. Okay, fine, point taken. But you're still my friend. And, you know, I've changed over the years too."

"Yeah, you don't drive a cool car and wear hippie skirts and tie dye t-shirts anymore. I've noticed."

"Oh geez, that car." Ellie remembered her banana yellow '76 Chevy Monte Carlo with the white wall tires. It was perfect for driving to concerts. And the clothes she used to wear... it was all so long ago.

"And for your information, I'm not trying to get my vicarious thrills through you."

"I guess you can just buy whatever thrills you want these days," Brandy commented, unable to resist taking the cheap shot at Ellie.

"I know you think I'm materialistic, and I admit I like things," Ellie replied. She thought for a few moments, deciding how much to share. "I guess you're right, I've become materialistic," she conceded. "But what I really want deep down is not things—it's people. In fact, I want more people—I want a family."

"El, I just tease you about that shit 'cause I can. I'm probably jealous of all your nice things—your shoes, your house, your car. But I don't really care. I know you work really hard and earn every dime. What *I* really want deep down isn't things either—it's space. I want space where people won't bother me and I can be somewhere outdoors, in nature. With a dog, maybe."

Ellie noticed Brandy hadn't included her children in her description of her perfect life.

She composed herself. The sauna was the place for confessionals. "Okay, so there's something I want to tell you too. It has to do with what happened to me at the crossroads."

"I know, I saw the nursery at your house. You don't have to talk about your miscarriage if you don't want to, Ellie."

"I didn't have a miscarriage. I had a son. His name was Michael. He was born last October and he lived for five weeks until he died suddenly. Sudden Infant Death Syndrome. He was our first child—he was a perfect, beautiful baby. I want to talk about him. I want people to know about him."

It was Brandy's turn to be stunned. Ellie had been holding in this fresh wound, putting on outward appearances of success and composure and control when, in fact, things were so out-of-control. Ellie helped others solve their problems and never once spoke of her own loss. Ellie *had* changed. And who she had become was so much more than a designer handbag or a pair of fancy shoes.

"I'm so, so sorry, El. I had no idea."

They both sat quietly for a few moments, inhaling the warm steam, thinking.

"Thank you for telling me," Brandy offered genuinely. "So... more people? Do you want to try to have more children?"

"I'm not sure," Ellie admitted. "Guess I'm scared. But we are going to have a new household member. Mike and I are inviting Ray to come live with us when we all get back home. I can't stand the idea of him going back to the shelter. He's like family to me now."

"That's awesome. I won't worry about him in rehab if I know he's living with you. Did he accept?"

"He said he would think about it. He's pretty down right now. I feel so bad about breaking down and spoiling his dream for him. And he was the one who saved me by singing that lullaby to me."

"He saved me too," Brandy said. "I was going to do some dope in that park, and then I heard him singing and thought about my kids, and I decided to quit. So I threw the dope away, but then I changed my mind and I tried to find it but the wild pig got to it before I could. And then Ray saved me from the wild pig."

Ellie brushed a strand of hair out of her face and stole a sideways glance at Brandy. One moment Brandy was lucid, and the next moment she was talking about the wild pig again. Ellie decided to let it go. She wondered again whether Brandy had purposely decided to get clean or had just run out of drugs. Perhaps it was a combination of both. Motive and opportunity, or in this case, lack of opportunity.

"Tell me about your kids. I don't even know your boys' names."

Brandy shifted and took a drink of water. "My oldest is Shawn. He's eleven. He's been with my mom since he was four. That's when things started going downhill for me, so she just stepped in. He's a great kid—smart, kind. But he's probably messed up; he saw a lot. Eddie is nine. Good kid too, kind of a clown, loves to play, roughhouse, tell jokes. And, of course, you know my little girl."

"Nevaeh's so sweet, Brandy, I just loved her. I'm sorry the boys weren't home when I stopped by your mom's house; I would have really liked to meet them too. Where is their dad?"

Brandy looked down, laughing with embarrassment. "Oh, oh, Ellie. I can't even imagine what you think of me. They all have different dads."

"Okay," Ellie nodded gamely, determined not to judge. She punched her friend playfully in the arm. "You always knew how to get around." They exchanged smiles. "So what's the story?"

"It's not too great a story. Shawn's father is in prison; Eddie's father, Razor, he's just a thug on the street; and Nevaeh's father, I did love him, he was a sweet guy..."

"Where is he?" Ellie pressed.

Brandy looked away. "He died. The lifestyle caught up to him."

Ellie processed this information. "Jesus. Sorry... were you with him when that happened? And Razor, isn't that the name of the guy that beat you up?"

Brandy started scratching at her skin, uncomfortable.

One of the clinicians popped her head into the sauna. "Time for your pedicures and manicures, ladies."

Brandy jumped up quickly and followed the woman out of the sauna, and Ellie resolved to back off. This was supposed to be a relaxing day; Brandy didn't need to be peppered with questions. Ellie didn't want to play the role of Brandy's therapist, her social worker or even her lawyer. She was just going to be her friend.

She grabbed her water bottle and followed, and they settled into the plush massage pedicure chairs, soaking their feet in the jet spa footbath.

"This must be the most wonderful thing in the world," Brandy exclaimed, enjoying the pumping jets swirling hot water around her feet.

"Totally agree," said Ellie. "I love pedicures. It'll cure whatever ails you."

After a bit, two clinicians appeared and started working on Brandy and Ellie's feet, sloughing off the dead skin and calluses with a sugar scrub, lathering on moisturizer.

"I do feel like a queen sitting here," Brandy giggled. "Just look at us."

El reached over and they held hands, Thelma & Louise-style, partners in crime. "Could you have predicted we'd end up here back in our party days?" Ellie said. She handed her phone to one of the pedicure ladies. "Would you mind taking a picture of us?"

"Some of us are still in our party days," Brandy quipped as the two women leaned in toward each other, smiling at the camera in their matching white bathrobes, hair wound up in white towels on their heads.

Ellie reviewed the photo. "It's good," she declared. "I'm gonna upload it to my Facebook page. I'll always remember our spa day together." She thought about tagging Brandy in the photo, but Brandy didn't have a Facebook account. She reached into her purse and pulled out her iPad and handed it to her friend. "Let's create a Facebook account for you. Then you'll have the photo too, and it'll make it easier for us to stay in touch."

"I don't have any gadgets though. I don't have a computer or a smarty-pants phone like you do."

Ellie had been thinking about this problem already. "When we get home I'm going to add you to my account and get you a phone. It's not that much more to add another user. It'll be my sobriety-gift for you, once you're done with rehab. You'll be able to set up an email account, get on the internet—look for a job, a place to live. And most importantly, you'll have a phone to call your kids. The only thing you need to promise me is you won't use it to hook up with drug dealers."

Brandy agreed to Ellie's terms and accepted the generous offer. They worked together to set up the Facebook account, and Brandy was intrigued with the concept of her own online identity. She worked on her profile, entering her hometown, her birthday, her likes and dislikes.

She entered her relationship status as "single and hopeful." When asked to enter her occupation she paused a few moments, thinking, and then typed in "human being." Ellie watched over her shoulder, grinning.

"Now you've got to send out some friend requests."

"Well, I don't know anybody," Brandy declared, defensive and angry again.

Ellie brushed off her objections. "You know more people than you think. How about me? Can I be your first friend? And everyone's on Facebook. You can be friends with people you sat next to in First Grade." Ellie helped Brandy brainstorm people they knew from their college days. Brandy was delighted as several requests she sent out were accepted. Her world was growing before her eyes.

"Hey, how about Evan?" Brandy brightened with the idea. "Do you think he's on here?" She searched and, sure enough, there was Evan, smiling next to Molasses in his profile photo. Brandy nodded with satisfaction. She was introducing herself to the world, and Ellie was delighted to see her friend blossoming.

Once their pedicures and manicures were finished, they progressed on to facials. After a lunch break, they would have their makeup done and then it would be time for hair.

"Do you think Ray is okay today?" Brandy wondered, sipping green tea. "Should we be checking on him?"

"I've got Steve from the bed & breakfast keeping an eye on him. He was more than happy to do it; probably wants to talk his head off about music. Hopefully he's not driving Ray crazy. Anyways, I think Ray's okay. He's just really, really disappointed. And I just don't know what more I can do for him."

"Well, what about the videos we posted?"

Ellie popped a chocolate-covered strawberry into her mouth. The responses to the Sally email account had dried up. Maybe they had exhausted the pool of Imposter Sally's out there, or maybe people just weren't paying attention anymore. Fads move quickly.

"I was really hoping Right Sally would see it and respond, but it just doesn't seem to be happening. I'm not sure why."

Brandy reached over for the iPad to see what was going on with the third video they had posted. It was still there, but there were significantly fewer "likes" or comments posted. Interest in Ray's plight had waned.

"What can we do to get more people to see this video?" Brandy wondered.

Ellie sat back, thinking. She fully believed the video was the key to finding Sally. In her law practice, she was a firm believer in the power of the sharing of information, and she was convinced it was the most critical component to solving any crime or mystery. When she had a tough legal question, reaching out to colleagues for ideas and tips was invaluable. But perhaps broadcasting the video to the world-at-large was casting too wide a net. They needed to target the right people. And then, the people seeing it had to realize the significance of what they were seeing. Even if they didn't know Ray or Sally, perhaps someone they knew would. Maybe someone would pass it along to a person who would recognize some connection to Ray's family. *Don't forget to think like a lawyer.* She thought back to Sally's shoebox, found in her own closet. Sally, or someone Sally was connected to, had been inside Ellie's own home.

"*I'm* the key," she said aloud.

"Huh?" Brandy asked distractedly, playing with her new Facebook account.

"I'm connected to my house, and my house is connected to Sally. Someone in my network has got to know how to get to Sally."

She watched Brandy on the iPad Facebook account. *You know more people than you think.* Information to be shared and targeted...

Ellie sat up straight, excited. "I've got it."

Brandy looked at her. "What have you got? And can I help?"

"Yes. We are both going to post Ray's three videos on our own Facebook accounts. We're going to write a plea and explain what we are trying to do; that we are searching for a Sally Eugenia Jones, born on October 14, 1964, whose father desperately wants to find her. We are going to beg people to *Please Help*. We're going to ask everyone we know to share the posting and pass it along, to their own friends and networks. We're going to create a special page for Ray's search, with the three videos, and we're going to ask everyone we know to "like" the page.

"But most importantly," she went on, "I need to share it with everyone in my network, and I need to increase my pool of friends so this reaches as many people as possible who have some connection to me. Or to Mike. Or anyone who used to live in my house, rent my house, work at my house, visit my house... or anything else you can think of. It has to go to that pool of people."

Brandy nodded, understanding, and they got to work. The video was posted on Ellie and Brandy's account, sent to all of their friends with requests to share and respond. Ellie mined all of Mike's friends, sent friend requests, and shared the video. She sifted through lists of friends from all her existing contacts, and sent friend requests to all of those people. She reached out to colleagues. She reached out to neighbors. She reached out to old schoolmates. She reached out to childhood friends. She reached out to her realtor. She thought of the prior owner, now deceased, and reached out to Ms. Goodworth's son, Bruce.

She called Jessica and explained the project. "Pull up the county auditor site for my house; I want the name of every prior owner going back to when the house was built. Share the videos with all of those prior owners and anyone you can mine in their networks. And, of course, share it on your own page too. And the page for our law firm."

"I'm on it," Jessica told her. "And speaking of our law firm, you know you have the McKenzie trial next week, right?"

Ellie assured her she would be home within a few days and ready for the trial. She would call her witnesses on the drive from Memphis to go over their testimony. Jessica was working on assembling the trial notebook, organizing subpoenaed documents so the exhibits would

be ready to enter into evidence. Ellie wanted to pour herself into helping Ray, but Jessica's point was well taken: she had responsibilities to
clients and couldn't ignore her work. Swarms of friend requests were
being accepted, and people Ellie hadn't caught up with for years were
flooding her inbox with well-wishes, photos and their own news. Her
number of friends had exploded from several hundred to well over one
thousand, and continued to climb. It was becoming almost instantly
unmanageable.

"I'll help monitor your page, as well as the Sally email account,"
Jessica told her. "You've got to delegate some of this stuff or you're
going to drown."

Brandy also agreed to help. An hour later, their lunch break was
done and they were satisfied they had reached out to every circle that
Ellie had some connection to which they could brainstorm. They high-
fived as they settled into adjoining chairs in front of big mirrors in the
salon. It was time for hair and makeup.

"All right, ladies," announced one of the beauticians brightly, "are
you feeling relaxed and renewed? Are you enjoying your spa day?
Ready to get beautiful?"

The friends looked at each other.

"Beautiful might be a stretch, but give it your best shot," said Brandy.
"We're as ready as we'll ever be."

**

Ray sat in the courtyard of the bed & breakfast, his back toward
the house, facing the perennial gardens. He had hardly moved in the
past three days except to transition quietly from his bed at night to this
spot in the garden. Ellie had given him some space to work through
his grief and crushed hopes, to soak up the sun and heal. He had given
her far away nods but not spoken much.

Today he sat with the guitar in his lap, humming in contemplation
and strumming gentle chords. He turned as Ellie and Brandy arrived.

"Ray, you're playing your music again," Ellie exclaimed, walking up to greet him.

But Ray wasn't looking at Ellie; he was staring at Brandy, his mouth hanging open in astonishment.

"*What*," Brandy demanded defensively, putting her hand on her hip and striking a haughty pose. "Do you think I look pretty? Or do you think I look like stupid?"

Ray looked her up and down in wonderment, a small, pleased smile creeping over his face. "Well, well, well, now look at our own gal, Blondie. Y'uns sure do clean up good. And yes, yes, of course you look pretty, but it's more than that..."

"What?" she demanded.

Ray searched for words that would do justice to New Brandy. "You look like you're back at the helm of your own life," he finally told her with satisfaction.

Brandy relaxed, proud. And Ray was right, Brandy's transformation was remarkable. Her hair was highlighted and styled into sleek, long, lovely beach curls. Her makeup made her look young and fresh, and hid any trace of the pockmarks and dark circles. Her nails were bright and cheery. She looked good in the new clothes. No one would ever be able to guess by looking at her what she had just gone through. She had spent several long moments staring into the full-length mirror at the salon, trying to reconcile the reflection of this new woman in the mirror with the fear she still felt inside. She was standing alone on a strange new island, not clear on whether she had swum there herself or the current had just carried her. If she was truly clean and sober, she was unsure what lie ahead and whether she even wanted to be clean and sober. The familiar shaking had started, but then Ellie gave her a hug and told her how great she looked. The shaking calmed. She wasn't on the island by herself. Maybe Ellie was right—maybe she should stop letting other people define her.

"And, Miss Ellie, you're looking mighty fine as well." Ray turned to his other friend. "Y'all got all dolled up, looking like fancy ladies today."

"Thanks Ray," Ellie said, taking a seat by the fountain and patting him on the back. "And how are *you*? You're playing the guitar again?"

"Yes, I'm playing again. I can't *not* play. You were right, Ellie, it's who I am, and I was foolish to think it was something I should bargain away. It didn't work anyway. Think you were right that I've had my daddy's voice in the back of my head all of these years, telling me music is something bad or evil, something to be ashamed of. That voice made me feel like music was to blame for that crash. But I've been doing a lot of thinking, and I realized I was just plain wrong about that. Been foolish and wrong about a lot of things."

"Ray," ventured Ellie, "I want to tell you that I'm sorry. I'm so sorry I ruined your Reverse-Robert Johnson."

He waved his hand. "Nah, Ellie, don't be sorry. I'm the one who owes an apology to the both of you. It's just a fool's errand I've had y'all on. There was simply no transaction for me to be had down at them crossroads. It wasn't real. Not a damn thing happened there. At least nothing happened to help me find my Sally."

"Well, maybe nothing happened to you, Ray, but something happened to me," Brandy spoke up. "I threw away my stash, and now look at me: I've come through the other side. I'm clean for three days now—and you're the one who helped me."

Ellie looked at the two of them, not understanding, but Ray was nodding along with Brandy. "Yes, Blondie, I had to pull you away from that feral boar; he was right there in your face. That big boy was mean and scary."

Ellie listened in surprise. Apparently, the wild pig had not been a figment of Brandy's imagination after all. It occurred to her that she was the only one in the group who had experienced a break with reality at the crossroads. She felt ashamed. She also knew she needed to open up to her friends.

"And you both know something happened to me too, and you both saved me. Thank you so very, very much, and there's something I want to show you." She reached into her purse and retrieved a photograph. Ray and Brandy leaned over to peer at the photo of Ellie's sweet baby boy. "This is Michael," she told them. "My son."

Brandy and Ray admired the picture. "Beautiful little boy," Ray told her. "I'm glad y'uns not holding that all inside anymore, Ellie. And I'm happy I was able to help both of you gals. Makes me feel proud, to tell you the truth. I haven't been much of a help to anyone for many years. Forgot what it felt like to feel useful."

"You don't need to be useful, you just need to be you," Ellie told him. "I'm so sorry we didn't find Sally, but I want you to know that we're going to keep looking. Even after we get home and you come live with us, we're going to keep searching."

"Finding her is what I want more than anything else in this life. I'm grateful, Ellie, to you and your husband for taking me in and keeping up the hope. I just don't want to be a burden to you folks..."

Ellie cut him off. "Having you in our home isn't a burden, or even something we're doing for you—you'll be doing something for us. You'll be helping us get through losing Michael. Mike and I want a family. We want you to join our family."

"I'm happy to help in any way I can," Ray told her. "And maybe I won't be too much of a burden after all—that feller who's staying here, the professor who studies music, Steve? He told me he wants to do some kind of study about me and the way I can remember and play so much music and play all the different types of instruments. He told me he'd come to Cleveland and interview me and give me some kind of psychological tests, then he's gonna do post-doctoral research and write a paper about me. Can you imagine that? And he said he'd be getting some grant money and he'd even be able to pay me for my trouble. Who'd have ever thunk something like that could happen to ole Ray Jones?"

Ellie and Brandy registered Ray's news, impressed. All of their lives would be changing, to some degree. Ray was finally embracing his musical talent and finding ways to put it to use for himself and the rest of the world.

"Anyways, I'm still sorry I spoiled the Reverse-Robert Johnson. But maybe the trip to the crossroads wasn't such a waste of time for us after all."

Brandy reached over, grasped Ray's hand, and then reached for Ellie's. "Maybe the crossroads isn't a place," said Brandy. "It's people. It's the three of *us*. We are the crossroads. We're a three-way intersection."

Ray nodded earnestly in agreement, smiling at the two women. "Good friends, with big dreams—just like The Gulch Jumpers." Then he reached again for the guitar and broke into song.

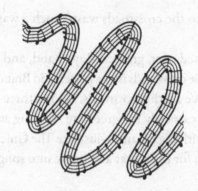

CHAPTER TWENTY-TWO

RIGHT SALLY

Later that night at the inn Ellie sipped wine and reviewed the trial documents Jessica had forwarded. Her window was open and crickets chirped in the darkness. A full moon hovered above the trees. It was still a warm summer night in Tennessee, but Labor Day weekend and autumn would be upon them before they knew it. She looked forward to getting back home and into Mike's arms. There was trepidation approaching the one-year anniversary of Michael's birth and death, but also some joy over the prospect of having Ray move in. She daydreamed how she would arrange the room down the hallway for Ray. The house would not feel so empty. She and Mike wouldn't just be a couple—they would be a family.

She checked one final case from her research and added a few notes to her trial preparation notebook. She would call her witnesses on the long return drive and be ready to jump back into her practice upon arrival in Cleveland. Practicing law was Ellie at her best—solving problems, standing up with clients in court, acting as a shield to deflect the blow of adversity when needed. She closed the web browser. *Done with law for the day.*

She checked the Sally email account, but there were no new

responses. She turned to her Facebook account and gasped at her overflowing inbox and the stream of entries. She hadn't realized that she knew so many people—or at least knew so many people who knew so many people. Jessica was right: there was no way she would have time to stay on top of so much incoming information. She wondered if she would eventually just need to shut down the account, if nothing panned out from the video posts.

It was almost midnight and they would be off to an early start in the morning, following a quick stop for Brandy's morning Methadone dose. Brandy had gone to bed early, grateful for rest following the brutal three days of detoxing in the hospital. Ellie hoped she was getting a good night's sleep and letting her body heal. She decided it was time to shut down her laptop and get some sleep as well.

An icon blinked to the side of her screen, indicating a friend was requesting a live chat. Ellie paused a moment, weighing curiosity versus sleep.

She clicked the icon and her heart started beating faster as she watched the message as it was being typed out in real time, letter by letter, word by word:

"Hello? I saw your video a few moments ago on my Facebook stream and just about jumped out of my chair. The man in the video... I think he's my father! He looks like me. The man he's singing and playing the guitar with—he looks like me too. I read the articles you filmed. My auntie Claire, who raised me, told me about Grandpa Sammy and Grandma Frances. And my mama, Doris. But I never knew anything about a father. Please, how can we check if I'm the daughter you're searching for?"

Sweat broke out on Ellie's forehead and she drew in a sharp breath. She had to be cautious... she had to be sure. *Follow the lyrics.* Her hands shook as she started typing:

"Did you listen to the lullaby? Ray used to sing it to his daughter when she was a baby and a little toddler. Is it familiar?"

She hit send and waited nervously. The screen remained blank; no response. Ellie held her breath, the moment stretching to an eternity.

Finally, a response appeared: "*Yes, I know it sounds impossible, but I DO think I remember. It feels very familiar—the words, the song, the way his deep voice rings out when he sings. It makes me feel safe. It feels like home.*"

Ellie quickly typed back: "Do you think you can remember how the next verse goes?"

After a few moments, the response came: "*I remember something about sassafras and huckleberry pie. Something about remembering mama and papa and the little house in the holler.*"

Ellie plastered her hand over her mouth to keep from screaming aloud. She kicked her feet into the air in a horizontal happy dance. Yes! All of her law papers and books went flying off the bed onto the floor.

She excitedly typed her next question: "May I ask if you have any birthmarks?"

"*Yes, I have a birthmark on the back of my left shin.*"

Ellie tried to maintain her composure. She had to be sure; she could not get Ray's hopes up again only to be disappointed by another Wrong Sally. *Think like a lawyer.* What was the connection between herself and this stranger she was chatting with? Who or what was the missing link?

"Do you remember the shoebox with the song lyrics that Ray showed in the video?" she typed.

"*Oh goodness yes! That was my little box of treasures; it went every-where with me when I was growing up. I used to keep my dolls in it too. I would lay out the dolls, and the jewelry, and the pages of songs. I would dress up my dolls and sing the verses to them. I guess I read that verse lots of times, so that's probably how I remember it, though I swear I can still hear a voice singing it to me. I lost the box, somehow, and I was just devastated. Auntie Claire tried to help me find it, but we never could figure out what happened. Like I said, I just about fell out of my chair when I recognized it in the videos. May I ask, where did you find it?*"

Ellie typed her reply: "I actually found it in the very back of a top shelf in my bedroom closet." She bravely pushed on. "I live on

Edgewater Boulevard on the west side of Cleveland. Does that ring any bells for you?"

Again, she waited several minutes, until she saw the reply being typed out:

"Auntie Claire used to clean some of the big houses for the white people in that neighborhood when I was a little girl, and sometimes I would come along. We would ride the bus over. If I was good, she would treat me to lunch on Saturdays, downtown at the fancy restaurant at Higbee's or Halle's Department Store. I think one of them was called the Silver Quill. But I did like coming over to the west side because I played with a boy named Bruce who lived in one of those houses. In fact, I think that house was on Edgewater. And I'm still Facebook friends with Bruce, though I haven't seen him for years."

The missing link. Ellie drew in her breath: "If you remember, can you describe the house?"

Goosebumps rose on Ellie's skin as she read along as Sally accurately described Ellie's own home, in detail. There was no doubt this person had been inside her house.

Ellie wanted to jump up and down on her bed. She wanted to run screaming down the hallway and bang on Ray's door, wake him up, envelope him in a huge hug and tell him she found Sally. She wanted to tell Brandy; she wanted to wake the whole bed & breakfast and run through the streets of Memphis ringing all the church bells. But she had to be absolutely sure this was the right person. If this was real, Ellie resolved she would do whatever it took to get Ray to Sally, and that it must happen tomorrow—she would drive any distance, she would put him on a plane. There was going to be a father-daughter reunion. Ray would not live one more day of his life without his daughter.

"Where are you, and can I call you?" she typed. "Do you still live in Cleveland?"

The response came a few moments later, and Ellie read with great interest. Then, with trembling hands, she picked up the phone and called Right Sally.

***

Ellie was up at dawn, energized and ecstatic. She quickly packed her things and loaded the car, waiting impatiently for Brandy and Ray to join her. "Do we want to sit down for one last southern breakfast before we depart for the North?" Ray suggested.

"Umm, I don't know, Ray; it's a pretty long drive today. Let's just grab a few things and munch on the way. I can always run us through a drive-thru for some donuts."

Ray agreeably acquiesced. "You're the driver, Miss Ellie. If you say it's time to hit the road, then it's time to hit the road. Are we gonna stay overnight in Louisville so Brandy can have her medicine stop there?"

"Oh yeah, sure, Louisville," Ellie answered distractedly as she threw the duffel bags in the back of the car.

Brandy floated downstairs in another one of her new outfits. She had done her hair and makeup again. She truly looked like a new person.

"Good morning, miss," said Greg respectfully as he held the door for Brandy.

Brandy tossed her hair, ignoring him as she walked past.

Ellie waited by the antique cherry secretary check-in area to settle their bill. "Do you need my credit card again to run through for the rooms?"

"No, we're all set here. I do thank you for staying at our little inn and hope you and your family had an enjoyable visit to Memphis." He paused a moment, waiting as Ellie signed off on the receipt, and then leaned forward and whispered in a conspiratorial tone. "Y'all ain't really family, are you? That's not really your dad and she's not really your sister, right?"

Ellie straightened up and looked him in the eye. "Thanks for your hospitality. The breakfasts were delightful and the rooms were very comfortable. I'm sure I'll be able to pen some kind of online review. But rest assured we will never stay here again. You know, you should never presume to define someone else's family." She grabbed a complimentary mint from the beveled glass dish and added, "Part of the bed & breakfast experience, you know."

She pulled the door shut behind her.

Brandy was fidgety and antsy but calmed down considerably after their quick stop at the detox wing. The Methadone took the edge off her cravings. "Think I can relax now and handle the ride," she confessed to the other two with embarrassment. "Sorry you got to put up with me."

"We're happy to put up with ya," Ray told her. "And really, there's no rush. We're not in any kind of great hurry today—are we, Ellie?"

Ray and Brandy turned to Ellie, but she was focused on the road and did not respond. They were used to seeing Ellie tense up at the wheel, but today Ellie's driving was surprisingly aggressive. Today, she was in the fast lane, speeding along well over the speed limit. She weaved in and out and around slower traffic, cutting off other drivers, and refusing to be boxed in by trucks.

Ellie was single-minded in her purpose as she advanced Ray mile by mile closer to his destiny. She forgot about the donut stop, and no one bothered to speak up to remind her. She tried to mind the speed limit but found it difficult to refrain from creeping up over eighty miles an hour. She watched the time, planning their arrival to coincide with the arrangement she had made with Right Sally the night before. She was bursting at the seams, attempting to contain her excitement. Ray watched her curiously.

They followed the highway north, out of Memphis and toward Nashville. The traffic moved along smoothly, and Ellie stopped only once for gas.

"Do you want me to use the smartphone app to look for cheap gas?" Brandy offered.

"No, we'll just hit the closest one to the exit," Ellie told her.

Soon they were on the highway bypass that circled Nashville. Ellie checked her GPS and took the exit toward the downtown district. The skyline of the Music City rose in the blue sky, sunshine and lazy

white clouds setting off the perfect day. They crossed the Cumberland
River and Ellie slowed as they passed the massive Bridgestone Arena,
the Country Music Hall of Fame and the walkway of the stars. Ray
leaned forward and gawked at the Hall of Fame and the huge oversize
guitar near the entrance. Across the street, on the Walk of Fame, step-
ping-stones were carved with the names of the superstars of country
music: Dolly Parton, Willie Nelson, Grandpa Jones, Patsy Cline, Bill
Monroe, Bob Wills and more.

"You should be in there, Ray," Ellie said. "There should be a Ray
Jones and The Gulch Jumpers exhibit, and you should be on the walk
of stars."

"Not in this lifetime, my friend," he demurred good-naturedly.

They cruised slowly through Printer's Alley, passing bustling bars,
honky-tonks and eateries. They cut a few blocks over to the Ryman
Hall, the original site of the Grand Ole Opry. Though it was early
afternoon on a weekday, there were still plenty of pedestrians and
tourists strolling through the historic, bustling downtown. Ellie pulled
into a parking lot. "Let's get out and walk around a bit. Let's go check
out the Ryman."

Ray looked at Ellie inquisitively. "Miss Ellie, why are you dragging
me to the Music City, of all places? I thought you were in a hurry to
get back home."

"Just humor me, Ray. Let's walk this way. Let's check this out."

They stood in the majestic lobby of the historic Ryman Hall, near
swirling staircases and the statue of Minnie Pearl and Roy Acuff.
Minnie's price tag hung from her hat. The auditorium itself was an
intimate two-tiered semi-circle of wooden church pew-like benches.
The famous red barn background and radio station microphone sat on
the stage. They wandered slowly through the great theater, admiring
photos and exhibits of all the iconic country and bluegrass stars who
had performed there throughout the years.

"Now *this* is a theater," Ray declared approvingly. "Used to listen to
those weekly live broadcasts from the Opry religiously; can't believe

I'm standing here now." He paused, hands on his hips, looking around with reverence.

Brandy stood alongside Ray. "We've sure come a long way from the Mission of Hope." Brandy was about to suggest checking the gift shop for some trinkets for her children, but Ellie was looking at her watch.

"Let's head back outside and walk down by the honky-tonks. Bet we can find some great live music down there."

"Ah, well, if you say so, Ellie," Ray agreed, exchanging a confused glance with Brandy.

They walked toward the strip, by the infamous Tootsies where Patsy Cline used to party with the fast crowd. Each bar and honky-tonk was buzzing with music, a jumble of sound spilling onto the noisy sidewalk. Echoes from the drums bounced off buildings across the street. Elvis impersonators strutted down the main drag, and women strolled along in skirts with cowboy boots. Cars and tour buses honked their horns as they added to the gridlock.

Ray became overwhelmed. He paused at the corner, coughing. The humidity of August in the South, compounded with the fumes from the cars, wasn't helping.

Ray looked at Ellie apologetically. "It's a busy, interesting place, that's for sure. But I can tell you without a shade of doubt that Nashville is the last place on earth I want to be right now. Please, Ellie, Brandy. This is awful. This is just the commercialized, cleaned-up version of bluegrass—it's not the down home, old-timey real thing. I just don't know what to make of all this."

"Hold on, wait. I think you're gonna feel better if we get you hooked up to your oxygen. I'll be right back." Without waiting for a reply, Ellie took off running, not walking, back to the car to retrieve Ray's oxygen tank.

"Lord Almighty, what's got into that gal today?" Ray watched Ellie running down the block.

Ellie reappeared with the oxygen tank, huffing and puffing as she ran, her hair sweaty and sticking to her forehead.

"El, what the hell?" Brandy leaned over and whispered to her.

"Trust me," Ellie whispered back.

She ushered them a few blocks further, and then stopped outside one of the smaller honky-tonks. Music spilled from this establishment as well, but it was acoustic rather than electric, with guitars and a fiddle offering a gentle melodic accompaniment. This music was softer, more bluegrass than country, and hauntingly beautiful. They paused and listened a moment, as the clear, sweet voice rang out:

> *"Traveled so far,*
>   *To see your sweet face;*
> *Mother, we yearn,*
>   *To know your embrace;*
> *Father working so hard,*
>   *His days steeped in coal;*
> *Brother studies the book,*
>   *For to nourish his soul;*
> *Sister spins at the wheel,*
>   *Yarn pools at her feet;*
> *Sings fondly of days,*
>   *Life t'was simple and sweet."*

Whoever was singing was very talented. Ray got a funny look on his face. He stood very still, listening intently. He took in long, deliberate breaths of oxygen, trying to gather himself.

Ellie watched him, concerned.

"Ray, shall we go inside? Shall we step in and listen to this band?"

His face contorted with emotion. "Ellie..." He started to back away from the entrance to the bar, shaking his head no.

"Ray. Don't walk away. Please trust me. You WANT to walk into this bar."

Ray stood paralyzed as self-doubt, guilt, and fear of rejection washed over him. The beauty of the pure, sweet voice reached their ears again. Ray stood speechless, looking at Ellie helplessly, fear in his eyes.

"Now we've traveled so far,
  Just to see your sweet face;
Love eternal reveal,
  Forgiveness and grace."

Brandy looked back and forth from Ray to Ellie as they hovered in a long moment of hesitation. Brandy tossed her newly highlighted hair across her shoulder and grabbed Ray's hand. "You were brave enough to try to make a deal with the devil at the crossroads but you're afraid of what's going to happen if you walk into this bar. Come on, old man. Don't forget you're at the helm of *your* life too."

She pulled him through the door. Ellie quickly grabbed the oxygen tank from Ray and left it sitting outside the entrance. She didn't want to risk an explosion if someone was smoking inside.

They blinked as their eyes adjusted from the sunlight to the interior. People perched on bar stools around a circular bar situated in the center of the room, drinking tequila, whiskey and beer. Small wooden tables were scattered across the wooden main floor. Waitresses scurried about, serving food and drink. Large windows at the front overlooked the street, and sunlight streamed through the windows, making it difficult to see the stage. Ellie saw the silhouette of a young woman on stage, between two men. All three were seated on stools, and the men were playing guitars while the young woman interspersed her singing with licks of bluegrass fiddle. Her voice was golden.

The light shifted and Ellie was finally able to see the woman's face. Ellie gasped. There were Ray's sad, smiling eyes—the exact same eyes! The girl's long dark hair hung down and lay across her honey-colored skin. This girl, this girl—she had to be Ray's. She looked just like him. But yet, something was off, something was not right. Ellie realized the girl was too young. She might be in her early twenties. Ellie stared, trying to comprehend what she was seeing. Could Sally really look that young for her age, even if she was in her forties? Was she just one of those people who took good care of themselves and was aging really well? She turned to Ray, opening her mouth to speak, but Ray had started moving forward, as if in a trance.

Ray made a sound, a guttural, primitive yell of grief and pleading, as he moved toward the stage. People looked up from their conversations to stare at the strange old man in the tattered suspenders, who was starting to disrupt the show. One of guitarists watched in alarm, with raised eyebrows, as Ray approached. Ray was focused on the young fiddle player as he moved closer. He was coming right at her. The girl kept singing, watching the old man with confusion and curiosity.

Tears started streaming down Ray's face. "Sally!" he screamed. He lunged toward the stage, stumbling, his arms reaching out toward her.

Ellie sprung into action and leaped forward to grab Ray, but the guitarist was faster and got there first. As he jumped off the stage to block Ray's advance toward the fiddle player, the guitar went crashing to the floor. Within seconds, the man tackled Ray to the ground and pinned him to the floor. The music had stopped and people screamed. Everyone was talking at once, and the serene laid-back mood the music had created was now replaced with chaos, yelling, and the sound of chairs scraping on the wood floor as people jumped up from their seats. "Call the police," someone yelled.

The young girl stood to the side, holding her fiddle, looking in bewilderment at the elderly man on the floor. "Sally," Ray cried again.

"It's okay, it's okay." Ellie breathlessly tried to pull the man off Ray. "He doesn't mean any harm!" As she struggled to break them up, another woman materialized next to her, also trying to help.

"Jay, back off, it's okay, get up off of him now," the woman said calmly. Ellie looked over in surprise, recognizing the voice.

The woman then reached her hand to Ray and gently pulled him to his feet. Ray stared in astonishment into the woman's sad, smiling eyes, looking from her to the girl with the fiddle.

"Dad," Sally said gently. "I'm Sally. And this young lady is your granddaughter, Caitlyn."

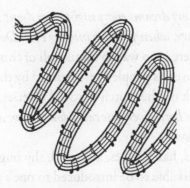

CHAPTER TWENTY-THREE

RAY

How does one compress a lifetime of yearning, grieving, regretting, repressing and searching into one moment? What does one say when one finally meets the one, the person, *your* person, the only person who can ever make everything whole again? How does one start explaining and apologizing for not stopping the unthinkable from happening? For not protecting? For not being there for the most important of moments, and for all the small day-to-day moments in between?

Where does one begin the conversation? *Do you know how much I love you, have always loved you, have thought about you every single day of my life since that day, the last happy day of my life? What did they tell you about me? What did they tell you about your mama? Do you know we created a home for you, built with our own hands? Do you know we created a family for you, even when our government said we couldn't? When all our families rejected us? We gave you love, gave you music, sang for you, danced with you. Did you feel loved, understand deep down how special you are? Was life kind to you? Did you find your way in the world? Can you ever forgive me for not finding you? I must know if you are all right, but if you're not, I can't bear to hear it, it will kill me. Do you know I rocked you to sleep, sang you to sweet dreams, and that you have been in my dreams every night since then? Do you see me, your family, your history, when you look into my eyes? Do you remember me?*

Turns out, there is no way to capture all of this in a moment. The mundane takes over, as people overwhelmed by the enormity of such an event fall back on the crutch of social niceties. *Let's sit down. We can take this table here. Everyone calm down, have a drink of water. We can order some food.*

Introductions, handshakes, awkward, shy hugs. Tears are wiped away. How remarkable to be introduced to one's very own child. To be introduced to one's very own grandchild—who you didn't even know existed. The possibility of such a thing had never even been considered. But wait, there's even more. Not just one grandchild, but two. There is a granddaughter and there is a grandson. They look like their grandmother, who they can never meet in this life. They have the eyes of their grandfather, who they never knew existed.

Is it an introduction, a new beginning, a first meeting—or a recap, a rewind, a remembering?

Conversation begins. It is halting, tentative and awkward at first, like a square boulder rolling clumsily down a slope, but then it picks up steam and starts hurtling, out of control, as everyone is trying to speak at once, with uncontrolled excitement, emotion finally pouring out, unstoppable. There aren't enough words now. So much to say, so much to tell, so much to ask. So much to listen to. It's hard not to just stare at them, taking in their faces. It would be enough just to be able to stare at their faces for a while, without the words. Time is suspended; there is nothing else. Other people, the bar, the sounds... they fade into periphery. We are glowing, light is emanating from us. One is aware of the little things; the way she laughs, the way her fingers curl around her glass. The way the grandson looks to her for approval. The way the granddaughter hums to the music in the background, tapping her foot along to the beat unconsciously, by second nature—the same way her grandmother did when she read her poetry in the late afternoons.

One wants to drink it all in, to take all of their hands and hold tight and never let go, to learn and memorize their stories: their birthdays, their names, their middle names, how old they are, what they like to do. One wants most of all to hear where she has been all of these years, and all of her stories. The details will surely be painful, there will have been near misses where it will be discovered that paths came close to crossing—cruel twists of fate: you were in the same state, you were in the same city after all, until she moved down South so the kids could be closer to the music of Nashville. She even worked as a nurse at a Cleveland hospital ten years ago. Pain buzzes around one's ears, making one dizzy and lightheaded as one staggers with that piece of information. There is almost a numbness as one determines that these most painful bits of information must be set aside, clinically, to think about and go over again later, when it is possible to bear it.

She speaks of her unanswered questions growing up and the hole in her heart, never meeting any cousins, aunts or uncles. Did "Auntie" Claire's relatives go with Auntie Claire's family or her own? She understood her coloring was different from theirs. Hours spent as a child sifting through the contents of her treasure box, looking at her mother's portrait, reading the rhymes and verses, wondering who wrote them. Where did her father go, and why? It all seemed just out of reach. The hole in her heart filled a bit when she found her calling in nursing, fell in love, married, had the children. She stopped thinking about the little box that had comforted her as a child and was lost over the years. But seeing and hearing Ray singing her lullaby in the video was a sensory bombardment. She knew those words and that melody. She knew her father. The hole rushed to fill.

And they have questions too—the young people want to know everything, want to learn who their grandfather is. She wants to learn her father all over again, to be taught, to be reminded. They are staring as well, studying one's face, really looking and seeing. I see you. I know you. You go with us; you fit in our group, right here in this spot. You are one of ours.

How inconceivable that one is not being rejected, one is not being blamed. One is not being questioned, doubted, or shamed. One is being welcomed, with unconditional love. One is wanted. Too much time lost, there's no time now for regrets and explaining the past. All that matters is now, and our time together, from here on out.

They want one to come live with them, they will not take no for an answer, and one readily agrees since it's unanimous—we are together now, we are repaired and made whole. We will go forward and build our family and allow no one to tear it apart again.

One is not alone in the world after all.

Ray Jones was homeless no more.

***

Ellie and Brandy sat quietly to the side, a few feet behind Ray and his family. Ellie watched and listened, a humbled, reverent spectator as Ray joyfully reunited with his family. It was unbelievable they had actually pulled it off. She realized she had never been overly confident they would actually find Sally, despite Ray's unshaken conviction that they would. She had certainly not thought the crossroads deal would amount to anything, and she was hopeful but unsure that the internet videos would work either. What were the chances?

But then again, why not? Ray had spent a lifetime paying for his loss; surely, he was due for some good karma to come his way. The dastardly deed Sammy and Frances had perpetrated was finally undone and, at last, there was justice. Ellie thought back to her posters about her favorite Supreme Court cases. The right to marry, a fundamental constitutional right. The right to raise one's children, also a fundamental constitutional right. The right to life, liberty and the pursuit of happiness—for everyone, just by virtue of their birth. Weren't these just fancy ways of saying "don't mess with me?" And sometimes all it took for an injustice to be confronted was for a person to stand up and challenge, question, push back, dig deeper, risk everything—and not give up.

She watched Sally and Ray embracing each other, holding hands, crying, laughing, talking all at once, excitedly making plans. Of course Ray would be staying with them. She knew this would happen. From the start, Ray had told her this was what he wanted more than anything in life. Ellie was happy for Ray, very happy for him, but it was bittersweet as well. There was a twinge of jealousy. Ray felt like her own dad. But he was only "play" family after all, just as Albert had spoken of. Brandy was just her "play" sister. The three of them had been playing house together—all make-believe. Brandy had real family; she had her mother, her three children. Brandy could finish rehab and rejoin her real family and she wouldn't need this patched-together pretend group anymore. Ray wouldn't need it either, now that he had the real thing. Ellie was the only one left playing house, by herself.

The extra bedrooms in her house would remain empty. She and Mike would go back to their old lives: working, quiet dinners, yard work, shopping, television.

But then again, perhaps they wouldn't. Now that they were finally talking about Michael, something had opened up. Something had shifted, and somehow there was now space available with potential to be filled. Perhaps there was a way for make-believe to become real. *I need more people.* For the first time in almost a year, Ellie considered the idea of trying to have another child. It would be scary, really scary, and perhaps she was just getting too old to try. Another idea hovered in her mind; it had been there for some time, on the sidelines, trying to get her attention, and she was finally ready to turn her head and look it in the eye: they could adopt. They could create the real thing, choose their family and make something new. Enthalpy: the creation of order out of disorder, atoms and matter coming together to create cells, life, organisms, families, societies, great achievements of art, music, literature—rather than entropy: atoms flying apart into tiny individual pieces of nothingness. It wasn't impossible at all. She and Mike could make it happen, if they had the will to do so. She remembered Ray's words to Brandy: *if you can come up with a dream for yourself in your head, that's the first step to making it happen in the real world.*

Still, she loved her new friends. It had been an extraordinary trip, and their three-way crossroads meant so much to her. She was happy for Ray, of course, but she would miss him terribly.

As if on cue, Ray looked up from his happy huddle with Sally and his grandchildren, as if just remembering where he was, looking for something he had forgotten about. Hours had gone by. His eyes met Ellie's. "Y'all excuse me a moment," he told his family, getting up to move his chair over close to Ellie.

"West Side..." he started gently, reaching his hand out to grasp hers.

"Ray, it's okay." She looked down. "I know you're not coming back to Cleveland to live with me, you don't have to say anything. I understand. This is where you belong. And I'm beyond happy for you."

"I'm so grateful to y'uns that I just don't know where to begin," he choked up. "No one has ever done nothing like what you have done to help me, Ellie. Ever. You listened to me, you heard out my silly half-baked plan, you drove me hundreds of miles, you used your brains, your technology, to solve my problem, and then you set all this up here today." He waved his hand, gesturing toward the table where Sally and her children sat. "What kind of person does all that? I just never dreamed a person could exist who could do all of that for another person."

Ellie grinned sheepishly. "Maybe you just needed a good lawyer after all."

He smiled. "And you are a good lawyer, no doubt about that. But you're more than that to me. Y'all know you're like a daughter to me, you both are." He looked to Brandy and reached for her hand as well. "Guess I got a chance to practice being a dad again with the two of you. How lucky can a man be?"

Brandy and Ellie exchanged flattered, congratulatory little smiles. Partners in crime could be partners in good deeds too.

"Just don't go breaking into some corny song now, old man," Brandy told him, excusing herself to use the restroom.

Ray and Ellie laughed, but Ray grew serious as Brandy left them alone for a few moments. "Our Blondie there, keep an eye on her now, okay? I worry about her. And I worry about you—I don't want to see you get your heart broken. She's got a very tough road ahead and, remember, that gal's been on drugs for years and years. It's a lot to change just based on a few days and a showdown with a wild hog in a thunderstorm. Day at the beauty shop can patch up the outside, but Ellie, she ain't fixed on the inside. *She ain't fixed on the inside*. You can only take her so far; Brandy's the only one who can decide to save Brandy."

Ellie nodded. "Okay, Ray. I'll remember. And you better come back up to visit us in Cleveland, or we're gonna be making lots of road trips down to Nashville."

"Sure, you better. I'm thinking this place ain't so bad after all. Look at all the live music going on, just within a few city blocks right here in this downtown. It's modern and amplified and all that, but it's the same good stuff I was raised on. How many guitars do y'uns think there are here just within a one-mile radius? Martin guitars, Gibson guitars, Epi guitars, Fender guitars. Everything under the sun. Steel guitars, bass guitars, double-neck guitars. Banjos, fiddles, ukuleles, pianos, everything. Look at all these people, so talented, singing and playing these instruments, making their own music. People of all ages. It's a living, breathing thing. Playing old time songs and playing new songs too. It's timeless."

Ray gazed in wonder at Sally and his grandchildren, his people, who had inherited the family jewel of musical talent. Ray was going to get more than his one hundred years after all, because the music would be passed down and live forever.

"Well, now, I guess Blondie's gonna be mad at me, but I do have to sing a song after all." He got up and walked over to Sally and the kids.

"It's a song I've been waiting a very long time to sing again, for the person it was written for. I hope you'll humor an old man."

They set Ray up in a chair on the stage and handed him a guitar. Sally moved her chair front and center, taking her rightful place as the guest of honor for Ray's concert. Ray, ever the entertainer, cleared his throat nervously as he tuned and shifted in his seat, preparing for the most important performance of his life. Other patrons, scattered around the bar, looked curiously up at the stage, no longer alarmed by the old man who apparently was not so crazy after all.

Ray glanced over in surprise as Caitlyn jumped up on the stage next to him and grabbed her fiddle. "Do you mind if I sit in and play along with you, Grandpa?"

"Well now, that would be a marvelous thing indeed, Caitlyn," he exclaimed, pleased. "Can ya just do that, with a song you don't know? Let's see, I believe this one is in the Key of D, common time, if that helps ya figure out how to improvise along. Do you want me to strum a few bars first, before we start?"

"That's okay, Grandpa, I don't need to know what key it's in. Just start the song and I'll come in. I can tell you that I *do* know my way around the strings of a bluegrass fiddle."

Ray gave a wickedly pleased chuckle.

The room fell to a hush as the sweet, comforting Mozart-like symmetry of the lullaby carried everyone to a place of love, safety, and the joys of the simpler things in life. Ray's deep, folksy voice resonated and rang, reverberating through the wood of the floors, the plants by the window, the cubes of ice twinkling in the glasses, the streams of late afternoon sunlight shining into the honky-tonk. Ellie felt it vibrate in her heart. Brandy felt it as a warm rush from her head to her toes, better than any drug. The guitar strummed softly and the fiddle sang along, light and exquisite. Ellie had given fleeting thought to suggesting to Ray and his family that they could have genetic testing done to ensure once and for all that they were related to one another. But now, as she listened, watching Ray and his granddaughter perform for the woman who was their daughter and mother, she understood there was no need. Science was airtight, but musical proof was stronger, at least in this family. Ellie realized she was a great, enthusiastic fan of the Ray-way of doing things after all.

Ray was completely focused on Sally, but at one point he looked over to Ellie and Brandy and gave a little wink and a nod. Sally began to sing along with Ray. Ray nodded, and then repeated the song and gestured to the crowd, inviting everyone to join in. Several dozen patrons in the bar listened, spellbound, lucky to hear a tiny taste of what might have been had things turned out differently for the musical career of Ray Jones and The Gulch Jumpers. They eagerly joined in.

"Baby child, baby o' mine,
*   We rock softly under the elms, the wind keeping time.*
Come evening I'll strike out, to earn me a dime,
*   Making music to bring home treats so fine.*
Catfish, cornbread, berries on the vine,
*   Common time with a walking beat, for sweet baby o' mine.*
With a song in your heart, and the sound of my voice,
*   Sing it out, little girl, in our love we rejoice.*
Sassafras, honey, huckleberry pie,
*   Don't need no coal in the ground, don't need no cry.*
Baby child, baby o' mine,
*   You'll always remember, the wind keeping time.*
Little house in the holler, where de sun always shine,
*   Golden melodies from mama and daddy,*
For sweet baby o' mine."

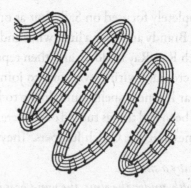

CHAPTER TWENTY-FOUR

WILD PIG

Brandy and Ellie checked into a nearby hotel, exhausted from the emotional day behind them. They had bid their farewell to Ray, unloading his stand-up string bass, guitar and duffel bag at Sally's home in Nashville. Ray had finally been able to present the shoebox to Sally, who gasped with pleasure to see her childhood treasure box again after so many years. Ellie marveled at how it had traveled from the back of her closet, to the shelter, into the past, into the South, and finally back to the present, all the way to its rightful owner.

The goodbyes were difficult. "I don't like goodbyes," Brandy told Ray as she hugged him.

"Then we won't say goodbye. We'll say 'till next time.' We'll stay in touch, that's just what we're going to do," he reassured. "And same to you, Miss Ellie. We tip our hats and bid each other 'till next time.'"

Ellie had nodded, hugged him quickly and turned back to her car, unable to speak. She liked Sally, Sally's husband, and their kids, and she knew how thrilled Ray was. It was a bonus that Sally, a nurse, understood Ray's medical condition. But leaving Ray behind was ripping her apart. She couldn't even think about how much she was going to miss him.

The trio was now reduced to a duo. Brandy and Ellie were quiet as they drove to the hotel. For the first time on the trip, Ellie paused at check-in, considering the idea of getting a double and sharing a room with Brandy. Ray's words echoed in her head: *She ain't fixed on the inside.*

"Stay up and watch old movies, final girl-pajama party, before we return to the real world?" she offered.

"Well..." Brandy considered. "Will I offend you if I have my own room? It's not that I don't want to hang out. It's just that I'm probably not going to have my own space or much privacy for a long time. Do you mind if I get to enjoy one more night in my own space?"

"Of course not. Totally understand. We'll meet up in the morning for breakfast. Then we'll push off."

They would leave early so Brandy could receive her Methadone dose in Louisville as soon as possible. And then, late tomorrow afternoon, they would be home. Ellie would drop Brandy off at the rehab center. Once Brandy was checked in, there would be another difficult goodbye, and then Ellie would be home.

They parted ways in the hallway by the elevator. Ellie started to unlock the door to her room.

"Hey, El," Brandy called over her shoulder as she unlocked her own door. "All those songs we've heard on this trip—songs Ray sang, songs on the radio, songs the bands in the bars were playing—why do you think no one writes a song about what it feels like to have a baby kicking inside of you?"

Ellie turned to face her friend, considering the question. "Maybe it's because men are writing the songs instead of women. Maybe women should write more songs."

Brandy smiled. "Goodnight, Ellie."

***

Brandy set her duffel bag on the luggage rack. She looked at her bed, looked at her bathroom. She turned the television on and turned it back off. She pulled the curtain aside and considered the view from her window, the lights of the city shining below. She paced back and forth a few moments, unsettled by Ray's departure from the group, nervous about entering the inpatient rehab center. Ninety days was a long time to live in an institution. It was a long time to have to follow rules about what time to get up, what to eat, what one could or couldn't do during the day. She wondered what the other women in the program would be like. What if they were rough and violent like the women in prison? What if the food was awful? What would the counselors be like? What if the treatment didn't work for her? And what if it did? Where would she go if she really could get sober? Would she really be able to find a job, a place to live? Would there be any way to repair her relationship with her kids? And what would they think if she tried the treatment but didn't make it? What would Ellie and Ray think? Everyone would know she had failed.

She paced, thinking. Downtown Nashville was exciting. The streets would be hopping by this time in the evening; people would be packed three-deep at the bars and clubs, listening to the bands, drinking and dancing. And it was all within walking distance. She could slip out just for a little while. Ellie wouldn't ever have to know. And if Brandy decided to have one last little celebratory high, before embarking on her life of sobriety, well what would be the harm? It was her life, wasn't it?

They had explained at the hospital how dangerous any additional opiates from street drugs could be on top of the Methadone dose, how it could push one into overdose territory. But Brandy didn't want to think about that. It would just be one more time.

Rationalizations made, she left the hotel and started walking toward the nightclub area. It took only a few blocks and a few brief inquiries to find what she was seeking. She looked around for a place to shoot up, away from the openness of the street.

Brandy was delighted to see a stray dog making its way along the sidewalk, no leash, no collar.

"Hey, buddy," she called to the brown furry mutt.

The dog turned into an alley. Brandy followed, curious to see where the dog had gone. The alley would be a perfect place to step away from the crowds to get high. She went a little farther, into the darkness, and then loaded her syringe, found a vein, and shot the drugs into her body. The dog appeared next to her. "There you are. Aren't you a good boy? Or are you a girl?"

The warm rush began, calming and enlightening. She leaned against the brick wall and slid down, taking a seat on the ground. The dog climbed into her lap.

Brandy looked into the dog's face, talking softly and petting around his ears. She looked into his big beautiful brown eyes. "Maybe you could come home with me...." she told him, the words coming out in slow motion. Her pupils constricted to pinpoints, and she tried to focus. She looked into the puppy's eyes and, for just a split second, she thought she saw the flashing red eyes of the angry wild boar. From very far away, she thought she heard someone screaming a warning: "Wild pig!" How strange the voice sounded like Ellie's. Ellie had never even seen that pig. But then the red eyes faded back into the soft, beautiful, big brown eyes, trusting and innocent. "Silly doggie," she slurred, "you're not a wild pig... silly doggie...."

Her breathing slowed, but it was okay, because she didn't need those breaths after all. She was driving the train, she was piloting the ship, she could choose which breaths she wanted to use and which ones she wanted to discard. She was on top of the world. It just couldn't ever, ever get any better than this. She was unbearably happy. Her breathing slowed even more and then stopped altogether. The colors were beautiful.

***

The two beat cops patrolling the downtown area on foot sauntered past the alley, but paused at the sound of a dog frantically barking.

"What's with this little guy—another stray? Guess we need to call the dog warden," commented the man, as the stray ran up to them barking excitedly and then turned and ran back into the alley. "He sure is barking up a storm down there. Think we should check it out?"

"Yeah, let's see what he's going crazy over in there," said the female cop.

They turned into the alley, pulling out their long flashlights.

"Oh, geez. Look what we got here. Is there a pulse?"

The woman checked while her partner called for an ambulance. "No pulse. She's cold." Their flashlights shined on the syringe, lying on the ground to the side.

"Another homeless junkie. Overdose, you think?"

"I guess," said the female cop as she panned her flashlight over the body. "But she looks pretty nice. See? Her hair and makeup are all done; she's dressed nicely." She shined the flashlight onto Brandy's feet. "And I can tell you I sure wouldn't be able to afford a pair of shoes like that on my cop salary. Maybe she's someone important."

They checked but found no purse, no identification. All they found was a plastic hotel room key in a pocket. "We can go canvass the rooms at that hotel, see if anyone has a person missing from their group who matches this description."

"Wait, there's something else in her pocket," the female cop said as she pulled out another paper and unfolded it. They leaned over and trained their flashlights on the photograph of the three smiling children. "Looks like our Jane Doe was a mother."

The male cop shook his head. "Oh, man. What a waste."

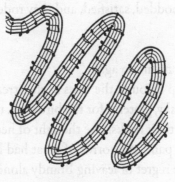

EPILOGUE

CUYAHOGA VALLEY NATIONAL PARK, OHIO

A YEAR LATER

Ellie, Mike and the three children set out over the bridge and the sparkling Cuyahoga River, onto the crushed limestone towpath of the National Park. The children's new bicycles glinted in the sunlight. Pedals turned as they hummed along the forested trail, keeping the river to their left and the canal to their right. It was Nevaeh's eighth birthday. The adoption had been finalized a month ago. The boys pulled ahead, hitting a good pace, and Mike accelerated to ride with them while Ellie rode compatibly next to the birthday girl, who was chatting excitedly. "Are we going to see Grandpa Ray at our picnic, Ellie?"

"Sure, Grandpa Ray will be up for Labor Day weekend, and I bet he's going to play the guitar and sing for you. He's going to be so happy to see you again, Nevaeh."

"Yes, I want him to sing songs for me," she declared. "Hey, Ellie, do you think we're riding fast enough? The boys are way up ahead of us."

"We are riding exactly the right speed. Don't worry about how anyone else is riding."

The little girl nodded, satisfied, and they rode on for a ways.

"Ellie?"

"Yes, Nevaeh."

"Tell me about my mom again."

Ellie looked up through the trees at the streams of sunlight, the magnificent blue sky, grateful for the birdsong, the quiet rush of the river, the wind at their backs. She thought of her friend, her partner in crime, and the pain and horror of what had happened. Each day she lived with the regret of leaving Brandy alone on that final night, just as she tried each day to rise to the honor of raising her friend's children. The comfortable speed of their cycling could never keep up with the dizzying speed of life's twists and turns over the past year, but this, above all else, Ellie understood: a family is not a static, fixed thing, rigidly defined by other people's rules. A family is a constantly evolving story. And where some stories are tragically cut short, other, new stories must take up. Ellie was determined that Brandy's stories would be told and passed down. Brandy was important. Brandy would be remembered. She would get more than her one hundred years.

"Your mom was strong. She was brave, so brave she even scared away a bear. She was funny; she loved to laugh. She was the best dancer I ever saw. She loved animals. She loved you, Shawn and Eddie. And she loved being outside in the woods, in nature—she would love it here by the river. She would be very happy we are riding our bikes here today."

"She can't be here." Nevaeh was matter-of-fact and sounded so grown-up, though her brow furrowed in concentration. "She *wants* to be here, but she *can't*. So she is...somewhere?... nowhere?"

"Somewhere," Ellie told her decidedly. "Her love for you is here."

Neveah nodded. "When I look into the windows of my little log cabin, I imagine she's in there."

Ellie looked at the child curiously. "And what is she doing inside the little log cabin?"

"She's in there taking care of Michael, your little boy, just like you're here taking care of me and my brothers."

Ellie swallowed, unable to speak. She looked in wonderment at this tiny person, wise beyond her years. Nevaeh cruised a little faster and changed gears, smoothly and perfectly, without even breaking her cadence.

"Look at you, Nevaeh, you're doing great, you're a natural!"

The child was pleased and sat up higher, proudly steering her bicycle.

"Ellie? How far do you think I can ride this bike?"

"Farther and farther than you can ever imagine."

THE END

ABOUT THE AUTHOR

Catherine Pomeroy (pronouns: She/Her/Hers) is a writer and child welfare attorney who lives with her husband in Chagrin Falls, Ohio. They are a blended family with four adult children. Over the span of a twenty-plus year legal career dedicated to the protection of children from abuse and neglect, Catherine has worked as a county prosecutor, guardian ad litem, and legal counsel for a child protective services agency. Catherine is an avid cyclist and an amateur musician. Music, love of family and adventure inspire her writing. *The Gulch Jumpers* is her first novel.

BOOK CLUB QUESTIONS FOR DISCUSSION

Why do you think Ellie initially avoids talking to her old friend Brandy after she recognizes her at the shelter? Is Ellie ashamed of her past party days? Do you think Ellie is embarrassed to be successful in her marriage and career in contrast to Brandy's misfortune?

Are Brandy and Ellie jealous of each other? What do they resent or admire about each other?

Ellie, Ray and Brandy are all parents who have lost their children, albeit in very different ways. Discuss how each character manifests this grief and the ways each character clings to hope. Do you think the characters demonstrate ambivalence about parenting?

What kinds of prejudice and obstacles do you imagine Ray and Doris faced as an interracial couple in 1960s Appalachia? How does music operate in the story to bring people of different races and cultural backgrounds together?

Why does Ray want to emulate Robert Johnson and the crossroads legend? Why does Ray reject more practical options to try to find his daughter?

Does the wild pig represent evil, and if so, what is the true evil in the story—racism? Heroin?

Why do you think Brandy immediately regretted throwing away her heroin in the park when the characters finally arrived at the crossroads in Mississippi? Do you have sympathy for Brandy as she struggled with addiction?

What roles does faith play in the story?

Did The Gulch Jumpers make you cry? Laugh? Did the story make you nostalgic or miss people in your own life?

How do the supporting characters—Jessica, Mike, Dottie, Evan, Wrong Sally, Alligator Joe, Right Sally, Nevaeh—contribute to the journey of Ray, Ellie and Brandy?

Discuss the animals in the story, such as Molasses, the wild pig, and the stray dog in the alley. What is Brandy's connection to animals?

The formation of his band The Gulch Jumpers helped Ray find his way in the world as a young man. Where did Ray draw his musical education and talent from? Did you learn anything about music and the history of American roots music from the story? Are there works of music that evoke strong emotional memories in your own life?

Have you visited any of the locations the characters traveled to? Imagine what your bucket list road trip would look like. Where would you go?

What do you think happens to Ellie after the novel ends?

RECIPES

Here are some fun recipes from the author that she suggests go with the story! Catherine also recommends that coffee and donuts immediately will always go well with this book!

My mother used to make fried oysters for Thanksgiving or special occasions:
-Dip drained oysters in 2 eggs, beaten, then in breadcrumbs or crushed saltine crackers with salt & pepper, coating each oyster thoroughly. Also okay to take a dip in buttermilk before the egg bath.
-Set aside to dry for about half an hour.
-Heat vegetable or olive oil in a cast iron frying pan.
-Fry the oysters until golden brown, 1-2 minutes on each side.
-Serve with lemon wedges, tartar sauce, cocktail sauce or hot sauce.

Country Potatoes - also a big hit in our family. Cubed cooked ham can be added, which goes with the "wild pig" in The Gulch Jumpers!
-Mix 2 lb Ore Ida southern style hash brown potatoes, 1 cup sour cream, 1 can cream of chicken soup, 1 chopped onion, 1/2 cup cheddar cheese and 1 stick of melted butter. Put in a 9 x 13 casserole dish.
-melt 4 tbs butter and mix with cornflake crumbs or crushed Honey Bunches of Oats cereal, and pour over the top.
-Bake at 350 degrees F for 1 hour.

Pineapples were a sign of hospitality in early America. Here's a comfort food pineapple casserole that goes great with a brunch:
- Mix in a bowl: 3 eggs beaten, 3/4 cups sugar, 1/2 cup milk, 1/3 cup butter, 1 can drained 15 1/2 oz of pineapple (or use fresh pineapple!), and 8 slices of bread cut in small pieces.
-put all the ingredients in a greased casserole dish and bake 450 deg F for 10 minutes, then reduce temp to 350 deg F and bake an

additional 30 minutes.

Okay, one more!

Corn & Onion casserole:
-Melt 1/2 cup butter in a skillet and add 2 sliced sweet onions and saute until golden. Remove from heat. Stir in 8 oz container sour cream and 1/2 cup shredded cheddar cheese. Set aside. In a medium bowl combine 7 oz pkg corn muffin mix, 1 beaten egg, 1/2 cup milk, 1 can creamed corn and 4 drops hot pepper sauce. Mix well. Turn muffin mixture into a greased 9 x 9 baking pan. Top with onion mixture, and sprinkle with a little more shredded cheddar cheese.
-Bake uncovered at 350 deg F for 1 hour.

(In the interest of full disclosure I found this one in a recipe book and have never tried it, but the hot sauce along with the corn muffin twist sounds southern to me).

CPSIA information can be obtained
at www.ICGtesting.com
Printed in the USA
LVHW042049301021
702001LV00003B/16

9 781955 431040